Samuel A. Drake

The Heart of the White Mountains

Their Legend and Scenery

Samuel A. Drake

The Heart of the White Mountains
Their Legend and Scenery

ISBN/EAN: 9783337154899

Printed in Europe, USA, Canada, Australia, Japan

Cover: Foto ©Andreas Hilbeck / pixelio.de

More available books at **www.hansebooks.com**

Tourist's Edition

THE HEART

OF THE

WHITE MOUNTAINS

THEIR LEGEND AND SCENERY

BY

SAMUEL ADAMS DRAKE

AUTHOR OF "NOOKS AND CORNERS OF THE NEW ENGLAND COAST"
"CAPTAIN NELSON" ETC.

WITH ILLUSTRATIONS BY

W. HAMILTON GIBSON

"Eyes loose; thoughts close"

NEW YORK

HARPER & BROTHERS, FRANKLIN SQUARE

1882

To JOHN G. WHITTIER:

An illustrious and venerated bard, who shares with you the love and honor of his countrymen, tells us that the poets are the best travelling companions. Like Orlando in the forest of Arden, they " hang odes on hawthorns and elegies on thistles."

In the spirit of that delightful companionship, so graciously announced, it is to you, who have kindled on our aged summits

> *" The light that never was on sea or land,*
> *The consecration and the poet's dream,"*

that this volume is affectionately dedicated by

THE AUTHOR.

PREFACE.

THE very flattering reception which the sumptuous holiday edition of "The Heart of the White Mountains" received on its *début* has decided the Messrs. Harper to re-issue it in a more convenient and less expensive form, with the addition of a Tourist's Appendix, and an Index farther adapting it for the use of actual travellers. While all the original features remain intact, these additions serve to render the references in the text intelligible to the uninstructed reader, and at the same time help to make a practical working manual. One or two new maps contribute to the same end.

I take the opportunity thus afforded me to say that, when "The Heart of the White Mountains" was originally prepared, I hoped it might go into the hands of those who, making the journey for the first time, feel the need of something different from the conventional guide-book of the day, and for whom it would also be, during the hours of travel or of leisure among the mountains, to some extent an entertaining as well as a useful companion. So far as author and publisher are concerned, that purpose is now realized.

Finally, I wrote the book because I could not help it.

SAMUEL ADAMS DRAKE.

MELROSE, *January*, 1882.

GENERAL CONTENTS.

FIRST JOURNEY.

SECOND JOURNEY.

THIRD JOURNEY.

ILLUSTRATIONS.

These Illustrations, excepting those marked *, were designed by W. HAMILTON GIBSON.

FIRST JOURNEY.

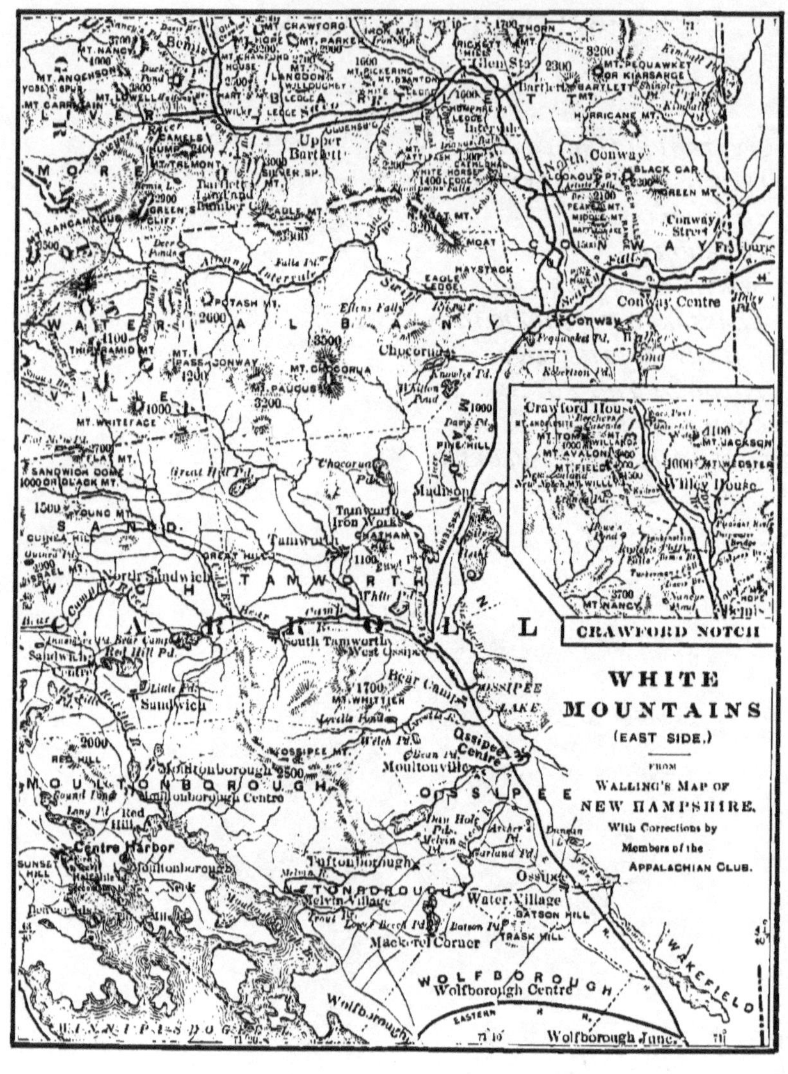

CRAWFORD NOTCH

WHITE
MOUNTAINS
(EAST SIDE.)

FROM

WALLING'S MAP OF
NEW HAMPSHIRE.

With Corrections by
Members of the
APPALACHIAN CLUB.

THE
HEART OF THE WHITE MOUNTAINS.

FIRST JOURNEY.

I.

MY TRAVELLING COMPANIONS.

"Si jeunesse savait! si vieillesse pouvait!"

ONE morning in September I was sauntering up and down the rail-way-station waiting for the slow hands of the clock to reach the hour fixed for the departure of the train. The fact that these hands never move backward did not in the least seem to restrain the impatience of the travellers thronging into the station, some with happy, some with anxious faces, some without trace of either emotion, yet all betraying the same eagerness and haste of manner. All at once I heard my name pronounced, and felt a heavy hand upon my shoulder.

"What!" I exclaimed, in genuine surprise, "is it you, colonel?"

"Myself," affirmed the speaker, offering his cigar-case.

"And where did you drop from"—accepting an Havana; "the Blue Grass?"

"I reckon."

"But what are you doing in New England, when you should be in Kentucky?"

"Doing, I? oh, well," said my friend, with a shade of constraint; then with a quizzical smile, "You are a Yankee; guess."

"Take care."

"Guess."

"Running away from your creditors?"

The colonel's chin cut the air contemptuously.

"Running after a woman, perhaps?"

My companion quickly took the cigar from his lips, looked at me with mouth half opened, then stammered, "What in blue brimstone put that into your head?"

"Evidently you are going on a journey, but are dressed for an evening party," I replied, comprising with a glance the colonel's black suit, lavender gloves, and white cravat.

"Why," said the colonel, glancing rather complacently at himself — "why we Kentuckians always travel so at home. But it's now your turn; where are you going yourself?"

"To the mountains."

"Good; so am I: White Mountains, Green Mountains, Rocky Mountains, or Mountains of the Moon, I care not."

"What is your route?"

"I'm not at all familiar with the topography of your mountains. What is yours?"

"By the Eastern to Lake Winnipiseogee, thence to Centre Harbor, thence by stage and rail to North Conway and the White Mountain Notch."

My friend purchased his ticket by the indicated route, and the train was soon rumbling over the bridges which span the Charles and Mystic. Farewell, Boston, city where, like thy railways, all extremes meet, but where I would still rather live on a crust moistened with east wind than cast my lot elsewhere.

When we had fairly emerged into the light and sunshine of the open country, I recognized my old acquaintance George Brentwood. At a gesture from me he came and sat opposite to us.

George Brentwood was a blond young man of thirty-four or thirty-five, with brown hair, full reddish beard, shrewdish blue eyes, a robust frame, and a general air of negligent repose. In a word, he was the antipodes of my companion, whose hair, eyebrows, and mustache were coal-black, eyes dark and sparkling, manner nervous, and his attitudes careless and unconstrained, though not destitute of a certain natural grace. Both were men to be remarked in a crowd.

"George," said I, "permit me to introduce my friend Colonel Swords."

After a few civil questions and answers, George declared his destination to be ours, and was cordially welcomed to join us. By way of breaking the ice, he observed,

"Apropos of your title, colonel, I presume you served in the Rebellion?"

The colonel hitched a little on his seat before replying. Knowing him to be a very modest man, I came to his assistance. "Yes," said I, "the colonel fought hard and bled freely. Let me see, where were you wounded?"

"Through the chest."

"No, I mean in what battle?"

"Spottsylvania."

"Left on the field for dead, and taken prisoner," I finished.

George is a fellow of very generous impulses. "My dear sir," said he, effusively, grasping the colonel's hand, "after what you have suffered for the old flag, you can need no other passport to the gratitude and friendship of a New-Englander. Count me as one of your debtors. During the war it was my fortune—my misfortune, I should say—to be in a distant country; otherwise we should have been found fighting shoulder to shoulder under Grant, or Sherman, or Sheridan, or Thomas.

The colonel's color rose. He drew himself proudly up, cleared his throat, and said, laconically, "Hardly, stranger, seeing that I had the honor to fight under the Confederate flag."

You have seen a tortoise suddenly draw back into his shell. Well, George as suddenly retreated into his. For an instant he looked at the Southron as one might at a confessed murderer; then stammered out a few random and unmeaning words about mistaken sense of duty— gallant but useless struggle, you know—drew a newspaper from his pocket, and hid his confusion behind it.

Fearing my fiery Kentuckian might let fall some unlucky word that would act like a live coal dropped on the tortoise's back, I hastened to interpose. "But really, colonel," I urged, returning to the charge, "with the Blue Ridge always at your back, I wager you did not come a thousand miles merely to see our mountains. Come, what takes you from Lexington?"

"A truant disposition."

"Nothing else?"

His dark face grew swarthy, then pale. He looked at me doubtfully a moment, and then leaned close to my ear. "You guessed it," he whispered.

"A woman?"

"Yes; you know that I was taken prisoner and sent North. Through the influence of a friend who had known my family before the war, I was allowed to pass my first days of convalescence in a beautiful little village in Berkshire. There I was cured of the bullet, but received a more mortal wound."

"What a misfortune!"

"Yes; no; confound you, let me finish."

"Helen, the daughter of the gentleman who procured my transfer from the hospital to his pleasant home" (the proud Southerner would not say his benefactor), "was a beautiful creature. Let me describe her to you."

"Oh," I hastened to say, "I know her." Like all lovers, that subject might have a beginning but no ending.

"You?"

"Of course. Listen. Yellow hair, rippling ravishingly from an alabaster forehead, pink cheeks, pouting lips, dimpled chin, snowy throat—"

The colonel made a gesture of impatience. "Pshaw, that's a type, not a portrait. Well, the upshot of it was that I was exchanged, and ordered to report at Baltimore for transportation to our lines. Imagine my dismay. No, you can't, for I was beginning to think she cared for me, and I was every day getting deeper and deeper in love. But to tell her! That posed me. When alone with her, my cowardly tongue clove to the roof of my mouth. Once or twice I came very near bawling out, 'I love you!' just as I would have given an order to a squadron to charge a battery."

"Well; but you did propose at last?"

"Oh yes."

"And was accepted."

The colonel lowered his head, and his face grew pinched.

"Refused gently, but positively refused."

"Come," I hazarded, thinking the story ended, "I do not like your Helen."

"Why?"

"Because either you are mistaken, or she seems just a little of a coquette."

"Oh, you don't know her," said the colonel, warmly; "when we parted she betrayed unusual agitation—for her; but I was cut to the quick by her refusal, and determined not to let her see how deeply I felt it. After the Deluge—you know what I mean—after the tragedy at Appomattox, I went back to the old home. Couldn't stay there. I tried New Orleans, Cuba. No use."

Something rose in the colonel's throat, but he gulped it down and went on:

"The image of that girl pursues me. Did you ever try running away from yourself? Well, after fighting it out with myself until I could endure it no longer, I put pride in my pocket, came straight to Berkshire, only to find Helen gone."

"That was unlucky; where?"

"To the mountains, of course. Everybody seems to be going there; but I shall find her."

"Don't be too sanguine. It will be like looking for a needle in a hay-stack. The mountains are a perfect Dædalian labyrinth," I could not help saying, in my vexation. Instead of an ardent lover of nature, I had picked up the "baby of a girl." But there was George Brentwood. I went over and sat by George.

It was generally understood that George was deeply enamored of a young and beautiful widow who had long ceased to count her love affairs, who all the world, except George, knew loved only herself, and who had therefore nothing left worth mentioning to bestow upon another. By nature a coquette, passionately fond of admiration, her self-love was flattered by the attentions of such a man as George, and he, poor fellow, driven one day to the verge of despair, the next intoxicated with the crumbs she threw him, was the victim of a species of slavery which was fast undermining his buoyant and generous disposition. The colonel was in hot pursuit of his adored Helen. Two words sufficed to acquaint me that George was escaping from his beautiful tormentor. At all events, I was sure of him.

"How charming the country is! What a delightful sense of freedom!" George drew a deep breath, and stretched his limbs luxuriously. "Shall we have an old-fashioned tramp together?" He continued, with assumed vivacity, "The deuce take me if I go back to town for a twelvemonth. How we creep along! I feel exultation in putting the long miles between me and the accursed city," said George, at last.

"You experience no regret, then, at leaving the city?"

George merely looked at me; but he could not have spoken more eloquently.

The train had just left Portsmouth, when the conductor entered the car holding aloft a yellow envelope. Every eye was instantly riveted upon it. Conversation ceased. For whom of the fifty or sixty occupants of the car had this flash overtaken the express train? In that moment the criminal realized the futility of flight, the merchant the uncertainty of his investments, the man of leisure all the ordinary contingencies of life. The conductor put an end to the suspense by demanding,

"Is Mr. George Brentwood in this car?"

In spite of an heroic effort at self-control, George's hand trembled as he tore open the envelope; but as he read his face became radiant. Had he been alone I believe he would have kissed the paper.

"Your news is not bad?" I ventured to ask, seeing him relapse into a fit of musing, and noting the smile that came and went like a ripple on still water.

"Thank you, quite the contrary; but it is important that I should immediately return to Boston."

"How unfortunate!"

George turned on me a fixed and questioning look, but made no reply.

"And the mountains?" I persisted.

"Oh, sink the mountains!"

I last saw George striding impatiently up and down the platform of the Rochester station, watch in hand. Without doubt he had received his recall. However, there was still the lovelorn colonel.

Never have I seen a man more thoroughly enraptured with the growing beauty of the scenery. I promised myself much enjoyment in his society, for his comments were both original and picturesque; so that by the time we arrived at Wolfborough I had already forgotten George and his widow.

There was the usual throng of idlers lounging about the pier with their noses in the air, and their hands in their pockets; perhaps more than the usual confusion, for the steamer merely touched to take and leave passengers. We went on board. As the bell tolled the colonel uttered an exclamation. He became all on a sudden transformed from a passive spectator into an excited and prominent actor in the scene. He gesticulated wildly, swung his hat, and shouted in a frantic way, apparently to attract the attention of some one in the crowd; failing in which he seized his luggage, took the stairs in two steps, and darting like a rocket among the astonished spectators, who divided to the right and left before his impetuous onset, was in the act of vigorously shaking hands with a hale old gentleman of fifty odd when the boat swung clear. He waved his unoccupied hand, and I saw his face wreathed in smiles. I could not fail to interpret the gesture as an adieu.

" Halloo!" I shouted, " what of the mountains?"

" Burn the mountains!" was his reply. The steamer glided swiftly down the little bay, and I was left to continue my journey alone.

II.

INCOMPARABLE WINNIPISEOGEE.

First a lake
Tinted with sunset, next the wavy lines
Of far receding hills.—WHITTIER.

WHEN the steamer glides out of the land-locked inlet at the bottom of which Wolfborough is situated, one of those pictures, forever ineffaceable, presents itself. In effect, all the conditions of a picture are realized. Here is the shining expanse of the lake stretching away in the distance, and finally lost among tufted islets and foliage - rounded promontories. To the right are the Ossipee mountains, dark, vigorously outlined, and wooded to their summits. To the left, more distant, rise the twin domes of the Belknap peaks. In front, and closing the view, the imposing Sandwich summits dominate the scene.

All these mountains seem advancing into the lake. They possess a special character of color, outline, or physiognomy which fixes them in the memory, not confusedly, but in the place appropriate to this beautiful picture, to its fine proportions, exquisite harmony, and general effectiveness. Even M. Chateaubriand, who maintains that mountains should only be seen from a distance—even he would have found in Winnipiseogee the perfection of his ideal *mise en scène;* for here they stand well back from the lake, so as to give the best effect of perspective.

Lovely as the lake is, the eye will rove among the mountains that we have come to see. They, and they alone, are the objects which have enticed us—entice us even now with a charm and mystery that we cannot pretend to explain. We do not wish it explained. We know that we are as free, as light of heart, as the birds that skim the placid surface of the lake, and coquet with their own shadows. The memory of those mountains is like snatches of music that come unbidden and haunt you perpetually.

Having taken in the grander features, the eye is occupied with its details. We see the lake quivering in sunshine. From bold summit to beautiful water the shores are clothed in most vivid green. The islands, which we believe to be floating gardens, are almost tropical in the luxuriance and richness of their vegetation. The deep shadows they fling down image each islet so faithfully that it seems, like Narcissus, gloating over its own beauty. Here and there a glimmer of water through the trees denotes secluded little havens. Boats float idly on the calm surface. Water-fowl rise and beat the glossy, dark water with startled wings. White tents appear, and handkerchiefs flutter from jutting points or headlands. Over all tower the mountains.

The steamer glided swiftly and noiselessly on, attended by the echo of her paddles from the shores. Dimpled waves, parting from her prow, rolled indolently in, and broke on the foam-fretted rocks. There was a warmth of color about these rocks, a pure transparency to the water, a brightness to the foliage, an invigorating strength in the mountains that exerted a cheerful influence upon our spirits.

As we advanced up the lake new and rare vistas rapidly succeeded. After leaving Long Island behind, the near ranges drew apart, holding us admiring and absorbed spectators of a moving panorama of distant summits. An opening appeared, through which Mount Washington burst upon us blue as lapis-lazuli, a chaplet of clouds crowning his imperial front. Slowly, majestically, he marches by, and now Chocorua scowls upon us. A murmur of admiration ran from group to group as these monumental figures were successively unveiled. Men kept silence, but women could not repress the exclamation, " How beautiful!" The two grandest types which these mountains enclose were thus displayed in the full splendor of noonday.

I should add that those who now saw Mount Washington for the first time, and whose curiosity was whetted by the knowledge that it was the highest peak of the whole family of mountains, openly manifested their disappointment. That Mount Washington! It was in vain to remind them that the eye traversed forty miles in its flight from lake to summit. Fault of perspective or not, the mountain was not nearly so high as they imagined. Chocorua, on the contrary, with its ashen spire and olive-green flanks, realized more fully their idea of a high mountain. One was near, the other far. Imagination fails to make a mountain higher than it looks. The mind takes its measure after the eye.

Our boat was now rapidly nearing Centre Harbor. On the right its progress gradually unmasking the western slopes of the Ossipee range, more fully opened the view of Chocorua and his dependent peaks. We were looking in the direction of Tamworth, Ossipee, and Conway. Red Hill, a detached mountain at the head of the lake, now moved into the gap, excluding further views of distant summits. Mooschillock, lofty but unimpressive, has for some time showed its flattened heights over the Sandwich Mountains, but is now sinking behind them. To the west, thronged with islands, is the long reach of water toward the outlet of the lake at Weirs.[1]

This lake was the highway over which Indian war-parties advanced or retreated during their predatory incursions from Canada. Many captives must have crossed it whom its mountain walls seemed forever destined to separate from friends and kindred. The Indians who inhabited villages at Winnipiseogee (Weirs), Ossipee, and Pigwacket (Fryeburg), were hostile; and from time to time during the old wars troops were marched from the English settlements to subdue them. These scouting-parties found the woods well stocked with bear, moose, and deer, and the lake with salmon-trout, some of which, according to the narrative before me, were three feet long, and weighed twelve pounds each.

Traces of Indian occupation remained up to the present century. Fishing-weirs and woodland paths were frequently discovered by the whites; but a greater curiosity than either is mentioned by Dr. Belknap, in his "History of New Hampshire," who there tells of a pine-tree, standing on the shore of Winnipiseogee River, on which was carved a canoe with two men in it, supposed to have been a mark of direction to those who were expected to follow. Another was a tree in Moultonborough, standing near a carrying-place between two ponds. On this tree was a representation of one of their expeditions. The number of killed and the prisoners were shown by rude drawings of human beings, the former being distinguished by the mark of a knife across the throat. Even the distinction of sex was preserved in the drawing.

Centre Harbor is advantageously situated for a sojourn more or less prolonged. Although settled as early as 1755, it is, in common with the other lake towns, barren of history or tradition. Its greatest impulse is,

---

[1] So called from the fishing-weirs of the Indians. The Indian name was Aquedahtan. Here is the Endicott Rock, with an inscription made by Massachusetts surveyors in 1652.

beyond question, the tide of tourists which annually ebbs and flows among the most sequestered nooks, enriching this charming region like an inundation of the Nile. An anecdote will, however, serve to illustrate the character of the men who first subdued this wilderness. Our anecdote represents its hero a man of resources. His career proves him a man of courage. Although a veritable personage, let us call him General Hampton.

The fact that General Hampton lived in that only half-cleared atmosphere following the age of credulity and superstition, naturally accounts for the extraordinary legend concerning him which, for the rest, had its origin among his own friends and neighbors, who merely shared the general belief in the practice of diabolic arts, through compacts with the arch-enemy of mankind himself, universally prevailing in that day—yes, prevailing all over Christendom. By a mere legend, we are thus able to lay hold of the thread which conducts us back through the dark era of superstition and delusion, and which is now so amazing.

The general, says the legend, encountered a far more notable adversary than Abenaki warriors or conjurers, among whom he had lived, and whom it was the passion of his life to exterminate.

In an evil hour his yearning to amass wealth suddenly led him to declare that he would sell his soul for the possession of unbounded riches. Think of the devil, and he is at your elbow. The fatal declaration was no sooner made—the general was sitting alone by his fireside—than a shower of sparks came down the chimney, out of which stepped a man dressed from top to toe in black velvet. The astonished Hampton noticed that the stranger's ruffles were not even smutted.

"Your servant, general," quoth the stranger, suavely, "but let us make haste, if you please, for I am expected at the governor's in a quarter of an hour," he added, picking up a live coal with his thumb and forefinger and consulting his watch with it.

The general's wits began to desert him. Portsmouth was five leagues, long ones at that, from Hampton House, and his strange visitor talked, with the utmost unconcern, of getting there in fifteen minutes. His astonishment caused him to stammer out,

"Then you must be the—"

"Tush! what signifies a name?" interrupted the stranger, with a deprecating wave of the hand. "Come, do we understand each other? is it a bargain or not?"

At the talismanic word "bargain" the general pricked up his ears. He had often been heard to say that neither man nor devil could get the better of him in a trade. He took out his jack-knife and began to whittle. The devil took out his, and began to pare his nails.

"But what proof have I that you can perform what you promise?" demanded Hampton, pursing up his mouth, and contracting his bushy eyebrows.

The fiend ran his fingers carelessly through his peruke; a shower of golden guineas fell to the floor, and rolled to the four corners of the room. The general quickly stooped to pick up one; but no sooner had his fingers closed upon it than he uttered a yell. It was red-hot.

The devil chuckled. "Try again," he said.

But Hampton shook his head, and retreated a step.

"Don't be afraid."

Hampton cautiously touched a coin. It was cool. He weighed it in his hand, and rung it on the table. It was full weight and true ring. Then he went down on his hands and knees, and began to gather up the guineas with feverish haste.

"Are you satisfied?" demanded Satan.

"Completely, your majesty."

"Then to business. By-the-way, have you anything to drink in the house?"

"There is some Old Jamaica in the cupboard."

"Excellent. I am as thirsty as a Puritan on election-day," said the devil, seating himself at the table and negligently flinging his mantle back over his shoulder.

Hampton brought a decanter and a couple of glasses from the cupboard, filled one and passed it to his infernal guest, who tasted it, and smacked his lips with the air of a connoisseur. Hampton watched every gesture. "Does your excellency not find it to his taste?" he ventured to ask.

"H'm, I have drunk worse; but let me show you how to make a salamander," replied Satan, touching the lighted end of the taper to the liquor, which instantly burst into a spectral blue flame. The fiend then raised the tankard, glanced approvingly at the blaze—which to Hampton's disordered intellect resembled an adder's forked and agile tongue —nodded, and said, patronizingly, "To our better acquaintance." He then quaffed the contents at a single gulp.

Hampton shuddered. This was not the way he had been used to seeing healths drunk. He pretended, however, to drink, for fear of giving offence, but somehow the liquor choked him. The demon set down the tankard, and observed, in a matter-of-fact way that put his listener in a cold sweat,

"Now that you are convinced I am able to make you the richest man in all the province, listen. In consideration of your agreement, duly signed and sealed, to deliver your soul"—here he drew a parchment from his breast—"I engage, on my part, on the first day of every month, to fill your boots with golden elephants like these before you. But mark me well," said Satan, holding up a forefinger glittering with diamonds; "if you try to play me any trick you will repent it. I know you, Jonathan Hampton, and shall keep my eye upon you. So beware!"

Hampton flinched a little at this plain speech; but a thought seemed to strike him, and he brightened up. Satan opened the scroll, smoothed out the creases, dipped a pen in the inkhorn at his girdle, and pointing to a blank space said, laconically, "Sign!"

Hampton hesitated.

"If you are afraid," sneered Satan, "why put me to all this trouble?" And he began to put the gold in his pocket.

His victim seized the pen, but his hand shook so he could not write. He gulped down a swallow of rum, stole a look at his infernal guest, who nodded his head by way of encouragement, and a second time approached his pen to the paper. The struggle was soon over. The unhappy Hampton wrote his name at·the bottom of the fatal list, which he was astonished to see numbered some of the highest personages in the province. "I shall at least be in good company," he muttered.

"Good!" said Satan, rising and putting the scroll carefully within his breast. "Rely on me, general, and be sure you keep faith. Remember!" So saying, the demon waved his hand, wrapped his mantle about him, and vanished up the chimney.

Satan performed his part of the contract to the letter. On the first day of every month the boots, which were hung on the crane in the fireplace the night before, were found in the morning stuffed full of guineas. It is true that Hampton had ransacked the village for the largest pair to be found, and had finally secured a brace of trooper's boots, which came up to the wearer's thigh; but the contract merely expressed boots, and the devil does not stand upon trifles.

Hampton rolled in wealth. Everything prospered. His neighbors regarded him first with envy, then with aversion, at last with fear. Not a few affirmed he had entered into a league with the Evil One. Others shook their heads, saying, "What does it signify? that man would out-wit the devil himself."

But one morning, when the fiend came as usual to fill the boots, what was his astonishment to find that he could not fill them. He poured in the guineas, but it was like pouring water into a rat-hole. The more he put in, the more the quantity seemed to diminish. In vain he persisted: the boots could not be filled.

The devil scratched his ear. "I must look into this," he reflected. No sooner said than he attempted to descend, but found his progress suddenly arrested. The chimney was choked up with guineas. Foam-ing with rage, the demon tore the boots from the crane. The crafty general had cut off the soles, leaving only the legs for the devil to fill. The chamber was knee-deep with gold.

The devil gave a horrible grin, and disappeared. The same night Hampton House was burnt to the ground, the general only escaping in his shirt. He had been dreaming he was dead and in hell. His precious guineas were secreted in the wainscot, the ceiling, and other hiding-places known only to himself. He blasphemed, wept, and tore his hair. Suddenly he grew calm. After all, the loss was not irrepara-ble, he reflected. Gold would melt, it is true; but he would find it all, of course he would, at daybreak, run into a solid lump in the cellar— every guinea. That is true of ordinary gold.

The general worked with the energy of despair clearing away the rubbish. He refused all offers of assistance: he dared not accept them. But the gold had vanished. Whether it was really consumed, or had passed again into the massy entrails of the earth, will never be known. It is certain that every vestige of it had disappeared.

When the general died and was buried, strange rumors began to circulate. To quiet them, the grave was opened; but when the lid was removed from the coffin, it was found to be empty.

Having reached Centre Harbor at two in the afternoon, there was still time to ascend Red Hill before sunset. This eminence would be called a mountain anywhere else. Its altitude is inconsiderable, but its situation at the head of the lake, on its very borders, is highly favora-ble to a commanding prospect of the surrounding lake region. There

are two summits, the northern and highest being only a
little more than two thousand
feet.

For such an excursion little
preparation is necessary. In fact a carriage-
road ascends within a mile of the superior summit; and from this point the path is one of the
easiest I have ever traversed. The value of a pure atmosphere is so
well understood by every mountain tourist that he will neglect no op-

portunity which this thrice-fickle element offers him. This was a day of days.

After a little promenade of two hours, or two hours and a half, I reached the cairn on the summit, from which a tattered signal-flag fluttered in the breeze. Without extravagance, the view is one of the most engaging that the eye ever looked upon. I had before me that beautiful valley extending between the Sandwich chain on the left and the Ossipee range on the right, the distance filled by a background of mountains. It was across this valley that we saw Mount Washington, while coming up the lake. But that noble peak was now hid.

The first chain trending to the west threw one gigantic arm around the beautiful little Squam Lake, which like a magnificent gem sparkled at my feet. The second stretched its huge rampart along the eastern shores of Winnipiseogee.

The surface of this valley is tumbled about in most charming disorder. Three villages crowned as many eminences in the foreground; three little lakes, half hid in the middle distance, blue as turquoise, lighted the fading hues of field and forest. Hamlets and farms, groves and forests innumerable, were scattered broadcast over this inviting landscape. The harvests were gathered, and the mellowed tints of green, orange, and gold resembled rich old tapestry. Men and animals looked like insects creeping along the roads.

From this point of view the Sandwich Mountains took far greater interest and character, and I remarked that no two summits were precisely alike in form or outline. Higher and more distant peaks peered curiously over their brawny shoulders from their lairs in the valley of the Pemigewasset; but more remarkable, more weird than all, was the gigantic monolith which tops the rock-ribbed pile of Chocorua. The more I looked, the more this monstrous freak of nature fascinated. As the sun glided down the west, a ruddy glow tinged its pinnacle; while the shadows lurking in the ravines stole up the mountain side and crouched for a final spring upon the summit. Little by little, twilight flowed over the valley, and a thin haze rose from its surface.

I had waited for this moment, and now turned to the lakes. Winnipiseogee was visible throughout its whole length, the multitude of islands peeping above it giving the idea of an inundation rather than an inland sea. On the farthest shores mere specks of white denoted houses; and traced in faint relief on the southern sky, so unsubstantial, indeed, as to render it doubtful if it were sky or mountain, was the Grand Monadnock, the fixed sentinel of all this august assemblage of mountains.

Glowing in sunset splendor, streaked with all the hues of the rainbow, the lake was indeed magnificent.

In vain the eye roved hither and thither seeking some foil to this peerless beauty. Everywhere the same unrivalled picture led it captive over thirty miles of gleaming water, up the graceful curves of the mountains, to rest at last among crimson clouds floating in rosy vapor over their notched summits.

Imagination must assist the reader to reproduce this ravishing spectacle. To attempt to describe it is like a profanation. Paradise seemed to have opened wide its gates to my enraptured gaze; or had I surprised the secrets of the unknown world? I stood silent and spellbound, with a strange, exquisite feeling at the heart. I felt a thrill of pain when a voice from the forest broke the solemn stillness which alone befitted this almost supernatural vision. Now I understood the pagan's adoration of the sun. My mind ran over the most striking or touching incidents of Scripture, where the sublimity of the scene is always in harmony with the grandeur of the event—the Temptation, the Sermon on the Mount, the Transfiguration—and memory brought to my aid these words, so simple, so tender, yet so expressive, "And he went up into the mountain to pray, himself, alone."

3

III.

CHOCORUA.

> " There I saw above me mountains,
> And I asked of them what century
> Met them in their youth."

AFTER a stay at Centre Harbor long enough to gain a knowledge of its charming environs, but which seemed all too brief, I took the stage at two o'clock one sunny afternoon for Tamworth. I had resolved, if the following morning should be clear, to ascend Chocorua, which from the summit of Red Hill seemed to fling his defiance from afar.

Following my custom, I took an outside seat with the driver. There being only three or four passengers, what is frequently a bone of contention was settled without that display of impudent selfishness which is seen when a dozen or more travellers are all struggling for precedence. But at the steamboat landing the case was different. I remained a quiet looker-on of the scene that ensued. It was sufficiently ridiculous.

At the moment the steamboat touched her pier the passengers prepared to spring to the shore, and force had to be used to keep them back until she could be secured. An instant after the crowd rushed pell-mell up the wharf, surrounded the stage, and began, women as well as men, a promiscuous scramble for the two or three unoccupied seats at the top.

Two men and one woman succeeded in obtaining the prizes. The woman interested me by the intense triumph that sparkled in her black eyes and glowed on her cheeks at having distanced several competitors of her own sex, to say nothing of the men. She beamed! As I made room for her, she said, with a toss of the head, " I guess I haven't been through Lake George for nothing."

Crack! We were jolting along the road, around the base of Red

Hill, the horses stepping briskly out at the driver's chirrup, the coach pitching and lurching like a gondola in a sea. What a sense of exhilaration, of lightness! The air so pure and elastic, the odor of the pines so fragrant, so invigorating, which we breathe with all the avidity of a convalescent who for the first time crosses the threshold of his chamber. Each moment I felt my body growing lighter. A delicious sense of self-ownership breaks the chain binding us to the toiling, struggling, worrying life we have left behind. We carry our world with us. Life begins anew, or rather it has only just begun.

The view of the ranges which on either side elevate two immense walls of green is kept for nearly the whole distance. As we climb the hill into Sandwich, Mount Israel is the prominent object; then brawny Whiteface, Passaconnaway's pyramid, Chocorua's mutilated spire advance, in their turn, into line. Sometimes we were in a thick forest, sometimes on a broad, sunny glade; now threading our way through groves of pitch-pine, now winding along the banks of the Bear-Camp River.

The views of the mountains, as the afternoon wore away, grew more and more interesting. The ravines darkened, the summits brightened. Cloud-shadows chased each other up and down the steeps, or, flitting slowly across the valley, spread thick mantles of black that seemed to deaden the sound of our wheels as we passed over them. On one side all was light, on the other all gloom. But the landscape is not all that may be seen to advantage from the top of a stage-coach.

From time to time, as something provoked an exclamation of surprise or pleasure, certain of the inside occupants manifested open discontent. They were losing something where they had expected to see everything.

While the horses were being changed, one of the insides, I need not say it was a woman, thrust her head out of the window, and addressed the young person perched like a bird upon the highest seat. Her voice was soft and persuasive:

" Miss!"

" Madam!"

" I'm so afraid you find it too cold up there. Sha'n't I change places with you?"

The little one gave her voice a droll inflection as she briskly replied, "Oh dear no, thank you; I'm very comfortable indeed."

" But," urged the other, "you don't look strong; indeed, dear, you don't. Aren't you very, *very* tired, sitting so long without any support to your back?"

" Thanks, no; my spine is the strongest part of me."

" But," still persisted the inside, changing her voice to a loud whisper, "to be sitting alone with all those men!"

" They mind their business, and I mind mine," said the little one, reddening; "besides," she quickly added, "you proposed changing places, I believe!"

" Oh!" returned the other, with an accent impossible to convey in words, "if you like it."

" I tell you what, ma'am," snapped the one in possession, "I've been all over Europe alone, and was never once insulted except by persons of my own sex."

This home-thrust ended the colloquy. The first speaker quickly drew in her head, and I remarked a general twitching of muscles on the faces around me. The driver shook his head in silent glee. The little woman's eyes emitted sparks.

From West Ossipee I drove over to Tamworth Iron Works, where I passed the night, and where I had, so to speak, Chocorua under my thumb.

This mountain being the most proper for a legend, it accordingly has one. Here it is in all its purity:

After the terrible battle in which the Sokokis were nearly destroyed, a remnant of the tribe, with their chief, Chocorua, fled into the fastnesses of these mountains, where the foot of a white man had never intruded. Here they trapped the beaver, speared the salmon, and hunted the moose.

The survivors of Lovewell's band brought the first news of their disaster to the settlements. More like spectres than living men, their haggard looks, bloodshot eyes, and shaking limbs, their clothing hanging about them in shreds, announced the hardships of that long and terrible march but too plainly.

Among those who had set out with the expedition were three brothers—one a mere stripling, the others famous hunters. The eldest of the three, having fallen lame on the second day, was left behind. His brethren would have conducted him back to the nearest village, but he promptly refused their proffered aid, saying,

"'Tis enough to lose one man; three are too many. Go; do my part as well as your own."

The two had gone but a few steps when the disabled ranger called the second brother back.

" Tom," said the elder, "take care of our brother."

"Surely," replied the other, in some surprise. "Surely," he repeated.

" I charge you," continued the first speaker, "watch over the boy as I would myself."

" Never fear, Lance; whatever befalls Hugh happens to me."

" Not so," said the other, with energy; "you must die for him, if need be."

" They shall chop me as fine as sausage-meat before a hair of the lad's head is harmed."

"God bless you, Tom!" The brothers then embraced and separated.

"What was our brother saying to you?" demanded the younger, when Tom rejoined him.

"He begged me, seeing he could not go with us, to shoot two or three redskins for him; and I promised." The two then quickened their pace in order to overtake their comrades.

Among those who succeeded in regaining the settlements was a man who had been wounded in twenty places. He was at once a ghastly and a pitiful object. Faint with hunger, fatigue, and loss of blood, he reeled, fell, slowly rose to his feet, and sunk lifeless at the entrance to the village. This time he did not rise again.

A crowd ran up. When they had wiped the blood and dirt from the dead man's face, a by-stander threw himself upon the body with the cry, "My God, it is Tom!"

The following day the surviving brother joined a strong party despatched by the colonial authorities to the scene of Lovewell's encounter, where they arrived after a forced march. Here, among the trampled thickets, they found the festering corpses of the slain. Among them was Hugh, the younger brother. He was riddled with bullets and shockingly mangled. Up to this moment, Lance had hoped against hope; now the dread reality stared him in the face. The stout ranger grew white, his fingers convulsively clutched the barrel of his gun, and something like a curse escaped through his clinched teeth; then, kneeling beside the body, he buried his face in his hands. Hugh's blood cried aloud for vengeance.

Thorough but unavailing search was made for the savages. They had disappeared, after applying the torch to their village. Silently and sadly the rangers performed the last service for their fallen comrades, and then, turning their backs upon the mountains, commenced their march homeward.

The next day the absence of Lance was remarked; but, as he was their best hunter, the rangers made no doubt he would rejoin them at the next halt.

Chocorua was not ignorant that the English were near. Like the vulture, he scented danger from afar. From the summit of the mountain he had watched the smoke of the hostile camp-fires stealing above the forest. The remainder of the tribe had buried themselves still deeper in the wilderness. They were too few for attack, too weak for defence.

One morning the chief ascended the pinnacle, and swept the horizon with his piercing eye. Far in the south a faint smoke told where the foe had pitched his last encampment. Chocorua's dark eye lighted with exultation. The accursed pale-faces were gone.

He turned to descend the mountain, but had not taken ten steps when a white hunter, armed to the teeth, started from behind the crags and barred his passage. The chief recoiled, but not with fear, as the muzzle of his adversary's weapon touched his naked breast. The white man's eyes shone with deadly purpose, as he forced the chieftain, step by step, back to the highest point of the mountain. Chocorua could not pass except over the hunter's dead body.

Glaring into each other's eyes with mortal hate, the two men reached the summit.

"Chocorua will go no farther," said the chief, haughtily.

The white man trembled with excitement. For a moment he could not speak. Then, in a voice husky with suppressed emotion, he exclaimed,

"Die, then, like a dog, thou destroyer of my family, thou incarnate devil! The white man has been in Chocorua's wigwam; has counted their scalps—father, mother, sister, brother. He has tracked him to the mountain-top. Now, demon or devil, Chocorua dies by my hand."

The chief saw no escape. He comprehended that his last moment was come. As if all the savage heroism of his race had come to his aid, he drew himself up to his full height, and stood erect and motionless as a statue of bronze upon the enormous pedestal of the mountain. His dark eye blazed, his nostrils dilated, the muscles of his bronzed forehead stood out like whip-cord. The black eagle's feather in his scalp-lock fluttered proudly in the cool morning breeze. He stood thus for a moment looking death sternly in the face, then, raising his bared arm with a gesture of superb disdain, he spoke with energy:

"Chocorua is unarmed; Chocorua will die. His heart is big and strong with the blood of the accursed pale-face. He laughs at death. He spits in the white man's face. Go; tell your warriors Chocorua died like a chief!"

With this defiance on his lips the chief sprung from the brink into the unfathomable abyss below. An appalling crash was followed by a death-like silence. As soon as he recovered from his stupor the hunter ran to the verge of the precipice and looked over. A horrible fascina-

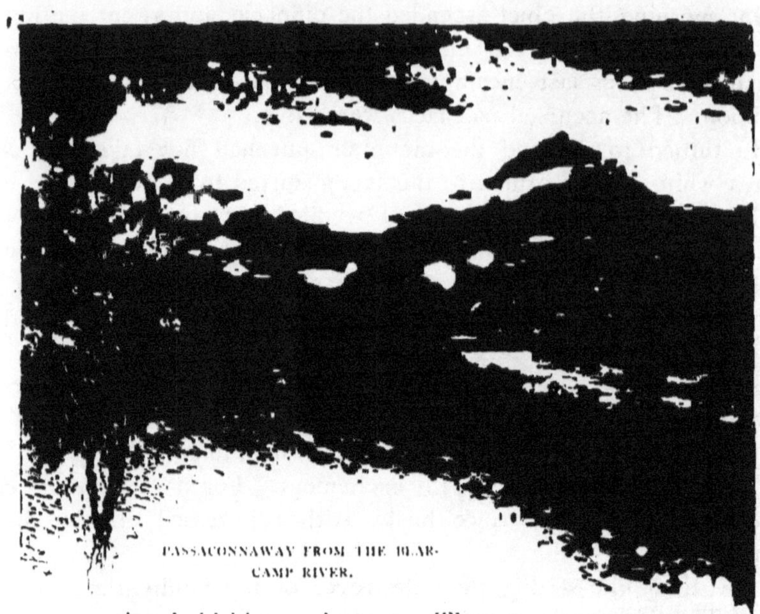

PASSACONNAWAY FROM THE BEAR-
CAMP RIVER.

tion held him an instant.   Then, shouldering his gun, he retraced his steps down the mountain, and the next day rejoined his comrades.

The general and front views of the Sandwich group, which may be had in perfection from the hill behind the Chocorua House, or from the opposite elevation, are very striking, embracing as they do the principal summits from Chocorua to the heavy mass of Black Mountain.   There are more distinct traits, perhaps, embodied in this range than in any other among the White Hills, except that incomparable band of peaks constituting the northern half of the great chain itself.   There seems, too, a special fitness in designating these mountains by their Indian titles — Chocorua, Paugus, Passaconnaway, Wonnalancet — a group of great sagamores, wild, grand, picturesque.[1]

------

[1] No tradition attaches to the last three peaks.   Passaconnaway was a great chieftain and conjurer of the Pennacooks.   It is of him the poet Whittier writes:

> Burned for him the drifted snow,
> Bade through ice fresh lilies blow,
> And the leaves of summer grow
> Over winter's wood.

This noted patriarch and necromancer, in whose arts not only the Indians but the English

The highway now skirted the margin of Chocorua Lake, a lovely little sheet of water voluptuously reposing at the foot of its overshadowing mountain. I cannot call Chocorua beautiful, yet of all the White Mountain peaks is it the most individual, the most aggressively suggestive. But the lake, fast locked in the embrace of encircling hills, bathed in all the affluence of the blessed sunlight, its bosom decorated with white lilies, its shores glassed in water which looks like a sheet of satin—ah, this was beautiful indeed! Its charming seclusion, its rare combination of laughing water and impassive old mountains; above all, the striking contrast between its chaste beauty and the huge-ribbed thing rising above, awakens a variety of sensations. It is passing strange. The mountain attracts, and at the same time repels you. Two sentiments struggle here for mastery—open admiration, energetic repulsion. For the first time, perhaps, in his life, the beholder feels an antipathy for a creation of inanimate nature. Chocorua suggests some fabled prodigy of the old mythology—a headless Centaur, sprung from the foul womb of earth. The lake seems another Andromeda exposed to a monster.

A beautiful Indian legend ran to the effect that the stillness of the lake was sacred to the Great Spirit, and that if a human voice was heard upon its waters the offender's canoe would instantly sink to the bottom.

Chocorua, as seen from Tamworth, shows a long, undulating ridge of white rising over one of green, both extending toward the east, and opening between a deep ravine, through which a path ascends to the summit. But this way affords no view until the summit is close at hand. Beyond the hump-backed ridge of Chocorua the tip of the southern peak of Moat Mountain peers over, like a mountain standing on tiptoe.

The mountain, with its formidable outworks, is constantly in view until the highway is left for a wood-road winding around its base into an interval where there is a farm-house. Here the road ends and the ascent begins.

Taking a guide here, who was strong, nimble, and sure-footed, but who proved to be lamentably ignorant of the topography of the country, we were in a few moments rapidly threading the path up the mountain.

---

seemed to have put entire faith, after living to a great age, was, according to the tradition, translated to heaven from the summit of Mount Washington, after the manner of Elias, in a chariot of fire, surrounded by a tempest of flame. Wonnalancet was the son and successor of Passaconnaway. Paugus, an under chief of the Pigwackets, or Sokokis, killed in the battle with Lovewell, related in the next chapter.

It ought to be said here that, with rare exceptions, the men who serve you in these ascensions should be regarded rather as porters than as guides.

In about an hour we reached the summit of the first mountain; for there are four subordinate ridges to cross before you stand under the single block of granite forming the pinnacle.

CHOCORUA.

When reconnoitring this pinnacle through your glass, at a distance of five miles, you will say to scale it would be difficult; when you have climbed close underneath you will say it is impossible. After surveying it from the bare ledges of Bald Mountain, where we stood letting the cool breeze blow upon us, I asked my guide where we could ascend. He pointed out a long crack, or crevice, toward the left, in which a few bushes were growing. It is narrow, almost perpendicular, and seemingly impracticable. I could not help exclaiming, "What, up there! nothing but birds of the air can mount that sheer wall!" It is, however, there or nowhere you must ascend.

The whole upper zone of the mountain seems smitten with palsy.

Except in the ravines between the inferior summits, nothing grew, nothing relieved the wide-spread desolation. Beyond us rose the enormous conical crag, scarred and riven by lightning, which gives to Chocorua its highly distinctive character. It is no longer ashen, but black with lichens. There was little of symmetry, nothing of grace; only the grandeur of power. You might as well pelt it with snow-balls as batter it with the mightiest artillery. For ages it has brushed the tempest aside, has seen the thunder-bolt shivered against its imperial battlements; for ages to come it will continue to defy the utmost power that can assail it. And what enemies it has withstood, overthrown, or put to rout! Not far from the base of the pinnacle evidence that the mountain was once densely wooded is on all sides. The rotted stumps of large trees still cling with a death-grip to the ledges, the shrivelled trunks lie bleaching where they were hurled by the hurricane. Many years ago this region was desolated by fire. In the night Old Chocorua, lighting his fiery torch, stood in the midst of his own funeral pyre. The burning mountain illuminated the sky and put out the stars. A brilliant circle of light, twenty miles in extent, surrounded the flaming peak like a halo; while underneath an immense tongue of forked flame licked the sides of the summit with devouring haste. The lakes, those bright jewels lying in the lap of the valleys, glowed like enormous carbuncles. Superstitious folk regarded the conflagration as a portent of war or pestilence. In the morning a few charred trunks, standing erect, were all that remained of the original forest. The rocks themselves bear witness to the intense heat which has either cracked them wide open, crumbled them in pieces, or divested them, like oysters, of their outer shell, all along the path of the conflagration.

The walk over the lower summits to the base of the peak occupied another hour, and is a most profitable feature of the ascent. On each side a superb panorama of mountains and lakes, of towns, villages, and hamlets, is being slowly unrolled; while every forward step develops the inaccessible character of the high summit more and more.

Having strayed from the path to gather blueberries, my companion set me again on the march by pointing out where a bear had been feeding not long before. Yet, while assuring me that Bruin was perfectly harmless at this season, I did not fail to remark that my guide made the most rapid strides of the day after this discovery. While feeling our way around the base of the pinnacle, in order to gain the ravine by

which it is attacked, the path suddenly stopped. At the right, projecting rocks, affording a hold for neither hand nor foot, rose like a wall;
before us, joined to the perpendicular rock, an unbroken ledge of bare
granite, smoothly polished by ice, swept down by a sharp incline hundreds of feet, and then broke off abruptly into profounder depths. To
advance upon this ledge, as steep as a roof, and where one false step
would inevitably send the climber rolling to the bottom of the ravine,
demands steady nerves. It invests the whole jaunt with just enough of
the perilous to excite the apprehensions, or provoke the enthusiasm of
the individual who stands there for the first time, looking askance at his
guide, and revolving the chances of crossing it in safety. While debat-
ing with myself whether to take off my boots, or go down on my hands
and knees and creep, the guide crossed this place with a steady step;
and, upon reaching the opposite side, grasped a fragment of rock with
one hand while extending his staff to me with the other. Rather than
accept his assistance, I passed over with an assurance I was far from
feeling; but when we came down the mountain I walked across with
far more ease in my stockings.[1]

When he saw me safely over, my conductor moved on, with the
remark,

"A skittish place."

"Skittish," indeed! We proceeded to drag ourselves up the ravine
by the aid of bushes, or such protruding rocks as offered a hold. From
the valley below we must have looked like flies creeping up a wall.
After a breathless scramble, which put me in mind of the escalade of
the Iron Castle of Porto Bello, where the English, having no scaling-lad-
ders, mounted over each other's shoulders, we came to a sort of plateau,
on which was a ruined hut. The view here is varied and extensive; but
after regaining our breath we hastened to complete the ascent, in order
to enjoy, in all its perfection, the prospect awaiting us on the summit.

Like Goethe's Wilhelm Meister, it is among mountains that my
knowledge of them has been obtained. I have little hesitation, then, in
pronouncing the view from Chocorua one of the noblest that can reward
the adventurous climber; for, notwithstanding it is not a high peak, and
cannot, therefore, unfold the whole mountain system at a glance, it yet

---

[1] Something has since been done by the Appalachian Club to render this part of the ascent less hazardous than it formerly was.

affords an unsurpassed view-point, from which one sees the surrounding mountains rising on all sides in all their majesty, and clothed in all their terrors.

Let me try to explain why Chocorua is such a remarkable and eligible post of observation.

One comprehends perfectly that the last high building on the skirts of a city embraces the largest unobstructed view of the surrounding country. This mountain is placed at the extremity of a range that abuts upon the lower Saco valley, and therefore overlooks all the hill-country on the east and south-east as far as the sea-coast. The arc of this circle of vision extends from the Camden Hills to Agamenticus, or from the Penobscot to the Piscataqua. The day being one of a thousand, I distinctly saw the ocean with the naked eye; not merely as a white blur on the horizon's edge, but actual blue water, over which smoke was curling. This magnificent *coup-d'œil* embraces the scattered villages of Conway, Fryeburg, Madison, Eaton, Ossipee, with their numerous lakes and streams. I counted seventeen of the former flashing in the sun.

In the second place, Chocorua stands at the entrance to the valley opening between the Sandwich and Ossipee chains, and commands, therefore, to the south-west, between these natural walls, the northern limb of Winnipiseogee and of Squam, which are seen glittering on each side of Red Hill. In the foreground, at the foot of the mountain, Chocorua Lake is beyond question the most enticing object in a landscape wonderfully lighted and enriched by its profusion of brilliant waters, which resemble so many highly burnished reflectors multiplying the rays of the sun. I was now looking back to my first station on Red Hill, only the range of vision was much more extensive. It is unnecessary to recapitulate the names of the villages and summits seen in this direction. Over the lakes, Winnipiseogee and Squam, the humid peaks of Mount Belknap and of Mount Kearsarge, in Warner, last caught the eye. These two sections of the landscape first meet the eye of the climber while advancing toward the peak, whose rugged head and brawny shoulders intercept the view to the north, only to be enjoyed when the mountain is fully conquered.

Upon the cap-stone crowning the pinnacle, supporting myself by grasping the signal-staff planted on the highest point of this rock, from which the wind threatened to sweep us like chaff, I enjoyed the third and final act of this sublime tableau, in which the whole company of

mountains is crowded upon the stage. Hundreds of dark and bristling
shapes confronted us. Like a horde of barbarians, they seemed silently
awaiting the signal to march upon the lowlands. As the wind swept
through their ranks, an impatient murmur rose from the midst. Each
mountain shook its myriad spears, and gave its voice to swell the sublime chorus. At first all was confusion; then I began to seek out the
chiefs, whose rock-helmed heads, lifted high above their grisly battalions,
invested each with a distinction and a sovereignty which yielded nothing except to that imperial peak over which attendant clouds hovered or
floated swiftly away, as if bearing a message to those distant encampments pitched on the farthest verge of the horizon.

At my left hand extended all the summits, forming at their western
extremity the valley of Mad River, and terminating in the immovable
mass of Black Mountain. The peaks of Tripyramid, Tecumseh, and
Osceola stretched along the northern course of this stream, and over
them gleamed afar the massive plateau-ridge of Mooschillock. From
my stand-point the great wall of the Sandwich chain, which from Tamworth presents an unbroken front to the south, now divided into ridges'
running north and south, separated by profound ravines. Paugus
crouched at my feet; Passaconnaway elevated his fine crest next; Whiteface, his lowered and brilliant front; and then Black Mountain, the giant
landmark of half a score of towns and villages.

Directly at my feet, to the north-west, the great intervale of Swift
River gleamed from the depths of this valley, like sunshine from a
storm-cloud. Following the course of this little oasis, the eye wandered
over the inaccessible and untrodden peaks of the Pemigewasset wilderness, resting last on the blue ridge of the Franconia Mountains. About
midway of this line one sees the bristling slopes of Mounts Carrigain
and Hancock, and the Carrigain Notch, through which a hardy pedestrian may pass from the Pemigewasset to the Saco by following the
course of the streams flowing out of it. Besides its solitary, picturesque
grandeur, Carrigain has the distinction of being the geographical centre
of the White Mountain group. Taking its peak for an axis, a radius
thirty miles long will describe a circle, including in its sweep nearly the
whole mountain system. In this sense Carrigain is, therefore, the hub
of the White Mountains.

Having explored the horizon thus far, I now turned more to the
north, where, by a fortunate chance, Chocorua dominates a portion of

the chain intervening between itself and the Saco Valley. I was looking straight up this valley through the great White Mountain Notch.
There was the dark spire of Mount Willey, and the scarred side of
Webster. There was the arched rock of Mount Willard, and over it
the liquid profile of Cherry Mountain. It was superb; it was idyllic.
Such was the perfect transparency of the air, that I clearly distinguished
the red color of the slides on Mount Webster without the aid of my
glass.

From this centre, outlined with a bold, free hand against the azure,
the undulations of the great White Mountains ascended grandly to the
dome of Mount Washington, and then plunged into the defiles of the
Pinkham Notch. Following this line eastward, the eye traversed the
mountains of Jackson to the half-closed aperture of the Carter Notch,
finally resting on the pinnacle of Kearsarge. Without stirring a single
step, we have taken a journey of three hundred miles.

Down in the valley the day was one of the sultriest; up here it was
so cold that our teeth chattered. We were forced to descend into the
hollow lying between the northerly foot of the peak and the first of the
bald knobs constituting the great white ridge of the mountain. Here
is a fine spring, and here, on either side of this singular rock-gallery, is
a landscape of rare beauty enclosed by its walls. Here, too, the mutilated pyramid of the peak rises before you like an antique ruin. One
finds, without effort, striking resemblances to winding galleries, bastions,
and battlements. He could pass days and weeks here without a single
wish to return to earth. Here we ate our luncheon, and perused the
landscape at leisure. Before us stretched the long course of the Saco,
from its source in the Notch to where, with one grand sweep to the east,
it takes leave of the mountains, flows awhile demurely through the lowlands, and in two or three infuriated plunges reaches the sea.

I do not remember when I have more fully enjoyed the serene calm
of a Sabbath evening than while wandering among the fragrant and
stately pines that skirt the shores of Lake Chocorua. Indeed, except
for the occasional sound of hoofs along the cool and shady road, or of
voices coming from the bosom of the lake itself, one might say a perpetual Sabbath reigned here. Yonder tall, athletic pines, those palms of
the north, through which the glimmer of water is seen, hum their monotonous lullaby to the drowsy lake. The mountains seem so many
statues to Silence. There is no use for speech here. The mute and

expressive language of two lovers, accustomed to read each others' secret thoughts, is the divine medium. Truant breezes ruffle the foliage in playful wantonness, but the trees only shake their green heads and murmur "Hush! hush!" A consecration is upon the mere, a hallowed light within the wood. Here is the place to linger over the pages of "Hyperion," or dream away the idle hours with the poets; and here, stretched along the turf, one gets closer to Nature, studying her with ever-increasing wonder and delight, or musing upon the thousand forms of mysterious life swarming in the clod under his hand.

Charming, too, are the walks by the lake-side in the effulgence of the harvest-moon; and enchanting the white splendor quivering on its dark waters. A boat steals by; see! its oars dip up molten silver. The voyagers troll a love-ditty. Dangerous ground this colonnade of woods and yonder sparkling water for self-conscious lovers! Love and the ocean have the same subtle sympathy with moonlight. The stronger its beams the higher rises the flood.

Very little of the world—but that little the best part—gets in here. It is out of the beaten path of mountain-travel, so that those only who have in a manner served their apprenticeship are sojourners. One small hotel and a few boarding-houses easily accommodate all comers. For people who like to refine their pleasures, as well as their society, or who have wearied of life at the great hotels, such a place offers a most tempting retreat. Display makes no part of the social regime. Mrs. P—— is not jealous of Mrs. Q——'s diamonds. Ladies stroll about unattended, gather water-lilies, cardinal-flowers, and rare ferns by brook or way-side. Gentlemen row, drive, climb the mountains, or make little pedestrian tours of discovery. Quiet people are irresistibly attracted to this kind of life, which, with a good degree of probability, they assert to be the true and only rational way of enjoying the mountains.

IV.

LOVEWELL.

Of worthy Captain Lovewell I purpose now to sing,
How valiantly he served his country and his king.
Old Ballad.

LET us make a détour to historic Fryeburg, leaving the cars at Conway, which in former times enjoyed a happy pre-eminence as the centre upon which the old stage-routes converged, and where travellers, going or returning from the mountains, always passed the night. But those old travellers have mostly gone where the name of Chatigee, by which both drivers and tourists liked to designate Conway, is going; only there is for the name, fortunately, no resurrection. No one knows its origin; none will mourn its decease.

It is here, at Conway, or Conway Corner, that first enrapturing view of the White Mountains bursts upon the traveller like a splendid vision. But we shall see it again on our return from Fryeburg. Moreover, I enjoyed this constant espionage from a distance before a nearer approach, this exchange of preliminary civilities before coming closer to the heart of the mountains.

Fryeburg stands on a dry and sandy plain, elevated above the Saco River. It lies behind the mountain range, which, terminating in Conway, compels the river to make a right angle. Turning these mountains, the river seems now to be in no hurry, but coils about the meadows in a manner that instantly recalls the famous Connecticut Ox-Bow. Chocorua and Kearsarge are the two prominent figures in the landscape.

The village street is most beautifully shaded by elms of great size, which, giving to each other an outstretched hand over the way, spring an arch of green high above, through which we look up and down. At one end justice is dispensed at the Oxford House—an inn with a pedigree; at the other learning is diffused in the academy where Webster

LOVEWELL'S POND.

once taught and disciplined the rising generation. A scroll over the inn door bears the date of 1763. The first school-house and the first framed house built in Fryeburg are still standing, a little way out of the village. On our way to the remarkable rock, emerging from the plain like a walrus from the sea, we linger a moment in the village graveyard to read the long inscription on the monument of General Joseph Frye, a veteran of the old wars, and founder of the town which bears his name. Ascending now the rock to which we just referred, called the Jockey Cap, we are lifted high above the plain, having the river meadows, the graceful loops of the river itself, the fine pyramid of Kearsarge on one side, and on the other the dark sheet of Lovewell's Pond stretched at our feet.

It was here, under the shadow of Mount Kearsarge, was fought one of the bloodiest and most obstinately contested battles that can be found in the annals of war; so terrible, indeed, that the story was repeated from fireside to fireside, and from generation to generation, as worthy a niche beside that of Leonidas and his band of heroes. Familiar as is the tale —and who does not know it by heart?—it can still send the blood throbbing to the temples, or coursing back to the heart. Unfortunately, the details are sufficiently meagre, but, in truth, they need no embellishment. Their very simplicity presents the tragedy in all its grandeur. It is an epic.

In April, 1725, John Lovewell, a hardy and experienced ranger of Dunstable, whose exploits had already noised his fame abroad, marched with forty-six men for the Indian villages at Pigwacket, now Fryeburg, Maine. At Ossipee he built a small fort, designed as a refuge in case of disaster. This precaution undoubtedly saved the lives of some of his men. He was now within two short marches of the enemy's village. The scouts having found Indian tracks in the neighborhood, Lovewell resumed his route, leaving one of his men who had fallen sick, his surgeon, and eight men, to guard the fort. His command was now reduced to thirty-four officers and men.

The rangers reached the shores of the beautiful lake which bears Lovewell's name, and bivouacked for the night.

The night passed without an alarm; but the sentinels who watched the encampment reported hearing strange noises in the woods. Lovewell scented the presence of his enemy.

In fact, on the morning of the 8th of May, while his band were on their knees seeking Divine favor in the approaching conflict, the report of a gun brought every man to his feet. Upon reconnoitring, a solitary Indian was discovered on a point of land about a mile from the camp.

The leader immediately called his men about him, and told them that they must now quickly decide whether to fight or retreat. The men, with one accord, replied that they had not come so far in search of the enemy to beat a shameful retreat the moment he was found. Seeing his band possessed with this spirit, Lovewell then prepared for battle. The rangers threw off their knapsacks and blankets, looked to their primings, and loosened their knives and axes. The order was then given, and they moved cautiously out of their camp. Believing the enemy was in his front, Lovewell neglected to place a guard over his baggage.

Instead of plunging into the woods, the Indian who had alarmed the camp stood where he was first seen until the scouts fired upon him, when he returned the fire, wounding Lovewell and one other. Ensign Wyman then levelled his musket and shot him dead. The day began thus unfortunately for the English. Lovewell was mortally wounded in the abdomen, but continued to give his orders.

After clearing the woods in their front without finding any more Indians, the rangers fell back toward the spot where they had deposited their packs. This was a sandy plain, thinly covered with pines, at the north-east end of the lake.

During their absence, the Indians, led by the old chief, Paugus, whose name was a terror throughout the length and breadth of the English frontiers, stumbled upon the deserted encampment. Paugus counted the packs, and, finding his warriors outnumbered the rangers,

the wily chief placed them in ambush: he divined that the English
would return from their unsuccessful scout sooner or later, and he prepared to repeat the tactics used with such fatal effect at Bloody Brook,
and at the defeat of Wadsworth. This consisted in arranging his savages in a semicircle, the two wings of which, enveloping the rangers,
would expose them to a murderous cross-fire at short musket-range.

Without suspecting their danger, Lovewell's men fell into the fatal
snare which the crafty Paugus had thus spread for them. Hardly had
they entered it when the grove blazed with a deadly volley, and resounded with the yells of the Indians. As if confident of their prey,
they even left their coverts, and flung themselves upon the English with
a fury nothing could withstand.

In this onset Lovewell, who, notwithstanding his wound, bravely encouraged his men with voice and example, received a second wound, and
fell. Two of his lieutenants were killed at his side; but with desperate
valor the rangers charged up to the muzzles of the enemy's guns, killing
nine, and sweeping the others before them. This gallant charge cost
them eight killed, besides their captain; two more were badly wounded.

Twenty-three men had now to maintain the conflict with the whole
Sokokis tribe. Their situation was indeed desperate. Relief was impossible; for they were fifty miles from the nearest English settlements.
Their packs and provisions were in the enemy's hands, and the woods
swarmed with foes. To conquer or die was the only alternative. These
devoted Englishmen despaired of conquering, but they prepared to die
bravely.

Ensign Wyman, on whom the command devolved after the death of
Lovewell, was his worthy successor. Seeing the enemy stealing upon
his flanks as if to surround him, he ordered his men to fall back to the
shore of the lake, where their right was protected by a brook, and their
left by a rocky point extending into the lake. A few large pines stood
on the beach between.

This manœuvre was executed under a hot fire, which still further
thinned the ranks of the English. The Indians closed in upon them,
filling the air with demoniac yells whenever a victim fell. Assailing the
whites with taunts, and shaking ropes in their faces, they cried out to
them to yield. But to the repeated demands to surrender, the rangers
replied only with bullets. They thought of the fort and its ten defend-
ers, and hoped, or rather prayed, for night. This hope, forlorn as it

seemed, encouraged them to fight on, and they delivered their fire with fatal precision whenever an Indian showed himself. The English were in a trap, but the Indians dared not approach within reach of the lion's claws.

While this long combat was proceeding, one of the English went to the lake to wash his gun, and, on emerging at the shore, descried an Indian in the act of cleansing his own. This Indian was Paugus.

The ranger went to work like a man who comprehends that his life depends upon a second. The chief followed him in every movement. Both charged their guns at the same instant. The Englishman threw his ramrod on the sand; the Indian dropped his.

" Me kill you," said Paugus, priming his weapon from his powder-horn.

" The chief lies," retorted the undaunted ranger, striking the breech of his firelock upon the ground with such force that it primed itself. An instant later Paugus fell, shot through the heart.

" I said I should kill you," muttered the victor, spurning the dead body of his enemy, and plunging into the thickest of the fight.

Darkness closed the conflict, which had continued without cessation since ten in the morning. Little by little the shouts of the enemy grew feebler, and finally ceased. The English stood to their arms until mid-night, when, convinced that the savages had abandoned the sanguinary field of battle, they began their retreat toward the fort. Only nine were unhurt. Eleven were badly wounded, but were resolved to march with their comrades, though they died by the way. Three more were alive, but had received their death-wounds. One of these was Lieutenant Robbins, of Chelmsford. Knowing that he must be left behind, he begged his comrades to load his gun, in order that he might sell his life as dearly as possible when the savages returned to wreak their vengeance upon the wounded.

I have said that twenty-three men continued the fight after the bloody repulse in which Lovewell was killed. There were only twenty-two. The other, whose name the reader will excuse me from mentioning, fled from the field and gained the fort, where he spread the report that Lovewell was cut to pieces, himself being the sole survivor. This intelligence, striking terror, decided the little garrison to abandon the fort, which was immediately done, and in haste.

This was the crowning misfortune of the expedition. The rangers now became a band of panic-stricken fugitives. After incredible hard-ships, less than twenty starving, emaciated, and footsore men, half of them badly wounded, straggled into the nearest English settlements.

The loss of the Indians could only be guessed; but the battle led to the immediate abandonment of their village, from which so many war-parties had formerly harassed the English. Paugus, the savage wolf, the implacable foe of the whites, was dead. His tribe forsook the graves of their fathers, nor rested until they had put many long leagues be-tween them and their pursuers. For them the advance of the English was the Juggernaut under whose wheels their race was doomed to per-ish from the face of the earth.

V.

NORTH CONWAY.

"Tall spire from which the sound of cheerful bells
Just undulates upon the listening ear,
Groves, heaths, and smoking villages remote."

THE entrance to North Conway is, without doubt, the most beautiful and imposing introduction to the high mountains.

Although the traveller has for fifty miles skirted the outlying ranges, catching quick-shifting glimpses of the great summits, yet, when at last the train swings round the foot of the Moat range into the Saco Valley, so complete is the transition, so charming the picture, that not even the most apathetic can repress a movement of surprise and admiration. This is the moment when every one feels the inadequacy of his own conceptions.

Nature has formed here a vast antechamber, into which you are ushered through a gate-way of mountains upon the numerous inner courts, galleries, and cloisters of her most secluded retreats. Here the mountains fall back before the impetuous flood of the Saco, which comes pouring down from the summit of the great Notch, white, and panting with the haste of its flight. Here the river gives rendezvous to several of its larger affluents — the East Branch, the Ellis, the Swift — and, like an army taking the field, their united streams, sweeping grandly around the foot of the last mountain range, emerge into the open country. Here the valley, contracted at its extremity between the gentle slope of Kearsarge and the abrupt declivities of Moat, encloses an ellipse of verdant and fertile land ravishing to behold, skirted on one side by thick woods, behind which precipices a thousand feet high rise black and threatening, overlooked on the other by a high terrace, along which the village is built. It is the inferior summit of Kearsarge, which descends by a long, regular slope to the intervale at its upper end, while a secondary ridge of the Moats, advancing on the opposite side, drops into it by a precipice. The superb silver-gray crest of Kearsarge is seen rising in a regular pyramid behind the right shoulder of its lower summit. Ordinarily the house perched on the top is seen as distinctly as those in the village. It is the last in the village.

Looking up through this verdant mountain park, at a distance of twenty miles, the imposing masses of the great summits seem scaling the skies. Then, heavily massed on the right, comes the Carter range, divided by the cup-shaped dip of the Carter Notch; then the truncated cone of Double-Head; and then, with outworks firmly planted in the valley, the glittering pinnacle of Kearsarge. The mountain in front of you, looking up the village street, is Thorn Mountain, on the other side of which is Jackson, and the way up the Ellis Valley to the Pinkham Notch, the Glen House, Gorham, and the Androscoggin.

The traveller, who is ushered upon this splendid scene with the rapidity of steam, perceives that he is at last among real mountains,

MOUNT WASHINGTON FROM THE SACO.

and quickly yields to the indefinable charm which from this moment surrounds and holds him a willing captive.

Looking across the meadow from the village street, the eye is stopped by an isolated ridge of bare, overhanging precipices. It is thrust out into the valley from Moat Mountain, of which it forms a part, presenting two singular, regularly arched cliffs, seven hundred to nine hundred and fifty feet in height toward the village. The green forest underneath contrasts vividly with the lustrous black of these precipitous walls, which glisten brightly in the sunshine, where they are wet by tiny streams flowing down. On the nearest of these is a very curious resemblance to the head and shoulders of a horse in the act of rearing, occasioned by a white incrustation on the face of the cliff. This accident gives to it the name of White Horse Ledge. All marriageable ladies, maiden or widow, run out to look at it, in consequence of the belief current in New England that if, after seeing a white horse, you count a hundred, the first gentleman you meet will be your future husband! Underneath this cliff a charming little lake lies hid.

Next beyond is the Cathedral Ledge, so called from the curious rock cavity it contains; and still farther up the valley is Humphrey's Ledge, one of the finest rock-studies of them all when we stand underneath it.

THE LEDGES, NORTH CONWAY.

But the reader now has a general acquaintance with North Conway, and with its topography. He begins his study of mountain beauty in a spirit of loving enthusiasm, which leads him on and on to the ripeness of an education achieved by simply throwing himself upon the bosom of indulgent Nature, putting the world as far as possible behind him.

But now from these masses of hard rock let us turn once more to the valley, where the rich intervales spread an exhaustless feast for the eye. If autumn be the season, the vase-like elms, the stacks of yellow corn, the golden pumpkins looking like enormous oranges, the floor-cloth of green and gold damasked with purple gorse and coppice, give the idea of an immense table groaning beneath its luxurious weight of fruit and flowers.

Turn now to the mountain presiding with such matchless grace and dignity over the village. Kearsarge, in the twilight, deserves, like Lorenzo di Medicis, to be called "the magnificent." The yellow and orange foliage looks, for all the world, like a golden shower fallen upon it. The gray ledges at the apex, which the clear, yellow light renders almost incandescent, are far more in harmony with the rest of the mountain than in the vernal season.

Are we yet in sympathy with that free-masonry of art through which our eminent landscape-painters recognized here the true picturesque point of view of the great mountains, the effective contrasts and harmonious *ensemble* of the near scenery—the grandest allied with the humblest objects of nature? One cannot turn in any direction without recognizing a picture he has seen in the studios, or in the saloons of the clubs.

The first persons I saw on the platform of the railway-station were my quondam companions, the colonel and George. We met like friends who had parted only half an hour before. During dinner it was agreed that we should pass our afternoon among the cliffs. This arrangement appeared very judicious; the distance is short, and the attractions many.

We accordingly set out for the ledges at three in the afternoon. The weather did not look promising, to be sure, but we decided it sufficiently so for this promenade of three or four hours.

While *en route*, let me mention a discovery. One morning, while sitting on the piazza of the Kearsarge House enjoying the dreamy influence of the warm atmosphere, which spun its soft, gossamer web about the mountains, I observed a peculiar shadow thrown by a jutting mass of the Cathedral Ledge upon a smooth surface, which exactly resembled a human figure standing upright. I looked away, then back again, to see if I was not the victim of an illusion. No, it was still there. Now it is always there. The head and upper part of the body were inclined slightly forward, the legs perfectly formed. At ten every forenoon, punctual to the hour, this phantom, emerging from the rock, stands, fixed and motionless, as a statue, in its niche. At every turn of the sun, this shade silently interrogates the feverish activity that has replaced the silence of ages. One day or another I shall demand of my phantom what it has witnessed.

The road we followed soon turned sharply away from the main street of the village, to the left, and in a few rods more plunged into the Saco, leaving us standing on the bank, looking askance at a wide expanse of water, choked with bowlders, around which the swift current whirled and foamed with rage. We decided it too shallow to swim, but doubted if it was not too deep to ford. We had reached our Rubicon.

"We must wade," said the colonel, with decision.

"Precisely my idea," assented George, beginning to unlace his shoes.

I put my hand in the river. Ugh! it was as cold as ice.

Having assured ourselves no one saw us, we divested ourselves of shoes, stockings, pantaloons, and drawers. We put our stockings in our pockets, disposed our clothing in a roll over the shoulder, as soldiers do on the march, tied our shoes together, and hung them around our necks. Then, placing our hands upon each others' shoulders, as I have seen gymnasts do in a circus, we entered the river, like candidates for baptism, feeling our way, and catching our breath.

"*Sans-culottes*," suggested the colonel, who knew a little French.

"Kit-kats," added George, who knows something of art, as the water rose steadily above our knees.

The treacherous bowlders tripped us up at every step, so that one or the other was constantly floundering, like a stranded porpoise in a frog-pond. But, thanks to our device, we reached the middle of the river without anything worse than a few bruises. Here we were fairly stopped. The water was waist-deep, and the current every moment threatened to lift us from our feet. How foolish we looked!

Advance or retreat? That was the question. One pointed up stream, another down; while, to aggravate the situation, rain began to patter around us. In two minutes the river was steaming. George, who is a great infant, suggested putting our hands in our pockets, to keep them warm, and our clothes in the river, to keep them dry.

"By Jove!" ejaculated the colonel, "the river is smoking."

"Let us join the river," said George, producing his cigar-case.

Putting our heads together over the colonel's last match, thus forming an antique tripod of our bodies, we succeeded in getting a light; and for the first time, I venture to affirm, since its waters gushed from the mountains, incense ascended from the bosom of the Saco.

"I'm freezing!" stuttered George.

I was pushing forward, to cut the dilemma short, when the colonel interposed with,

"Stop; I want to tell you a story."

"A story? here—in the middle of the river?" we shouted.

"In the middle of the river; here—a story!" he echoed.

"I would like to sit down while I listen," observed George.

Evidently the coldness of the water had forced the blood into our friend's head. He was ill, but obstinate. We therefore resigned ourselves to hear him.

"This river and this situation remind me of the Potawatamies," he began.

"Potawatamies!" we echoed, with chattering teeth. "Go on; go on."

"When I was on the Plains," continued the colonel, "I passed some time among those Indians. During my stay, the chief invited me to accompany him on a buffalo-hunt. I accepted on the spot; for of all things a buffalo-hunt was the one I was most desirous of seeing. We set out at daybreak the next morning. After a few hours' march, we came to a stream between deep banks, and flowing with a rapid current, like this one—"

"Go on; go on!" we shiveringly articulated.

"At a gesture from the chief, a young squaw dismounted from her pony, advanced to the edge of the stream, and began, timidly, to wade it. When she hesitated, as she did two or three times, the chief said something which encouraged her to proceed. All at once she stopped, threw up her arms, and screamed something in the Indian dialect; at which all the braves burst into a loud laugh, the squaws joining in.

"'What does she say?' I asked of the chief.

"'Up to the middle,' he replied, pushing his pony into the stream."

The stream grew shallower, so that we soon emerged from the water upon the opposite bank. Here we poured the water from our shoes, and resumed our wet clothing. Everything was cooled, except our ardor.

As we approached nearer, the ledges were full of grim recesses, rude rock-niches, and traversed by perpendicular cracks from brow to base. "Take care!" I shouted; "there is a huge piece of the cliff just ready to fall."

In some places the rock is sheer and smooth, in others it is broken regularly down, for half its whole height, to where it is joined by rude buttresses of massive granite. The lithe maples climb up the steepest ravines, but cannot pass the waste of sheer rock stretching between them and the firs, which look down over the brink of the precipice. Rusted purple is the prevailing color, blotched here and there with white, like the drip oozing from limestone. We soon emerged on the shore of Echo Lake.

Hovering under the great precipices, which lie heavily shadowed on its glossy surface, are gathered the waters flowing from the airy heights above—the little rills, the rivulets, the cascades. The tremendous shadow the cliff flings down seems lying deep in the bosom of the lake, as if perpetually imprinted there. Slender birches, brilliant foliage, were daintily etched upon the surface, like arabesques on polished steel. The water is perfectly transparent, and without a ripple. Indeed, the breezes playing around the summit, or humming in the tree-tops, seem forbidden

ECHO LAKE, NORTH CONWAY.

to enter this haunt of Dryads. The lake laps the yellow strand with a light, fluttering movement. The place seems dedicated to silence itself.

To destroy this illusion, a man came out of a booth and touched off a small cannon. The effect was like knocking at half a dozen doors at once. And the silence which followed seemed all the deeper. Then the aged rock was pelted with questions, and made to jeer, laugh, menace, or curse by turns, or all at once. How grandly it bore all these petty insolences! How presumptuous in us thus to cover its hoary front with obloquy! We could never get the last word. We did not even come off in triumph. How ironically the mountain repeated, "Who are you?" and "What am I!" With what energy it at last vociferated, "Go to the devil!" To the Devil's Den we accordingly go.

Following a woodland path skirting the base of the cliffs, we were very soon before the entrance of the Devil's Den, formed by a huge piece of the cliff falling upon other detached fragments in such a way as to leave an aperture large enough to admit fifty persons at once. A ponderous mass divides the cavern into two chambers, one of which is light, airy, and spacious, the other dark, gloomy, and contracted—a mere hole. This might well have been the lair of the bears and panthers formerly roaming, unmolested, these woods.

The Cathedral is a recess higher up in the same cliff, hollowed out by the cleaving off of the lower rock, leaving the upper portion of the precipice overhanging. The top of the roof is as high as a tall tree. Some maples that have grown here since the outer portion of the rock fell, assist, with their straight-limbed, columnar trunks, the resemblance to a chancel. A little way off this cavity has really the appearance of a gigantic shell, like those fossils seen imbedded in subterranean rocks. We did not miss here the delicious glimpses of Kearsarge, and of the mountains across the valley which, now that the sun came out, were all in brilliant light, while the cool afternoon shadows already wrapped the woods about us in twilight gloom.

Still farther on we came upon a fine cascade falling down a long, irregular staircase of broken rock. One of these steps extends, a solid mass of granite, more than a hundred feet across the bed of the stream, and is twenty feet high. Unless the brook is full, it is not a single sheet we see, but twenty, fifty crystal streams gushing or spirting from the grooves they have channelled in the hard granite, and falling into basins they have hollowed out. It is these curious, circular stone cavities, out of which the freshest and cleanest water constantly pours, that give to the cascade the name of Diana's Baths. The water never dashes itself noisily down, but slips, like oil, from the rocks, with a pleasant, purling sound no single word of our language will correctly describe. From here we returned to the village in the same way that we came.[1]

The wild and bristling little mountain range on the east side of North Conway embodies a good deal of picturesque character. It is there our way lies to Artists' Falls, which are on a brook issuing from these Green Hills. I found the walk, following its windings, more remunerative than the falls themselves. The brook, flowing first over a smooth granite ledge, collects in a little pool below, out of which the

---

[1] The Saco has since been bridged, and is traversed with all ease.

pure water filters through bowlders and among glittering pebbles to a gorge between two rocks, down which it plunges. The beauty of this cascade consists in its waywardness. Now it is a thin sheet, flowing demurely along; now it breaks out in uncontrollable antics; and at length, as if tired of this sport, darts like an arrow down the rocky fissure, and is a mountain brook again.

The ascent of Kearsarge and of the Moats fittingly crowns the series of excursions which are the most attractive feature of out-of-door life at North Conway. The northern peak of Moat is the one most frequently climbed, but the southern affords almost equally admirable views of the Saco, the Ellis, and the Swift River valleys, with the mountain chains enclosing them. The prospect here is, however, much the same as that obtained from Chocorua, which is seen rising beyond the Swift River valley. To that description I must, therefore, refer the reader, who is already acquainted with its principal features.

The high ridge is an arid and desolate heap of summits stripped bare of vegetation by fire. When this fire occurred, twenty odd years ago, it drove the bears and rattlesnakes from their forest homes in great numbers, so that they fell an easy prey to their destroyers. A depression near its centre divides the ridge in two, constituting, in effect, two mountains. We crossed the range in its whole length, and, after newly refreshing ourselves with the admirable views had from its greater elevation, descended the northern peak to Diana's Baths. Probably the most striking view of the Moats is from Conway. Here the summits, thrown into a mass of lawless curves and blunted, prong-like protuberances, rear a blackened and weird-looking cluster on high. But for a wide region they divide with Chocorua the honors of the landscape, constituting, at Jackson especially, a large and imposing background, massively based and buttressed, and cutting through space with their trenchant edge.

In the winter of 1876, finding myself at North Conway, I determined to make the attempt to ascend Mount Kearsarge, notwithstanding two-thirds of the mountain were shrouded in snow, and the bare shaft constituting the spire sheathed in glittering ice. The mountain had definitively gone into winter-quarters.

I was up early enough to surprise, all at once, the unwonted and curiously-blended effect of moonlight, starlight, and the twilight of dawn. The new moon, with the old in her arms, balanced her shining

KEARSARGE IN WINTER.

crescent on the curved peak of Moat Mountain. All these high, surrounding peaks, carved in marble and flooded with effulgence, impressed
the spirit with that mingled awe and devotion felt among the antique
monuments of some vast cemetery. The sight thrilled and solemnized
by its chaste magnificence. Glittering stars, snow-draped summits, black
mountains casting sable draperies upon the dead white of the valley,
constituted a scene of sepulchral pomp into which the supernatural entered unchallenged. One by one the stars went out. The moon grew
pale. A clear emerald, overspreading the east, was reflected from lofty
peak and tapering spire.

Day broke bright, clear, and crisp. There, again, was the same matchless array of high and noble summits, sitting on thrones of alabaster whiteness. While the moon still lingered in the west, the broad red disk of the sun rose over the wooded ridges in the east. So sun and moon, monarch and queen, saluted each other. One gave the watchword, and descended behind the moated mountain; the other ascended the vacant throne. Thus night and day met and exchanged majestic salutation in the courts of the morning.

The mercury stood at three degrees below zero in the village, when I set out on foot for the mountain. A light fall of snow had renewed the Christmas decorations. The trees had newly-leaved and blossomed. Beautiful it was to see the dark old pines thick-flaked with new snow, and the same feathery substance lodged on every twig and branchlet, tangle of vines, or tuft of tawny yellow grass. Fir-trees looked like gigantic azaleas; thickets like coral groves. Nothing too slender or too fragile for the white flight to alight upon. Talk of decorative art! Even the telegraph-wires hung in broad, graceful festoons of white, and the poor washer-woman's clothes-line was changed into the same immaterial thing of beauty.

The ascent proved more toilsome than I had anticipated, as my feet broke through the frozen crust at every step. But if the climb had been difficult when in the woods, it certainly presented few attractions when I emerged from them half a mile below the summit. I found the surface of the bare ledges, which now continue to the top of the mountain, sheeted in ice, smooth and slippery as glass.

Many a time have I laughed heartily at the feverish indecision of a dog when he runs along the margin of a pond into which he has been urged to plunge. He turns this way and that, whines, barks, crouches for the leap, laps the water, but hesitates. Imagine, now, the same animal chasing some object upon slippery ice, his feet spread widely apart; his frantic efforts to stop; the circles described in the air by his tail. Well, I experienced the same perplexity, and made nearly the same ridiculous evolutions.

After several futile attempts to advance over it, and as often finding myself sliding backward with entire loss of control of my own movements, I tried the rugged ravine, traversing the summit, with some success, steadying my steps on the iced bowlders by grasping the bushes which grew there among clefts of the rock. But this way, besides being extremely fatiguing, was decidedly the more dangerous of the two; and I was glad, after a brief trial, to abandon it for the ice, in which, here and there, detached stones, solidly embedded, furnished points of support, if they could be reached. By pursuing a zigzag course from stone to stone, sometimes—like a pious Moslem approaching the tomb of the Prophet—upon my hands and knees, and shedding tears from the force of the wind, I succeeded in getting over the ledges after an hour's obstinate battle to maintain an upright position, and after several mishaps had taught me a degree of caution closely approaching timidity. By far the most treacherous ground was where fresh snow, covering the smooth ice, spread its pitfalls in the path, causing me several times to measure my length; but at last these obstacles were one by one surmounted; I groped my way, foot by foot, up the sharp rise of the pinnacle, finding myself at the front door of the house which is so conspicuous an object from the valley.

Never was air more pure, more crisp, or more transparent. Besides, what air can rival that of winter? I felt myself rather floating than walking. Certainly there is a lightness, a clearness, and a depth that belongs to no other season. At no other season do we behold our native skies so blue, so firm, or so brilliant as when the limpid ether, winnowed by the fierce north wind to absolute purity, presents objects with such marvellous clearness, precision, and fidelity, that we hardly persuade ourselves they are forty, fifty, or a hundred miles distant. To realize this rare condition was all the object of the ascent—an object attained in a measure far beyond any anticipations I had formed.

As may easily be imagined, the immediate effect was bewildering in the extreme. In the first place, the direct rays of the noonday sun covered the mountain-top with dazzling brilliancy. The eye fairly ached with looking at it. In the second, the intensity of the blue was such as to give the idea that the grand expanse of sky was hard frozen. Nothing more coldly brilliant than this immense azure dome can be conceived. There was not the faintest trace of a cloud anywhere; nothing but this splendid void. Under this high-vaulted dome, imagine now a vast expanse of white etched with brown—a landscape in sepia. Such was the general effect.

But the inexpressible delight of having all this admirable scene to one's self! Taine asks, " Can anything be sweeter than the certainty of being alone? In any widely known spot, you are in constant dread of an incursion of tourists; the hallooing of guides, the loud-voiced admiration, the bustle, whether of unfastening horses, or of unpacking provisions, or of airing opinions, all disturb the budding sensation; civilization recovers its hold upon you. But here, what security and what silence! nothing that recalls man; the landscape is just what it has been these six thousand years."

The view from this mountain is justly admired. Stripped of life and color, I found it sad, pathetic even. Dead white and steel blue rudely repulsed the sensitive eye. The north wind, cold and cutting, drove me to take shelter under glaring rocks. The cracking of ice first on one side, then on the other, diverted the attention from the landscape, as if the mountain was continually snapping its fingers in disdain. I had constantly the feeling that some *one* or some *thing* was at my elbow. What childishness! But where now was the lavish summer, the barbaric splendors of autumn—its arabesques of foliage, its velvet shadows, its dappled skies, its glow, mantling like that of health and beauty? All-pervading gloom and defoliation were rendered ten times more melancholy by the splendid glare. Winter flung her white shroud over the land to hide the repulsiveness of death.

I looked across the valley where Moat Mountain reared its magnificent dark wave. Passing to the north side, the eye wandered over the wooded summits to the silvery heap of Washington, to which frozen, rose-colored mists were clinging. A great ice-cataract rolled down over the edge of Tuckerman's Ravine, its wave of glittering emerald. It shone with enchanting brilliancy, cheating the imagination with the idea that it moved; that the thin, spectral vapor rose from the depths of the ice-cold gorge below. There gaped, wide open, the enormous hole of Carter Notch; there the pale-blue Saco wound in and out of the hills, with hamlets and villages strung along its serpentine course; and, as the river grows, villages increase to towns, towns to cities. There was the sea sparkling like a plain of quicksilver, with ponds and lakes innumerable between. There, in the south-west, as far as the eye could reach, was Monadnock demanding recognition; and in the west, Mooschillock, Lafayette, Carrigain peaks, lifted with calm superiority above the chaos of mountains, like higher waves of a frozen sea. Finally, there were the snow-capped summits of the great range seen throughout their whole extent, sunning their satin sides in indolent enjoyment.

This view has no peer in these mountains. Indeed, the mountain seems expressly placed to command in one comprehensive sweep of the eye the most impressive features of any mountain landscape. Being a peak of the second order — that is to say, one not dominating all the chains — while it does not unfold the topography of the region in its whole extent, it is sufficiently elevated to permit the spectator to enjoy that increasing grandeur with which the distant ranges rise, tier upon tier, to their great central spires, without lessening materially their loftiness, or the peculiar and varied expression of their contours. The peak of Kearsarge peeps down over one shoulder into New Hampshire, over the other into Maine. It looks straight up through the open door of the Carter Notch, and boldly stares Washington in the face. It sees the sun rise from the ocean, and set behind Mount Lafayette. It patronizes Moat, measures itself proudly with Chocorua, and maintains a distant acquaintance with Monadnock. It is a handsome mountain, and, as such, is a general favorite with the ladies and the artists. Like a careful shepherd, it every morning scans the valleys to see that none of its flock of villages has wandered. For these villagers it is a sun-dial, a weather-vane, an almanac; for the wayfarer, a sure guide; and for the poet, a mountain with a soul.

The cold was intense, the wind piercing. On its north side the house was deeply incrusted with ice-spars—windows and all. I feel that only scant justice can be done to their wondrous beauty. All the scrubby bushes growing out of interstices of the crumbling summit—wee twig and slender filament—were stemmed with ice; while the rocks bristled with countless frost feathers. With my pitch-cakes and a few twigs I lighted a fire, which might be seen from the half-dozen villages clustered about the foot of the mountain, and pleased myself with imagining the astonishment with which a smoke curling upward from this peak would be greeted for fifty miles around. I then prepared to descend—I say prepared to descend, for the thing at once so easy to say and so difficult of performance suddenly revived the recollection of the hazardous scramble up the ledges, and made it seem child's play by comparison. For a brief hour I had forgotten all this. However, go down I must. But how? The first step on the ice threatened a descent more rapid than flesh and blood could calmly contemplate. I had no hatchet to cut steps in the ice; no rope to attach to the rocks, and thus lower myself, as is practised in crossing the glaciers of the Alps; and there was no foothold. For a moment I seriously thought of forcing an entrance into the house, and, making a signal of distress, resign myself to the possibility of help from below. But while sitting on a rock looking blankly at the glassy declivity stretching down from the summit, a bright idea came to my aid. I remembered having read in Bourrienne's " Memoirs " that Bonaparte — the great Bonaparte — was forced to slide down the summit of the Great St. Bernard *seated*, while making his

SLIDING DOWN KEARSARGE.

famous passage of the Alps. Yes, the great Corsican really advanced to the conquest of Italy in this undignified posture. But never did great example find more unworthy imitator. Seating myself, as the Little Corporal had done, using my staff as a rudder, and steering for protruding stones in order to check the force of the descent from time to time, I slid down with a celerity the very remembrance of which makes my head swim, arriving safe, but breathless and much astonished, at the first irregular patch of snow. The pleasure of standing erect on something the feet could grasp was one not to be translated into words.

Upon reaching the hotel, I procured another pair of pantaloons of my host, and some court-plaster from the village apothecary. If any of my readers think my dignity compromised, I beg him to remember the example of the great Napoleon, and his famous expedient for circumventing the Great St. Bernard.

VI.

Raleigh.—" Fain would I climb, but that I fear to fall."
Queen Elizabeth.—" If thy heart fail thee, climb thou not at all."

AFTER the storm, we had a fine lunar bow. The corona in the centre was a clear silver, the outer circle composed of pale green and orange fires. Over the moon's disk clouds swept a continuous stormy flight. The great planet resembled a splendid decoration hung high in the heavens.

Having now progressed to terms of easy familiarity with the village, it was decided to pay our respects to the Intervale, which unites it with the neighboring town of Bartlett.

The road up the valley first skirts a wood, and through this wood are delicious glimpses of Mount Adams. During the heat of the day or cool of the evening this extensive and beautiful forest has always been a favorite haunt. Tall, athletic pines, that bend in the breeze like whalebone, lift their immense clusters of impenetrable foliage on high. The sighs of lovers are softly echoed in their green tops; voices and laughter issue from it. We, too, will swing our hammock here, and breathe the healing fragrance that is so grateful.

In a little enclosure of rough stone, on the Bigelow place, lie the remains of the ill-fated Willey family, who were destroyed by the memorable slide of 1826. The inscription closes with this not too lucid figure:

> " We gaze around, we read their monument ;
> We sigh, and when we sigh we sink."

Where the high terrace, making one grand sweep to the right, again unveils the same superb view of the great summits, now wholly unobstructed by houses or groves, we halt before that picture, unrivalled in these mountains, not surpassed, perhaps, upon earth, and which we never

CONWAY MEADOWS.

tire of gazing upon. Its most salient
features have already been described;
but here in their very midst, from their
very heart, nature seems to have snatched
a garden-spot from the haggard mountains arrested in their advance by
the command, " Thus far, and no farther !" The elms, all grace, all refinement of form, bend before the fierce blasts of winter, but stir not. The
frozen east wind flies shrieking through, as if to tear them limb from
limb. The ground is littered with their branches. They bow meekly
before its rage, but stir not. Really, they seem so many sentinels jeal-
ously guarding that repose of which the vale is so eloquently the expression. The vale regards the stormy summits around with the unconcern
of perfect security. It is rest to look at it.

Again we scan the great peaks which in clear days come boldly down and stand at our very doors, but on hazy ones remove to a vast distance, keeping vaguely aloof day in and day out. Sometimes they are in the sulks, sometimes bold and forward. By turns they are graciously condescending, or tantalizingly incomprehensible. One time they muffle themselves in clouds from head to foot, so we cannot detect a suggestive line or a contour; another, throwing off all disguise, they expose their most secret beauties to the free gaze of the multitude. This is to set the beholder's blood on fire with the passion to climb as high as those gray shafts of everlasting rock that so proudly survey the creeping leagues beneath them.

Nowhere is the unapproachable grandeur of Mount Washington more fully manifested than here. This large and impressive view is at once suggestive of that glorious pre-eminence always associated with high mountains. There are mountains, respectable ones too, in the middle distance; but over these the great peak lords it with undisputed sway. The bold and firm, though gradual, lines of ascent culminating at the apex, extend over leagues of sky. After a clear sunset, Mount Washington takes the same dull lead-color of the clouds hovering like enormous night-birds over its head.

North Conway permits, to the tourist, a choice of two very agreeable excursions, either of which may be made in a day, although they could profitably occupy a week. One is to follow the course of the Saco, through the great Notch, to Fabyans, where you are on the westward side of the great range, and where you take the rail to the summit of Mount Washington. The other excursion is to diverge from the Saco Valley three or four miles from North Conway, ascending the valley of Ellis River—one of the large affluents of the Saco—through the Pinkham Notch to the Glen House, where you are exactly under the eastern foot of Mount Washington, and may ascend it, by the carriage-road, in a coach-and-four. We had already chosen the first route, and as soon as the roads were a little settled we began our march.

The storm was over. The keen north wind drove the mists in utter rout before it. Peak after peak started out of the clouds, glowered on us a moment, and then muffled his enormous head in fleecy vapor. The clouds seemed thronged with monstrous apparitions, struggling fiercely with the gale, which in pure wantonness tore aside the magic drapery that rendered them invisible, scattering its tattered rags far and wide over the valley.

Now the sun entered upon the work begun by the wind. Quicker than thought, a ray of liquid flame transfixed the vapors, flashed upon the vale, and, flying from summit to summit, kindled them with new-born splendor. One would have said a flaming javelin, hurled from high heaven, had just cleft its dazzling way to earth. The mists slunk away and hid themselves. The valley was inundated with golden light. Even the dark faces of the cliffs brightened and beamed upon the vale,

BARTLETT BOWLDER.

where the bronzed foliage flut-tered, and the river leaped for joy. In a little time nothing was left but scattered clouds winging their way toward the low-lands.

Near Glen Station is one of those curiosities—a transported bowlder —which was undoubtedly left while on its travels through the moun-tains, poised upon four smaller ones, in the position seen in the en-graving.

Three miles below the village of Bartlett we stopped before a farm-house, with the gable-end toward the road, to inquire the distance to the next tavern, where we meant to pass the night. A gruff voice from the inside growled something by way of reply; but as its owner, whoever he might be, did not take the trouble to open his door, the answer was unintelligible.

" The churl !" muttered the colonel. " I have a great mind to teach him to open when a gentleman knocks."

"And I advise you not to try it," said the voice from the inside.

The one thing a Kentuckian never shrinks from is a challenge. He only said, "Wait a minute," while putting his broad shoulder against the door; but now George and I interfered. Neither of us had any desire to signalize our entry into the village by a brawl, and after some trouble we succeeded in pacifying our fire-eater with the promise to stop at this house on our way back.

" I shall know it again," said the colonel, looking back, and nibbling his long mustache with suppressed wrath; "something has been spilled on the threshold—something like blood."

We laughed heartily. The blood, we concluded, was in the colonel's eyes.

Some time after nightfall we arrived in the village, having put thirteen miles of road behind us without fatigue. Our host received us with a blazing fire—what fires they do have in the mountains, to be sure!—a pitcher of cider, and the remark, " Don't be afraid of it, gentlemen."

All three hastened to reassure him on this point. The colonel began with a loud smack, and George finished the jug with a deep sigh.

" Don't be afraid of it," repeated the landlord, returning presently with a fresh pitcher. " There are five barrels more like it in the cellar."

" Landlord," quoth George, " let one of your boys take a mattress, two blankets, and a pillow to the cellar. I intend to pass the night there."

" I only wish your well was full of it," said the colonel, taking a second pull at the jug, and making a second explosion with his lips.

"Gentlemen," said I, " we have surely entered a land of milk and honey."

" You shall have as much of both as you desire," said our host, very affably. " Supper is ready, gentlemen."

After supper a man came in for whom I felt, upon the instant, one of those secret antipathies which are natural to me. The man was an utter stranger. No matter: the repugnance seized me all the same.

After a tour of the tap-room, and some words with our landlord in an undertone, the stranger went out with the look of a man who had asked for something and had been refused.

"Where have I heard that man's voice?" said the colonel, thoughtfully.

Our landlord is one of the most genial to be found among the mountains. While sitting over the fire during the evening, the conversation turned upon the primitive simplicity of manners remarked among mountaineers in general; and our host illustrated it with this incident:

"You noticed, perhaps, a man who left here a few moments ago?" he began.

We replied affirmatively. It was my antipathy.

"Well, that man killed a traveller a few years back."

We instinctively recoiled. The air seemed tainted with the murderer's presence.

"Yes; dead as a mutton," continued the landlord, punching the logs reflectively, and filling the chimney with sparks. "The man came to his house one dark and stormy night, and asked to be admitted. The man of the house flatly refused. The stranger pleaded hard, but the fellow ordered him away with threats. Finding entreaties useless, the traveller began to grow angry, and attempted to push open the door, which was only fastened by a button, as the custom is. The man of the house said nothing, but took his gun from a corner, and when the intruder crossed the threshold he put three slugs through him. The wounded man expired on the threshold, covering it with his blood."

"Murdered him, and for that? Come, come, you are joking!" ejaculated George, with a half smile of incredulity.

"Blowed him right through, just as I tell you," reiterated the narrator, without heeding the doubt George's question implied.

"That sounds a little like Old Kentuck," observed the colonel, coolly.

"Yes; but listen to the sequel, gentlemen," resumed the landlord. "The murderer took the dead body in his arms, finding, to his horror, that it was an acquaintance with whom he had been drinking the day before; he took up the body, as I was saying, laid it out upon a table, and then went quietly to bed. In the morning he very honestly exhibited the corpse to all who passed his door, and told his story as I tell it to you. I had it from his own lips."

"That beats Kentucky," asseverated the colonel. For my own part, I believed the landlord was amusing himself at our expense.

"I don't know about Kentucky," observed the landlord; "I was never there in my life; but I do know that, when the dead man was buried, the man who killed him went to the funeral like any curious or indifferent spectator."

This was too much. George rose from his chair, and began to be interested in a placard on the wall. "And you say this happened near here?" he slowly inquired; "perhaps, now, you could show us the very house?" he finished, dryly.

"Nothing easier. It's only three miles back on the road you came. The blood-stain is plain, or was, on the threshold."

We exchanged glances. This was the house where we halted to inquire our way. The colonel's eyes dilated, but he said nothing.

"But was there no trial?" I asked.

"Trial? oh yes. After several days had run by, somebody thought of that; so one morning the slayer saddled his horse and rode over to the county-seat to inquire about it. He was tried at the next sessions, and acquitted. The judge charged justifiable homicide; that a man's house is his fort; the jury did not leave their benches. By-the-bye, gentlemen, that is some of the man's cider you are drinking."

I felt decided symptoms of revolt in my stomach; George made a grimace, and the colonel threw his unfinished glass in the fire. During the remainder of the evening he rallied us a good deal on the subject of New England hospitality, but said no more about going back to chastise the man of the red house.[1]

The sun rose clear over the right shoulder of Kearsarge. After breakfast the landlord took us out and introduced us to his neighbors, the mountains. While he was making the presentation in due form, I jotted down the following, which has, at least, the merit of conciseness:

Upper Bartlett: an ellipse of fertile land; three Lombardy poplars; a river murmuring unseen; a wall of mountains, with Kearsarge looking up, and Carrigain looking down the intervale. *Item:* the cider is excellent.

We had before us the range extending between Swift River and the Saco, over which I looked from the summit of Chocorua straight to Mount Washington. To the east this range is joined with the out-

---

[1] The sequel to this strange but true story is in keeping with the rest of its horrible details. Perpetually haunted by the ghost of his victim, the murderer became a prey to remorse. Life became insupportable. He felt that he was both shunned and abhorred. Gradually he fell into a decline, and within a few years from the time the deed was committed he died.

works of Moat. Then come Table, Bear, Silver Spring (Bartlett Haystack), and Tremont, in the order named. Then comes the valley of Sawyer's River, with Carrigain rising between its walls; then, crossing to the north side of the Saco, the most conspicuous object is the bold Hart's Ledge, between which and Sawyer's Rock, on the opposite bank, the river is crowded into a narrow channel. The mountain behind the hotel is Mount Langdon, with Crawford more distant. Observe closely the curious configuration of this peak. Whether we go up or down, it nods familiarly to us from every point of approach.

But Kearsarge and Carrigain are the grand features here. One gives his adieu, the other his welcome. One is the perfection of symmetry, of grace; the other simply demands our homage. His snowy crown, dazzling white against the pure blue, was the badge of an incontestable superiority. These two mountains are the presiding genii of this charming intervale. You look first at the massive lineaments of one, then at the flowing lines of the other, as at celebrated men, whose features you would strongly impress upon the memory.

From the village street we saw the sun go down behind Mount Carrigain, and touch with his glittering sceptre the crest of Hancock. We looked up the valley dominated by the giant of the Pemigewasset wilderness with feelings of high respect for this illustrious hermit, who only deigns to show himself from this single point, and whose peak long yielded only to the most persevering and determined climbers.

Two days were formerly required for the ascent of this mountain, but a long day will now suffice, thanks to the path constructed under the direction of the Appalachian Club. The mountain is four thousand six hundred and twenty-five feet above the sea, and is wooded to its summit. The valley of Sawyer's River drains the deep basin between Carrigain and Hancock, entering the Saco near the railroad station called Livermore. The lumbermen have now penetrated this valley to the foot of the mountain, with their rude logging roads, offering a way soon, it is hoped, to be made plainer for future climbers than it was our lot to find it.

Thoroughly imbued with the spirit of the mountains, we now regarded distances with disdain, and fatigue with indifference. We had learned to make our toilets in the stream, and our beds in the fragrant groves. Truly, the bronzed faces that peered at us as we bent over some solemn, pine-shaded pool were not those we had been accustomed to seeing at home; but having solved the problem of man's true existence, we only laughed at each other's tawny countenances while shouldering our packs and tightening our belts for the day's march.

Leaving Bartlett at an early hour, we turned aside from the highway a little beyond the bridge which spans Sawyer's River, and were soon following a rough and stony cart-way ascending the banks of this stream, which thundered along its rocky bed, making the woods echo with its roar. The road grew rapidly worse, the river wilder, the forest gloomier, until, at the end of two miles, coming suddenly out into the sun, we entered a rude street of unpainted cabins, terminating at some saw-mills. This hamlet, which to the artistic eye so disadvantageously replaces the original forest, is the only settlement in the large township of Livermore. Its mission is to ravage and lay waste the adjacent mountains. Notwithstanding the occupation is legitimate, one instinctively rebels at the waste around him, where the splendid natural forest, literally hewed and hacked in pieces, exposes rudely all the deformities of the mountains. But this lost hamlet is the first in which a genuine emotion of any kind awaits the traveller. Ten to one it is like nothing he ever dreamed of; his surprise is, therefore, extreme. The men were rough, hardy-looking fellows; the women appeared contented, but as if hard work had destroyed their good looks prematurely. Both announced, by their looks and their manner, that the life they led was no child's play; the men spoke only when addressed; the women stole furtive glances at us; the half-dressed children stopped their play to stare at the strangers. Here was neither spire nor bell. One cow furnished all the milk for the commonalty. The mills being shut, there was no sound except the river plashing over the rocks far down in the gorge below; and had I encountered such a place on the sea-coast or the frontier, I should at once have said I had stumbled upon the secret hold of outlaws and smugglers, into which signs, grips, and passwords were necessary to procure admission. To me, therefore, the hamlet of Livermore was a wholly new experience.

From this hamlet to the foot of the mountain is a long and uninteresting tramp of five miles through the woods. We found the walking good, and strode rapidly on, coming first to a wood-cutter's camp pitched on the banks of Carrigain Brook, and next to the clearing they had made at the mountain's foot. Here the actual work of the ascent began in earnest.

Carrigain is solid, compact, massive. It is covered from head to foot with forest. No incident of the way diverts the attention for a single moment from the severe exertion required to overcome its steeply inclined side; no breathing levels, no restful outlooks, no gorges, no precipices, no cascades break the monotony of the escalade. We conquer, as Napoleon's grenadiers did, by our legs. It is the most inexorable of mountains, and the most exasperating. From base to summit you cannot obtain a cup of water to slake your thirst.

Two hours of this brought us out upon the bare summit of the great northern spur, beyond which the true peak rose a few hundred feet higher. Carrigain, at once the desire and the bugbear of climbers, was beneath our feet.

We have already examined, from the rocks of Chocorua, the situation of this peak. We then entitled it the Hub of the White Mountains. It reveals all the magnitude, unfolds the topography of the woody wilderness stretching between the Saco and the Pemigewasset valleys. As nearly as possible, it exhibits the same amazing profusion of unbroken forest, here and there darkly streaked by hidden watercourses, as when the daring foot of the first climber pressed the unviolated crest of the august peak of Washington. In all its length and breadth there is not one object that suggests, even remotely, the presence of man. We saw not even the smoke of a hunter's camp. All was just as created; an absolute, savage, unkempt wilderness.

Heavens, what a bristling array of dark and shaggy mountains! Now and then, where water gleamed out of their hideous depths, a great brilliant eye seemed watching us from afar. We knew that we had only to look up to see a dazzling circlet of lofty peaks drawn around the horizon, chains set with glittering stones, clusters sparkling with antique crests; still we could not withdraw our eyes from the profound abysses sunk deep in the bowels of the land, typical of the uncovered bed of the primeval ocean, sad and terrible, from which that ocean seemed only to have just receded.

But who shall describe all this solitary, this oppressive grandeur? and what language portray the awfulness of these untrodden mountains? Now and then, high up their bleak summits, a patch of forest had been plucked up by the roots, or shaken from its hold in the throes of the mountain, laid bare a long and glittering scar, red as a half-closed wound. Such is the appearance of Mount Lowell, on the other side of the gap dividing Carrigain from the Notch mountains. We saw where the dark slope of Mount Willey gives birth to the infant Merrimack. We saw the confluent waters of this stream, so light of foot, speeding through the gloomy defiles, as if fear had given them wings. We saw the huge mass of Mount Hancock force itself slowly upward out of the press. Unutterable lawlessness stamped the whole region as its own.

That I have thus dwelt upon its most extraordinary feature, instead of examining the landscape in detail, must suffice for the intelligent reader. I have not the temerity to coolly put the dissecting-knife into its heart. To science the things which belong to science. Besides, to the man of feeling all this is but secondary. We are not here to make a chart.

After a visit to the high summit, where some work was done in the interest of future climbers, we set out at four in the afternoon, on our return down the mountain. A second time we halted on the spur to glance upward at the heap of summits over which Mount Washington lifts a regular dome. The long line of peaks, ascending from Crawford's, seems approaching it by a succession of huge steps. It was after dark when we saw the lights of the village before us, and were again warmly welcomed by the rousing fire and smoking viands of mine host.

6

VII.

With our faint heart the mountain strives;
Its arms outstretched, the Druid wood
Waits with its benedicte.—*Sir Launfal.*

AT eight o'clock in the morning we resumed our march, with the intention of reaching Crawford's the same evening. The day was cold, raw, and windy, so we walked briskly—sharp air and cutting wind acting like whip and spur.

I retain a vivid recollection of this morning. Autumn had passed her cool hand over the fevered earth. Soft as three-piled velvet, the green turf left no trace of our tread. The sky was of a dazzling blue, and frescoed with light clouds, transparent as gauze, pure as the snow glistening on the high summits. On both sides of us audacious mountains braced their feet in the valley; while others mounted over their brawny shoulders, as if to scale the heavens.

But what shall I say of the grand harlequinade of nature which the valley presented to our view? I cannot employ Victor Hugo's odd simile of a peacock's tail; that is more of a witticism than a description. The death of the year seemed to prefigure the glorious and surprising changes of color in a dying dolphin—putting on unparalleled beauty at the moment of dissolution, and so going out in a blaze of glory.

From the meagre summits enfiladed by the north wind, and where a solitary pine or cedar intensified the desolation, to the upper forests, the mountains bristled with a scanty growth of dead or dying trees. Those scattered birches, high up the mountain side, looked like quills on a porcupine's back; that group, glistening in the morning sun, like the pipes of an immense organ. From this line of death, which vegetation crossed at its peril, the eye dropped down over a limitless forest of dark evergreen spotted with bright yellow. The effect of the sunlight on this foliage was magical. Myriad flambeaux illuminated the deep gloom, doubling the intensity of the sun, emitting rays, glowing, resplendent. This splendid light, which the heavy masses of orange seemed to absorb, gave a velvety softness to the lower ridges and spurs, covering their hard, angular lines with a magnificent drapery. The lower forests, the valley, were one vast sea of color. Here the bewildering melange of green and gold, orange and crimson, purple and russet, produced the effect of an immense Turkish rug—the colors being soft and rich, rather than vivid or brilliant. This quality, the blending of a thousand tints, the dreamy grace, the sumptuous profusion, the inexpressible tenderness, intoxicated the senses. Earth seemed no longer earth. We had entered a garden of the gods.

From time to time a scarlet maple flamed up in the midst of the forest, and its red foliage, scattered at our feet by the wind, glowed like flakes of fire beaten from an anvil. A tangled maze of color changed the road into an avenue bordered with rare and variegated plants. Autumn's bright sceptre, the golden-rod, pointed the way. Blue and white daisies strewed the greensward.

After passing Sawyer's River, the road turned abruptly to the north, skirting the base of the Nancy range. We were at the door of the second chamber in this remarkable gallery of nature.

Before crossing the threshold it is expedient to allude to the incident which has given a name not only to the mountain, but to the torrent we see tearing its impetuous way down from the upper forests. The story of Nancy's Brook is as follows:

In the latter part of the last century, a maiden, whose Christian name of Nancy is all that comes down to us, was living in the little hamlet of Jefferson. She loved, and was betrothed to a young man of the farm. The wedding-day was fixed, and the young couple were on the eve of setting out for Portsmouth, where their happiness was to be consummated at the altar. In the trustfulness of love, the young girl confided the small sum which constituted all her marriage-portion to her lover. This man repaid her simple faith with the basest treachery. Seizing his opportunity, he left the hamlet without a word of explanation or of adieu. The deserted maiden was one of those natures which cannot quietly sit down under calamity. Urged on by the intensity of her feelings, she resolved to pursue her recreant lover. He could not resist her prayers, her entreaties, her tears! She was young, vigorous, intrepid.

With her to decide and to act were the same thing. In vain the family attempted to dissuade her from her purpose. At nightfall she set out.

A hundred years ago the route taken by this brave girl was not, as to-day, a thoroughfare which one may follow with his eyes shut. It was only an obscure path, little travelled by day, deserted by night. For thirty miles, from Colonel Whipple's, in Jefferson, to Bartlett, there was not a human habitation. The forests were filled with wild beasts. The

NANCY IN THE SNOW.

rigor of the season—it was December—added its own perils. But nothing could daunt the heroic spirit of Nancy; she had found man more cruel than all besides.

The girl's hope was to overtake her lover before dawn at the place where she expected he would have camped for the night. She found the camp deserted, and the embers extinguished. Spurred on by hope or despair, she pushed on down the tremendous defile of the Notch, fording the turbulent and frozen Saco, and toiling through deep snows and over rocks and fallen trees, until, feeling her strength fail, she sunk exhausted on the margin of the brook which seems perpetually bemoaning her sad fate. Here, cold and rigid as marble, under a canopy of evergreen which the snow tenderly drooped above, they found her. She was wrapped in her cloak, and in the same attitude of repose as when she fell asleep on her nuptial couch of snow-crusted moss.

The story goes that the faithless lover became a hopeless maniac on learning the fate of his victim, dying in horrible paroxysms not long after. Tradition adds that for many years, on every anniversary of her death, the mountains resounded with ravings, shrieks, and agonized cries, which the superstitious attributed to the unhappy ghost of the maniac lover.[1]

It was not quite noon when we entered the beautiful and romantic glen under the shadow of Mount Crawford. Upon our left, a little in advance, a solidly-built English country-house, with gables, stood on a terrace well above the valley. At our right, and below, was the old Mount Crawford tavern, one of the most ancient of mountain hostelries. Upon the opposite side of the vale rose the enormous mass of Mount Crawford; and near where we stood, a humble mound, overgrown with bushes, enclosed the mortal remains of the hardy pioneer whose monument is the mountain.

We had an excusable curiosity to see a man who, in the prime of life, had forsaken the city, its pleasures, its opportunities, and had come to pass the rest of his life among these mountains; one, too, whose enormous possessions procured for him the title of Lord of the Valley. We heard with astonishment that our day's journey, of which we had completed the half only, was wholly over his tract—I ought to say his dominions—that is, over thirteen miles of field, forest, and mountain. This being equal to a small principality, it seemed quite natural and proper to approach the proprietor with some degree of ceremony.

A servant took our cards at the door, and returned with an invitation to enter. The apartment into which we were conducted was the most singular I have ever seen; certainly it has no counterpart in this world, unless the famous hut of Robinson Crusoe has escaped the ravages of time. It was literally crammed with antique furniture, among which was a high-backed chair used in dentistry; squat little bottles, containing chemicals; and a bench, on which was a spirit-lamp; a turning-lathe, a small portable furnace, and a variety of instruments or tools of

---

[1] Dr. Jeremy Belknap relates that, on his journey through this region in 1784, he was besought by the superstitious villagers to lay the spirits which were still believed to haunt the fastnesses of the mountains.

which we did not know the use.   A few prints and oil-paintings adorned
the walls.   A cheerful fire burnt on the hearth.

"Were we in the sixteenth century," said George, "I should say this
was the laboratory of some famous alchemist."

Further investigation was cut short by the entrance of our host, who
was a venerable-looking man, turned of eighty, with a silver beard falling
upon his breast, and a general expression of benignity.   He stooped a

ABEL CRAWFORD.

little, but seemed hale and hearty, notwithstanding the weight of his
fourscore years.

Doctor Bemis received us graciously.   For an hour he entertained
us with the story of his life among the mountains, "to which," said he,
" I credit the last forty-five years—for I at first came here in pursuit of
health."   After he had satisfied our curiosity concerning himself, which
he did with perfect *bonhomie,* I asked him to describe Abel Crawford,
the veteran guide of the White Hills.

"Abel," said the doctor, "was six feet four; Erastus, the eldest son, was six feet six, or taller than Washington; and Ethan was still taller, being nearly seven feet. In fact, not one of the sons was less than six feet; so you may imagine what sort of family group it was when 'his boys,' as Abel loved to call them, were all at home. Ah, well!" continued the doctor, with a sigh, "that kind of timber does not flourish in the mountains now. Why, the very sight of one of those giants inspired the timid with confidence. Ethan, called in his day the Giant of the Hills, was a man of iron frame and will. Fear and he were strangers. He would take up an exhausted traveller in his sinewy arms and carry him as you would a baby, until his strength or courage returned. The first bridle-path up the mountain was opened by him in—let me see— ah! I have it, it was in 1821. Ethan, with the help of his father, also built the Notch House above.[1]

"Abel was long-armed, lean, and sinewy. Doctor Dwight, whose 'Travels in New England' you have doubtless read, stopped with Crawford, on his way down the Notch, in 1797. His nearest neighbor then, on the north, was Captain Rosebrook, who lived on or near the site of the present Fabyan House. Crawford's life of hardship had made little impression on a constitution of iron. At seventy-five he rode the first horse that reached the summit of Mount Washington. At eighty he often walked to his son's (Thomas J. Crawford), at the entrance of the Notch, before breakfast. I recollect him perfectly at this time, and his appearance was peculiarly impressive. He was erect and vigorous as one of those pines on yonder mountain. His long white hair fell down upon his shoulders, and his fresh, ruddy face was always expressive of good-humor.

"The destructive freshet of 1826," continued the doctor, "swept everything before it, flooding the intervale, and threatening the old house down there with instant demolition. During that terrible night, when the Willey family perished, Mrs. Crawford was alone with her young children in the house. The water rose with such rapidity that she was driven to the upper story for safety. While here, the thud of floating trees, driven by the current against the house, awakened new terrors. At every concussion the house trembled. Wooden walls could not long

---

[1] This house stood just within the entrance to the Notch, from the north, or Fabyan side. It was for some time kept by Thomas J., one of the famous Crawfords. Travellers who are a good deal puzzled by the frequent recurrence of the name "Crawford's" will recollect that the present hotel is now the only one in this valley bearing the name.

stand that terrible pounding. The heroic woman, alive to the danger, seized a stout pole, and, going to the nearest window, kept the side of the house exposed to the flood free from the mass of wreck-stuff collected against it. She held her post thus throughout the night, until the danger had passed. When the flood subsided, Crawford found several fine trout alive in his cellar."

"When do the great freshets usually occur?" I asked.

"In the autumn," replied our host. "It is not the melting snows, but the sudden rainfalls that we fear."

"Yes," resumed he, reflectively, "the Crawfords were a family of athletes. With them the race of guides became extinct. Soon after settling here, Abel went with his wife to Bartlett on some occasion, leaving their two boys in the care of a hired man. When they had gone, this man took what he could find of value and decamped. When Abel returned, which he did on the following day, he immediately set out in pursuit of the thief, overtook him thirty miles from here, in the Franconia forests, flogged him within an inch of his life, and let him go."

"Sixty miles on foot, and alone, to recover a few stolen goods, and punish a thief!" cried the astonished colonel; "that beats Daniel Boone."

"Yes; and what is more, the boys were brought up to face hunger, cold, fatigue, with Indian stoicism, and even to encounter bears, lynxes, and wolves with no other weapons than those provided by nature. There, now, was Ethan, for example," said the doctor, smiling at the recollection. "One day he took it into his head to have a tame bear for the diversion of his guests. Well, he caught a young one, half grown, and remarkably vicious, in a trap. But how to get him home! At length Ethan tied his fore and hind paws together so he couldn't scratch, and put a muzzle of withes over his nose so he couldn't bite. Then, shouldering his prize as he would a bag of meal, the guide started for home, in great glee at the success of his clever expedient. He had not gone far, however, before Bruin managed to get one paw wholly and his muzzle partly free, and began to scratch and struggle and snap at his captor savagely. Ethan wanted to get the bear home terribly; but, after having his clothing nearly torn off his back, he grew angry, and threw the beast upon the ground with such force as to kill him instantly."

"Report," said I, "credits you with naming most of the mountains which overlook the intervale."

" Yes," replied the doctor, " Resolution, over there "—indicating the mountain allied to Crawford, and to the ridge which forms one of the buttresses of Mount Washington—" I named in recognition of the perseverance of Mr. Davis, who became discouraged while making a path to Mount Washington in 1845."

" Is the route practicable ?" I asked.

" Practicable, yes ; but nearly obliterated, and seldom ascended. Have you seen Frankenstein ?" demanded the doctor, in his turn.

We replied in the negative.

" It will repay a visit. I named it for a young German artist who passed some time with me, and who was fascinated by its rugged picturesqueness. Here is some of his work," pointing to the paintings which, apparently, formed the foundation of the collection on the walls.

Our host accompanied us to the door with a second injunction not to forget Frankenstein.

" You have something there good for the eyes," I observed, indicating the green carpet of the vale beneath us.

" True ; but you should have seen it when the deer boldly came down the mountain and browsed quietly among the cattle. That was a pretty sight, and one of frequent occurrence when I first knew the place. At that time," he continued, " the stage passed up every other day. Sometimes there were one or two, but seldom three passengers."

Proceeding on our way, we now had a fine view of the Giant's Stairs, which we had already seen from Mount Carrigain, but less boldly outlined than they appear from the valley, where they really look like two enormous steps cut on the very summit of the opposite ridge. No name could be more appropriate, though each of the degrees of this colossal staircase demands a giant not of our days; for they are respectively three hundred and fifty, and four hundred and fifty feet in height. It was over those steps that the Davis path ascended.

A mile or a mile and a half above the Crawford Glen, we emerged from behind a projecting spur of the mountain which hid the upper valley, when, by a common impulse, we stopped, fairly stupefied with admiration and surprise.

Thrust out before us, athwart the pass, a black and castellated pile of precipices shot upward to a dizzy height, and broke off abruptly against the sky. Its bulging sides and regular outlines resembled the clustered towers and frowning battlements of some antique fortress built to command the pass. Gashed, splintered, defaced, it seemed to have withstood for ages the artillery of heaven and the assaults of time. With what solitary grandeur it lifted its mailed front above the forest, and seemed even to regard the mountains with disdain! Silent, gloomy, impregnable, it wanted nothing to recall those dark abodes of the Thousand and One Nights, in which malignant genii are imprisoned for thousands of years.

This was Frankenstein. We at once accord it a place as the most suggestive of cliffs. From the other side of the valley the resemblance to a mediæval castle is still more striking. It has a black gorge for a moat, so deep that the head swims when crossing it; and to-day, as we crept over the cat's-cradle of a bridge thrown across for the passage of the railway, and listened to the growling of the torrent far down beneath, the whole frail structure seemed trembling under us.

But what a contrast! what a singular freak of nature! At the foot of this grisly precipice, clothing it with almost superhuman beauty, was a plantation of maples and birches, all resplendent in crimson and gold. Never have I seen such masses of color laid on such a background. Below all was light and splendor; above, all darkness and gloom. Here the eye fairly revelled in beauty, there it recoiled in terror. The cliff was like a naked and swarthy Ethiopian up to his knees in roses.

We walked slowly, with our eyes fixed on these cliffs, until another turn of the road—we were now on the railway embankment—opened a vista deserving to be remembered as one of the marvels of this glorious picture-gallery.

The perfection and magnificence of this truly regal picture, the gigantic scale on which it is presented, without the least blemish to mar its harmony or disturb the impression of one grand, unique whole, is a revelation to the least susceptible nature in the world.

Frankenstein was now a little withdrawn, on our left. Upon the right, fluttering its golden foliage as if to attract our attention, a plantation of tall, satin-stemmed birches stretched for some distance along the railway. Between the long buttress of the cliff and this forest lay open the valley of Mount Washington River, which is driven deep into the heart of the great range. There, through this valley, cutting the sapphire sky with their silver silhouette, were the giant mountains, surmounted by the splendid dome of Washington himself.

Passing beyond, we had a fine retrospect of Crawford, with his curved horn; and upon the dizzy iron bridge thrown across the gorge beneath

STORM ON MOUNT WILLEY.

Frankenstein, striking views are obtained of the mountains below. They seemed loftier and grander, and more imposing than ever.

Turning our faces toward the north, we now beheld the immense bulk and superb crest of Willey. On the other side of the valley was the long battlement of Mount Webster. We were at the entrance of the great Notch.

VIII.

THROUGH THE NOTCH.

Around his waist are forests braced,
The avalanche in his hand.—BYRON.

THE valley, which had continually contracted since leaving Bartlett, now appeared fast shut between these two mountains; but on turning the tremendous support which Mount Willey flings down, we were in presence of the amazing defile cloven through the midst, and giving entrance to the heart of the White Hills.

These gigantic mountains divided to the right and left, like the Red Sea before the Israelites. Through the immense trough, over which their crests hung suspended in mid-air, the highway creeps and the river steals away. The road is only seen at intervals through the forest; a low murmur, like the hum of bees, announces the river.

I have no conception of the man who can approach this stupendous chasm without a sensation of fear. The idea of imminent annihilation is everywhere overwhelming. The mind refuses to reason, or rather to fix itself, except on a single point. What if the same power that commanded these awful mountains to remove should hurl them back to ever-during fixedness? Should, do I say? The gulf seemed contracting under our very eyes—the great mountains toppling to their fall. With an eagerness excited by high expectation, we had pressed forward; but now we hesitated.

This emotion, which many of my readers have doubtless partaken, was our tribute to the dumb but eloquent expression of power too vast for our feeble intellects to measure. It was the triumph of matter over mind; of the finite over the infinite.

Below, it was all admiration and surprise; here, all amazement and fear. The more the mountains exalted themselves, the more we were abased. Trusting, nevertheless, in our insignificance, we moved on, looking with all our eyes, absorbed, silent, and almost worshipping.

The wide split of the Notch, which we had now entered, had on one side Mount Willey, drawn up to his full height; and on the other Mount Webster, striped with dull red on dingy yellow, like an old tiger's skin. Willey is the highest; Webster the most remarkable. Willey has a conical spire; Webster a long, irregular battlement. Willey is a mountain; Webster a huge block of granite.

For two miles the gorge winds between these mountains to where it is apparently sealed up by a sheer mass of purple precipices lodged full in its throat. This is Mount Willard. The vast chasm glowed with the gorgeous colors of the foliage, even when a passing cloud obscured the sun. These general observations made, we cast our eyes down into the vale reposing at our feet. We had chosen for our point of view that to which Abel Crawford conducted Sir Charles Lyell in 1845. The scientist has made the avalanche bear witness to the glacier, precisely as one criminal is made to convict another under our laws.

Five hundred feet below us was a little clearing, containing a hamlet of two or three houses. From this hamlet to the storm-crushed crags glistening on the summit of Mount Willey the track of an old avalanche was still distinguishable, though the birches and alders rooted among the débris threatened to obliterate it at no distant day.

We descended by this still plain path to the houses at the foot of the mountain. One and the other are associated with the most tragic event connected with the history of the great Notch.

We found two houses, a larger and smaller, fronting the road, neither of which merits a description; although evidence that it was visited by multitudes of curious pilgrims abounded on the walls of the unoccupied building.

Since quite early in the century, this house was kept as an inn; and for a long time it was the only stopping-place between Abel Crawford's below and Captain Rosebrook's above—a distance of thirteen miles. Its situation, at the entrance of the great Notch, was advantageous to the public and to the landlord, but attended with a danger which seems not to have been sufficiently regarded, if indeed it caused successive inmates particular concern. This fatal security had a lamentable sequel.

In 1826 this house was occupied by Samuel Willey, his wife, five children, and two hired men. During the summer a drought of unusual

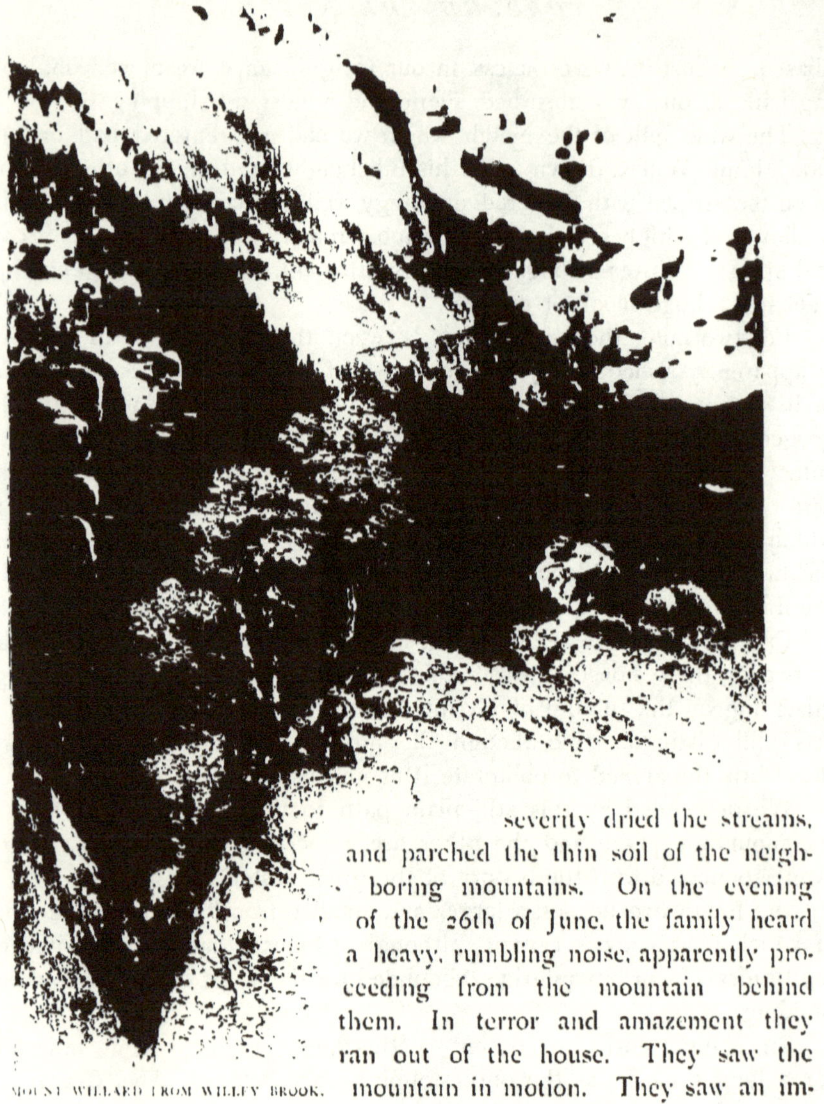

severity dried the streams, and parched the thin soil of the neighboring mountains. On the evening of the 26th of June, the family heard a heavy, rumbling noise, apparently proceeding from the mountain behind them. In terror and amazement they ran out of the house. They saw the mountain in motion. They saw an immense mass of earth and rock detach itself and move toward the valley, at first slowly, then with gathered and irresistible momentum. Rocks, trees, earth, were swooping down upon them from the heights in three destroying streams. The spectators stood rooted to the spot. Before they could recover their presence of mind the avalanche was upon them. One torrent crossed the road only ten rods from the house; another a little distance beyond; while the third and largest portion took a different direction. With great labor a way was made over the mass of rubbish for the road. The avalanche had shivered the largest trees, and borne rocks weighing many tons almost to the door of the lonely habitation.

This awful warning passed unheeded. On the 28th of August, at dusk, a storm burst upon the mountains, and raged with indescribable fury throughout the night. The rain fell in sheets. Innumerable torrents suddenly broke forth on all sides, deluging the narrow valley, and bearing with them forests that had covered the mountains for ages. The swollen and turbid Saco rose over its banks, flooding the Intervales, and spreading destruction in its course.

Two days afterward a traveller succeeded in forcing his way through the Notch. He found the Willey House standing uninjured in the midst of woful desolation. A second avalanche, descended from Mount Willey during the storm, had buried the little vale beneath its ruins. The traveller, affrighted by the scene around him, pushed open the door. As he did so, a half-famished dog, sole inmate of the house, disputed his entrance with a mournful howl. He entered. The interior was silent and deserted. A candle burnt to the socket, the clothing of the inmates lying by their bedsides, testified to the haste with which this devoted family had fled. The death-like hush pervading the lonely cabin—these evidences of the horrible and untimely fate of the family—the appalling scene of wreck all around, froze the solitary intruder's blood. In terror he, too, fled from the doomed dwelling.

On arriving at Bartlett, the traveller reported what he had seen. Assistance was despatched to the scene of disaster. The rescuers came too late to render aid to the living, but they found, and buried on the spot, the bodies of Mr. and Mrs. Willey, and the two hired men. The remaining children were never found.

It was easily conjectured that the terrified family, alive at last to the appalling danger that menaced them, and feeling the solid earth tremble in the throes of the mountain, sought safety in flight. They only rushed to their doom. The discovery of the bodies showed but too plainly the manner of their death. They had been instantly swallowed up by the avalanche, which, in the inexplicable order of things visible in great calamities, divided behind the house, leaving the frail structure unharmed, while its inmates were hurried into eternity.[1]

For some time after the disaster a curse seemed to rest upon the old Notch House. No one would occupy it. Travellers shunned it. It remained untenanted, though open to all who might be driven to seek its inhospitable shelter, until the deep impression of horror which the fate of the Willey family inspired had, in a measure, effaced itself.

The effects of the cataclysm were everywhere. For twenty-one miles, almost its entire length, the turnpike was demolished. Twenty-one of the twenty-three bridges were swept away. In some places the meadows were buried to the depth of several feet beneath sand, earth, and rocks; in others, heaps of great trees, which the torrent had torn up by the roots, barricaded the route. The mountains presented a ghastly spectacle. One single night sufficed to obliterate the work of centuries, to strip their summits bare of verdure, and to leave them with shreds of forest and patches of shrubbery hanging to their stark and naked sides. Thus their whole aspect was altered to an extent hardly to be realized to-day, though remarked with mingled wonder and dread long after the period of the convulsion.

From the house our eyes naturally wandered to the mountain, where quarrymen were pecking at its side like yellow-hammers at a dead sycamore. All at once a tremendous explosion was heard, and a stream of loosened earth and bowlders came rattling down the mountain. So unexpected was the sound, so startling its multiplied echo, it seemed as if the mountain had uttered a roar of rage and pain, which was taken up and repeated by the other mountains until the uproar became deafening. When the reverberation died away in the distance, we again heard the metallic click of the miners' hammers chipping away at the gaunt ribs of Mount Willey.

How does it happen that this catastrophe is still able to awaken the liveliest interest for the fate of the Willey family? Why is it that the

---

[1] A portion of the slide touching the house, even moved it a little from its foundations before being stopped by the resistance it opposed to the progress of the débris.

oft-repeated tale seems ever new in the ears of sympathetic listeners? Our age is crowded with horrors, to which this seems trifling indeed. May we not attribute it to the influence which the actual scene exerts on the imagination? One must stand on the spot to comprehend; must feel the mysterious terror to which all who come within the influence of the gorge submit. Here the annihilation of a family is but the legitimate expression of that feeling. It seems altogether natural to the place. The ravine might well be the sepulchre of a million human beings, instead of the grave of a single obscure family.

We reached the public-house, at the side of the Willey house, with appetites whetted by our long walk. The mercury had only risen to thirty-eight degrees by the thermometer nailed to the door-post. We went in.

In general, the mountain publicans are not only very obliging, but equal to even the most unexpected demands. The colonel, who never brags, had boasted for the last half-hour what he was going to do at this repast. In point of fact, we were famishing.

A man was standing with his back to the fire, his hands thrust underneath his coat-tails, and a pipe in his mouth. Either the pipe illuminated his nose, or his nose the pipe. He also had a nervous contraction of the muscles of his face, causing an involuntary twitching of the eyebrows, and at the same time of his ears, up and down. This habit, taken in connection with the perfect immobility of the figure, made on us the impression of a statue winking. We therefore hesitated to address it — I mean *him* — until a moment's puzzled scrutiny satisfied us that it—I mean the strange object—was alive. He merely turned his head when we entered the room, wagged his ears playfully, winked furiously, and then resumed his first attitude. In all probability he was some stranger like ourselves.

I accosted him. "Sir," said I, "can you tell us if it is possible to procure a dinner here?"

The man took the pipe from his mouth, shook out the ashes very deliberately, and, without looking at me, tranquilly observed,

"You would like dinner, then?"

"Would we like dinner? We breakfasted at Bartlett, and have passed six hours fasting."

"And eleven miles. You see, a long way between meals," interjected George, with decision.

"It's after the regular dinner," drawled the apathetic smoker, using his thumb for a stopper, and stooping for a brand with which to relight his pipe.

"In that case we are willing to pay for any additional trouble," I hastened to say.

The man seemed reflecting. We *were* hungry; that was incontestable; but we were also shivering, and he maintained his position astride the hearth-stone, like the fabled Colossus of old.

"A cold day," said the colonel, threshing himself.

"I did not notice it," returned the stranger, indifferently.

"Only thirty-eight at the door," said George, stamping his feet with unnecessary vehemence.

"Indeed!" observed our man, with more interest.

"Yes," George asserted; "and if the fireplace were only larger, or the screen smaller."

The man hastily stepped aside, knocking over, as he did so, a blazing brand, which he kicked viciously back into the fire.

Having carried the outworks, we approached the citadel. "Perhaps, sir," I ventured, "you can inform us where the landlord may be found?"

"You wanted dinner, I believe?" The tone in which this question was put gave me goose-flesh. I could not speak. George dropped into a chair. The colonel propped himself against the chimney-piece. I shrugged my shoulders, and nodded expressively to my companions, who returned two glances of eloquent dismay. Evidently nothing was to be got out of this fellow.

"Dinner for one?" continued the eternal smoker.

"For three!" I exclaimed, out of all patience.

"For four; I shall eat double," added the colonel.

"Six!" shouted George, seizing the dinner-bell on the mantel-piece.

"Stop," said the man, betraying a little excitement; "don't ring that bell."

"Why not?" demanded George; "we want to see the landlord; and, by Jove," brandishing the bell aloft, "see him we will!"

"He stands before you, gentlemen; and if you will have a little patience I will see what can be done." So saying, he put his pipe on the chimney-piece, wiped his mouth with the back of his hand, and went out, muttering, as he did so, "The world was not made in a day."

In three-quarters of an hour we sat down to a funereal repast, the bare recollection of which makes me ill, but which was enlivened by the following conversation:

"How many inhabitants are in your tract?" I asked of the man who waited on us.

"Do you mean inhabitants?"

"Certainly, I mean inhabitants."

"Well, that's not an easy one."

"How so?"

"Because the same question not only puzzled the State Legislature, but made the attorney-general sick."

We became attentive.

"Explain that, if you please," said I.

"Why, just look at it: with only eight legal voters in the tract" (he called it track), "we cast five hundred ballots at the State election."

"Five hundred ballots! then your voters must have sprung from the ground or from the rocks."

"Pretty nearly so."

"Actual men?"

"Actual men."

"You are jesting."

My man looked at me as if I had offered him an affront. The supposition was plainly inadmissible. He was completely innocent of the charge.

"You hear those men pounding away up the hill?" he demanded, jerking his thumb in the direction indicated.

"Yes."

"Well, those are the five hundred voters. On election morning they came to the polling-place with a ballot in one hand, and a pick, a sledge, or a drill in the other. Our supervisor is a very honest, blunt sort of man: he refused their ballots on the spot."

"Well?"

"Well, one of them had a can of nitro-glycerine and a coil of wire. He deposited his can in a corner, hitched on the wire, and was going out with his comrades, when the supervisor, feeling nervous, said,

"'The polls are open, gentlemen.'"

"Ingenious," remarked George.

The man looked astounded.

"He means dangerous," said I; "but go on."

" I will. When the votes were counted, at sundown, it was found that our precinct had elected two representatives to the General Court. But when the successful candidates presented their certificates at Concord, some meddlesome city fellow questioned the validity of the election. The upshot of it was that the two nitro-glycerites came back with a flea in each ear."

" And the five hundred were disfranchised," said George.

" Why, as to that, half were French Canadians, half Irish, and the devil knows what the rest were; I don't."

" Never mind the rest. You see," said George, rising, " how, with the railway, the blessings of civilization penetrate into the dark corners of the earth."

The colonel began his sacramental, " That beats—" when he was interrupted by a second explosion, which shook the building. We paid our reckoning, George saying, as he threw his money on the table, " A heavy charge."

" No more than the regular price," said the landlord, stiffly.

" I referred, my dear sir, to the explosion," replied George, with the sardonic grin habitual to him on certain occasions.

" Oh!" said the host, resuming his pipe and his fireplace.

We spent the remaining hours of this memorable afternoon sauntering through the Notch, which is dripping with cascades, and noisy with mountain torrents. The Saco, here nothing but a brook, crawls languidly along its bed of broken rock. From dizzy summit to where they meet the river, the old wasted mountains sit warming their scarred sides in the sun. Looking up at the passage of the railway around Mount Willey, it impressed us as a single fractured stone might have done on the Great Pyramid, or a pin's scratch on the face of a giant. The locomotive, which groped its way along its broken shelf, stopped, and stealthily moving again, seemed a mouse that the laboring mountain had brought forth. But when its infernal clamor broke the silence, what demoniacal yells shook the forests! Farewell to our dream of inviolable nature. The demon of progress had forced his way into the very sanctuary. There were no longer any White Mountains.

We passed by the beautiful brook Kedron, flung down from the utmost heights of Willey, between banks mottled with colors. Then, high up on our right, two airy water-falls seemed to hang suspended from the summit of Webster. These, called respectively the Silver

THE CASCADES, MOUNT WEBSTER.

Cascade, and the Flume withdrew the
attention from every other object, until
a sharp turn to the right brought the overhanging precipice of Mount Willard full upon us.
This enormous mass of granite, rising seven hundred feet above the road, stands in the very jaws of
the gorge, which it commands from end to end.

Here the railway seems fairly stopped ; but with a graceful

sweep it eludes the mountain, and glides around its massive shoulder, giving, as it does so, a hand to the high-road, which comes straggling up the sharp ascent. The river, now shrunken to a rivulet, is finally lost to view beneath heaped-up blocks of granite, which the infuriated old mountain has hurled down upon it. It is heard painfully gurgling under the ruins, like a victim crushed, and dying by inches.

Now and here we entered a close, dark defile hewn down between cliffs, ascending on the right in regular terraces, on the left in ruptured masses. These terraces were fringed at the top with tapering evergreens, and displayed gaudy tufts of maple and mountain-ash on their cool gray. Those on the right are furthermore decorated with natural sculptures, indicated by sign-boards, which the curious investigate profitably or unprofitably, according to their fertility of imagination.

For a few rods this narrow cleft continues; then, on a sudden, the rocks which lift themselves on either side shut together. An enormous mass has tumbled from its ancient location on the left side, and, taking a position within twenty feet of the opposite precipice, forms the natural gate of the Notch, through which a way was made for the common road with great labor, through which the river frays a passage, but where no one would imagine there was room for either. The railway has made a breach for itself through the solid rock, greatly diminishing the native grandeur of the place. All three emerge from the shadow and gloom of the pass into the cheerful sunshine of a little prairie, at the extremity of which are seen the white walls of a hotel.

The whole route we had traversed is full of contrasts, full of surprises; but this sudden transition was the most picturesque, the most startling of all. We seemed to have reached the end of the world.

IX.

CRAWFORD'S.

The seasons alter: hoary-headed frosts
Fall in the fresh lap of the crimson rose.
SHAKSPEARE.

ALL who have passed much time at the mountains have seen the elephant—near the gate of the Notch.

Though it is only from Nature's chisel, the elephant is an honest one, and readily admitted into the category of things curious or marvellous constantly displayed for our inspection. Standing on the piazza of the hotel, the enormous forehead and trunk seem just emerging from the shaggy woods near the entrance to the pass. And the gray of the granite strengthens the illusion still more. From the Elephant's Head, a title suggestive of the near vicinity of a public-house, there is a fine view down the Notch for those who cannot ascend Mount Willard.

The Crawford House, being built at the highest point of the pass, nearly two thousand feet above the sea, is not merely a hotel—it is a water-shed. The roof divides the rain falling upon it into two streams, flowing on one side into the Saco, on the other into the Ammonoosuc. Here the sun rises over the Willey range, and sets behind Mount Clinton. The north side of the piazza enables you to look over the forests into the valley of the Ammonoosuc, where the view is closed by the chain dividing this basin from that of Israel's River. But we are not yet ready to conduct the reader into this Promised Land.

My window overlooked a grassy plain of perhaps half a mile, the view being closed by the Gate of the Notch, now disfigured by snow-sheds built for the protection of the railway. The massive, full-rounded bulk of Webster rose above, the forests of Willard tumbled down into the ragged fissure. Half-way between the hotel and the Gate, over-borne by the big shadow of Mount Clinton, extends the pretty lakelet

ELEPHANT'S HEAD, WINTER.

which is the fountain-head of the Saco. Beyond the lake, and at the left, is where the old Notch House stood. This lake was once a beaver-pond, and this plain a boggy meadow, through which a road of corduroy and sods conducted the early traveller. The highway and railway run amicably side by side, dividing the little vale in two.

This pass, which was certainly known to the Indians, was, in 1771, rediscovered by Timothy Nash, a hunter, who was persuaded by Benjamin Sawyer, another hunter, to admit him to an equal share in the discovery. In 1773 Nash and Sawyer received a grant of 2184 acres, skirting the mountains on the west, as a reward. With the prodigality characteristic of their class, the hunters squandered their large acquisition in a little time after it was granted. Both the Crawford and Fabyan hotels stand upon their tract.

Of many excursions which this secluded retreat offers, that to the summit of Mount Washington, by the bridle-path opened in 1840 by Thomas J. Crawford, and that to the top of Mount Willard, are the principal. The route to the first begins opposite to the hotel, at the left; the latter turns from the glen a quarter of a mile below, on the right. Supposing Mount Washington a cathedral set on an eminence, you are here on the summit of the eminence, with one foot on the immense staircase of the cathedral.

Our resolve to ascend by the bridle-path was already formed, and we regarded the climb up Mount Willard as indispensable. As for the cascades, which lulled us to sleep, who shall describe them? We could not lift our eyes to the heights above without seeing one or more fluttering in the play of the breeze, and making rainbows in pure diversion. President Dwight, in his "Travels," has no more eloquent passage than that describing the Flume Cascade. How many since have thrown down pen or pencil in sheer despair of reproducing, by words or pigments, the aërial lightness, the joyous freedom; above all, the exuberant, unquenchable vitality that characterize mountain water-falls! Down the Notch is a masterpiece, hidden from the eye of the passer-by, called Ripley Falls, which fairly revels in its charming seclusion. Only a short walk from the hotel, by a woodland path, there is another, Beecher's Cascade, whose capricious leaps and playful somersaults, all the while volubly chattering to itself, like a child alone with its playthings, fascinates us, as sky, water, and fire charm the eyes of an infant. It is always tumbling down, and as often leaping to its feet to resume its frolicsome gambols, with no loss of sprightliness or sign of weariness that we can detect. Only a lover may sing the praises of these mountain cascades falling from the skies:

"The torrent is the soul of the valley. Not only is it the Providence or the scourge, often both at once, but it gives to it a physiognomy; it gladdens or saddens it; it lends it a voice; it communicates life to it. A valley without its torrent is only a hole."

They give the name of Idlewild to the romantic sylvan retreat, reached by a winding path, diverging near the hotel, on the left. I visited it in company with Mr. Atwater, whose taste and enthusiasm for the work have converted the natural disorder of the mountain side into a trysting-place fit for elves and fairies; but where one encounters ladies in elegant toilets, enjoying a quiet stroll among the fern-draped rocks. Some fine vistas of the valley mountains have been opened through the woods—beautiful little bits of blue, framed in illuminated foliage. One notes approvingly the revival of an olden taste in the cutting and shaping of trees into rustic chairs, stairways, and arbors.

After a day like ours, the great fires and admirable order of the hotel were grateful indeed. If it is true that the way to man's heart lies through his stomach, the cherry-lipped waiter-girl, who whispered her seductive tale in my too-willing ear at supper, made a veritable conquest. My compliments to her, notwithstanding the penalty paid for lingering too long over the griddle-cakes.

The autumn nights being cool, it was something curious to see the parlor doors every now and then thrown wide open, to admit a man who came trundling in on a wheelbarrow a monster log fit for the celebration of Yule-tide. The city guest, accustomed to the economy of wood at home, because it is dear, looks on this prodigality first with consternation, and finally with admiration. When the big log is deposited on the blazing hearth amid fusees of sparks, the easy-chairs again close around the fireplace a charmed circle; and while the buzz of conversation goes on, and the faces are illuminated by the ruddy glow, the wood snaps, and hisses, and spits as if it had life and sense of feeling. The men talk in drowsy undertones; the ladies, watching the chimney-soot catch fire and redden, point out to each other the old grandame's pictures of "folks coming home from meeting." This scene is the counterpart of a warm summer evening on the piazza—both typical of unrestrained, luxurious indolence. How many pictures have appeared in that old fireplace! and what experiences its embers revived! Water shows us only our own faces in their proper mask—nothing more, nothing less; but fire, the element of the supernatural, is able, so at least we believe, to unfold the future as easily as it turns our eyes into the past. If only we could read!

When we arose in the morning, what was our astonishment to see the surrounding mountains white with snow. Like one smitten with sudden terror, they had grown gray in a night. Striking, indeed, was the transformation from yesterday's pomp; beautiful the contrast between the dark green below and the dead white of the upper zones. Thickly incrusted with hoar-frost, the stiffened foliage of the pines and firs gave those trees the unwonted appearance of bursting into blossom. Over all a dull and brooding sky shed its cold, wan light upon the glen, forbidding all thought of attacking the high summits, at least for this day.

Dismissing this, therefore, as impracticable, we nevertheless determined on ascending Mount Willard—an easy thing to do, considering you have only to follow a good carriage-road for two miles and a half to reach the precipices overlooking the Saco Valley.

Startling, indeed, by its sublimity was the spectacle that rewarded our trouble a thousand-fold. Still, the sensations partook more of wonder than admiration — much more. The unpractised eye is so utterly confounded by the immensity of this awful chasm of the Notch, yawning in all its extent and all its grandeur far down beneath, that, powerless to grasp the fulness and the vastness thus suddenly encountered, it stupidly stares into those far-retreating depths. The scene really seems too tremendous for flesh and blood to comprehend. For an instant, while standing on the brink of the sheer precipice,

LOOKING DOWN THE NOTCH.

which here suddenly drops seven or eight hundred feet, my head swam and my knees trembled.

First came the idea that I was looking down into the dry bed of some primeval cataract, whose mighty rush and roar the imagination summoned again from the tomb of ages, and whose echo was in the cascades, hung like two white arms on the black and hairy breast of the adjacent mountain. This idea carries us back to the Deluge, of which science pretends to have found proofs in the basin of the Notch. What am I saying? to the Deluge! it transports us to the Beginning itself, when "*Darkness was upon the face of the deep. And the Spirit of God moved upon the face of the waters.*"

You see the immense walls of Mount Willey on one side, and of Webster on the other, rushing downward thousands of feet, and meeting in one magnificently imposing sweep at their bases. This vast natural inverted archway has the heavens for a roof. The eye roves from the shaggy head of one mountain to the shattered cornices of the other. One is terrible, the other forbidding. The naked precipices of Willey, furrowed by avalanches, still show where the fatal slide of 1826 crushed its way down into the valley, traversing a mile in only a few moments. Far down in the distance you see the Willey hamlet and its bright clearing. You see the Saco's silver.

Such, imperfectly, are the more salient features of this immense cavity of the Notch, three miles long, two thousand feet deep, rounded as if by art, and as full of suggestions as a ripe melon of seeds. I recall few natural wonders so difficult to get away from, or that haunt you so perpetually.

Like ivy on storied and crumbling towers, so high up the cadaverous cliffs of Willey the hardy fir-tree feels its way, insinuating its long roots in every fissure where a little mould has crept, but mounting always like the most intrepid of climbers. Upon the other side, the massed and plumed forest advances boldly up the sharp declivity of Webster; but in mid-ascent is met and ploughed in long, thin lines by cataracts of stones, poured down upon it from the summit. Only a few straggling bushes succeed in mounting higher; and far up, upon the very edge of the crumbling parapet, one solitary cedar tottered. The thought of imminent destruction prevailed over every other. Indeed, it seemed as if one touch would precipitate the whole mass of earth, stones, and trees into the vale beneath.

Between these high, receding walls, which draw widely apart at the outlet of the pass, mountains rise, range upon range. Over the flattened Nancy summits, Chocorua lifts his crested head once more into view. We pass in review the summits massed between, which on this morning were of a deep blue-black, and stood vigorously forth from a sad and boding sky.

From the ledges of Mount Willard, Washington and the peaks between are visible in a clear day. This morning they were muffled in clouds, which a strong upper current of air began slowly to disperse. We, therefore, secured a good position, and waited patiently for the unveiling.

Little by little the clouds shook themselves free from the mountain, and began a slow, measured movement toward the Ammonoosuc Valley. As they were drawn out thinner and thinner, like fleeces, by invisible hands, we began to be conscious of some luminous object behind them, and all at once, through a rift, there burst upon the sight the grand mass of Washington, all resplendent in silvery whiteness. From moment to moment the trooping clouds, as if pausing to pay homage to the illustrious recluse, encompassed it about. Then moving on, the endless procession again and again disclosed the snowy crest, shining out in unshrouded effulgence. To look was to be wonder-struck—to be dumb.

As the clouds unrolled more and more their snowy billows, other and lower summits rose above, as on that memorable morn after the Deluge, where they appeared like islands of crystal floating in a sea of silvery vapor. We gazed for an hour upon this unearthly display, which derived unique splendor from fitful sun-rays shot through the folds of surrounding clouds, then drawing off, and again darting unawares upon the stainless white of the summits. It was a dream of the celestial spheres to see the great dome, one moment glittering like beaten silver, another shining with the dull lustre of a gigantic opal.

I have since made several journeys through the Notch by the railway. The effect of the scenery, joined with some sense of peril in the minds of the timid, is very marked. Old travellers find a new and veritable sensation of excitement; while new ones forget fatigue, drop the novels they have been reading, maintaining a state of breathless suspense and admiration until the train vanishes out at the rocky portal, after an ascent of nearly six hundred feet in two miles.

In effect, the road is a most striking expression of the maxim, "*L'audace, et toujours de l'audace,*" as applied to modern engineering skill. From Bemis's to Crawford's its way is literally carved out of the side of the mountain. But if the engineers have stolen a march upon it, the thought, how easily the mountain could shake off this puny, clinging thing, prevailing over every other, announces that the mountain is still the master.

There are no two experiences which the traveller retains so long or so vividly as this journey through the great Notch, and this survey from the ledges of Mount Willard, which is so admirably placed to command it. To my mind, the position of this mountain suggests the doubt whether nature did not make a mistake here. Was not the splitting of the mountains an after-thought?

X.

THE ASCENT FROM CRAWFORD'S.

On a throne of rocks, in a robe of clouds,
With a diadem of snow.—*Manfred.*

AT five in the morning I was aroused by a loud rap at the door. In an instant I had jumped out of bed, ran to the window, and peered out. It was still dark; but the heavens were bright with stars, so bright that there was light in the room. Now or never was our opportunity. Not a moment was to be lost.

I began a vigorous reveille upon the window-pane. George half opened one sleepy eye, and asked if the house was on fire. The colonel pretended not to have heard.

" Up, sluggards!" I exclaimed; "the mountain is ours!"

" Do you know who first tempted man to go up into a high mountain?" growled George.

" Satan!" whined a smothered voice from beneath the bedclothes.

The case evidently was one which demanded heroic treatment. In an instant I whipped off the bedclothes; in another I received two violent blows full in the chest, which compelled me to give ground. The pillows were followed by the bolster, which I parried with a chair, the bolster by a sortie of the garrison *in puris naturalibus.* For a few seconds the mêlée was furious, the air thick with flying missiles. By a common instinct we drew apart, with the intention of renewing the combat, when we heard quick blows upon the partition at the left, and scared voices from the chamber at the right demanding what was the matter. George dropped his pillow, and articulated in a broken voice, " Malediction! I am awake."

" Come, gentlemen," I urged, "if you are sufficiently diverted, dress yourselves, and let us be off. At the present moment you remind me of the half-armed warriors on the pediment of the Parthenon."

"I take it you mean the frieze," said George, with chattering teeth.

The colonel was on all fours, picking up the different articles of his wardrobe from the four corners of the chamber. "My stocking," said he, groping among the furniture.

"What do you call this?" inquired George, fishing the dripping article from the water-pitcher.

"Eh! where the deuce is my watch?" redemanded the colonel, still seeking.

"Perhaps this is yours?" George again suggested, drawing it, with mock dexterity, as he had seen Hermann do, from a boot-leg.

We quickly threw on our clothes, but at the moment of starting George put his hand into his breast and made a frightful grimace.

"What is it?" we both asked in one breath. "What is the matter?"

"My pocket-book is gone."

After five minutes' ransacking in every hole and corner of the room, and after shaking the bedclothes carefully, all to no purpose, it was discovered that George and myself had exchanged coats. We then went down-stairs into the great hall, where a solitary jet of gas burnt blue, and a sleepy watchman dozed on a settee. The morning air was more than chilly: it was "a nipping and an eager air." There were two or three futile attempts at pleasantry, but hunger, darkness, and the cold quickly silenced them. A man is never himself when roused at five in the morning. No matter how desirable the excursion may have looked the night before, turning out of a warm bed to hurry on your clothes by candle-light, and to take the road fasting, strips it of all glamour.

Day broke disclosing a clear sky, up which the rosy tints of sunrise were streaming. The last star trembled in the zone of dusky blue above the grand old hills, like a tear-drop on the eyelids of the night. The warm color flowed over the frosted heads of the pines, mantling their ghastly white with the warm glow of reviving life. Then the eye fell upon the lower forests, still wrapped in deep shadows, the tiny lake, the boats, and, lastly, the oval plain, or vestibule of the Notch, above which ascended the shaggy sides of Mount Willard, and the retreating outline of Mount Webster. The little plain was white with hoar-frost: the frozen fountain dripped slowly into its basin, like a penitent telling its beads.

After a hasty breakfast, despatched with mountain appetites, behold us at half-past six entering the forest in Indian file! My companions again found their accustomed gayety, and soon the solemn old woods echoed with mirth. Our hopes were as high as the mountain itself.

A détour as far as Gibbs's Falls cost a good half-hour in recovering the bridle-path; but we were at length *en route*, myself at the head, George behind. The colonel carried the flask, and marched in the middle. He was considered the most incorruptible of the three; but this precaution was deemed an indispensable safeguard, should he, in a moment of forgetfulness, carry the flask to his lips.

The side of Mount Clinton, which we were now climbing, is very steep. The name of bridle-path, which they give the long gully we had entered, is a snare for pedestrians, but a greater delusion for cavaliers. The rains, the melting snows, have so channelled it as to leave little besides interlaced roots of old trees and loose bowlders in its bed. Higher up it is nothing but the bare course of a mountain torrent.

The long rain had thoroughly soaked the earth, rendering it miry and slippery to the feet; the heavy air, compounded of a thousand odors, hindered, rather than assisted, the free play of the lungs. Our progress was slow, our breathing quick and labored. Every leaf trembled with rain-drops, so that the flight of a startled bird overhead sprinkled us with fine spray. Finches chattered in the tree-tops, squirrels scolded us sharply from fallen logs.

Looking up was like looking through some glorious, illuminated window—the changed foliage seemed to have fixed the gorgeous hues of the sunset. Through its crimson and gold, violet and green, patches of blue sky greeted us with fair promise for the day. Looking ahead, the path zigzagged among ascending trees, plunged into the sombre depths above our heads, and was lost. One impression that I received may be, yet I doubt, common to others. On either side of me the forest seemed all in motion; the dusky trunks striding silently and stealthily by, moving when we moved, halting when we halted. The greenwood was as full of illusions as the human heart. I can never repress a certain fear in a forest, and to-day this seemed peopled with sprites, gnomes, and fauns. Once or twice a crow rose lazily from the top of a dead pine, and flew croaking away; but we thought not of omens or auguries, and pushed gayly on up the sharp ascent.

It was a wild woodland walk, with few glimpses out of the forest. For about a mile we steered toward the sun, climbing one of the long braces of the mountain. Stopping near here, at a spring deliciously pure and cold, we soon turned toward the north. As we advanced up the mountain the sun began to gild the tree-tops, and stray beams to play at hide-and-seek among the black trunks. We saw dells of Arcadian loveliness, and we heard the noise of rivulets, trickling in their depths, that we did not see.

Wh-r-r-r! rose a startled partridge, directly in our path, bringing us to a full stop. Another and another took flight.

"Gad!" muttered the colonel, wiping his forehead, "I was dreaming of old times; I declare I thought the mountain had got our range, and was shelling us."

"*Salmis* of partridge; *sauce aux champignons*," said George, licking his lips, and looking wistfully after the birds. You see, one spoke from the head, the other from the stomach.

Half an hour's steady tramp brought us to an abandoned camp, where travellers formerly passed the night. A long stretch of corduroy road, and we were in the region of resinous trees. Here it was like going up rickety stairs, the mossed and sodden logs affording only a treacherous foothold. Evidence that we were nearing the summit was on all sides. Patches of snow covered the ground and were lodged among the branches. From these little runlets made their way into the path, as the most convenient channel. There were many dead pines, having their curiously distorted limbs hung with the long gray lichen called "old man's beard." Multitudes of great trees, prostrated by the wind, lay rotting along the ground, or had lodged in falling, constituting a woful picture of wreck and ruin. Here was not only the confusion and havoc of a primitive forest, untouched by the axe, but the battle-ground of ages, where frost, fire, and flood had steadily and pitilessly beaten the forest back in every desperate effort made to scale the summit. Prone upon the earth, stripped naked, or bursting their bark, the dead trees looked like fallen giants despoiled of their armor, and left festering upon the field. But we advanced to a scene still more weird.

The last mile gives occasional glimpses into the Ammonoosuc Valley, of Fabyan's, of the hamlet at the base of Washington, and of the mountains between Fabyan's and Jefferson. The last half-mile is a steady planting of one foot before another up the ledges. We left the forest for a scanty growth of firs, rooted among enormous rocks, and having their branches pinned down to their sides by snow and ice. The whole forest had been seized, pinioned, and cast into a death-like stupor.

Each tree seemed to keep the attitude in which it was first overtaken; each silvered head to have dropped on its breast at the moment the spell overcame it. Perpetual imprisonment rewarded the temerity of the forest for thus invading the dominion of the Ice King. There it stood, all glittering in its crystal chains!

But as we threaded our way among these trees, still as statues, the sun came valiantly to the rescue. A warm breath fanned our cheeks and traversed the ice-locked forest. Instantly a thrill ran along the mountain. Quick, snapping noises filled the air. The trees burst their fetters in a trice. Myriad crystals fluttered overhead, or fell tinkling on the rocks at our feet. Another breath, and tree after tree lifted its bowed head gracefully erect. The forest was free.

George, who began by asking every few rods how much farther it was, now repeated the question for the fiftieth time; but we paid no attention.

We now entered a sort of liliputian forest, not higher than the knee, but which must have presented an almost insuperable barrier to early explorers of the mountain. In fact, as they could neither go through it nor around it, they must have walked over it, the thick-matted foliage rendering this the only alternative. No one could tell how long these trees had been growing, when a winter of unheard-of severity destroyed them all, leaving only their skeletons bleaching in the sun and weather. Wrenched, twisted, and made to grow the wrong way by the wind, the branches resembled the cast-off antlers of some extinct race of quadrupeds which had long ago resorted to the top of the mountain. The girdle of blasted trees below was piteous, but this was truly a strange spectacle. Indeed, the pallid forehead of the mountain seemed wearing a crown of thorns.

Getting clear of the dwarf-trees, or knee-wood, as it is called in the Alps, we ran quickly up the bare summit ledge. The transition from the gloom and desolation below into clear sunshine and free air was almost as great as from darkness to light. We lost all sense of fatigue; we felt only exultation and supreme content.

Here we were, we three, more than four thousand feet above the sea, confronted by an expanse so vast that no eye but an eagle's might grasp it, so thronged with upstarting peaks as to confound and bewilder us out of all power of expression. One feeling was uppermost—our own insignificance. We were like flies on the gigantic forehead of an elephant.

However, we had climbed and were astride the ridge-pole of New England. The rains which beat upon it descend on one side to the Atlantic, on the other to Long Island Sound. The golden sands which are the glory of the New England coast have been borne, atom by atom, grain by grain, from this grand laboratory of Nature; and if you would know the source of her great industries, her wealth, her prosperity, seek it along the rivers which are born of these skies, cradled in these ravines, and nourished amid the tangled mazes of these impenetrable forests. How, like beautiful serpents, their sources lie knotted and coiled in the heart of these mountains! How lovingly they twine about the feet of the grand old hills! Too proud to bear its burdens, they create commerce, building cities, scattering wealth as they run on. No barriers can stay, no chains fetter their free course. They laugh and run on.

We stood facing the south. Far down beneath us, at our left, was the valley of Mount Washington River. A dark, serpentine rift in the unbroken forest indicated the course of the stream. Mechanically we turned to follow it up the long gorge through which it flows, to where it issues, in secret, from the side of Mount Washington itself. In front of us arose the great Notch Mountains; beyond, mountains were piled on mountains; higher still, like grander edifices of some imperial city, towered the pinnacles of Lafayette, Carrigain, Chocorua, Kearsarge, and the rest. Yes, there they were, pricking the keen air with their blunted spears, fretting the blue vault with the everlasting menace of a power to mount higher if it so willed, filling us with the daring aspiration to rise as high as they pointed. Here and there something flashed brightly upon the eye; but it was no easy thing to realize that those little pools we saw glistening among the mountains were some of the largest lakes in New England.

Leaving the massive Franconia group, the eye swept over the Ammonoosuc basin, over the green heights of Bethlehem and Littleton, overtopped by the distant Green Mountains; then along the range dividing the waters flowing from the western slopes of the great summits into separate streams; then Whitefield, Lancaster, Jefferson; and, lastly, rested upon the amazing apparition of Washington, rising two thousand feet above the crags on which we stood. Perched upon the cap-stone of this massive pile, like a dove-cot on the cupola of St. Peter's, we distinctly saw the Summit House. Between us and our goal rose the brown heads of Pleasant, Franklin, and Monroe, over which our path lay. All these peaks and their connecting ridges were freely spattered with snow.

"By Jove!" ejaculated the colonel at last; "this beats Kentucky!"

It is necessary to say two words concerning a spectacle equally novel and startling to dwellers in more temperate regions, and which now held us in mingled astonishment and admiration. We could hardly believe our eyes. This bleak and desolate ridge, where only scattered tufts of coarse grass, stinted shrubs, or spongy moss gave evidence of life, which seemed never to have known the warmth of a sunbeam, was transformed into a garden of exquisite beauty by the frozen north wind.

We remarked the iced branches of dwarf firs inhabiting the upper zone of the mountain as we passed them; but here, on this summit, the surfaces of the rocks actually bristled with spikes, spear-heads, and lance-points, all of ice, all shooting in the direction of the north wind. The forms were as various as beautiful, but most commonly took that of a single spray, though sometimes they were moulded into perfect clusters of berries, branching coral, or pendulous crystals. Common shrubs were transformed to diamond aigrettes, coarse grasses into bird-of-paradise plumes, by the simple adhesion of frost-dust. The iron rocks attracted the flying particles as the loadstone attracts steel. Cellini never fashioned anything half so marvellous as this exquisite workmanship of a frozen mist. Yet, though it was all surpassingly beautiful, it was strangely suggestive of death. There was no life—no, not even the chirrup of an insect. No wonder our eyes sought the valley.

Hardly had we time to take in these unaccustomed sights, when, to our unspeakable dismay, ominous streakings of gray appeared in the southern and eastern horizons. The sun was already overclouded, and emitted only a dull glare. For a moment a premonition of defeat came over me; but another look at the summit removed all indecision, and, without mentioning my fears to my companions, we all three plunged into the bushy ravine that leads to Mount Pleasant.

Suddenly I felt the wind in my face, and the air was filled with whirling snow-flakes. We had not got over half the distance to the second mountain, before the ill-omened vapors had expanded into a storm-cloud that boded no good to any that might be abroad on the mountain. My idea was that we could gain the summit before it overtook us. I accordingly lengthened my steps, and we moved on at a pace which brought us quickly to the second mountain. But, rapidly as we had marched, the storm was before us.

Here began our first experience of the nature of the task in hand. The burly side of Mount Pleasant was safely turned, but beyond this snow had obliterated the path, which was only here and there indicated by little heaps of loose stones. It became difficult, and we frequently lost it altogether among the deep drifts. We called a halt, passed the flask, and attempted to derive some encouragement from the prospect.

The storm-cloud was now upon us in downright earnest. Already the flying scud drifted in our faces, and poured, like another Niagara, over the ridge one long, unbroken billow. The sun retreated farther and farther, until it looked like a farthing dip shining behind a blanket. Another furious blast, and it disappeared altogether. And now, to render our discomfiture complete, the gigantic dome of Washington, that had lured us on, disappeared, swallowed up in a vortex of whirling vapor; and presently we were all at once assailed by a blinding snow-squall. Henceforth there was neither luminary nor landmark to guide us. None of us had any knowledge of the route, and not one had thought of a guide. To render our situation more serious still, George now declared that he had sprained an ankle.

If I had never before realized how the most vigorous travellers had perished within a few paces of the summit, I understood it this day.

Bathed in perspiration, warned by the fresh snow that the path would soon be lost beyond recovery, we held a brief council upon the situation before and behind us. It was more than aggravating either way.

All three secretly favored a retreat. Without doubt it was not only the safest, but the wisest course to pursue; yet to turn back was to give in beaten, and defeat was not easy to accept. Even George, notwithstanding his ankle, was pluckily inclined to go on. There was no time to lose, so we emerged from the friendly shelter of a jutting ledge upon the trackless waste before us.

From this point, at the northern foot of Pleasant, progress was necessarily slow. We could not distinguish objects twenty paces through the flying scud and snow, and we knew vaguely that somewhere here the mountain ridge suddenly broke off, on both sides, into precipices thousands of feet down. George, being lame, kept the middle, while the colonel and I searched for stone-heaps at the right and left.

We were marching along thus, when I heard an exclamation, and saw the colonel's hat driven past me through the air. The owner ran rapidly over to my side.

"Take care!" I shouted, throwing myself in his path; "take care!"

"But my hat!" cried he, pushing on past me. The wind almost drowned our voices.

"Are you mad?" I screamed, griping his arm, and forcing him backward by main strength.

He gave me a dazed look, but seemed to comprehend nothing of my excitement. George halted, looking first at one, then at the other.

"Wait," said I, loosening a piece of ice with my boot. On both sides of us rose a whirlpool of boiling clouds. I tossed the piece of ice in the direction the hat had taken—not a sound; a second after the first—the same silence; a third in the opposite direction. We listened intently, painfully, but could hear nothing except the loud beating of our own hearts. A dozen steps more would have precipitated our companion from the top to the bottom of the mountain.

I looked at the man whose arm I still tightly grasped. He was as pale as a corpse.

"This must be Oakes's Gulf," I ventured, in order to break the silence, after we had all taken a pull at the flask.

"This is Oakes's Gulf—agreed; but where in perdition is my hat?" demanded the colonel, wiping the big drops from his forehead.

After he had tied a handkerchief around his head, we crossed this Devil's Bridge, with the caution of men fully alive to the consequences of a false step, and with that tension of the nerves which announces the terrible or the unknown.[1]

We had not gone far when a tremendous gust sent us reeling toward the abyss. I dropped on my hands and knees, and my companions followed suit. We arose, shook off the snow, and slowly mounted the long, steep, and rocky side of Franklin. Upon gaining the summit, the walking was better. We were also protected by the slope of the mountain.

---

[1] I have since passed over the same route without finding those sensations to which our inexperience, and the tempest which surrounded us, rendered us peculiarly liable. In reality, the ridge connecting Mount Pleasant with Mount Franklin is passed without hesitation, in good weather, by the most timid; but when a rod of the way cannot be seen the case is different, and caution necessary. The view of this natural bridge from the summit of Mount Franklin is one of the imposing sights of the day's march.

The worst seemed over. But what fantastic objects were the big rocks, scattered, or rather lying in wait, along our route! What grotesque appearances continually started out of the clouds! Now it was an enormous bear squatted on his haunches; now a dark-browed sphinx; and more than once we could have sworn we saw human beings stealthily watching us from a distance. How easy to imagine these weird objects lost travellers, suddenly turned to stone for their presumptuous invasion of the domain of terrors! It really seemed as if we had but to stamp our feet to see a legion of demons start into life and bar our way.

Say what you will, we could not shake off the dread which these unearthly objects inspired; nor could we forbear, were it at the risk of being turned to stone, looking back, or peering furtively from side to side when some new apparition thrust its hideous suggestions before us. What would you have? Are we not all children who shrink from entering a haunted chamber, and shudder in the presence of death? Well, the mountain was haunted, and death seemed near. We forgot fatigue, forgot cold, to yield to this mysterious terror, which daunted us as no peril could do, and froze us with vague presentiment of the unknown.

Covered from head to foot with snow, bearded with icicles, tracking this solitude, which refused the echo of a foot-fall, like spectres, we seemed to have entered the debatable ground forever dedicated to spirits having neither home on earth nor hope in heaven, but doomed to wander up and down these livid crags for an eternity of woe. The mountain had already taken possession of our ʼphysicalʼ, now it seized upon our moral nature. Neither the one nor the other could resist the impressions which naked rock, furious tempest, and hidden danger stamped on every foot of the way.

In this way we reached Mount Monroe, last of the peaks in our route to the summit, where we were forced to pick our way among the rocks, struggling forward through drifts frequently waist deep.

It was here that, finding myself some distance in advance of the others—for poor George was lagging painfully—I halted for them to come up. I was choking with thirst, aggravated by eating the damp snow. As soon as the colonel was near enough—the wind only could be heard —I made a gesture of a man drinking. He did not seem to understand, though I impatiently repeated the pantomime. He came to where I stood.

"The flask!" I exclaimed.

He drew it slowly from his pocket, and handed it to me with a hang-dog look that I failed for the moment to interpret. I put it to my lips, shook it, turned it bottom up. Not a drop!

And, nevertheless, this was the man in whom I had trusted. Cæsar only succumbed to the dagger of Brutus; but I had not the courage to fall with dignity under this new misfortune, and so stood staring at the flask and the culprit alternately.

"Say that our cup is now full," suggested the incorrigible George. "The paradox strikes me as ingenious and appropriate."

It really was too bad. Snow and sleet had wet us to the skin, and clung to our frozen garments. Our hands and faces were swollen and inflamed; our eyes half closed and blood-shot. Even this short minute's halt set our teeth chattering. George could only limp along, and it was evident could not hold out much longer. Just now my uneasiness was greater than my sympathy. He was an accessory before the fact; for, while I was diligently looking out the path, he had helped the colonel to finish the flask.

We were nearing the goal: so much was certain. But the violence of the gale, increasing with the greater altitude, warned us against delay. We therefore pushed on across the stony terraces extending beyond, and were at length rewarded by seeing before us the heaped-up pile of broken granite constituting the peak of Washington, and which we knew still rose a thousand feet above our heads. The sight of this towering mass, which seems formed of the débris of the Creation, is well calculated to stagger more adventurous spirits than the three weary and foot-sore men who stood watching the cloud-billows, silently rolling up, dash themselves unceasingly against its foundations. We looked first at the mountain, then in each other's faces, then began the ascent.

For near an hour we toiled upward, sometimes up to the middle in snow, always carefully feeling our way among the treacherous pitfalls it concealed. Compelled to halt every few rods to recover breath, the distance traversed could not be great. Still, with dogged perseverance, we kept on, occasionally lending each other a helping hand out of a drift, or from rock to rock; but no words were exchanged, for the stock of gayety with which we set out was now exhausted. The gravity of the situation began to create uneasiness in the minds of my companions. All at once I heard my name called out. I turned. It was the colonel, whose halloo in midst of this stony silence startled me.

"You pretend," he began, "that it's only a thousand feet from the plateau to the top of this accursed mountain?"

"No more, no less. Professor Guyot assures us of the fact."

"Well, then, here we have been zigzagging about for a good hour, haven't we?"

"An hour and twenty minutes," said I, consulting my watch.

"And not a sign of the houses or the railway, or any other creeping thing. Do you want my opinion?"

"Charmed."

"We have passed the houses without seeing them in the storm, and are now on the side of the mountain opposite from where we started."

"So that you conclude—?"

"We are lost."

This was, of course, mere guesswork; but we had no compass, and might be travelling in the wrong direction, after all. A moment's reflection, however, reassured me. "Is that your opinion, too, George?" I asked.

George had taken off his boot, and was chafing his swollen ankle. He looked up.

"My opinion is that I don't know anything about it; but as you got us into this scrape, you had better get us out of it, and be spry about it too, for the deuce take me if I can go much farther."

"Why," croaked the colonel, "I recollect hearing of a traveller who, like us, actually walked by the Summit House without seeing it, when he was hailed by a man who, by mere accident, chanced to be outside, and who imagined he saw something moving in the fog. In five minutes the stranger would inevitably have walked over a precipice with his eyes open."

"And I remember seeing on the wall of the tavern where we stopped, at Bartlett, a placard offering a reward for a man who, like us, set out from Crawford's, and was never heard of," George put in.[1]

"And I read of one who, like us, almost reached the summit, but mistaking a lower peak for the pinnacle, losing his head, crawled, exhausted, under a rock to die there," I finished, firing the last shot.

Without another word both my comrades grappled vigorously with

---

[1] The remains of this ill-fated climber have since been found at the foot of the pinnacle. See chapter on Mount Washington.

the mountain, and for ten minutes nothing was heard but our labored breathing. On whatever side we might be, so long as we continued to ascend I had little fear of being in the wrong road. Our affair was to get to the top.

At the end of ten minutes we came suddenly upon a walled enclosure, which we conjectured to be the corral at the end of the bridle-path. We hailed it like an oasis in the midst of this desert. We entered, brushed the snow from a stone, and sat down.

Up to this time my umbrella had afforded a good deal of merriment to my companions, who could not understand why I encumbered myself with it on a day which began as this one did, perfectly clear and cloudless. Since the storm came on, the force of the wind would at any time have lifted off his feet the man who attempted to spread it, and even if it had not, as well might one have walked blindfolded in that treacherous road as with an open umbrella before him. Now it was my turn, or, rather, the turn of the abused umbrella. A few moments of rest were absolutely necessary; but the wind cut like a cimeter, and we felt ourselves freezing. I opened the umbrella, and, protected by it from the wind, we crouched under its friendly shelter, and lighted our cigars. Never before did I know the luxury of a smoke like that.

"Now," said I, complacently glancing up at our tent, "ever since I read how an umbrella saved a man's life, I determined never to go on a mountain without one."

"An umbrella! How do you make that out?" demanded both my auditors.

"It is very simple. He was lost on this very mountain, under conditions similar to those we are now experiencing, except that his carrying an umbrella was an accident, and that he was alone. He passed two nights under it. But the story will keep."

It may well be imagined that we had not the least disposition to be merry; yet for all that there was something irresistibly comical in three men sitting with their feet in the snow, and putting their heads together under a single umbrella. Various were the conjectures. We could hear nothing but the rushing wind, see nothing but driving sleet. George believed we were still half a mile from the summit; the colonel was not able to precisely fix his opinion, but thought us still a long way off. After diligent search, in which we all joined, I succeeded in finding something like a path turning to the right, and we again resumed our slow clambering over the rocks.

Perhaps ten minutes passed thus, when we again halted and peered anxiously into the whirling vapor — nothing, neither monument nor stone, to indicate where we were. A new danger confronted us; one I had hitherto repulsed because I dared not think of it. The light was failing, and darkness would soon be here. God help any that this night surprised on the mountain! While we eagerly sought on all sides some evidence that human feet had ever passed that way, a terrific blast, that seemed to concentrate the fury of the tempest in one mighty effort, dashed us helpless upon the rocks. For some seconds we were blinded, and could only crouch low until its violence subsided. But as the monstrous wave recoiled from the mountain, a piercing cry brought us quickly to our feet.

"Look!" shouted George, waving his hat like a madman — "look there!" he repeated.

Vaguely, through the tattered clouds, like a wreck driving miserably before the tempest, we distinguished a building propped up by timbers crusted with thick ice. The gale shook and beat upon it with demoniacal glee, but never did weary eyes rest on a more welcome object. For ten seconds, perhaps, we held it in view; then, in a twinkling, the clouds rolled over it, shut together, and it was gone — swallowed up in the vortex.

A moment of bewilderment succeeded, after which we made a simultaneous rush in the direction of the building. In five minutes more we were within the hotel, thawing our frozen clothing before a rousing fire.

It provokes a smile when I think of it. Here, in this frail structure, perched like another Noah's Ark on its mountain, and which every gust threatened to scatter to the winds of heaven, a grand piano was going in the parlor, a telegraphic instrument clicked in a corner, and we sat down to a *menu* that made the colonel forget the loss of his hat.

" By the bones of Daniel Boone! I can say as Napoleon did on the Great St. Bernard, ' I have spoiled a hat among your mountains ; well, I shall find a new one on the other side,' " observed the colonel, uncorking a second bottle of champagne.

SECOND JOURNEY.

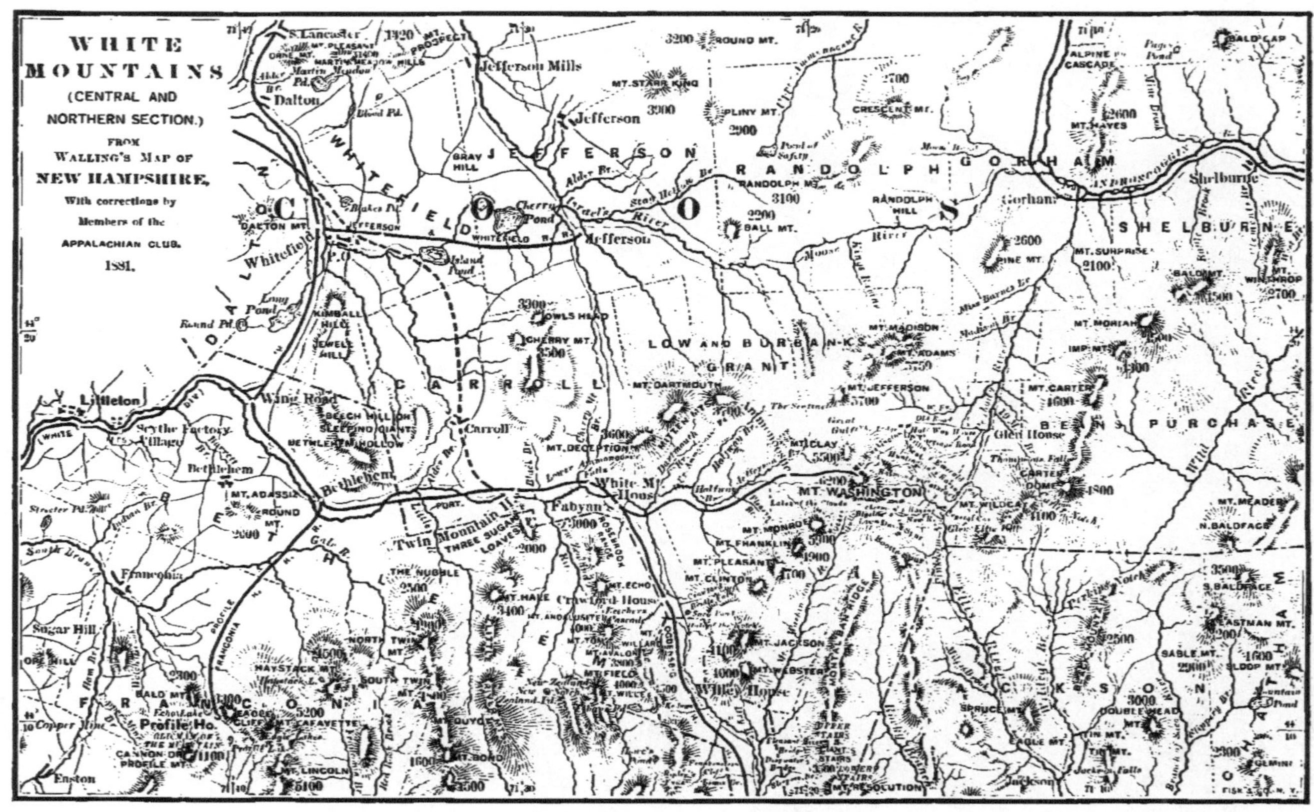

WHITE MOUNTAINS
(CENTRAL AND NORTHERN SECTION.)
FROM WALLING'S MAP OF NEW HAMPSHIRE,
With corrections by Members of the APPALACHIAN CLUB.
1881.

SECOND JOURNEY.

I.

LEGENDS OF THE CRYSTAL HILLS.

> My lord, I will hoist saile; and all the wind
> My bark can beare shall hasten me to find
> A great new world.—SIR W. DAVENANT.

WHEN Cabot, in the *Mathew*, of Bristol, was sailing by the New England coast, and the amazed savage beheld a pyramid of white sails rising, like a cloud, out of the sea, the navigator saw from the deck of his ship, rising out of the land, a cluster of lofty summits cut like a cameo on the northern sky.

The Indian left his tradition of the marvellous apparition, which he at first believed to be a mass of trees wrapped in faded foliage, drifting slowly at the caprice of the waves; but, as he gazed, fire streamed from the strange object, a cloud shut it from his view, and a peal like distant thunder was wafted on the breeze to his startled ears. That peal announced the doom of his race. He was looking at the first ship.

Succeeding navigators, Italians, Portuguese, French, English — a roll of famous names—sailed these seas, and, in their turn, hailed the distant summits. They became the great distinguishing landmarks of this corner of the New World. They are found on all the maps traced by the early geographers from the relations of the discoverers themselves. Having thus found form and substance, they also found a name—the Mountains of St. John.

Ships multiplied. Men of strange garb, speech, complexion, erected their habitations along the coast, the unresisting Indian never dreaming that the thin line which the sea had cast up would speedily rise to an inundation destined to sweep him from the face of the earth. Then began that steady advance, slow at first, gathering momentum with the years, before which he recoiled step by step, and finally disappeared forever. His destiny was accomplished. To-day only mountains and streams transmit to us the certainty that he ever did exist. They are his monument, his lament, his eternal accusation.

The White Mountains stood for the Indian not only as an image, but as the actual dwelling-place of Omnipotence. His dreaded Manitou, whose voice was the thunder, whose anger the lightning, and on whose face no mortal could look and live, was the counterpart of the terrible Thor, the Icelandic god, throned in a palace of ice among frozen and inaccessible mountain peaks, over which he could be heard urging his loud chariot amid the rage of the tempest. Frost and fire, plague and famine were the terrific natural agents common to the Indian and to the Norse mythology; and to his god of terrors the Indian conjurer addressed his prayers, his incantations, and his propitiatory offerings, when some calamity had befallen or threatened his tribe. But to cross the boundary which separated him from the abiding-place of the Manitou! plant his audacious foot within the region from which Nature shrunk back affrighted! Not all the wealth he believed the mountain hoarded would have tempted him to brave the swift and terrible vengeance of the justly offended, all-powerful Manitou. So far, then, as he was concerned, the mountain remained inviolate, inviolable, as a kind of hell, filled with the despairing shrieks of those who in an evil hour transgressed the limits sacred to immortals.[1]

As a pendant to this superstition, in which their deity is with simple grandeur throned on the highest mountain peak, it is curious to remember the Indian tradition of the Deluge; for, like so many peoples, they had their tradition, coming from a remote time, and having strong family resemblance with that of more enlightened nations. According to it, all

---

[1] This analogy of belief may be carried farther still, to the populations of Asia, which surround the great "Abode of Snow"—the Himalayas. It would be interesting to see in this similarity of religious worship a link between the Asiatic, the primitive man, and the American—the most recent, and the most unfortunate. Our province is simply to recount a fact to which the brothers Schlaginweit ("Exploration de la Haute Asie") bear witness:

"It is in spite of himself, under the enticement of a great reward, that the superstitious Hindoo decides to accompany the traveller into the mountains, which he dreads less for the unknown dangers of the ascent than for the sacrilege he believes he is committing in approaching the holy asylum, the inviolable sanctuary of the gods he reveres; his trouble becomes extreme when he sees in the peak to be climbed not the mountain, but the god whose name it bears. Henceforth it is by sacrifice and prayer alone that he may appease the profoundly offended deity."

the inhabitants of the earth were drowned, except one Powaw and his wife, who were preserved by climbing to the top of the White Mountains, and who were the progenitors of the subsequent races of man. The Powaw took with him a hare, which, upon the subsiding of the waters, he freed, as Noah did the dove, seeing in its prolonged absence the assurance that he and his companion might safely descend to earth. The likeness of this tradition with the story of Deucalion, and Pyrrha, his wife, as related by Ovid, is very striking. One does not easily consent to refer it to accident alone.

There is one thing more. When asked by the whites to point out the Indian's heaven, the savage stretched his arm in the direction of the White Hills, and replied that heaven was just beyond. Such being his religion, and such the influence of the mountain upon this highly imaginative, poetic, natural man, one finds himself drawn legitimately in the train of those marvels which our ancestors considered the most credible things in the world, and which the sceptical cannot explain by a sneer.

According to the Indians, on the highest mountain, suspended from a crag overlooking a dismal lake, was an enormous carbuncle, which many declared they had seen blazing in the night like a live coal. Some even asserted that its ruddy glare lighted the livid rocks around like the fire of a midnight encampment, while by day it emitted rays, like the sun, dazzling to look upon. And this extraordinary sight they declared they had not only seen, but seen again and again.

It is true that the Indians did not hesitate to declare that no mortal hand could hope to grasp the great fire-stone. It was, said they, in the special guardianship of the genius of the mountain, who, on the approach of human footsteps, troubled the waters of the lake, causing a dark mist to rise, in which the venturesome mortal became bewildered, and then hopelessly lost. Several noted conjurers of the Pigwackets, rendered foolhardy by their success in exorcising evil spirits, so far conquered their fears as to ascend the mountain; but they never returned, and had, no doubt, expiated their folly by being transformed into stone, or flung headlong down some stark and terrible precipice.

This tale of the great carbuncle fired the imagination of the simple settlers to the highest pitch. We believe what we wish to believe, and, notwithstanding their religion refused to admit the existence of the Indian demon, its guardian, they seem to have had little difficulty in crediting the reality of the jewel itself. At any rate, the belief that the mountain shut up precious mines has come down to our own day; we are assured by a learned historian of fifty years ago that the story of the great carbuncle still found full credence in his.[1]   We are now acquainted with the spirit of the time when the first attempt to scale the mountain, known to us, was rewarded with complete success.   But the record is of exasperating brevity.

Among the earliest settlers of Exeter, New Hampshire, was a man by the name of Darby Field.   The antecedents of this obscure personage are securely hidden behind the mists of more than two centuries.

A hundred and twenty-five years before the ascent of Mont Blanc by Jacques Balmat, Darby Field successfully ascended to the summit of the "White Hill," to-day known as Mount Washington; but the exploit of the adventurous Irishman is far more remarkable in its way than that of the brave Swiss, since he had to make his way for eighty miles through a wilderness inhabited only by beasts of prey, or by human beings scarcely less savage, before he reached the foot of the great range; while Balmat lived under the very shadow of the monarch of the Alps, so that its spectre was forever crossing his path.   Furthermore, the greater part of the ascent of Mont Blanc was already familiar ground to the guides and chamois-hunters of the Swiss Alps.   On the contrary, according to every probability, Field was the first human being whose daring foot invaded the hitherto inviolable seclusion of the illustrious hermit of New England.

For such an adventure one instinctively seeks a motive.   I did not long amuse myself with the idea that this explorer climbed merely for the sake of climbing; and I have little notion that he dreamed of posthumous renown.   It is far more probable that the reports brought by the Indians of the fabulous treasures of the mountains led to Field's long, arduous, and really perilous journey.   It is certain that he was possessed of rare intrepidity, as well as the true craving for adventure. That goes without saying; still, the whole undertaking — its inception, its pursuit to the end in the face of extraordinary obstacles, which he had no means of measuring or anticipating—announces a very different sort of man from the ordinary, a purpose before which all dangers disappear.

In June, 1642, that is to say, only twelve years after the Puritan set-

---

[1] Sullivan: "History of Maine."

tlements in Massachusetts Bay, Field set out from the sea-coast for the White Hills.

So far as known, he prosecuted his journey to the Indian village of Pigwacket, the existence of which is thus established, without noteworthy accident or adventure. Here he was joined by some Indians, who conducted him within eight miles of the summit, when, declaring that to go farther would expose them to the wrath of their great Evil Spirit, they halted, and refused to proceed. The brave Irishman was equal to the emergency. To turn back, baffled, within sight of his goal was evidently not an admitted contingency. Leaving the Indians, therefore, squatted upon the rocks, and no doubt regarding him as a man rushing upon a fool's fate, Field again resolutely faced the mountain, when, seeing him equally unmoved by their warnings as unshaken in his determination to reach the summit, two of the boldest warriors ran after him, while the others stoically made their preparations to await a return which they never expected to take place. They watched the retreating figures until lost among the rocks.

In the language of the original narration, the rest of the ascent was effected by "a ridge between two valleys filled with snow, out of which came two branches of the Saco River, which met at the foot of the hill, where was an Indian town of two hundred people." ... "By-the-way, among the rocks, there were two ponds, one a blackish water, and the other reddish." ... "Within twelve miles of the top was neither tree nor grass, but low savins, which they went upon the top of sometimes."

The adventurous climber pushed on. Soon he was assailed by thick clouds, through which he and his companions resolutely toiled upward. This slow and labored progress through entangling mists continued until within four miles of the summit, when Field emerged above them into a region of intense cold. Surmounting the immense pile of shattered rocks which constitute the spire, he at last stood upon the unclouded summit, with its vast landscape outspread beneath him, and the air so clear that the sea seemed not more than twenty miles distant. No doubt the daring explorer experienced all the triumph natural to his successful achievement. It is not difficult to imagine the exultation with which he planted his audacious foot upon the topmost crag, for, like Columbus, Cabot, Balboa, he, too, was a real discoverer. The Indians must have regarded him, who thus scornfully braved the vengeance of their god of terrors, as something more than man. I have often pictured him standing there, proudly erect, while the wonder-struck savages crouched humbly at his feet. Both, in their way, felt the presence of their God; but the white man would confront his as an equal, while the savage adored with his face in the dust.

The three men, after their first emotion of ecstasy, amazement, or fear, looked about them. For the moment the great carbuncle was forgotten. Field had chosen the best month of the twelve for his attempt, and now saw a vast and unknown region stretching away on the north and east to the shores of what he took for seas, but what were really only seas of vapor, heaped against the farthest horizons. He fancied he saw a great water to the north, which he judged to be a hundred miles broad, for no land was beyond it. He thought he descried the great Gulf of Canada to the east, and in the west the great lake out of which the river of Canada came. All these illusions are sufficiently familiar to mountain explorers; and it must not be forgotten that in Field's day geographical knowledge of the interior of the country was indeed limited. In fact, he must have brought back with him the first accurate knowledge respecting the sources of those rivers flowing from the eastern slopes of the mountains. The great gulf on the north side of Mount Washington is truly declared to be such a precipice that they could scarce discern to the bottom; the great northern wilderness as "daunting terrible," and clothed with "infinite thick woods." Such is its aspect to-day.

The day must have been so far spent that Field had but little time in which to prosecute his search. He, however, found "store of Muscovy glass" and some crystals, which, supposing them to be diamonds, he carefully secured and brought away. These glittering masses, congealed, according to popular belief, like ice on the frozen regions of the mountains, gave them the name of the Crystal Hills—a name the most poetic, the most suggestive, and the most fitting that has been applied to the highest summits since the day they were first discovered by Englishmen.

Descending the mountain, Field rejoined his Indians, who were doubtless much astonished to see him return to them safe and sound; for, while he had been making the ascent, a furious tempest, sent, as these savages believed, to destroy the rash pale-face and his equally reckless companions, burst upon the mountain. He found them drying themselves by a fire of pine-knots; and, after a short halt, the party took their way down the mountain to the Indian village.

Before a month elapsed, Field, with five or six companions, made a second ascent; but the gem of inestimable value, by whose light one might read at night, continued to elude his pursuit. The search was not, however, abandoned. Others continued it. The marvellous story, as firmly believed as ever by the credulous, survived, in all its purity, to our own century, to be finally transmitted to immortality by Hawthorne's tale of "The Great Carbuncle." It may be said here that great influence was formerly attributed to this stone, which the learned in alchemy believed prevailed against the dangers of infection, and was a sure talisman to preserve its owner from peril by sea or by land.

A tradition is ten times a tradition when it has a fixed locality. Without this it is a myth, a mere vagabond of a tradition. Knowing this, I searched diligently for the spot where the great carbuncle, like the eye of a Cyclop, shed its red lustre far down the valley of the Saco; and if the little mountain tarn to-day known as Hermit Lake, over which the gaunt crags rise in austere grandeur, be not the place, then I am persuaded that further seeking would be unavailing. I cannot go so far as to say that it never existed.

What seems passing strange is that the feat performed by Field,[1] the fame of which spread throughout the colony, should have been nearly, if not wholly, forgotten before the lapse of a century. Robert Rogers, one of the most celebrated hunters of the White Mountains, subsequently a renowned partisan leader in the French and Indian wars, uses the following language concerning them :

" I cannot learn that any person was ever on the top of these mountains. I have been told by the Indians that they have often attempted it in vain, by reason of the change of air they met with, which I am inclined to believe, having ascended them myself 'til the alteration of air was very perceptible; and even then I had not advanced half way up; the valleys below were then concealed from view by clouds."

It is not precisely known when or how these granite peaks took the name of the White Mountains. We find them so designated in 1672 by Josselyn, who himself performed the feat of ascending the highest

---

[1] Field's second ascension (July, 1642) was followed in the same year by that of Vines and Gorges, two magistrates of Sir F. Gorges's province of Maine, within which the mountains were believed to lie. Their visit contributed little to the knowledge of the region, as they erroneously reported the high plateau of the great chain to be the source of the Kennebec, as well as of the Androscoggin and Connecticut rivers.

summit, of which a brief record is found in his " New England's Rarities."   One cannot help saying of this book that either the author was a liar of the first magnitude, or else we have to regret the degeneracy of Nature, exhausted by her long travail; for this narrator gravely tells us of frogs which were as big as a child of a year old, and of poisonous serpents which the Indians caught with their bare hands, and ate alive with great gusto.   These are rarities indeed.

The first mention I have met with of an Indian name for the White Mountains is in the narrative of John Gyles's captivity, printed in Boston in 1736, saying:

" These White Hills, at the head of Penobscot River, are by the Indians said to be much higher than those called Agiockochook,¹ above Saco."

The similitude between the names White Mountains and Mont Blanc suggests the same idea, that color, rather than character, makes the first and strongest impression upon the beholder.   Thus we have White Mountains and Green Mountains, Red Mountains and Black Mountains, the world over.   The eye seizes a color before the mind fixes upon a distinctive feature, or the imagination a resemblance.   It is stated, on the authority of Schoolcraft, that the Algonquins called these summits " White Rocks."   Mariners, approaching from the open sea, descried what seemed a cloud-bank, rising from the landward horizon, when twenty leagues from the nearest coast, and before any other land was visible from the mast-head.   Thirty leagues distant in a direct line, in a clear midsummer day, the distant summits appeared of a pearly

---

¹ It also occurs, reduced to Agiochook, in the ballad, of unknown origin, on the death of Captain Lovewell.   One of these was, doubtless, the authority of Belknap.   Touching the signification of Agiochook, it is the opinion of Dr. J. Hammond Trumbull that the word which Captain Gyles imperfectly translated from sound into English syllables is Algonquin for "at the mountains on that side," or "over yonder."   "As to the generally received interpretations of Agiockochook, such as 'the abode of the Great Spirit,' 'the place of the Spirit of the Great Forest,' or, as one writer prefers, 'the place of the Storm Spirit,' " says Dr. Trumbull, " it is enough to say that no element of any Algonkin word meaning 'great,' 'spirit,' 'forest,' 'storm,' or 'abode,' or combining the meaning of any two of these words, occurs in 'Agiockochook.' The only Indian name for the White Hills that bears internal evidence of genuineness is one given on the authority of President Alden, as used 'by one of the eastern tribes,' that is, Waumbekketmethna, which easily resolves itself into the Kennebec-Abnaki waubeghiket-amadinar, 'white greatest mountain.'   It is very probable, however, that this synthesis is a mere translation, by an Indian, of the English 'White Mountains.'   I have never, myself, succeeded in obtaining this name from the modern Abnakis."

whiteness; observed again from a church steeple on the sea-coast, with the sky partially overcast, they were whitish-gray, showing that the change from blue to white, or to cool tones approximating with white, is due to atmospheric conditions. The early writers succeed only imperfectly in accounting for this phenomenon, which for six months of the year at least has no connection whatever with the snows that cover the highest peaks only from the middle of October to the middle of April, a period during which few navigators of the sixteenth and seventeenth centuries visited our shores, or, indeed, ventured to put to sea at all.[1]

---

[1] Here is what Douglass says in his "Summary" (1748-'53): "The White Hills, or rather mountains, inland about seventy miles north from the mouth of Piscataqua Harbor, about seven miles west by north from the head of the Pigwoket branch of Saco River; they are called white not from their being continually covered with snow, but because they are bald atop, producing no trees or brush, and covered with a whitish stone or shingle: these hills may be observed at a great distance, and are a considerable guide or direction to the Indians in travelling that country."

And Robert Rogers ("Account of America," London, 1765) remarks that the White Mountains were "so called from that appearance which is like snow, consisting, as is generally supposed, of a white flint, from which the reflection is very brilliant and dazzling."

II.

JACKSON AND THE ELLIS VALLEY.

Once more, O mountains of the North, unveil
Your brows, and lay your cloudy mantles by!—WHITTIER.

IT is Petrarch who says, "A journey on foot hath most pleasant commodities; a man may go at his pleasure; none shall stay him, none shall carry him beyond his wish, none shall trouble him; he hath but one labor, the labor of nature, to go." Every true pedestrian ought to render full faith to the poet's assertion; and should he chance to have his Laura, he will see her somewhere, or, rather, everywhere, I promise him. But that is his affair.

There are two ways of reaching Jackson from North Conway. One route leaves the travelled highway a short distance beyond the East Branch of the Saco, and ascends Thorn Hill; another diverges from it near Glen Station, in Bartlett. The Thorn Hill way is the longer; but, as the views are unsurpassed, I unhesitatingly chose it in preference to the easier and shorter road.

The walk from the Intervale over Thorn Hill gives ravishing backward glimpses, opening to a full and broad panorama of the Saco meadows and of the surrounding mountains. Needless to call them by name. One might forget names, but the image never. Then, advancing to the summit, full upon the charmed eye comes that glorious vision of the great mountains, elevated to an immense height, and seeming, in their benevolence, to say, "Approach, mortals!" Underneath is the village.

We have left the grand vestibule of the Saco to enter an amphitheatre. Washington, in his snowy toga, occupies the place of high honor. Adams flaunts his dainty spire over the Pinkham Notch, at the monarch's left hand. Then comes an embattled wall, pierced through its centre by the immense hollow of the Carter Notch.

Jackson is the ideal mountain village. From Thorn Hill it looked a little elysium, with its handful of white houses huddled around its one little church spire, like a congregation sitting at the feet of their pastor. You perceive neither entrance nor exit, so completely is the deep vale shut in by mountains. The streams, that make two veins of silver in the green floor, seem vainly seeking a way out. One would think Nature had locked the door and thrown away the key. The first stream is the Wildcat, coming from the Carter Notch; the second, the Ellis, from the Pinkham Notch. They unite just below the village, and, like a forlorn-hope, together cut their way out of the mountains.

Getting down into the village, the high mountains now sink out of sight, and I saw only the nearer and less elevated ones immediately surrounding — on the north, Eagle and Wildcat; on the east, Tin and Thorn; on the west, Iron Mountain. The latter has fine, bold cliffs. Over its smooth slope I again saw the two great steps of the Giant's Stairs, mounting the long ridge which conducts to the great plateau of Mount Washington.

The village has a bright, pleasant look, but is not otherwise remarkable in itself. Three hotels, the church, and a score or so of houses, constitute the central portion. But if the village is small, the township is large; and what is the visitor's astonishment, on opening his eyes some fine morning, to see farms and farm-houses scattered along the very summit of Thorn Mountain, whence they appear to regard the little world below with a lofty disdain. How came they there? is the question one feels inclined to ask; for in this enchanted air he loses the desire, almost the faculty, of thinking for himself. The inhabitants of this little colony seem to prize their seclusion, and only descend to earth at the call of necessity. Their neighbors are the eagles. Surely this is *Ultima Thule.* Alas! no; the tax-gatherer mounts even here.

The people of Jackson are above all anxious for the development of the mineral resources of the place. They have iron and tin, and claim also the existence of copper and even of gold ores. Yet it is probable that the vein most profitable for them, the one most likely to yield satisfactory returns, is that on which the summer hotels have been located and opened. So far, the mountains refuse to give up the wealth they hoard.

The Wildcat cuts the village in two. It is a perfect highwayman of a stream. The very air is tremulous with its rush and roar. I halted

GIANT'S STAIRS, FROM THORN MOUNTAIN.

awhile on the little bridge that spans it, from which, looking down the long pathway it makes, I enjoyed a fine retrospect of the Moats, and, looking up, saw the torrent come bounding toward me. Here it makes a swift descent over granite ledges, clean and fresh from constant scrubbing, as the face of a country urchin, and as freckled. See how hard every rod of its course is beset by huge hump-backed bowlders! A river in fetters!

Just above the bridge the stream plunges, two white streaks of water, twenty to thirty feet obliquely down. Now it is dark, now light; sometimes tinged a pale emerald, sometimes a rich amber, where it falls down in thin sheets. For half a mile the ledges look as if an earthquake had ripped them up to make a channel for this tempest of water. It is from these ledges, looking down the course of the stream, that Moat Mountain is so incomparably fine. It stretches itself luxuriously along the rich meadows, like a Sybarite upon his couch of velvet, lifting its head high enough to embrace the landscape, of which itself is the most attractive feature. And the tall pines rise above the framework of forest, as if to look at the beautiful mountain, clothed with the light of the morning, and reclining with such infinite grace.

Sprays of trembling foliage droop or stretch themselves out over the stream in search of the fine dew it sends up. They seem endeavoring to hide the broad scar made through the forest. The clear sun illuminates their green leaves, and makes the cool rocks emit a sensible warmth. It also illuminates the little fountains of water. Ferns and young willows shoot from crevices, delicate mosses attach themselves to the grim bowlders. I found the perfect print of a human foot sunk in the hardest rock; also cavities as cleverly rounded as if pebbles had been taken from the granite. On the banks, under the thick shade of the pines, I gathered a handful of the showy pappoose flower, the green leaves of which are edible. Little mauve butterflies fluttered at our knees like violets blown about by the wind.

The crest of the fall is split, and broken up in huge fragments. The main stream gains an outlet by a deep channel it has cut in the rock; then turns a mill; then shoots down the face of the ledge. Above the high ledge the bed of the river widens to about two hundred feet. Higher up, where it is broken in long regular steps over which fifty cascades tumble, I thought it most beautiful.

Besides Jackson Falls, so called, there is a fine cataract on the Ellis, known as Goodrich Falls. This is a mile and a half out of the village, where the Conway road passes the Ellis by a bridge; and, being directly upon the high-road, is one of the best known. The river here suddenly pours its whole volume over a precipice eighty feet high, making the earth tremble with the shock. I made my way down the steep bank to the bed of the river below the fall, from which I saw, first, the curling wave, large, regular, and glassy, of the dam, then three wild and foaming pitches of broken water, with detached cascades gushing out from the rocks at the right—all falling heavily into the eddying pool below. Where the water was not white, or filliped into fine spray, it was the color of pale sherry, and opaque, gradually changing to amber gold as the light penetrated it and the descending sheet of the fall grew thinner. The full tide of the river showed the fall to the best possible advantage. But spring is the season of cascades—the only season when one is sure of seeing them at all.

One gets strongly attached to such a stream as the Ellis. If it has been his only comrade for weeks, as it has been mine, the liking grows stronger every day—the sense of companionship is full and complete: the river is so voluble, so vivacious, so full of noisy chatter. If you are dull, it rouses and lifts you out of yourself; if gay, it is as gay as you. Besides, there is the paradox that, notwithstanding you may be going in different directions, it never leaves you for a single moment. One

MOAT MOUNTAIN, FROM JACKSON FALLS.

talks as it runs, one listens as he walks. A secret, an indefinable sympathy springs up. You are no longer alone.

Among other stories that the river told me was the following:

Once, while on their way to Canada through these mountains, a war-party of Indians, fresh from a successful forray on the sea-coast, halted with their prisoners on the banks of a stream whose waters stopped their way. For weeks these miserable captives had toiled through trackless forests, through swollen and angry torrents, sometimes climbing mountains on their hands and knees—they were so steep—and at night stretching their aching limbs on the cold ground, with no other roof than the heavens.[1]

The captives were a mother, with her new-born babe, scarcely fourteen days old, her boy of six, her two daughters of fourteen and sixteen years, and her maid. Two of her little flock were missing. One little prattler was playing at her knee, and another in the orchard, when thirteen red devils burst in the door of their happy home. Two cruel strokes of the axe stretched them lifeless in their blood before her frenzied eyes. One was killed to intimidate, the other was despatched because he was afraid, and cried out to his mother. There was no time for tears—none even for a parting kiss. Think of that, mothers of the nineteenth century! The tragedy finished, the hapless survivors were hurried from the house into the woods. There was no resistance. The blow fell like a stroke of lightning from a clear sky.

This mother, whose eyes never left the embroidered belt of the chief, where the reeking scalps of her murdered babes hung; this mother, who had tasted the agony of death from hour to hour, and whose incomparable courage not only supported her own weak frame, but had so far miraculously preserved the lives of her little ones, now stood shivering on the shores of the swollen torrent with her babe in her arms, and holding her little boy by the hand. In rags, bleeding, and almost famished, her misery should have melted a heart of stone. But she well knew the mercy of her masters. When fainting, they had goaded her on with blows, or, making a gesture as if to snatch her little one from her arms, significantly grasped their tomahawks. Hope was gone; but the mother's instinct was not yet extinguished in that heroic breast.

But at this moment of sorrow and despair, what was her amazement to hear the Indians accost her daughter Sarah, and command her to sing them a song. What mysterious chord had the wild, flowing river touched in those savage breasts? The girl prepared to obey, and the Indians to listen. In the heart of these vast solitudes, which never before echoed to a human voice, the heroic English maiden chanted to the plaintive refrain of the river the sublime words of the Psalmist:

" By the rivers of Babylon, there we sat down, yea, we wept, when we remembered Zion.

---

[1] Captivity of Elizabeth Hanson, taken at Dover, New Hampshire, 1724.

"We hanged our harps upon the willows in the midst thereof.

"For there they that carried us away captive required of us a song; and they that wasted us required of us mirth."

As she sung, the poor girl's voice trembled and her eyes filled, but she never once looked toward her mother.

When the last notes of the singer's voice died away, the bloodiest devil, he who murdered the children, took the babe gently from the mother, without a word; another lifted her burden to his own shoulder; another, the little boy; when the whole company entered the river.

Gentlemen, metaphysicians, explain that scene, if you please: it is no romance.

As this tale plunged me in a train of sombre reflection, the river recounted one of those marvellous legends which contain more poetry than superstition, and which here seem so appropriate.

According to the legend, a family living at the foot of a lofty peak had a daughter more beautiful than any maiden of the tribe, possessing a mind elevated far above the common order, and as accomplished as beautiful. When she reached a proper age, her parents looked around them for a suitable match, but in vain. None of the young men of the tribe were worthy of so peerless a creature. Suddenly this lovely wildflower of the mountains disappeared. Diligent was the search, and loud the lamentations when no trace of her light moccasin could be found in forest or glade. The tribe mourned her as lost. But one day some hunters, who had penetrated into the fastnesses of the mountain, discovered the lost maiden disporting herself in the limpid waters of a stream with a beautiful youth, whose hair, like her own, flowed down below his waist. On the approach of the intruders, the youthful bathers vanished from sight. The relatives of the maiden recognized her companion as one of the kind spirits of the mountain, and henceforth looked upon him as their son. They called upon him for moose, bear, or whatever creature they desired, and had only to go to the water-side and signify their desire, when, behold! the animal came swimming toward them. This legend strongly reminded me of one of those marvellous fables of the Hartz, in which a princess of exceeding beauty, destroyed by the arts of a wicked fairy, was often seen bathing in the river Ilse. If she met a traveller, she conducted him into the interior of the mountain and loaded him with riches. Each legend dimly conveys its idea of the wealth believed to reside in the mountain itself.

The Ellis continues to guide us farther and farther into the mountains. If we turn in the direction of the Glen House, a mile out of the village the Giant's Stairs come finely into view, and are held for some distance. Then bewitching vistas of Mount Washington, with snow decorating his huge sides, rise and sink, appear and disappear, until we reach an open vale, where the stream is spanned by a rude bridge. The route offers nothing more striking in its way than the view of the Pinkham Notch, which lies open at this point.

One of my walks extending as far as the last house on this road, permitted me to gratify a strong desire to see something of the in-door life of the poorer class of farmers. That desire was fully satisfied. There was nothing remarkable about the house itself; but the room in which I rested would have furnished Meyer von Bremen a capital subject for one of his characteristic interiors—it carried me back a century at least. In one corner a woman upward of seventy, I should say, sat at a spinning-wheel. She rose, got my bread-and-milk, and then resumed her spinning. A young mother, with a babe in her lap and two tow-headed urchins at her knee, occupied a high-backed rocking-chair. To judge from appearances, the river which flowed by the door was completely forgotten. Her efforts to hush the babe being interrupted by the peevish whining of one of the brats, she dealt him a sound box on the ear, upon which the whole pack howled in unison, while the mother, very red with the effect of her own anger, dragged the culprit from the room. There was still another occupant, a young girl, so silently plying her needle that I did not at first notice her. The floor was bare. A rickety chair or two and a cradle finished the meagre inventory of the apartment. The general appearance of things was untidy and unthrifty, rather than squalid; but I could not help recalling Sir William Davenant's remark, " that those tenants never get much furniture who begin with a cradle."

In such rambles, romantic and picturesque, in such dreams, the time runs away. The weeks are long days, the days moments. Every one asks himself why he finds Jackson so enticing, but no one is able to answer the question. *Cui bono?* When I am happy, shall I make myself miserable searching for the reason? Not if I know it.

Like bees to the sweetest flowers, the artists alight on the choicest bits of scenery by instinct. One runs across their umbrellas almost everywhere, spread like gigantic mushrooms; but some of them seem only to live and have their true artistic being here. In general, they are gentle, unobtrusive, and rather subdued in the presence of their beloved mountains. Some among them, however, develop actual rapacity in the search for new subjects, as, with a pencil between their teeth, they creep in ambush to surprise and carry off some mountain beauty which you or I are to ransom. Does a traveller contemplate some arduous exploration in an unvisited region? the artist knocks him over by quietly remarking, "I camped there several days last year."

In France they maintain that high mountains cannot be painted. Consequently, the modern French landscape is almost always a dead level: an illimitable plain, through which a placid stream quietly meanders, with a thick wood of aged trees at the left, a snug hamlet in the middle distance, some shrubbery on the right, and a clumsy ox-cart with peasants, in the foreground. All these details are sufficiently common-place; but they appeal strongly to our human yearning for a life of perfect peace—a sanctuary the world cannot enter. Turner knew that he must paint a mountain with its head in the clouds, and its feet plunged in unfathomable abysses. Imagination would do the rest, and imagination governs the universe.

Photography cannot reproduce the true relation of distant mountains to the landscape. The highest summits look like hills. For want of color, too, it is always twilight. Even running water has a frozen look, and rocks emit a dead, sepulchral glare. But for details—every leaf of the tree, or shadow of the leaf—it is faultless; it is the thing itself. True, under the magnifying-glass the foliage looks crisped, as is noticed after a first frost. In short, the photograph of mountain scenery is like that of a friend taken in his coffin. We say with a shiver that is he, but, alas, how changed! A body without a soul. Again, photography cannot suggest movement. Perfect immobility is a condition indispensable to a successful picture. A successful picture! A petrified landscape!

"In the morning to the mountain," says the proverb, as emblematic of high hopes. For two stations embodying the best features the vicinity of Jackson can offer, the crest of Thorn Mountain and the ledges above Fernald's Farm are strongly commended to every sojourner. Both are easily reached. On the first, you are a child lifted above the crowd on the shoulders of a giant; the mountains have come to you. On the second, you have taken the best possible position to study the form and structure of Mount Washington. You see all the ravines, and can count all the gigantic feelers the immense mountain throws down into the gorge of the Ellis.   In this way, step by step, we continue to master the topography of the region visited as we take our chocolate, one sip at a time.

I prepared to continue my journey to the Glen House by the valley of the Wildcat and the Carter Notch, which is a sort of side entrance to the Peabody Valley.   Two passes thus lie on alternate sides of the same mountain chain.   Before doing so, however, two words are necessary.

III.

THE CARTER NOTCH.

Stranger, if thou hast learned a truth which needs
No school of long experience, that the world
Is full of guilt and misery, and hast seen
Enough of all its sorrows, crimes, and cares,
To tire thee of it, enter this wild wood
And view the haunts of nature.—BRYANT.

WHAT traveller can pass beyond the crest of Thorn Hill without paying his tribute of silent admiration to the splendid pageant of mountains visible from this charmed spot! Before him the great rampart, bristling with its countless towers, is breached as cleanly as if a cannon-ball had just crashed through it. It is an immense hole; it is the cavity from which, apparently, one of those great iron teeth has just been extracted. Only it does not disfigure the landscape. Far from it. It really exalts the surrounding peaks. They are enormously aggrandized by it. You look around for a mountain of proper size and shape to fill it. That gives the true idea. It is a mountainous hole.

The little river, tumbling step by step down its broken ledges into Jackson, comes direct from the Notch, and its stream is the thread which conducts through the labyrinth of thick woods. I dearly love the companionship of these mountain streams. They are the voices of the wilderness, singing high or low, softly humming a melodious refrain to your thoughts, or, joining innumerable cascades in one grand chorus, they salute the ear with a gush of sound that strips the forest of its loneliness and awe. This same madcap Wildcat runs shouting and hallooing through the woods like a stream possessed.

By half-past seven of a bright and crisp morning I was climbing the steep hill-side over which Jackson Falls pour down. Here was a genuine surprise. On arriving at the top, instead of entering a difficult and confined gorge, I found a charming and tolerably wide vale, dotted with farms, extending far up into the midst of the mountains. You hardly realize that the stream flowing so demurely along the bottom of the valley is the same making its entry into the village with such noise and tumult. Half a mile above the falls the snowy cupola of Washington showed itself over Eagle Mountain for a few moments. Then, farther on, Adams was seen, also white with snow. For five miles the road skirts the western slopes of the valley, which grows continually deeper, narrower, and higher. Spruce Mountain is now on our left, the broad flanks of Black Mountain occupy the right side of the valley. Beyond Black Mountain Carter Dome lifts its ponderous mass, and between them the dip of the Perkins Notch, dividing the two ranges, gives admittance to the Wild River Valley, and to the Androscoggin, in Shelburne. Before me the grand, downward curves of Carter Notch opened wider and wider.

I picked up, *en route*, the guide of this locality, who lives on the side of the mountain near where the road is left for the woods. Our business was transacted in two words. While he was strapping on his knapsack I had leisure to observe the manner of man he was.

The guide, whose Christian name is Jonathan, is known in all the country round as " Jock " Davis. He was a medium-sized, muscular man, whiskered to his eyes, with a pair of bare arms the color of unglazed earthen-ware, and a step like a panther. As he strode silently on before, with his dog at his heels, I was reminded of the Jibenainosay and his inseparable Little Peter. He was steady as a clock, careful, and a capital forester, but a trifle taciturn. From time to time, as he drew my attention to the things noticeable or interesting by the way, his face grew animated, and his eyes sparkled. By the same token I believed I detected that dormant perception of beauty and grandeur which is inborn, and which travellers are in general too much disposed to deny any existence among the natives of these mountains. It is true, one cannot express his feelings with the vivacity of the other; but if there is such a thing as speech in silence, the honest guide's looks spoke volumes.

He told me that he was accustomed to get his own living in the woods, like an old bear. He had trapped and gummed all through the region we were in; the slopes of the great range, and the Wild River wilderness, which he declared, with a shake of the head, to be " a horrid

THE CARTER NOTCH.

hole." Now and then, without halting, he took a step to the right or left to look into his fox and sable traps, set near the foot-path. When he spoke of "gumming" on Wildcat Mountain, I was near making an awkward mistake; I understood him to say "gunning." So I very innocently asked what he had bagged. He opened his eyes widely and replied, "Gum."[1]

---

[1] No Yankee girl need be told for what purpose spruce gum is procured; but it will doubtless be news to many that the best quality is worth a dollar the pound. Davis told me he had gathered enough in a single season to fetch ninety dollars.

Seeing me ready, Davis whistled to his dog, and we entered the logging-road in Indian file. We at once took a brisk pace, which in a short time brought us to the edge of a clearing, now badly overgrown with bramble and coppice, and showing how easily nature obliterates the mark of civilization when left alone. In this clearing an old cellar told its sad story but too plainly. Those pioneers who first struck the axe into the noble pines here are all gone. They abandoned in consternation the effort to wring a scanty subsistence from this inhospitable and unfruitful region. Even the poor farms I had seen encroaching upon the skirts of this wilderness seemed fighting in retreat.

We quickly came to a second opening, where the axe of God had smote the forest still more ruthlessly than that of man. The ground was encumbered with half-burnt trees, among which the gaudy fire-weed grew rank and tall. Divining my thought, the guide explained in his quaint, sententious way, "Fire went through it; then the wind harricaned it down." A comprehensive sweep of his staff indicated the area traversed by the whirlwind of fire and the tornado. This opening disclosed at our left the gray cliffs and yawning aperture of the Notch—by far the most satisfactory view yet obtained, and the nearest.

Burying ourselves in deeper solitudes, broken only by the hound in full cry after a fox or a rabbit, we descended to the banks of the Wildcat at a point one and a half miles from the road we had left. We then crossed the rude bridge of logs, keeping company with the gradually diminishing river, now upon one bank, now on the other, making a gradual ascent along with it, frequently pausing in mid-stream to glance up and down through the beautiful vistas it has cut through the trees. Halt at the third crossing, traveller, and take in the long course through the avenue of black, moss-draped firs! one so sombre and austere, the other gliding so bright and blithesome out of its shadow and gloom. Just above this spot a succession of tiny water-falls comes like a procession of nymphs out of an enchanted wood.

We were now in a colder region. The sparseness of the timber led me to look right and left for the stumps of felled trees, but I saw nothing of the kind. To the rigorous climate and extreme leanness of the soil they attribute the scanty, undersized growth. I did not see fifty good timber trees along the whole route. Where a large tree had been prostrated by the wind, its upturned and matted roots showed a pitiful quantity of earth adhering. Finding it impossible to grow downward more than a few poor inches, they spread themselves laterally out to a great distance. But the fir, with its flame-shaped point, is a symbol of indomitable pluck. You see it standing erect on the top of some huge bowlder, which its strong, thick roots clutch like a vulture's talons. How came it there? Look at those rotting trunks, so beautifully covered with the lycopodium and partridge-plum! The seed of a fir has taken root in the bark. A tiny tree is already springing from the rich mould. As it grows, its roots grasp whatever offers a support; and if the decaying tree has fallen across a bowlder, they strike downward into the soil beneath it, and the rock is a prisoner during the lifetime of the tree. Its resin protects it from the icy blasts of winter, and from the alternate freezing and thawing of early spring. It is emphatically the tree of the mountains.

An hour and a half of pretty rapid walking brought us to the bottom of a steep rise. We were at length come to close quarters with the formidable outworks of Wildcat Mountain. The brook has for some distance poured a stream of the purest water over moss of the richest green, but now it most mysteriously vanishes from sight. From this point the singular rock called the Pulpit is seen overhanging the upper crags of the Dome.[1]

We drank a cup of delicious water from a spring by the side of the path, and, finding direct access forbidden by the towering and misshapen mass before us, turned sharply to the left, and attacked the side of Wildcat Mountain. We had now attained an altitude of nearly three thousand feet above the sea, or two thousand two hundred and fifty above the village of Jackson; we were more than a thousand higher than the renowned Crawford Notch.

On every side the ground was loaded down with huge gray bowlders, so ponderous that it seemed as if the solid earth must give way under them. Some looked as if the merest touch would send them crashing down the mountain. Undermined by the slow action of time, these fragments have fallen one by one from the high cliffs, and accumulated at the base. Among these the path serpentined for half a mile more, bringing us at last to the summit of the spur we had been climbing, and to the broad entrance of the Notch. We passed quickly over the level

---

[1] I use the name, as usually applied, to the whole mountain. In point of fact, the Dome is not visible from the Notch.

ground we were upon, stopped by the side of a well-built cabin of bark, threw off our loads, and then, fascinated by the exceeding strangeness of everything around me, I advanced to the edge of the scrubby growth in front of the camp, in order to command an unobstructed view.

Shall I live long enough to forget this sublime tragedy of nature, enacted Heaven knows when or how? How still it was! I seemed to have arrived at the instant a death-like silence succeeds the catastrophe. I saw only the bare walls of a temple, of which some Samson had just overthrown the columns — walls overgrown with a forest, ruins overspread with one struggling for existence.

Imagine the light of a mid-day sun brightening the tops of the mountains, while within a sepulchral gloom rendered all objects—rocks, trees, cliffs—all the more weird and fantastic. I was between two high mountains, whose walls enclose the pass. Overhanging it, fifteen hundred feet at least, the sunburnt crags of the Dome towered above the highest precipices of the mountain behind me. These stately barriers, at once so noble and imposing, seemed absolutely indestructible. Impossible to conceive anything more enduring than this imperishable rock. So long as the world stands, those mountains will stand. And nothing can shake this conviction. They look so strong, so confident in their strength, so incapable of change.

But what, then, is this dusky gray mass, stretching huge and irregular across the chasm from mountain to mountain, completely filling the space between, and so effectually blockading the entrance that we were compelled to pick our way up the steep side of the mountain in order to turn it?

Picture to yourself acres upon acres of naked granite, split and splintered in every conceivable form, of enormous size and weight, yet pitched, piled, and tumbled about like playthings, tilted, or so poised and balanced as to open numberless caves, which sprinkled the whole area with a thousand shadows—figure this, I repeat, to yourself—and the mind will then grasp but faintly the idea of this colossal barricade, seemingly built by the giants of old to guard their last stronghold from all intrusion. At some distance in front of me a rock of prodigious size, very closely resembling the gable of a house, thrusting itself half out, conveyed its horrible suggestion of an avalanche in the act of ingulfing a hamlet. And all this one beholds in a kind of stupefaction.

Whence came this colossal débris? I had at first the idea that the great arch, springing from peak to peak, supported on the Atlantean shoulders of the two mountains, had fallen in ruins. I even tried to imagine the terrific crash with which heaven and earth came together in the fall. Easy to realize here Schiller's graphic description of the Jungfrau:

"One walks there between life and death. Two threatening peaks shut in the solitary way. Pass over this place of terror without noise; dread lest you awaken the sleeping avalanche."

It is evident, however, as soon as the eye attaches itself to the side of the Dome, that one of its loftiest precipices, originally measuring an altitude as great as any yet remaining, has precipitated itself in a crushed and broken mass into the abyss. Nothing is left of the primitive edifice except these ruins. It is easily conceived that, previous to the convulsion, the interior aspect of the Notch was quite different from what is seen to-day. It was doubtless narrower, gloomier, and deeper before the cliff became dislodged. The track of the convulsion is easily traced. From top to bottom the side of the mountain is hollowed out, exposing a shallow ravine, in which nothing but dwarf spruces will grow, and in which the erratic rocks, arrested here and there in their fall, seem endeavoring to regain their ancient position on the summit. There is no trace whatever of the rubbish ordinarily accompanying a slide—only these rocks.

Seeing that all this happened long ago, I asked the guide why the larger growth we saw on both sides of the hollow had not succeeded in covering the old scar, as is the case with the Willey Slide; but he was unable to advance even a conjecture. The spruce, however, loves ruins, spreading itself out over them with avidity.

We felt our way cautiously and slowly out over the bowlders; for the moment one quits the usual track he risks falling headlong upon the sharp rocks beneath. In the midst of these grisly blocks stunted firs are born, and die for want of sustenance, making the dreary waste bristle with hard and horny skeletons. The spruce, dwarfed and deformed, has established itself solidly in the interstices; a few bushes spring up in the crannies. With this exception, the entire area is denuded of vegetation. The obstruction is heaped in two principal ridges, traversing its greatest breadth, and opening a broad way between. This is one of the most curious features I remarked. From a flat rock on the summit of the first we obtained the best idea of the general configuration of the

Notch; and from this point, also, we saw the two little lakes beneath us which are the sources of the Wildcat. Beyond, and above the hollow they occupy, the two mountains meet in the low ridge constituting the true summit of Carter Notch. Far down, under the bowlders, the Wildcat gropes its way out; but, notwithstanding one or the other was continually dropping out of sight into the caverns with which they are filled, we could neither hear nor see anything to indicate its route. It is buried out of sight and sound.

No incident of the whole excursion is more curiously inexplicable than the total disappearance of the brook at the mountain's foot. Notice that it was last seen gushing from the side we ascended, half a mile below the camp. Whence does it come? When we were on top of the bowlders, looking down on the water of the two little lakes, we wonderingly ask, "Where does it go? How does it get out?" The mystery is, however, solved by the certainty that their waters flow out underneath the barrier, so that this mammoth pile of débris, which could destroy a city, was unable to arrest the flow of a rivulet.

But all this wreck and ruin exerts a saddening influence; it seems to prefigure the Death of the Mountain. So one gladly turns to the landscape—a very noble though not extensive one—enclosing all the mountains and valleys to the south of us lying between Kearsarge and Moat.

After this tour of the rocks, we returned to the hut and ate our luncheon. Here the Pulpit Rock, which is sure to catch the eye whenever it wanders to the cliffs opposite, looks very much like the broken handle of a jug. Davis explained that, by advancing fifteen or twenty paces upon it, it would be possible to hang suspended over the thousand feet of space beneath. While thus occupied, the dog received his share of the bread and meat; nor was the little tame hawk that came and hopped so fearlessly at our feet forgotten. This bird and a cross-bill were the only living things I saw.[1]

---

[1] The guide knew no other name for the larger bird than meat-hawk; but its size, plumage, and utter fearlessness are characteristic of the Canada jay, occasionally encountered in these high latitudes. I cannot refrain from reminding the reader that the cross-bill is the subject of a beautiful German legend, translated by Longfellow. The dying and forsaken Saviour sees a little bird striving to draw the nail from his bleeding palm with his beak :

"And the Saviour spoke in mildness:
 'Blest be thou of all the good!
Bear, as token of this moment,
Marks of blood and holy rood !'

"And the bird is called the cross-bill:
Covered all with blood so clear,
In the groves of pine it singeth
Songs like legends, strange to hear "

Being fully rested and refreshed, we started on a second exploration of the upper part of the Notch. Thus far our examination had been confined to the lower portion only. Descending the spur upon which the hut is situated, we were, in a few moments, at the bottom of the deep cavity lying between the Giants' Barricade and the little mountain forming the northern portal. This area is undoubtedly the original floor of the pass. We had now reached a position between the lakes. Looking backward, the barricade lifted a black and frowning wall a hundred and fifty feet above our heads. Looking down, the water of the lakes seemed "an image of the Dead Sea sleeping at the foot of Jerusalem destroyed." While I stood looking into them, a passing cloud, pausing in astonishment at seeing itself reflected from these shadowy depths, darkened the whole interior. Deprived all at once of sunlight, the scene became one of great and magnificent solemnity. The pass assumed the appearance of a vast cavern. The ponds lay still and cold below. The air grew chill, the water black as ink. The ruddy color faded from the cliffs. They became livid. I saw the thousands upon thousands of fir-trees, rigid and sombre, ranged tier on tier like spectators in an immense circus, who are awaiting the signal for some terrible spectacle to begin. When the cloud tranquilly resumed its journey, a load seemed lifted off. It was Nature repeating to herself,

> "Put out the light, and then put out the light."

We had reached the camp at half-past ten. At half-past twelve we began the ascent of the Dome. It is not so much the height as the steepness of this mountain that wins our respect. The path goes straight up to the first summit, deflects a little to reach the Pulpit, and then, turning more northerly, ascends for a mile and a half more by a much easier rise to the highest peak. There are no open ledges on the route. The path is cut through a wood from base to summit; and, with the exception of a few trees felled to open an outlook in the direction of the main range, was covered on the summit itself with a dense growth of fir-trees from twelve to fifteen feet high. To obtain a view of the whole horizon, it was necessary, at the time of my visit, to climb one of these trees.

I will not fatigue the reader with any detailed account of the ascent. Suffice it to say that it was a slow and toilsome lifting of one heavy foot after another for three-quarters of an hour. Sometimes the slope was so near the vertical that we could ascend only a few rods at a time. I improved these halts by leaning against a tree, and panting like a doe pursued by the hunter. Davis threw himself upon the ground and watched me attentively, but without speaking. If he expected me to give out, I disappointed him by giving the signal to move on. I had already served my apprenticeship on Carrigain. It was difficult to maintain an upright position. Once, indeed, on looking up, I perceived that the guide had abandoned in disgust the idea of walking erect, and was creeping on all-fours, like his dog. This breathless scramble continued for three-quarters of an hour, at the end of which we turned into the short by-path conducting to the Pulpit.

Near the Pulpit is a cleared space large enough to afford standing room for fifteen or twenty persons. This Pulpit is a huge, rectangular rock, jutting out from the face of the cliff on which we stood, and is not at all unworthy of the name given to it by the guide. It is a fine station from which to survey the deep rent in the side of the mountain, as well as the mammoth stone-heap, which it overlooks. The black side of Mount Wildcat, ploughed from top to bottom with four deep gashes,

> "The least a death to nature,"

is also seen to excellent advantage across the airy space between the mountains. The fluttering of a handkerchief at the door of the little cabin greatly enlivened the solitary scene, and drew from us the same signal in return.

At first sight the ascent by the chasm seems feasible ; but Davis, who has twice performed this difficult feat, declared with a shrug that nothing would tempt him to do it again. Those who have ever come to close quarters with the shrubby growth of these ruins will know how to leave it in undisputed possession of its own chosen ground. The dwarf spruce is the Cossack of the woods.

What a beautiful landscape is that from the Pulpit! The southern horizon is now widely opened. The mountains around Jackson have dwindled to hills. Especially curious are the flattened top and distorted contour-lines of Iron Mountain. Another singular feature is the way we look through the cloven summit of Doublehead to Kearsarge's stately pyramid. Here are strips of the Ellis and Saco Valleys, and all of the Wildcat. The lakes in Ossipee are dazzling to look upon. Old Chocorua lifts his brilliant spire; then Moat his iron bulwarks. Crawford,

Resolution, and the Giants' Stairs extend on the right, behind Iron. The view is then cut off by the burly form of Wildcat. Far back in the picture are the notched walls of the Franconia and Sandwich chains, topped by pale blue peaks.

Continuing the ascent for about three-fourths of a mile, we came to a point only a rod or two distant from the head of the great slide of 1869, and from the top of a tree here was the most thrilling prospect of Washington and the great northern peaks I ever beheld. All the summits as far south as Monroe are included in the view.

Over the right shoulder of Wildcat appeared the dazzling summit of Washington, having at his left the noble cone of Jefferson, the matchless shaft of Adams, and the massive pyramid of Madison. Each gray head was profusely powdered with snow. Dark clouds, heavily charged with frost, partially intercepted the sun's rays, and, enveloping the great mountains in their shadows, cast over them a mantle of the deepest blue; but enough light escaped to gild the arid slopes of the great ravines a rich brown gold, and to pierce through, and beautifully expose, against the dark bulk of Adams, a thin veil of slowly falling snow. Imagine an Ethiopian wrapped from head to foot in lace!

A chapter could not give the thousand details of this grand picture. One devours it with avidity. He sees to the greatest possible advantage the magnificent proportions of Washington, with his massive slopes rolling up and up, like petrified storm-clouds, to the final summit. He sees the miles of carriage-road, from where it leaves the woods, as far as the great northern plateau. He looks deep down into the depths of Tuckerman's and Huntington's ravines, and between them sees Raymond's Cataract crusting the bare cliffs with a vein of quicksilver. The massive head-wall of Tuckerman's was freely spattered with fresh snow; the Lion's Head rose stark and forbidding; the upper cliffs of Huntington's,

"With twenty trenched gashes in his head,"

the great billows of land rushing downward into the dark gulfs, resembled the vortex of a frozen whirlpool.

But for refinement of form, delicacy of outline, and a predominant, inexplicable grace, Adams stands forth here without a rival. Washington is the undisputed monarch, but Adams is the highest type of mountain beauty here. That splendid, slightly concave, antique shaft, rising in unconscious symmetry from the shoulders of two supporting mountain-peaks, which seem prostrating themselves at its feet, changes the emotion of awe and respect to one of admiration and pleasure. Our elevation presented all the great summits in an unrivalled attitude for observation or study; and whoever has once beheld them—banded together with bonds of adamant, their heads in the snow, and their feet in the impenetrable shades of the Great Gulf; with every one of their thousands of feet under his eye—every line as firm and strong, and every contour true as the Great Architect drew it—without loss or abatement; vigorous in old age as in youth; monuments of one race, and silent spectators of the passing of another; victors in the battle with Time; chronicles and retrospect of ages; types of the Everlasting and Unchangeable—will often try to summon up the picture of the great peaks, and once more marshal their towering battlements before the memory.

The descent occupied less than half an hour, so rapidly is it made. We had nothing whatever to do with regulating our speed, but were fully occupied in so placing our feet as to avoid pitching headlong, or sitting suddenly down in a miry place. We simply tumbled down the mountain, like two rocks detached from its peak.

After a last survey of the basin of the Notch, from the clearing above the upper lake, we crossed the little mountain at its head, taking the path leading to the Glen House. We descended the reverse side together, to the point where the great slide referred to came thundering down from the Dome into the gorge of Nineteen Mile Brook. This landslip, which happened October 4th, 1869, was one of the results of the disastrous autumnal storms, which deluged the mountains with rain, and set in motion here an enormous quantity of wreck and débris. It was at this time that Mr. Thompson, the proprietor of the Glen House, lost his life in the Peabody River, in a desperate effort to avert the destruction of his mill.

Here I parted from my guide; and, after threading the woods for two hours more, following the valley of Nineteen Mile Brook, came out of their shadowy embrace into the stony pastures above the Glen House.

IV.

THE PINKHAM NOTCH.

Levons les yeux vers les saintes montagnes.—RACINE.

THE Glen House is one of the last strongholds of the old ways of
travel. Jackson is twelve, Randolph seven, and Gorham eight miles
distant. These are the nearest villages. The nearest farm-houses are
Copp's, three miles on the road to Randolph, and Emery's, six on the
road to Jackson. The nearest railway-station is eight miles off, at Gorham. The nearest steam-whistle is there. So much for its seclusion.

Being thus isolated, the Glen House is naturally the point of direction for the region adjacent. Situated at the base of Carter Mountain,
on a terrace rising above the Peabody River, which it overlooks, it has
only the valley of this stream — a half mile of level meadow here — between it and the base of Mount Washington. The carriage-road to the
summit, which, in 1861, superseded the old bridle-path, is seen crossing
this meadow. This road occupied six years in building, is eight miles
long, and is as well and solidly built as any similar piece of highway in
New England.

When it is a question of this gigantic mass, which here offers such
an easy mode of ascent, the interest is assured. Respecting the appearance of Mount Washington from the Glen House itself, it is a received
truth that neither the height nor the proportions of a high mountain are
properly appreciated when the spectator is placed exactly at the base.
The same is true here of Mount Washington, which is too much foreshortened for a favorable estimate of its grandeur or its elevation. The
Dome looks flat, elongated, obese. But it is only a step from the hotel
to more eligible posts of observation, say the clearings on Mount Carter, or, better still, the slopes of Wildcat, which are easily reached over
a good path.

Still, Mount Washington is surveyed with more astonishment, perhaps, from this point, than from any other. Its lower section is covered with a dense forest, out of which rise the successive and stupendous undulations culminating at last in the absolutely barren summit, which the nearer swells almost conceal. The true peak stands well to the left, indicated by a white building when the sun is shining, and a dark one when it is not. As seen from this spot, the peculiar formation of the mountain gives the impression of a semi-fluid mass, first cooled to hardness, then receiving successive additions, which, although eternally united with its bulk, have left the point of contact forever visible. When the first mass cooled, it received a second, a third, and a fourth. One believes, so to speak, certain 'intervals to have elapsed in the process of solidifying these masses, which seem, to me at least, not risen above the earth, but poured down upon it.

It is related that an Englishman, seated on the balcony of his hotel at Chamouni, after having conscientiously followed the peripatetics of a sunset, remarked, "Very fine, very fine indeed! but it is a pity Mont Blanc hides the view." In this sense, Mount Washington "hides the view" to the west. No peak dares show its head in this direction.

From the vicinity of the hotel, Wildcat Mountain allows the eye to embrace, at the left, Mount Washington as far as Tuckerman's Ravine. Only a few miles of the valley can be traced on this side; but at the right it is open for nearly its whole length, fully exposing that magnificent sweep of the great northern peaks, here bending majestically to the north-east, and exhibiting their titanic props, deep hollows, soaring peaks, to the admiring scrutiny of every wayfarer. It is impossible to appreciate this view all at once. No one can pretend to analyze the sensations produced by looking at mountains. The bare thought of them causes a flutter of enthusiasm wherever we may be. At such moments one lays down the pen to revel in the recollection.

Among these grandees, Adams looks highest. It is indispensable that this mountain should be seen from some higher point. It is only half seen from the Glen, although the view here is by far the best to be had in any valley enclosing the great chain. Ascend, therefore, even at the risk of some toil, one of the adjacent heights, and this superb monument will deign to show the true symmetrical relation of summit to base.

I have already said that most travellers approach this charming mountain nook by the Pinkham defile, instead of making their début by the Carter Notch. It will be well worth our while to retrace at least so much of this route, through the first-named pass, as will enable us to gain a knowledge, not so much of what it shows as of what it hides. By referring to the chapter on Jackson, we shall then have seen all that can be seen on the travelled highway.

The four miles back through the Pinkham forest deserve to be called the Avenue of Cascades. Not less than four drop from the mountain tops, or leap down the confined gorges. Let us first walk in this direction.

Two miles from the hotel we meet a sprightly and vigorous brook coming down from Wildcat Mountain to swell the Peabody. A short walk up this stream brings us to Thompson's Falls, which are several pretty cascades slipping down a bed of granite. The ledges over which they glide offer a practicable road to the top of the falls, from which is a most interesting view into Tuckerman's Ravine, and of the summit of Mount Washington.

Some overpowering, some unexplained fascination about these dark and mysterious chambers of the mountain arouses in us a desire strangely like to that intense craving for a knowledge of futurity itself. We think of the Purgatory of the ancients into which we would willingly descend if, like Dante holding the hand of Virgil, we might hope to return unscathed to earth. " This is nothing but an enormous breach in the mountain," you say, weakly attempting to throw off the spell by ridiculing the imagination. Be it so. But it has all the terrible suggestiveness of a descent into the world of the dead. When we walk in the dark we say that we are afraid of falling. It is a falsehood. We are afraid of a *Presence.*

That dark curling lip of the south wall, looking as if the eternal adamant of the hills had been scorched and shrivelled by consuming flame, marks the highest curve of the massive granite spur rooted deep in the Pinkham defile. It is named Boott's Spur. The sky-line of the ravine's head-wall is five thousand feet above the sea, on the great plateau over which the Crawford trail passes. That enormous crag, rising like another Tower of Famine, on the north and east divides the ravine proper from the collateral chamber, known as Huntington's, out of which the source of the Peabody gushes a swift torrent, and near which the carriage-road winds its devious way up to the summit. In the depression of this craggy ridge, between the two ravines, sufficient water is collected to form the beautiful cataract known as Raymond's, which is seen from all those elevations commanding the ravine itself.

The ravine also furnishes a route to the summit of Mount Washington in so far that the ascent may be continued from the head of the chasm to the high plateau, and so up the pinnacle, by the old Crawford trail, or over the crag on the right to the carriage-road; but it is not to be highly recommended on that account, except to strong climbers. It should be visited for itself, and for what is to be seen going or returning by the different paths. I have also descended from the Summit House

THE EMERALD POOL.

to the ravine and returned by the same route; an excursion growing in favor with those tourists having a day or two on their hands, and who approach the mountain from the west or opposite side. In that case a return to the summit saves a long détour.

Before we come to Thompson's Falls a well-trod path leads to the Emerald Pool, which Bierstadt's painting has rendered famous. At first one sees only a deep hollow, with a dark and glassy pool at the bottom, and a cool light coming down through the high tree-tops. Two large rocks tightly compress the stream which fills it, so that the water gushes out with sufficient force to whiten a little, without disturbing the placid repose of the pool. This gives the effect of milk poured upon ink. Above these rocks we look up the stony bed of the frantic river and meet the blue mass of a distant mountain. Rocks are picturesquely dropped about the margin. Upon one side a birch leans far out over the basin, whose polished surface brilliantly reflects the white light of its bark. One sees the print of foliage on the black water, like that of ferns and grasses upon coal; or, rather, like the most beautiful Italian mosaics — black marble inlaid with arabesques of color. The illusion is more perfect still when the yellow and scarlet of the maples is reflected, as in autumn.

The contrast between the absolutely quiet pool and the feverish excitement of the river is singular. It is that of a life: one, serene and unmoved, receives the other in its bosom and calms its excitement. It then runs out over the pebbles at a steadier pace, soothed, tranquillized, and strengthened, to meet its destiny by this one moment of peace and rest.

Doubtless many turn languidly into this charming sylvan retreat with only a dim perception of its beauty. Few go away except to sing its praises with heart and tongue. Solitude is here. Repose is here. Peace is omnipresent. And, freed from the excitements of city life, "Peace at any price" is the cry of him whom care pursues as with a knotted scourge. If he find not rest here, 'tis his soul "is poor." For him the smell of the earth, the fragrance of the pines, the very stones, have healing or strength. He grows drowsy with the lullaby of the brook. A delicious languor steals over him. A thousand dreamy fancies float through his imagination. He is a child again; or, rather, he is born again. The artificial man drops off. Stocks and bonds are clean forgotten. His step is more elastic, his eye more alert, his heart lighter. He departs believing he has read, "Let all who enter here leave care behind." And all this comes of seeing a little shaded mountain pool consecrated by Nature. He has only experienced her religion and received her baptism.

Burying ourselves deeper in the pass, the trees, stirred by the breeze, shake out their foliage like a maiden her long tresses. And the glory of one is the glory of the other. We look up to the greater mountains, still wrapped in shadows, saying to those whom its beams caress, "Out of my sun!"

At the third mile a guide-board at the right announces the Crystal Cascade. We turn aside here, and, entering the wood, soon reach the banks of a stream. The last courtesy this white-robed maid makes on crossing the threshold of her mountain home is called the Crystal Cascade. It is an adieu full of grace and feeling.

The Crystal Cascade divides with Glen Ellis the honor of being the most beautiful water-fall of the White Mountains. And well may it claim this distinction. These two charming and radiant sisters have each their especial admirers, who come in multitudes every year, like pilgrims to the shrine of a goddess. In fact, they are as unlike as two human countenances. Every one is astonished at the changes effected by simple combinations of rocks, trees, and water. One shrinks from

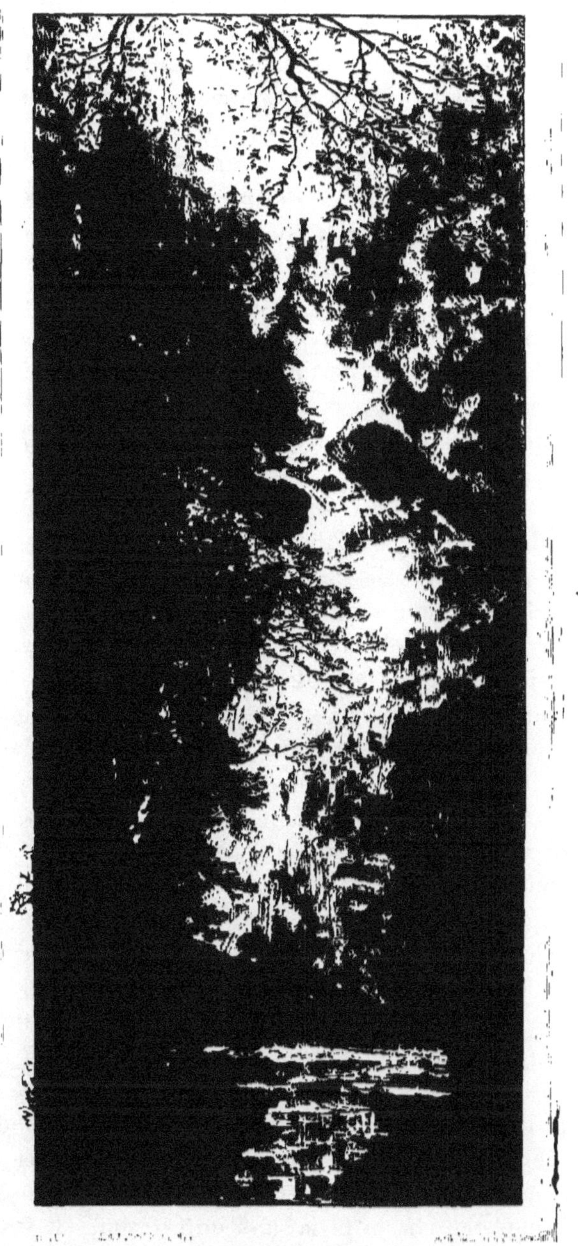

THE CRYSTAL CASCADE.

11*

a critical analysis of what appeals so strangely to his human sympathies. Indeed, he should possess the language of a Dumas or a Ruskin, the poetry of a Longfellow or a Whittier, the pencil of a Turner or a Church, to do justice to this pre-eminently beautiful of cascades.

Look around. On the right bank of the stream, where a tall birch leans its forked branches out over the pool below, a jutting rock embraces in one glance the greater part of the fall. The cliffs, rising on both sides, make a most wild and impressive setting. The trees, which shade or partly screen it, exclude the light. The ferns and shrubbery trace their arabesques of foliage upon the cold, damp rocks. The sides of the mountain, receding into black shadows, seem set with innumerable columns, supporting a roof of dusky leafage. All this combines to produce the effect of standing under the vault of some old dimly-lighted cathedral — a subdued, a softened feeling. A voice seems whispering, " God is here!"

Through these sombre shades the cascade comes like a gleam of light : it redeems the solitude. High up, hundreds of feet up the mountain, it boils and foams; it hardly seems to run. How it turns and tosses, and writhes on its hard bed! The green leaves quiver at its struggles. Birds fly silently by. Down, down, and still down over its shattered stairs falls the doomed flood, until, lashed and broken into a mere feathery cloud, it reaches a narrow gorge between abrupt cliffs of granite. A little pellucid basin, half white, half black water, receives it in full career. It then flows out by a pretty water-fall of twenty feet more. But here, again, the sharp, wedge-shaped cliff, advancing from the opposite bank, compresses its whole volume within a deep and narrow trough, through which it flies with the rapidity of light, makes a right angle, and goes down the mountain, uttering loud complaints. From below, the jagged, sharp-edged cliff forms a kind of vestibule, behind which the cascade conceals itself. Behind this, farther back, is a rock, perfectly black, and smooth as polished ebony, over which the surplus water of the fall spreads a tangled web of antique lace. Some very curious work has been going on here since the stream first made its way through the countless obstacles it meets in the long miles to its secret fountains on Mount Washington. One carries away a delightful impression of the Crystal Cascade. To the natural beauty of falling water it brings the charm of lawless unrestraint. It scorns the straight and narrow path; has stolen interviews with secret nooks on this side or that;

is forever coquettishly adjusting its beautiful dishabille. What power has taken one of those dazzling clouds, floating over the great summit, and pinned it to the mountain side, from which it strives to rise and soar away?

We are now in the wildest depths of the Pinkham defile. The road is gloomy enough, edging its way always through a dense wood around a spur of Mount Washington, which it closely hugs. Upon reaching the summit, thirteen hundred and fifty feet above the Saco, at Bartlett, a sign-board showed where to leave the highway, but now the noise of the fall coming clearer and clearer was an even surer guide.

The sense of seclusion is perfect. Stately pines, funereal cedars, sombre hemlocks, throng the banks, as if come to refresh their parched foliage with the fine spray ascending from the cataract. This spray sparkles in the sun like diamond-dust. Through the thick-set, clean-limbed tree-trunks jets of foam can be seen in mad riot along the rocky gorge. They leap, toss their heads, and tumble over each other like young lambs at play. Backward up the stream, downward beyond the fall, we see the same tumult of waters in the midst of statuesque immobility; we hear the roar of the fall echoing in the tops of the pines; we feel the dull earth throb with the superabundant energy of the wild river.

Making my way to the rocks above the cataract, I saw the torrent swiftly descending in two long, arching billows, flecked with foam, and tossing myriad diamonds to the sun. Two large masses of rock, loosened from the cliffs that hang over it, have dropped into the stream, turning it a little from its ancient course, but only to make it more picturesque and more tumultuous. On the left of the gorge the rocks are richly striped with black, yellow, and purple. The water is crystal clear, and cold as ice, having come, in less time than it takes to write, from the snows of Tuckerman's Ravine. The variegated hues of the rocks, glistening with spray, of the water itself seizing and imprisoning, like flies in amber, every shadow these rocks let fall, the roar of the cataract, make a deep and abiding impression of savage force and beauty.

But I had not yet seen the fall. Descending by slippery stairs to the pool beneath it, I saw, eighty feet above me, the whole stream force its way through a narrow cleft, and stand in one unbroken column, superbly erect, upon the level surface of the pool. The sheet was as white as marble, the pool as green as malachite. As if stunned by the fall, it turns slowly round; then, recovering, precipitates itself down the rocky gorge with greater passion than ever.

On its upper edge the curling sheet of the fall was shot with sunlight, and shone with enchanting brilliancy. All below was one white, feathery mass, gliding down with the swift and noiseless movement of an avalanche of fresh snow. No sound until the moment of contact with the submerged rocks beneath; then it finds a voice that shakes the hoary forest to its centre. How this exquisite white thing fascinates! One has almost to tear himself away from the spot. Undine seems beckoning us to descend with her into the crystal grottoes of the pool. From the tender dalliance of a sunbeam with the glittering mists constantly ascending was born a pale Iris. Exquisitely its evanescent hues decorated the virgin drapery of the fall. Within these mists two airy forms sometimes discover themselves, hand-in-hand.

The story runs that the daughter of a sagamore inhabiting the little vale, now Jackson, was secretly wooed and won by a young brave of another and neighboring tribe. But the haughty old chief destined her for a renowned warrior of his own band. Mustering his friends, the preferred lover presented himself in the village, and, according to Indian usage, laying

> "—at her father's feet that night
> His softest furs and wampum white,"

demanded his bride. The alliance was too honorable to permit an abrupt refusal. Smothering his wrath, the father assembled his braves. The matter was debated in solemn council. It was determined that the rivals should settle their dispute by a trial of skill, the winner to carry off the beautiful prize. A mark was set up, the ground carefully measured, and the two warriors took their respective places in the midst of the assembled tribe. The heart of the Indian maiden beat with hope when her lover sent his arrow quivering in the edge of the target; but it sunk when his rival, stepping scornfully to his place, shot within the very centre. A shout of triumph rewarded the skill of the victor; but before it died away the defeated warrior strode to the spot where his mistress was seated and spoke a few hurried words, intended for her ear alone. The girl sprung to her feet and grasped her lover's hand. In another moment they were running swiftly for the woods. They were hotly pursued. It became a matter of life and death. Perceiving escape impossible, rendered desperate by the near approach of their pursuers, the fugitives, still holding fast each other's hand, rushed to the verge of the cataract and flung themselves headlong into its deadly embrace.

Over the pool the gray and gloomy wall of Wildcat Mountain seems stretching up to an incredible height. The astonishing wildness of the surroundings affects one very deeply. You look up. You see the firs surmounting those tall cliffs sway to and fro, as if growing dizzy with the sight of the abyss beneath them.

The Ellis Cascade is not so light as those mountain sylphs in the great Notch, which a zephyr lifts from their feet, and scatters far and wide; it is a vestal hotly pursued by impish goblins to the brink of the precipice, transformed into a water-fall. For an instant the iron grip of the cliff seems clutching its snowy throat, but with a mocking courtesy the fair stream eludes the grasp, and so escapes.

While returning from Glen Ellis, I saw, not more than a quarter of a mile from this fall, a beautiful cascade come streaming down a long trough of granite from a great height, and disappear behind the tree-tops that skirt the narrow gorge. I had never before seen this cascade, it being usually dry in summer. The sight of glancing water among the shaggy upper forests of the mountain—for you hear nothing—is a real pleasure to the eye. The rock down which this cascade flows is New River Cliff.

Before leaving the Ellis, which I did regretfully, it is proper to recall an incident which gave rise to one of its affluents. In 1775, says Sullivan, in his "History of Maine," the Saco was found to swell suddenly, and in a singular manner. As there had not been rain sufficient to account for this increase of volume, people were at a loss how to explain the phenomenon, until it was finally discovered to be occasioned by a new river having broken out of the side of the White Mountains.

When this river issued from the mountains, in October, 1775, a mixture of iron-ore gave the water a deep red color, and this singular, and to them most startling, appearance led the people inhabiting the upper banks of the Saco to declare that the river ran blood — a circumstance which these simple-minded folk regarded as of evil omen for the success of their arms in the struggle then going on between the Colonies and Great Britain. Except for illustrating a marked characteristic the incident would possess little importance. Considerable doubt exists as to the precise course of this New River, by which it is conjectured that the ascents of Cutler, Boott, Bigelow, and perhaps others, early in this century, were made to the summit of Mount Washington.   But this is merely conjecture.[1]

After Glen Ellis one has had enough, for the day at least, of waterfalls and cascade.   Its excitement is strangely infectious and exhilarating.   At the same time, it casts a sweet and gentle spell over the spirits.   If he be wise, the visitor will not exhaust in a single tour of the sun the pleasures yet in store, but, after a fall, try a ravine or a mountain ascent, thus introducing that variety which is the spice of all our pleasures.

----

[1] Peabody River is said to have originated in the same manner, and in a single night.   It is probable, however, that as long as there has been a valley there has also been a stream.

V.

The crag leaps down, and over it the flood:
Know'st thou it, then?
'Tis there! 'tis there
Our way runs. . . . Wilt thou go?—GOETHE.

AT the mountains the first look of every one is directed to the heavens, not in silent adoration or holy meditation, but in earnest scrutiny of the weather. For here the weather governs with absolute sway; and nowhere is it more capricious. Morning and evening skies are, therefore, consulted with an interest the varied destinies of the day may be supposed to suggest. From being a merely conventional topic, the weather becomes one of the first importance, and such salutations as " A fine day," or " A nice morning," are in less danger of being coupled with a wet day or a scowling forenoon. To sum up the whole question, where life in the open air is the common aim of all, a rainy day is a day lost, and everybody knows that a lost day can never be recovered. Sun worship is, therefore, universal.

The prospect being duly weighed and pronounced good, or fair, or fairly good, *presto!* the hotel presents a scene of active preparation. Anglers, with rod and basket, betake themselves to the neighboring trout brooks, artists to the woods or the open. Mountain wagons clatter up to the door with an exhilarating spirit and dash. Amid much laughter and cracking of jokes, these strong, yet slight-looking vehicles are speedily filled with parties for the summit, the Crystal Cascade, or Glen Ellis; knots of pedestrians, picturesquely dressed, move off with elastic tread for some long-meditated climb among the hills or in the ravines; while the regular stages for Gorham or Glen Station depart amid hurried and hearty leave-takings, the flutter of handkerchiefs, and the sharp crack of the driver's whip. Now they are off, and quiet settles once more upon the long veranda.

My own plans included a trip in and out of Tuckerman's Ravine; in by the old Thompson path, out by the Crystal Cascade. It is necessary to depart a little from the order of time, as my first essay (during the first week of May) was frustrated by the deep snows then effectually blockading the way above Hermit Lake. The following July found me more fortunate, and it is this excursion that I shall now lay before the reader for his approval.

I chose a companion to whom I unfolded the scheme, while reconnoitring the ravine through my glass. He eagerly embraced my proposal, declaring his readiness to start on the instant. Upon a hint I let fall touching his ability to make this then fatiguing march, he observed, rather stiffly, " I went through one Wilderness with Grant; guess I can through this."

" Pack your knapsack, then, comrade, and you shall inscribe ' Tuckerman's ' along with Spottsylvania, Cold Harbor, and Petersburg."

" Bless me! is it so very tough as all that? No matter, give me five minutes to settle my affairs, and I'm with you."

Let us improve these minutes by again directing the glass toward the ravine.

The upper section of this remarkable ravine — that portion lifted above the forest line—is finely observed from the neighborhood of the Crystal Cascade, but from the Glen House the curiously distorted rim and vertical wall of its south and west sides, the astonishing crag standing sentinel over its entrance, may be viewed at full leisure. It constitutes quite too important a feature of the landscape to escape notice. Dominated by the towering mass of the Dome, infolded by undulating slopes descending from opposite braces of Mount Washington, and resembling gigantic draperies, we see an enormous, funnel-shaped, hollow sunk in the very heart of the mountain. We see, also, that access is feasible only from the north-east, where the entrance is defended by the high crag spoken of. Behind these barriers, graven with a thousand lines and filled with a thousand shadows, the amphitheatre lifts its formidable walls into view.

For two miles our plain way led up the summit-road, but at this distance, where it suddenly changes direction to the right, we plunged into the forest. Our course now lay onward and upward over what had at some time been a path—now an untrodden one—encumbered at every few rods with fallen trees, soaked with rain, and grown up with moose-

wood. Time and again
we found the way
barred by these ex-
asperating windfalls,
and their thick *abatis* of
branches, forcing us alternately to go down on all-
fours and creep underneath,
or to mount and dismount,
like recruits, on the wooden
horse of a cavalry school.

But to any one loving
the woods—and this

THE PATH, TUCKERMAN'S RAVINE.

day I loved not
wisely, but too well—
this walk is something to be
taken, but not repeated, for fear
of impairing the first and most
abiding impressions. One cannot
have such a revelation twice.

I recall no mountain-path that is so richly diversified with all the wildest forms of mountain beauty. At first our progress through primitive groves of pine, hemlock, and birch was impeded by nothing more remarkable than the giant trees stretching interminably, rank upon rank, tier upon tier. But these woods, these countless gray and black and white trunks, and outspread framework of branches, supported a canopy of thick foliage, filled with voices innumerable. Something stirred in the top of a lofty pine; and then, like an alguazil on a watch-tower, a crow, apparent sentinel of all the feathered colony, rose clumsily on his talons, flapped two sable wings, and thrice hoarsely challenged, "Caw! caw! caw!" What clamor, what a liliputian Babel ensued! Our ears fairly tingled with the calls, outcries, and objurgations apparently flung down at us by the multitudinous population overhead. Hark to the woodpecker's rat-tat-tat, the partridge's muffled drum! List to the bugle of the wood-thrush, sweet and clear! Now sounds the cat-bird's shrill alarm, the owl's hoot of indignant surprise. Then the squirrels, those little monkeys of our northern woods, grated their teeth sharply at us, and let fall nuts on our heads as we passed underneath. Never were visitors more unwelcome.

Before long we came to a brook, then to another. Their foaming waters shot past like a herd of wild horses. These we crossed. We now began to thread a region where the forest was more open. The moss we trampled underfoot, and which here replaces the grass of the valleys, was beating the tallest trees in the race for the mountain-top. It was the old story of the tortoise and the hare over again. But this moss: have you ever looked at it before your heel bruised the perfumed flowers springing from its velvet? Here are tufts exquisitely decorated with coral lichens; here the violet and anemone nestle lovingly together; here it creeps up the gray trunks, or hides the bare roots of old trees. Tread softly! This is the abode of elves and fairies. Step lightly! you expect to hear the crushed flowers cry out with pain.

These enchanting spots, where stones are couches and trees canopies, tempted us to sit down on a cushioned bowlder, or throw ourselves upon the thick carpet into which we sunk ankle-deep at every step. Even the bald, gray rocks were tapestried with mosses, lichens, and vines. All around, under the thick shade, hundreds of enormous trees lay rotting; yet exquisitely the prostrate trunks were overspread with robes of softest green, effectually concealing the repulsiveness, the suggestions of decay. Now and then the dead tree rose into new life through the sturdy roots of a young fir, or luxuriant, plumed ferns growing in its bark. This inexpressible fecundity, in the midst of inexpressible wastefulness, declared that for Nature there is no such thing as death. And they tell us the day of miracles has passed! Upon this dream of elf-land the cool morning light fell in oblique streams through the tree-trunks, as through grated windows, filling all the wood with a subdued twilight glimmer, leaving a portion of its own gleams on the moss-grown rocks, while the trees stretched their black shadows luxuriously along the thick-piled sward, like weary soldiers in a bivouac.

We proceeded thus from chamber to chamber, and from cloister to cloister, at times descending some spur of the mountain into a deep-shaded dell, and again climbing a swift and miry slope to better ground, until we crossed the stream coming from the high spur spoken of. From here the ground rapidly rose for half a mile more, when we suddenly came out of the low firs full upon the Lion's Head crag, rising above Hermit Lake, and visible from the vicinity of the Glen House. To be thus unexpectedly confronted by this wall of imperishable rock stirs one very deeply. For the moment it dominates *us*, even as it does the little tarn so unconsciously slumbering at its feet. It is horribly mutilated and defaced. Its sides are thickly sowed with stunted trees, that bury their roots in its cracks and rents with a gripe of iron. In effect it is the barbican of the great ravine. Crouched underneath, by the shore of the lake, is a matted forest of firs and spruces, dwindled to half their usual size, grizzled with long lichens, and occupying, as if by stealth, the debatable ground between life and death. It is, in fact, more dead than alive. Deeply sunk beneath is the lake.

Hermit Lake — a little pool nestling underneath a precipice — demands a word. Its solitary state, its waters green and profound, and the thick shades by which it was covered, seemed strangely at variance with the intense activity of the foaming torrents we had seen, and could still hear rushing down the mountain. It was too small for a lake, or else it was dwarfed by the immense mass of overshadowing rock towering above it, whose reflected light streamed across its still and glossy surface. Here we bid farewell to the forest.

We had now gained a commanding post of observation, though there was yet rough work to do. We saw the whole magnificent sweep of the ravine, to where it terminates in a semicircle of stupendous cliffs that seem hewn perpendicularly a thousand feet down. Lying against the western wall we distinguished patches of snow; but they appeared of trifling extent. Great wooded mountain slopes stretched away from the depths of the gorge on either side, making the iron lineaments of the giant cliffs seem harder by their own softness and delicacy. Here and there these exquisite draperies were torn in long rents by land-slips. In the west arose the shattered peak of Monroe—a mass of splintered granite, conspicuous at every point for its irreclaimable deformity. It

HERMIT LAKE.

seemed as if the huge open maw of the ravine might swallow up this peak with ease. There was a Dantesque grandeur and solemnity everywhere. With our backs against the trees, we watched the bellying sails of a stray cloud which intercepted in its aerial voyage our view of the great summit; but it soon floated away, discovering the whitish-gray ledges to the very capstone of the dome itself. Looking down and over the thick woods beyond, we met again the burly Carter Mountains, pushed backward from the Pinkham Notch, and kept back by an invisible yet colossal strength.

From Hermit Lake the only practicable way was by clambering up the bed of the mountain brook that falls through the ravine. The whole expanse that stretched on either side was a chaos of shattered granite, pitched about in awful confusion. Path there was none. No matter what way we turned, "no thoroughfare" was carved in stolid stone. We tried to force a passage through the stunted cedars that are mistaken at a mile for greensward, but were beaten back, torn and bleeding, to the brook. We then turned to the great bowlders, to be equally buffeted and abused, and finally repulsed upon the brook, which seemed all the while mocking our efforts. Once, while forcing a route, inch by inch, through the scrub, I was held suspended over a deep crevice, by my belt, until extricated by my comrade. At another time he disappeared to the armpits in a hole, from which I drew him like a blade from a scabbard. At this moment we found ourselves unable either to advance or retreat. The dwarf trees squeezed us like a vise. Who would have thought there was so much life in them? At our wits' end, we looked at our bleeding hands, then at each other. The brook was the only clew to such a labyrinth, and to it, as from Scylla to Charybdis, we turned as soon as we recovered breath. But to reach it was no easy matter; we had literally to cut our way out of the jungle.

When we were there, and had rested awhile from the previous severe exertions, my companion, alternately mopping his forehead and feeling his bruises, looked up with a quizzical expression, and ejaculated, "Faith, I am almost as glad to get out of this wilderness as the other! In any case," he gayly added, "I have lost the most blood here; while in Virginia I did not receive a scratch."

After this rude initiation into the mysteries of the ravine, we advanced directly up the bed of the brook. But the brook is for half a mile nothing but a succession of leaps and plunges, its course choked with bowlders. We however toiled on, from rock to rock, first boosting, then hoisting each other up; one moment splashing in a pool, the next halting in dismay under a cascade, which we must either mount like a chamois or ascend like a trout. The climber here tastes the full enjoyment of an encounter with untamed nature, which calls every thew and sinew into action. At length the stream grew narrower, suddenly divided, and we stood at the mouth of the Snow Arch, confronted by the vertical upper wall of the ravine.

We stood in an arena "more majestic than the circus of a Titus or a Vespasian." The scene was one of awful desolation. A little way below us the gorge was heaped with the ruins of some unrecorded convulsion, by which the precipice had been cloven from base to summit, and the enormous fragments heaved into the chasm with a force the imagination is powerless to conceive. In the interstices among these blocks rose thickets of dwarf cedars, as stiff and unyielding as the livid rock itself. It was truly an arena which might have witnessed the gladiatorial combats of immortals.

We did not at first look at the Snow Arch. The eye was irresistibly fascinated by the tremendous mass of the precipice above. From top to bottom its tawny front was covered with countless little streams, that clung to its polished wall without once quitting their hold. They twined and twisted in their downward course, like a brood of young serpents escaping from their lair; nor could I banish the idea of the ghastly head of a Gorgon clothed with tresses of serpents. A poetic imagination has named this tangled knot of mountain rills, " The fall of a thousand streams." At the foot of the cliff the scattered waters unite, before entering the Snow Arch, in a single stream. Turning now to the right, the narrowing gorge, ascending by a steep slope as high as the upper edge of the precipice, points out the only practicable way to the summit of Mount Washington in this direction. But we have had enough of such climbing, for one day, at least.

Partial recovery from the stupefaction which seizes and holds one fast is doubtless signalized in every case by an effort to account for the overwhelming disaster of which these ruins are the mute yet speaking evidence. We need go no farther in the search than the innocent-looking little rills, first dripping from the Alpine mosses, then percolating through the rocks of the high plateau, and falling over its edge in a thousand streams. Puny as they look, before their inroads the plateau line has doubtless receded, like the great wall of rock over which Niagara pours the waters of four seas. With their combined forces—how long ago cannot be guessed; and what, indeed, does it signify?—knitted together by frost into Herculean strength, they assailed the granite cliffs that were older than the sun, older than the moon or the stars, mined and countermined year by year, inch by inch, drop by drop, until—honey-combed, riddled, and pierced to its centre, and all was ready for its final overthrow—winter gave the signal. In a twinkling, yielding to the stroke, and shattered into a thousand fragments, the cliffs laid

their haughty heads
low in the dust. After-
ward the accumulated
waters tranquilly continued the process
of demolition, and of removing the soil
from the deep excavation they had made,
until the floor of the ravine had sunk to
its present level. In California a man   SNOW ARCH, TUCKERMAN'S RAVINE.
with a hose washes away mountains to
get at the gold deposits. This principle of hydraulic force is borrowed,
pure and simple, from a mountain cataract.

Osgood, the experienced guide, who had visited the ravine oftener
than anybody else, assured me that never within his remembrance had

this forgotten forgement of winter, the Snow Arch, been seen to such advantage. We estimated its width at above two hundred feet, where it threw a solid bridge of ice over the stream, and not far from three hundred in its greatest length, where it lay along the slope of the gorge. Summer and winter met on this neutral ground. Entering the Arch was joining January and July with a step. Flowers blossomed at the threshold. We caught water, as it dripped ice-cold from the roof, and pledged Old Winter in his own cellarage. The brook foamed at our feet. Looking up, there was a pretty picture of a tiny water-fall pouring in at the upper end and out at the ragged portal of the grotto. But I think we were most charmed with the remarkable sculpture of the roof, which was a groined arch fashioned as featly as was ever done by human hands. What the stream had begun in secret the warm vapors had chiselled with a bolder hand, but not altered. As it was formed, so it remained—a veritable chapel of the hills, the brook droning its low, monotonous chant, and the dripping roof tinkling its refrain unceasingly. If the interior of the great ravine impressed us as the hidden receptacle of all waste matter, this lustrous heap of snow, so insignificant in its relation to the immensity of the chasm that we scarcely looked at it at first, now chased away the feeling of mingled terror and aversion — of having stolen unawares into the one forbidden chamber—and possessed us with a sense of the beautiful, which remained long after its glittering particles had melted into the stream that flowed beneath. So under a cold exterior is nourished the principle of undying love, which the aged mountain gives that earth may forever renew her fairest youth.

The presence of this miniature glacier is a very simple matter. The fierce winds of winter which sweep over the plateau whirl the snows before them, over its crest, into the ravine, where they are lodged at the foot of the precipice, and accumulate to a great depth. As soon as released by spring, the little streams, falling down this wall, seek their old channels, and, being warmer, succeed in forcing a passage through the ice. By the end of August the ice usually disappears, though it sometimes remains even later.

After picking up some fine specimens of quartz, sparkling with mica, and uttering a parting malediction on the black flies that tormented us, we took our way down and out of the ravine, following the general course of the stream along its steep valley, and, after an uneventful march of two hours, reached the upper waters of the Crystal Cascade.

VI.

That lonely dwelling stood among the hills
By a gray mountain stream.—SOUTHEY.

AFTER the events described in the last chapter, I continued, like
the navigator of unknown coasts, my tour of the great range.
Half a mile below the Glen House, the Great Gulf discharges from its
black throat the little river rising on the plateau at its head. The head
of this stupendous abyss is a mountain, and mountains wall it in. Its
depths remain unexplored except by an occasional angler or trapper.

Two and a half miles farther on a road diverges to the left, crosses
the Peabody by a bridge, and stretches on over a depression of the range
to Randolph, where it intersects the great route from Lancaster and Jefferson to Gorham. Over the river, snugly ensconced at the foot of
Mount Madison, is the old Copp place. Commanding, as it does, a noble
prospect up and down the valley, and of all the great peaks except
Washington, its situation is most inviting; more than this, the picture
of the weather-stained farm-house nestling among these sleeping giants
revives in fullest vigor our preconceived idea of life in the mountains,
already shaken by the balls, routs, and grand toilets of the hotels. The
house, as we see by Mistress Dolly Copp's register, has been known to
many generations of tourists. The Copps have lived here about half a
century.

Travellers going up or down, between the Glen House and Gorham,
usually make a détour as far as Copp's, in order to view the Imp to better advantage than can be done from the road. Among these travellers
some have now and then knocked at the door and demanded to see the
Imp. The hired girl invariably requests them to wait until she can call
the mistress.

THE IMP.

Directly opposite the farm-house the inclined ridge of Imp Mountain is broken down perpendicularly some two hundred feet, leaving a jagged cliff, resembling an immense step, facing up the valley. This is a mountain of the Carter chain, sloping gradually toward the Glen House. Upon this cliff, or this step, is the distorted human profile which gives the mountain its name. A strong, clear light behind it is necessary to bring out all the features, the mouth especially, in bold relief against the sky, when the expression is certainly almost diabolical. One imagines that some goblin, imprisoned for ages within the mountain, and suddenly liberated by an earthquake, exhibits its hideous countenance, still wearing the same look it wore at the moment it was entombed in its mask of granite. The forenoon is the best time, and the road, a few rods back from the house, the best point from which to see it. The coal-black face is then in shadow.

The Copp farm-house has a tale of its own, illustrating in a remarkable manner the amount of physical hardship that long training, and familiarity with rough out-of-door life, will occasionally enable men to endure. Seeing two men in the door-yard, I sat down on the chopping-block, and entered into conversation with them.

By the time I had taken out my note-book I had all the members of the household and all the inmates of the barn-yard around me. I might add that all were talking at once. The matron stood in the door-way, which her ample figure quite filled, trifling with the beads of a gold necklace. A younger face stared out over her shoulder; while an old man, whose countenance had hardened into a vacant smile, and one of forty or thereabouts, alternately passed my glass one to the other, with an astonishment similar to that displayed by Friday when he first looked through Crusoe's telescope.

"Which of you is named Nathaniel Copp?" I asked, after they had satisfied their curiosity.

"That is my name," the younger very deliberately responded. "Really," thought I, "there is little enough of the conventional hero in that face;" therefore I again asked, "Are you the same Nathaniel Copp who was lost while hunting in the mountains, let me see, about twenty-five years ago?"

"Yes; but I wasn't lost after I got down to Wild River," he hastily rejoined, like a man who has a reputation to defend.

"Tell me about it, will you?"

I take from my note-book the following relation of the exploit of this mountain Nimrod, as I received it on the spot. But I had literally to draw it out of him, a syllable at a time.

On the last day of January, 1855, Nathaniel Copp, son of Hayes D. Copp, of Pinkham's Grant, near the Glen House, set out from home on a deer hunt, and was out four successive days. On the fifth day he again left to look for a deer killed the previous day, about eight miles from home. Having found it, he dragged the carcass (weighing two hundred and thirty pounds) home through the snow, and at one o'clock P.M. started for another he had tracked near the place where the former was killed, which he followed until he lost the track, at dark. He then found that he had lost his own way, and should, in all probability, be obliged to spend the night in the woods, with the temperature ranging from 32° to 35° below zero.

Knowing that to remain quiet was certain death, and having nothing with which to light a fire, the hunter began walking for his life. The moon shone out bright and clear, making the cold seem even more intense. While revolving in his mind his unpleasant predicament he heard a deer bleat. He gave chase, and easily overtook it. The snow was too deep for the animal to escape from a hunter on snow-shoes. Copp leaped upon his back, and despatched him with his hunting-knife. He then dressed him, and, taking out the heart, put it in his pocket, not for a trophy, but, as he told me, to keep starvation at arm's-length. The excitement of the chase made him forget cold until he perceived himself growing benumbed. Rousing himself, he again pushed on, whither he knew not, but spurred by the instinct of self-preservation. Daylight found him still striding on, with no clew to a way out of the thick woods, which imprisoned him on every side. At length, at ten in the morning, he came out at or near Wild River, in Gilead, forty miles from home, having walked twenty one consecutive hours without rest or food, the greater part of the time through a tangled growth of underbrush.

His friends at home becoming alarmed at his prolonged absence during such freezing weather, three of them, Hayes D. Copp, his father, John Goulding, and Thomas Culhane, started in search of him. They followed his track until it was lost in the darkness, and, by the aid of their dog, found the deer which young Copp had killed and dressed. They again started on the trail, but with the faintest hope of ever finding the lost man alive, and, after being out twenty-six hours in the extreme cold, found the object of their search.

No words can do justice to the heroic self-denial and fortitude with which these men continued an almost hopeless search, when every moment expecting to find the stiffened corpse of their friend. Goulding froze both feet; the others their ears.

When found, young Copp did not seem to realize in the least the great danger through which he had passed, and talked with perfect unconcern of hunts that he had planned for the next week. One of his feet was so badly frozen, from the effect of too tightly lacing his snow-shoe, that the toes had to be amputated.

Until reaching the bridge, within two miles of Gorham, I saw no one, heard nothing except the strokes of an axe, borne on the still air from some logging-camp, twittering birds, or chattering river. Ascending the hill above the bridge, I took my last look back at Mount Washington, over whose head rose-tinted clouds hung in graceful folds. The summit was beautifully distinct. The bases of all the mountains were floating in that delicious blue haze, enrapturing to the artist, exasperating to the climber. Turning to my route, I had before me the village of Gorham, with the long slopes of Mount Hayes meeting in a regular pyramid behind it. Against the dusky wall of the mountain one white spire stood out clean and sharp. At my right, along the river, was a cluster of saw-mills, sheds, and shanties; beyond, an irregular line of forest concealing the town — all except the steeple; beyond that the mountain. As I entered the village, the shrill scream of a locomotive pierced the still air, and, like the horn of Ernani, broke my dream of forgetfulness with its fatal blast. Adieu, dreams of delusion! we are once more manacled with the city.

I loitered along the river road, hoping, as the sky was clear, to see the sun go down on the great summits. Nor was I disappointed. As I walked on, Madison, the superb, gradually drew out of the Peabody Glen, and soon Washington came into line over the ridge of Moriah, whose highest precipices were kindled with a ruddy glow, while a wonderful white light rested, like a halo, on the brow of the monarch. Of a sudden, the crest of Moriah paled, then grew dark; night rose from the black glen, twilight descended from the dusky heavens. For an instant the humps of Clay reddened in the afterglow. Then the light went out, and I saw only the towering forms of the giant mountains dimly traced upon the sky. A star fell. At this signal the great dome sparkled with myriad lights. Night had ascended her mountain throne.

Gorham is situated on the Grand Trunk Railway, between Paris and Berlin, with Milan just beyond — names a trifle ambitious for villages with the bark on, but conferring distinction upon half a hundred otherwise obscure villages scattered from Maine to California.

Gorham is also situated in one of those natural parks, called intervales, in an amphitheatre of hills, through which the Androscoggin flows with a strong, steady tide. The left bank is appropriated by Mount Hayes, the right by the village — a suspension bridge giving access from one to the other. This mountain rises abruptly from the river to a broad summit-plateau, from which a wide and brilliant prospect rewards the climber. The central portion of Gorham is getting to be much too busy for that rest and quietude which is so greatly desired by a large class of travellers to the mountains, but, on the other hand, its position with respect to the highest summits is more advantageous than that of any other town lying on the skirts of the mountains, and accessible by railway. In one hour the tourist can be at the Glen

House, in three on the summit of Mount Washington. Being at the very end of the great chain, in the angle where its last elevation abuts on the Androscoggin, the valley conducting around the northerly side of the great eminences, through the settlements of Randolph and Jefferson, furnishes another and a charming avenue of travel into the region watered by the Connecticut. As the great tide of travel flows in from the west and south, Gorham has profited little by the extension of railways furnishing more direct communication with the heart of the mountains.

Mount Hayes is the guardian of the village, erecting its rocky rampart over it, like the precipices of Cape Diamond over Quebec. The hill in front is called Pine Mountain, though it is only a mountain by brevet. The tip of the peak of Madison peers down into the village over this hill. I plainly saw the snow up there from my window. To the left, and over the low slope of Pine Mountain, rise the Carter summits, which here make a remarkably imposing background to the picture, and in conjunction with the great range form the basin of the Peabody. I saw this stream, making its final exit from the mountains, throw itself exhausted with its rapid course into the Androscoggin, half a mile below the hotel. North-west of the village street, drawn up in line across the valley, extend the Pilot peaks.

The Carter group is said to have been named after a hunter. According to Farmer, the Pilot Mountains were so called from a dog. Willard, a hunter, had been lost two or three days on these mountains, on the east side of which his camp was situated. Every day he observed that Pilot, his dog, regularly left him, as he supposed in search of game; but toward nightfall would as regularly return to his master. This at length excited the attention of the hunter, who, when nearly exhausted with fatigue and hunger, decided to commit himself to the guidance of Pilot, and in a short time was conducted by the intelligent animal in safety to his camp.

My first morning at Gorham was a beautiful one, and I prepared to improve it to the utmost by a walk around the northern base of Madison, neither knowing nor caring whither it might lead me. Spring was in her most enchanting mood. A few steps, and I was amid the marvels of a new creation, the tasselled birches, the downy willows, the oaks in gosling-gray. Even the gnarled and withered apple-trees gave promise of blossoming, and the young ferns, pushing aside the dead leaves, came forth with their tiny fists doubled for the battle of life. Why did not Nature so order it that mankind might rest like the trees, or shall we, like them, come forth at last strong, vigorous, beautiful, from that long refreshing slumber?

Leaving the village, at the end of a mile and a half I took the road turning to the left, where Moose River falls into the Androscoggin, at the point where the latter, making a remarkable bend, turns sharply away to the north. Moose River is a true mountain stream, clear and limpid, foaming along a bed of sand and pebbles.

From this spot the whole extent of the Pilot range was unrolled at my right, while at the left, majestic among the lower hills, Madison and Adams were massed in one grand pyramid. · The snows glistening on the summits seemed trophies torn from winter.

About a mile from the turning, at Lary's, I found the best station for viewing the statuesque proportions of Madison. The foreground a swift mountain stream, white as the snows where it takes its rise. Beyond, a strip of meadow land, covered with young birches and poplars, just showing their tender, trembling foliage. Among these are scattered large, dead trees, relics of the primeval forest; the middle. ground a young forest, showing in its dainty wicker-work of branchlets that beady appearance which belongs to spring alone, and is so exquisitely beautiful. Above this ascends, mile upon mile, the enormous bulk of the mountain, ashen-gray at the summit, dusky olive-green below. Stark precipices, hedged about with blasted pines, and seamed with snow, capped the great pile. Over this a pale azure, deepening in intensity toward the zenith, unrolled its magnificent drapery.

After the ascent of Mount Hayes, which Mr. King has fittingly described as " the chair set by the Creator at the proper distance and angle to appreciate and enjoy " the kingly prominence of Mount Washington, the two things best worth seeing in the neighborhood are the falls of the Androscoggin at Berlin, and the beautiful view of the loftiest of the White Mountain peaks from what is called here the Lead Mine Bridge. To get to the falls you must ascend the river, and to obtain the view you must descend a few miles. I consecrated a day to this excursion.

With a head already filled with the noise of half a hundred mountain torrents, water-falls, or cascades, I set out after breakfast for Berlin Falls, feeling that the passage of a body of water such as the Androscoggin is at Gorham, through a narrow gorge, must be something different from the common.

A word about Berlin. Its situation is far more picturesque than that of Gorham. There is the same environment of mountains, and, in addition to the falls, a magnificent view of Madison, Adams, Jefferson, and of the Carter range. The precipices of Mount Forist, which overhang railway and village, are noticeable among a thousand. Here Dead River falls into the Androscoggin, and here the Grand Trunk Railway, taking leave of this river, turns to the north-west, crosses over to the Upper Ammonoosuc, twists and twines along with it among the northern mountains, and at last emerges upon the level meadows of the Connecticut.

Berlin has another aspect. Lumber is its business; lumber its staple of conversation; people go to bed to dream of lumber. In a word, lumber is everywhere. The lumberman admires a tree in his way quite as much as you or I. No eye like his to estimate its height, its girth, its thickness. But as ships to Shylock, so trees to him are naught but boards—so many feet. So that there is something almost ferocious in the lumberman's or mill-owner's admiration for the forest; something almost startling in the idea that this out-of-the-way corner is devouring the forests at the rate of twenty car-loads a day. In plain language, this village cuts up a good-sized grove every day, and rejoices over it with a new house or a new barn.

At the risk of being classed with the sentimental and the unpractical, every one who is alive to the consequences of converting our forests into deserts, or worse than deserts, should raise a voice of warning against this wholesale destruction. The consequences may be remote, but they are certain. For the most part, the travelled routes have long since been stripped of their valuable timber trees. Now the mills are fast eating their way into the hitherto inaccessible regions, leaving a track of desolation behind wherever they go, like that of a destroying army. What cannot be carried away is burnt. Fires are seen blazing by the side of every saw-mill, in which all the waste material is carefully consumed. A trifle? Enough is consumed every year in this way to furnish the great city of New York with its fuel. I speak with moderation. Not a village but has its saw-mills; while at Whitefield, Bethlehem, Livermore, Low, and Burbank's Grant, and many other localities, the havoc is frightful. Forest fires, originating chiefly in the logging-camps, annually desolate leagues of forest land. How long is this to continue?

The mountain labors incessantly to re-create, but what can it do against such fearful odds? and what shall we do when it can no longer furnish pine to build our homes, or wood to warm them? Delve deeper and deeper under the Alleghanies? In about two hundred and fifty years the noble forests, which set the early discoverers wild with enthusiasm, have been steadily driven farther and farther back into the interior, until "the forest primeval" exists not nearer than a hundred miles inland. Then the great northern wilderness began at the sea-coast. It is now in the vicinity of Lake Umbagog. Still the warfare goes on. I do not call occasional bunches of wood forests. All this means less and less moisture; consequently, more and more drouth. The tree draws the cloud from heaven, and bestows it on the earth. The summer of 1880 was one of almost unexampled dryness. Large rivers dwindled to pitiful rivulets, brooks were dried up, and the beautiful cascades in many instances wholly disappeared. The State is powerless to interfere. Not so individuals, or combinations of individuals for the preservation of such tracts of woodland as the noble Cathedral woods of North Conway. In the West a man who plants a tree is a public benefactor; is he who saves the life of one in the East less so? America, says Berthold Auerbach, is no longer "the Promised Land for the Old World;" if she does not protect her woods, she will become "waste and dry," like the Promised Land of the ancients—Palestine itself. Look on this picture of Michelet:

"On the shores of the Caspian, for three or four hundred leagues, one sees nothing, one encounters nothing, but midway an isolated and solitary tree. It is the love and worship of every passing wayfarer. Each one offers it something; and the very Tartar, in default of every other gift, will snatch a hair from his beard or his horse's mane."

The season when the great movement of lumber from the northern wilderness to the sea begins is one of great activity. The logs are floated down the Androscoggin from Lake Umbagog with the spring freshets, when those destined to go farther are "driven," as the lumbermen's phrase is, over the falls and through the rapids here, to be picked up below. It may well be believed that the passage of the falls by a "drive" is a sight worth witnessing. Sometimes the logs get so tightly jammed in the narrow gorge of the river that it seems impossible to extricate them; but the dam they form causes the river to rise behind it, when the accumulated and pent-up waters force their way through the obstruction, tossing huge logs in the air as if they were straws. A squad of lumbermen — tough, muscular, handy fellows they are — accompanies each drive, just as *vaqueros* do a Texan herd; and the herd of logs, like the herd of cattle, is branded with the owner's mark. After making the drive of the falls, the men move down below them, where they find active and, so far as appearance goes, dangerous work in disentangling the snarls of logs caught among the rocks of the rapids. Against a current no ordinary boat could stem for a moment; they dart hither and thither in their light bateaux, as the herdsman does on his active little mustang. If a log grounds in the midst of the rapids, the bateaux dashes toward it. One river-driver jumps upon it, and holds the boat fast, while another grapples it with a powerful lever called a cant-dog. In a moment the log rolls off the rocks with a loud splash, and is hurried away by the rapid tide.

During the drive the lumberman is almost always wet to the skin, day in and day out. When a raft of logs is first started in the spring the men suffer from the exposure; but after a little time the work seems to toughen and harden them, so that they do not in the least mind the amphibious life they are forced to lead. Rain or shine, they get to their work at five in the morning, leaving it only when it is too dark to see longer. Each squad — for the whole force is divided into what may be called skirmishers, advanced-guards, main body, and rear-guard, each having its appointed work to perform — then repairs to its camp, which is generally a tent pitched near the river, where the cook is waiting for their arrival with a hot supper of fried doughnuts and baked beans — the lumberman's diet of preference. They pass the evening playing euchre, telling stories, or relating the experiences of the day, and are as simple, hearty, happy-go-lucky fellows as can be found in the wide world.

To say that the Berlin Falls begin two miles below the village is no more than the truth, since at this distance the river was sheeted in foam from shore to shore. For these two miles its bed is so thickly sown with rocks that it is like a river stretched on the rack. The whole river, every drop of it, is hemmed in by enormous masses of granite, forming a long, narrow, and rocky gorge, down which it bursts in one mad plunge, tossing and roaring like the Maelstrom. What fury! What force! The solid earth shakes, and the very air trembles. It is a saturnalia. A whirlwind of passion, swift, uncontrollable, and terrible.

The best situation I could find was upon a jutting ledge below the little foot-bridge thrown from rock to rock. Several turns in the long course of the cataract prevent its whole extent being seen all at once; but it starts up hither and thither among the rocks, boiling with rage at being so continually hindered in its free course, until, at last, madness seizes it, and, flying straight at the throat of the gorge, it goes down in one long white wave, overwhelming everything in its way. It reaches the foot of the rocks in fleeces, darts wildly hither and thither, shakes off the grasp of concealed rocks, and, racing on, stretches itself on its wide and shallow bed, uttering a tremulous wail.

From the village at the falls, and from Berlin Mills, are elevations from which the great White Mountains are grandly conspicuous. The view is similar to that much extolled one from Milan, the town next to Berlin. Here the three great mountains, closed in mass, display a triple crown of peaks, Washington being thrown back to the left, and behind Madison, with Adams on his right. Best of all is the blended effect of early morning, or of the afterglow, when a few light clouds sail along the crimson sky, and their shadows play hide-and-seek on the mountain sides.

In the afternoon, while walking down the road to Shelburne, I met an apparently honest farmer, with whom I held some discourse. He was curious about the great city he had known half a century before, when it was in swaddling clothes; I about the mountains above and around us, that had never known change since the world began. An amiable contest ensued, in which each tried to lead the other to talk of the topic most interesting to himself. The husbandman grew eloquent upon his native State and its great man. "But what," I insisted, "do you think of your greatest mountain there?" pointing to the splendid peak.

"Oh, drat the mountains! I never look at 'em. Ask the old woman."

Some enticing views may be had from the Shelburne intervales, embracing Madison on the right, and Washington on the left. It is, therefore, permitted to steal an occasional look back until we reach the Lead Mine Bridge, and stand over the middle of the flashing Androscoggin.

The dimpled river, broad here, and showing tufts of foliage on its satin surface, recedes between wooded banks to the middle distance,

where it disappears. Swaying to and fro, without noise, the lithe and
slender willows on the margin continually dipped their budding twigs
in the stream, as if to show its clear transparency, while letting fall, drop
by drop, its crystal globules. They gently nodded their green heads,
keeping time to the low music of the river.

Beyond the river, over gently meeting slopes of the valley, two magnificent shapes, Washington and Madison, rose grandly. Those truly

THE ANDROSCOGGIN AT SHELBURNE.

regal summits still wore their winter ermine. They were drawn so
widely apart as to show the familiar peaks of Mount Clay protruding
between them. It is hardly possible to imagine a more beautiful picture of mountain scenery. Noble river, hoary summits, blanched precipices, over whose haggard visages a little color was beginning to steal,
eloquently appealed to every perception of the beautiful and the sublime.
Much as the view from this point is extolled, it can hardly be over-
praised. True, it exhibits the same objects that we see from Berlin and
Milan; but the order of arrangement is not only reversed, but so altered
as to render any comparison impossible. In this connection it may be
remarked that a short removal usually changes the whole character of
a mountain landscape. No two are precisely alike.

The annals of Shelburne, which originally included Gorham within its
limits, are sufficiently meagre; but they furnish the same story of struggle

with hardship—often with danger—common to the early settlements in this region. Shelburne was settled, just before the breaking out of the Revolution, by a handful of adventurous pioneers, who were attacked in 1781 by a prowling band of hostile Indians. This incursion is memorable as one of the last recorded in the long series going back into the first decade of the New England colonies. · It was one of the boldest. The histories place the number of Indians at only six. After visiting Bethel, where they captured three white men, and Gilead, where they killed another, they entered Shelburne. Here they killed and scalped Peter Poor, and took a negro prisoner. Such was the terror inspired by this audacious onset, that the inhabitants, making no defence, fled, panic-struck, to Hark Hill, where they passed the night, leaving the savages to plunder the village at their leisure. The next day the refugees continued their flight, stopping only when they reached Fryeburg, fifty-nine miles from the scene of disaster.

Before taking leave of the Androscoggin Valley, which is an opulent picture-gallery, and where at every step one finds himself arrested before some masterpiece of Nature, the traveller is strongly advised to continue his journey to Bethel, the town next below Shelburne. Bethel is one of the loveliest and dreamiest of mountain nooks. Its expanses of rich verdure, its little steeple, emerging from groves of elm-trees, its rustic bridge spanning the tireless river, its air of lethargy and indolence, captivate eye and mind; and to eyes tired with the hardness and glare of near mountains, the distant peaks become points of welcome repose.

13

VII.

ASCENT BY THE CARRIAGE-ROAD.

Where the huge mountain rears his brow sublime,
On which no neighboring height its shadow flings,
Led by desire intense the steep I climb.

PETRARCH.

THE first days of May, 1877, found me again at the Glen House, prepared to put in immediate execution the long-deferred purpose of ascending Mount Washington in the balmy days of spring. Before separating for the night, my young Jehu, who drove me from Gorham in an hour, said, with a grin,

"So you are going where they cut their butter with a chisel, and their meat with a hand-saw?"

"What do you mean?"

"Oh, you will learn to-morrow."

"Till to-morrow, then."

"Good-night."

"Good-night."

At six in the morning, while the stars were yet twinkling, I stood in the road in front of the Glen House. Everything announced a beautiful day. The rising sun crimsoned, first, the dun wall of Tuckerman's Ravine, then the high summits, and then flowed down their brawny flanks —his first salutation being to the monarch. In ten minutes I was alone in the forest with the squirrels, the partridges, the woodpeckers, and my own thoughts.

As bears are not unfrequently seen at this season of the year, I kept my eyes about me. One of the old drivers related to me that one morning, while going up this road with a heavy load of passengers, his horses suddenly stopped, showing most unmistakable signs of terror. The place was a dangerous one, where the road had been wholly excavated from the steep side of the mountain, so, keeping one eye upon his fractious team, he threw quick glances right and left with the other; while the passengers, alarmed by the sudden stop, the driver's shouts to his animals, and the still more alarming backward movement of the coach, thrust their heads out of the windows, and with white faces demanded what was the matter.

"By thunder!" ejaculated Jehu, "there was my leaders all in a lather, an' backin' almost atop of the fill-horses, and them passengers a-shoutin' like lunatics let out on a picnic. 'Look! darn it all,' sez I, a-pintin' with my whip. My hosses was all in a heap, I tell ye, rarin' and charging, when a little Harvard student, with his head sand-papered, sung out. 'All right, Cap, I've chucked your hind wheels:' and then he made for the leaders' heads. Them college chaps ain't such darned fools arter all, they ain't."

"What was it?"

"A big black bear, all huddled up in a bunch, a-takin' his morning observation on the scenery from the top of a dead sycamore. You see the side of the hill was so slantin' steep that he wa'n't more'n tew rod from the road."

"What did you do?"

"Dew?" echoed the driver, laughing—"dew?" he repeated, "why, them crazy passengers, when they found the bear couldn't get at *them*, just picked up rocks and hove them at the old cuss. When one hit him a crack, Lord, how he'd shake his head and growl! But, you see, he couldn't get at 'em, so they banged away, until Mr. Bruin couldn't stan' it any longer, an' slid right down the tree as slick as grease, and as mad as Old Nick. It tickled me most to death to see him a-makin' toothpicks fly from that tree."

"Was that your only encounter with bears?" I asked, willing to draw him out.

"Waal, no, not exactly," he replied, chuckling to himself, gleefully, at some recollection the question revived. "There used to be a tame bear over to the Alpine House. One night the critter got loose, and we all cal'lated he'd took to the woods. Anyhow we hunted high and low; but no bear. Waal, you see, one forenoon our hostler Mike—his real name was Pat, but there was another Pat came afore him, so we called t'other Mike—went up in the barn-chamber to pitch some hay down to the hosses." Here he stopped and began to choke.

"Well, go on; what has that to do with the bear?"

"Just you hold your hosses a minnit, stranger. Mike hadn't no sooner jabbed his pitchfork down, so as to git a big bunch, when it struck something soft-like, and then, before he knew what ailed him, the hay-mow riz rite up afore him, with the almightiest growl comin' out on't was ever heerd in any maynagery this side of Noah's Ark."

Here the driver broke down utterly, gasping, "Oho! aha! oh Lord! ah! ha! ha! ha! ha! ho! ho! Mike!" until his breath was quite gone, and the big tears rolled down his cheeks. Then he heaved a deep sigh, attempted to go on, but immediately went off in a second hysterical explosion. I waited for his recovery.

"Waal," he at length resumed, "the long and short of it was this: that air bear had buried himself under the hay-mow, and was a-snoozin' it comfortable and innocent as you please, when Mike prodded him in the ribs with the pitchfork. The fust any of us knew we saw Mike come a-flyin' out of the barn-chamber window and the bear arter him. Mike led him a length. Maybe that Irishman didn't streak it for the house! Bless you, he never teched the ground arter he struck it! The boys couldn't do anything for laughing, and Mick was so scart he forgot to yell. That bear was so hoppin' wild we had to kill him; and if you wanted to make Mike fightin' mad any time, all you had to do was to ask him to go up in the barn-chamber and pitch down a bear."

The first four miles are merely toilsome. It is only when emerging upon the bare crags above the woods that the wonders of the ascent begin, and the succession of views, dimly seen through my eyes in this chapter, challenges the attention at every step. There is one exception. About a mile up, the road issues upon a jutting spur of the mountain, from which the summit, with the house on the highest point, is seen in clear weather.

Suddenly I came out of the low firs, the scrubby growth of birches, upon the fear-inspiring desolation of the bared and wintry summit. The high sun poured down with dazzling brightness upon the white ledges, which, rising like a wall above the solitary cabin before me, thrust their jagged edges in the way, as if to forbid farther progress. Out of this glittering precipice dead trees thrust huge antlers. This formless mass overhanging the Half-Way House, known as The Ledge, is one of the most terrific sights of the journey.

Until clear of the woods, my uneasiness, inspired by the recollection of the ascent from Crawford's, was extreme; but I now stood, in the full blaze of an unclouded sun, upon a treeless wilderness of rock, a gratified spectator of one of the most extraordinary scenes it has ever fallen to man's lot to witness. But what a frightful silence! Not a murmur; not a rustling leaf; but all still as death. I was half-afraid.

At my feet yawned the measureless void of the Great Gulf, torn from the entrails of the mountain by Titanic hands. Above my head leaped up the endless pile of granite constituting the dome of Washington. It had now exchanged its gray cassock for pale green. All around was unutterable desolation. Crevassed with wide splits, encompassed round by lofty mountain walls, the gorge was at once fascinating and forbidding, grand yet terrible. The high-encircling steeps of Clay and Jefferson, Adams and Madison, enclosing it with one mighty sweep, ascended out of its depths and stretched along the sky, which seemed receding before their daring advance. Peering down into the abyss, where the tallest pines were shrubs and their trunks needles, the earth seemed split to its centre, and the feet of these mountains rooted in the midst. To confront such a spectacle unmoved one should be more, or less than human.

Looking backward over the forest through which I had come, the eye caught a blur of white and a gleam of blue in the Peabody Glen. The white was the hotel, the blue the river. Following the vale out to its entrance upon the Androscoggin meadows, the same swift messenger ascended Moriah, and, traversing the confederate peaks to the summit of Mount Carter, stopped short at its journey's end.

As I slowly mounted the Ledge the same unnatural appearance was everywhere—the same wreck, same desolation, same discord. The dead cedars, bleaching all around, looked like an army of gigantic crabs crawling up the mountain side, which universal ruin overspread, and which even the soft sunshine rendered more ghastly and more solemn. I looked eagerly along the road; listened. Not a human being; not a sound. I was alone upon the mountain.

From here I no longer walked upon earth but on air. Respiration became more and more difficult. Not even a zephyr stirred, while the glare was painful to eyes already overtaxed in the endeavor to grasp the full meaning of this most unaccustomed scene. The road, steadily ascending, showed its zigzags far up the mountain. Now and then a rude receptacle had been dug, or rather built up, by the road-side, in

MOUNT ADAMS AND THE GREAT GULF.

which earth to mend the road was stored; and this soil, wholly composed of disintegrated rock, must be scraped from underneath the ledges, from crevices, from hollows, and husbanded with care. "As cheap as dirt," was a saying without significance here. As I neared the summit the melting snows had, in many places, swept it bare, exposing the naked ledge; and here earth must be brought up from lower down the mountain. But the pains bestowed upon it equals the incessant demand for its preservation, and had I not seen with my own eyes I could scarcely have believed so excellent a specimen of road-making existed in this desert.

But how long will the mountain resist the denuding process constantly going on, and what repair the gradual but certain disintegration of the peak? It is a monument of human inability to act upon it in any way. Be it so. The snows, the frosts, the rains, pursue their work none the less surely. You see in the deep gullies, the avalanches of stones, the sands of the sea-shore—so many evidences of the forces which, sooner or later, will accomplish the miracle and remove the mountain.

From my next halting-place I perceived that I had been traversing a promontory of the mountain jutting boldly out into the Great Gulf, above the Half-Way House; and, looking down over the parapet-wall, a mile or more of the road uncoiled its huge folds, turning hither and thither, doubling upon itself like a bewildered serpent, and, like the serpent, always gaining a little on the mountain. This is one of the strangest sights of this strange journey; but, in order to appreciate it at its full value, one should be descending by the stage-coach, when the danger, more apparent than real, is intensified by the swift descent of the mountain into the gulf below, over which the traveller sees himself suspended with feelings more poignant than agreeable. The fact that there has never been a fatal accident upon the carriage-road speaks volumes for the caution and skill of the drivers; but, as one of the oldest and most experienced said to me, "There should be no fooling, no chaffing, and no drinking on that road."[1]

---

[1] Since the above was written, a deplorable accident has given melancholy emphasis to these words of warning. I leave them as they are, because they were employed by the very person to whom the disaster was due: "The first accident by which any passengers were ever injured on the carriage-road, from the Glen House to the summit of Mount Washington, occurred July 3d, 1880, about a mile below the Half-Way House. One of the six-horse mountain wagons, containing a party of nine persons—the last load of the excursionists from Michigan to make the descent of the mountain—was tipped over, and one lady was killed and five others injured. Soon after starting from the summit the passengers discovered that the driver had been drinking while waiting for the party to descend. They left this wagon a short distance from the summit and walked to the Half-Way House, four miles below, where

Continuing to ascend, the road once more took a different direction, curving around that side of the mountain rising above the Pinkham forest. This détour brought the Carter chain upon my left, instead of on my right.

Thus far I had encountered little snow, though the rocks were everywhere crusted with ice; but now a sudden turning brought me full upon an enormous bank, completely blocking the road, which here skirted the edge of a high precipice. Had a sentinel suddenly barred my way with his bayonet, I could not have been more astonished. I was brought to a dead stand. I looked over the parapet, then at the snow-bank, then at the mountain. The first look made me shudder, the second thoughtful, the third gave me a headache.

At this spot the side of the mountain was only a continuation of the precipice, bent slightly backward from the perpendicular, and ascending several hundred feet higher. The snow, extending a hundred feet or more above, and conforming nearly with the slope of the mountain, filled the road for thrice that distance. I saw that it was only prevented from sliding into the valley by the low wall of loose stones at the edge of the road; but how long would that resist the great pressure upon it? The snow-bank had already melted at its edges, so that I could crawl some distance underneath, and hear the drip of water above and below, showing that it was being steadily undermined. In fact, the whole mass seemed on the point of precipitating itself over the precipice. I could neither go around it nor under it; so much was certain.

What to do? I had only a strong umbrella, the inseparable companion of my mountain jaunts, and the glacier was as steep as a roof. What assurance was there that if I ventured upon it the whole sheet, dislodged by my weight, might not be shot off the mountain side, carrying me with it to the bottom of the abyss? But while I felt no desire to add mine to the catalogue of victims already claimed by the moun-

one of the employés of the Carriage-road Company assured them that there was no bad place below that, and that he thought it would be safe for them to resume their seats with the driver, who was with them. Soon after passing the Half-Way House, in driving around a curve too rapidly, the carriage was overset, throwing the occupants into the woods and on the rocks. Mrs. Ira Chichester, of Allegan, Michigan, was instantly killed, her husband, who was sitting at her side, being only slightly bruised. Of the other occupants, several were more or less injured. The injured were brought at once to the Glen House, and received every possible care and attention. Lindsey, the driver, was taken up insensible. He had been on the road ten years, and was considered one of the safest and most reliable drivers in the mountains."

tain, the idea of being turned back was inadmissible. Native caution put the question, " Will you ?" and native persistency answered, " I will."

When a thing is to be done, the best way is to do it. I therefore tried the snow, and, finding a solid foothold, resolved to venture; had it been soft, I should not have dared. Using my umbrella as an alpenstock, I crossed on the parapet, where the declivity was the least, and without accident, but slowly and breathlessly, until near the opposite side, when I passed the intervening space in two bounds, alighting in the road with the blood tingling to my fingers' ends.

A sharp turn around a ledge, and the south-east wall of Tuckerman's Ravine rose up, like a wraith, out of the forest. Nearer at hand was the head of Huntington's, while to the right the cone of Washington loomed grandly more than a thousand feet higher. A little to the left you look down into the gloomy depths of the Pinkham defile, the valley of Ellis River, the Saco Valley to North Conway, where the familiar figure of Kearsarge is the presiding genius. The blue course of the Ellis, which is nothing but a long cascade, the rich green of the Conway intervales, the blanched peak of Chocorua, the sapphire summits of the Ossipee Mountains, were presented in conjunction with the black and humid walls of the ravine, and the iron-gray mass of the great dome. The crag on which I stood leans out over the mountain like a bastion, from which the spectator sees the deep-intrenched valleys, the rivers which wash the feet of the monarch, and the long line of summits which partake his grandeur while making it all the more impressive.[1]

Turning now my back upon the Glen, the way led in the opposite direction, and began to look over the depression between Clay and Jefferson into the world of blue peaks beyond. From here the striking spectacle of the four great northern peaks, their naked summits, their sides seamed with old and new slides, and flecked with snow, constantly enlarged. There were some terrible rents in the side of Clay, red as half-closed wounds; in one place the mountain seemed cloven to its centre. It was of this gulf that the first climber said it was such a precipice he could scarce discern to the bottom. The rifts in the walls of the ravine, the blasted fir-trees leaning over the abyss, and clutching

---

[1] A stone bench, known as Willis's Seat, has been fixed in the parapet wall at the extreme southern angle of the road, between the sixth and seventh miles. It is a fine lookout, but will need to be carefully searched for.

the rocks with a death-gripe, the rocks themselves, tormented, formidable, impending, astound by their vivid portrayal of the formless, their suggestions of the agony in which these mountains were brought forth.

I was now fairly upon the broad, grass-grown terrace at the base of the pinnacle, sometimes called the Cow Pasture. The low peak rising upon its limits is a monument to the fatal temerity of a traveller who, having climbed, as he supposed, to the top of the mountain, died from hunger or exposure, or from both, at this inhospitable spot.[1]   A skeleton in rags was found, at the end of a year, huddled under some rocks. Farther down the mountain a heap of stones indicates the place where Doctor Ball, of Boston, was found by the party sent in search of him, famished, exhausted, and almost delirious.   When rescued, he had passed two nights upon the mountain, without food, fire, or shelter, after as many days of fruitless wandering up and down, always led astray by his want of knowledge, and mocked by occasional glimpses of snowy peaks above, or the distant Glen below.   More dead than alive, he was supported down the mountain as far as the camp at The Ledge, whence he was able to ride to the Glen House.   His reappearance had the effect of one risen from the dead.   In reality, the rescuing party took up with them materials for a rude bier, expecting to find a dead body stiffening in the snow.[2]

Besides this almost unheard of resistance to hunger, cold, and exhaustion combined, and notwithstanding the fortitude which enabled the lost man to continue his desperate struggle for life until rescued, all would doubtless have been to no purpose without the aid of an umbrella, which, by a lucky chance, he took at setting out.   This umbrella was his only protection during the two terrible vigils he made upon the mountain.   How, is related in the chapter on the ascent from Crawford's.

Crossing the terrace, where even the road seems glad to rest after its laborious climb of seven miles, and where the traveller may also relax his efforts, preparatory to his arduous advance up the pinnacle, I came upon the railway, still solidly embedded in snow and ice.

Still making a route for itself among massy blocks, tilted at every conceivable angle, but forming, nevertheless, a symmetrical cone,

---

[1] Benjamin Chandler, of Delaware, in August, 1856.
[2] Dr. B. L. Ball's "Three Days on the White Mountains," in October, 1855.

the carriage-road winds up the steep ascent, to which the railway is nailed. While traversing the plateau, with the Summit House now in full view, my eye caught, far above me, the figure of a man pacing up and down before the building, like a sentinel on his post. I swung my hat in the air; again; but he did not see me. Nevertheless, I experi-

WINTER STORM ON THE SUMMIT.

enced a thrill of pleasure at seeing him, so acutely had the sense of loneliness come over me in these awful solitudes. It put such vigor into my steps that in half an hour I crossed the last rise, when the solitary pedestrian, making an about-face at the end of his beat, suddenly discovered a strange form and figure emerging from the rocks before him. He stopped short, took the pipe from his teeth, looking with open-mouthed astonishment, then, as I continued to approach, he hastened toward me, met me half-way, and, between rapid questions and answers, led the way into the signal station.

Behold me installed in the cupola of New England! While I was resting, my host, a tall, bronzed, bearded man, bustled about the two or three apartments constituting this swallow's nest. He put the kettle on the stove, gave the fire a stir, spread a cloth upon the table, and took some plates, cups, and saucers from a locker, some canned meats and fruit from a cupboard, I, meanwhile, following all these movements with an interest easily imagined. His preparations completed, my host first ran his eye over them approvingly, then, presenting a pen, requested me to inscribe my name in the visitors' book. I did so, noticing that the last entry was in October—that is, five months had elapsed since the last climber wended his solitary way down the mountain. My hospitable entertainer then, with perfect politeness, begged me to draw my chair to the table and fall to. I did not refuse. While he poured out the tea, I asked,

"Whom have I the pleasure of addressing?" and he modestly replied,

"Private Doyle, sir, of the United States Signal Service. Have another bit of devilled ham? No? Try these peaches."

"Thank you. At least Uncle Sam renders your exile tolerable. Is this your ordinary fare?"

"Oh, as to that, you should see us in the dead of winter, chopping our frozen meat with a hatchet, and our lard with a chisel."

This, then, was what my young Jehu had meant. Where was I? I glanced out of the window. Nothing but sky, nothing but rocks; immensity and desolation. I disposed my ideas to hear my companion ask, "What is the news from the other world?"

VIII.

MOUNT WASHINGTON.

The soldiers from the mountain Theches ran from rear to front, breaking their ranks, crowding tumultuously upon each other, laughing and shouting, "The sea! the sea!"—XENOPHON'S *Anabasis.*

AFTER the repast we walked out, Private Doyle and I, upon the narrow platform behind the house. According to every appearance I had reached *Ultima Thule.*

For some moments—moments not to be forgotten—we stood there silent. Neither stirred. The scene was too tremendous to be grasped in an instant. A moment was needed to recover one's moral equipoise, as well as for the unpractised eye to adjust itself to the vastness of the landscape, and to the multitude of objects, strange objects, everywhere confronting it. My own sensations were at first too vague for analysis, too tumultuous for expression. The flood choked itself.

All seemed chaos. On every side the great mountains fell away like mists of the morning, dispersing, receding to an endless distance, diminishing, growing more and more vague, and finally vanishing on a limitless horizon neither earth nor sky. Never before had such a spectacle offered itself to my gaze. The first idea was of standing on the threshold of another planet, and of looking down upon this world of ours outspread beneath; the second, of being face to face with eternity itself. No one ever felt exhilaration at first. The scene is too solemnizing.

But by degrees order came out of this chaos. The bewildering throng of mountains arranged itself in chains, clusters, or families. Hills drew apart, valleys opened, streams twinkled in the sun, towns and villages clung to the skirts of the mountains or dotted the rich meadows; but all was mysterious, all as yet unreal.

Comprehending at last that all New England was under my feet, I began to search out certain landmarks. But this investigation is fatiguing: besides, it conducts to nothing—absolutely nothing. Pointing to a scrap of blue haze in the west, my companion observed, " That is Mount Mansfield ;" and I, mechanically, repeated, "Ah! that is Mount Mansfield." It was nothing. Distance and Infinity have no more relation than Time and Eternity. It sufficed for me, God knows, to be admitted near the person of the great autocrat of New England, while under skies so fair and radiant he gave audience to his imposing and splendid retinue of mountains.

But still, independent of the will, the eye flitted from peak to peak, from summit to summit, making the slow circuit of this immense horizon, hovering at last over a band of white gleaming far away in the southeast like a luminous cloud, on whose surface objects like birds reposed. It was the sea, and the specks ships sailing on the main. With the aid of a telescope we could even tell what sails the vessels carried. In these few seconds the eye had put a girdle of six hundred miles about.'

I consider this first introduction to what the peak of Mount Washington looks down upon an epoch in any man's life. I saw the whole noble company of mountains from highest to lowest. I saw the deep depressions through which the Connecticut, the Merrimac, the Saco, the Androscoggin, wind toward the lowlands. I saw the lakes which nurse the infant tributaries of those streams. I saw the great northern forests, the notched wall of the Green Mountains, the wide expanse of level land, flat and heavy like the ocean, and finally the ocean itself. And all this was mingled in one mighty scene.

The utmost that I can say of this view is that it is a marvel. You receive an impression of the illimitable such as no other natural spectacle—no, not even the sea—can give. Astonishment can go no farther. Nevertheless, the truth is that you are on too high a view-point for the most effective grasp of mountain scenery. This immense height renders near objects indistinct, obscures the more distant. Seldom, indeed, is the land seen, even under favoring conditions, except through a soft haze, which, you are surprised to notice, becomes more and more transparent as you descend. The eye explores this *clair-obscur*, and gradually dis-

---

' Considering the pinnacle of Mount Washington as the centre of a circle of vision, the greatest distance I have been able to see with the naked eye, in nine ascensions, did not probably much exceed one hundred miles. This being half the diameter, the circumference would surpass six hundred miles. It is now considered settled that Katahdin, one hundred and sixty miles distant, is not visible from Mount Washington.

cerns this or that object. It is true that you see to a great distance, but you do not distinguish anything clearly. This is the rule, derived from many observations, to which the crystal air of autumn and winter makes the rare and fortunate exception.

There is a more cogent reason why the view from Mount Washington is inferior to that from other and lower summits. Everything is below you, and, naturally, therefore, any picture of these mountains not showing the cloud-capped dome of the monarch, attended by his cortége of grand peaks—the central, dominating, perfecting group—must be essentially incomplete. Imagine Rome without St. Peter's, or, to come nearer home, Boston without her State House! One word more: from this lofty height you lose the symmetrical relation of the lesser summits to the grand whole. Even these signal embodiments of heroic strength—the peaks of Jefferson, Adams, and Madison — so vigorously self-asserting that what they lose in stature they gain by a powerful individuality, even these suffer a partial eclipse; but the summits stretching to the southward are so dwarfed as to be divested of any character as typical mountain structures. What fascinates us is the "sublime chaos of trenchant crests, of peaks shooting upward;" and the charm of the view—such at least is the writer's conviction—resides rather in the immediate surroundings than in the extent of the panorama, great as that unquestionably is.

One thing struck me with great force—the enormous mass of the mountain. The more you realize that the dependent peaks, stretching eight miles north, and as many south, are nothing but buttresses, the more this prodigious weight amazes. Two long spurs, divided by the valley of the Rocky Branch, also descend into the Saco Valley as far as Bartlett; and another, shorter, but of the same indestructible masonry, is traced between the valleys of the Ammonoosuc and of Israel's River. In a word, as the valleys lie and the roads run, we must travel sixty or seventy miles around in order to make the circuit of Mount Washington at its base.

Even here one is not satisfied if he sees a stone ever so little above him.[1] The best posts for an outlook, after the signal station, are upon a

---

[1] The highest point, formerly indicated by a cairn and a beacon, is now occupied by an observatory, built of planks, and, of course, commanding the whole horizon. It is desirable to examine this vast landscape in detail, or so much of it as the eye embraces at once, and no more.

point of rocks behind the old Tip-Top House, and from the end of the hotel platform, where the railway begins its terrifying descent. From all these situations the view was large and satisfying. From the first station one overlooks the southern summits; from the second, the northern. A movement of the head discloses, in turn, the ocean, the lakes and lowlands of Maine and New Hampshire, the broad highlands of Massachusetts, the fading forms of Monadnock and Wachusett, the highest peaks of Vermont and New York, and, finally, the great Canadian wilderness.

After all this, the eye dwells upon the hideous waste of rock blackened by ages of exposure, corroded with a green incrustation, like *verd-antique*, constituting the dome. It is at once mournful and appalling. Time has dealt the mountain some crushing blows, as we see by these ghastly ruins, bearing silent testimony to their own great age. It is necessary to step with care, for the rocks are sharp-edged. The green appearance is due to lichens which bespatter them. Greedy little spiders inhabit them. Truly this is a spot disinherited by Nature.

Noticing many boards scattered helter-skelter about the top and sides of the mountain, I drew my companion's attention to them, and he explained that what I saw was the result of the great January gale, which had blown down the shed used as an engine-house, demolished every vestige of the walk leading from the hotel to the signal station, and distributed the fragments as if they had been straws far and wide, as I saw them.

The same gale had swept the coast from Hatteras to Canso with destructive fury. I begged Private Doyle to give me his recollections of it. We returned to the station, and he began as follows:

"At the time of the tornado I was sick, and my comrade, Sergeant M——, who is now absent on leave, had to do my turn as well as his own. 'Uncle Sam,' you know, keeps two of us here, for fear of accidents."[1]

"It surprised me to find you here alone," I assented.

"This is the third day." Then, resuming his narrative, "During the forenoon preceding the gale we observed nothing very unusual; but the clouds kept sinking and sinking, until, in the afternoon, the summit alone

---

[1] One poor fellow (Private Stevens) did die here in 1872. His comrade remained one day and two nights alone with the dead body before help could be summoned from below.

was above them. For miles around nothing could be seen but one vast ocean of frozen vapor, with peaks sticking out here and there, like icebergs floating in this ocean—all being cased in snow and ice. I cannot tell you how curious this was. Later in the day the density of the clouds became such that they reflected the colors of the spectrum: and that too was beautiful beyond description. It was about this time Sergeant M—— came to where I was lying, and said, 'There is going to be the devil to pay; so I guess I'll make everything snug.'

"By nine in the evening the wind had increased to one hundred miles an hour, with heavy sleet, so that no observation could be safely made from without. At midnight the velocity of the storm was one hundred and twenty miles, and the exposed thermometer recorded 24° below zero. We could hardly get it above freezing inside the house. With the stove red, water froze within three feet of the fire; in fact, where you are now sitting.

"At this time the uproar outside was deafening. About one o'clock the wind rose to one hundred and fifty miles. It was now blowing a hurricane. That carpet (indicating the one in the room where we were) stood up a foot from the floor, like a sail. The wind, gathering up all the loose ice on top of the mountain, dashed it against the house in one continuous volley. I lay wondering how long we should stand this terrific pounding, when all at once there came a crash. M—— shouted to me to get up; but I had tumbled out in a hurry on hearing the glass go. You see I was ready-dressed, to keep myself warm in bed.

"Our united efforts were hardly equal to closing the storm-shutters from the inside; but we succeeded, finally, though the lights were out, and we worked in the dark." He rose in order to show me how the shutters, made of thick oak planks, were secured by a bar, and by strong wooden buttons screwed in the window-frame.

"We had scarcely done this," resumed Doyle, "and were shivering over the fire, when a heavy gust of wind again burst open the shutters as easy as if they had never been fastened at all. We sprang to our feet. After a hard tussle we again secured the windows by nailing a cleat to the floor, against which we fixed one end of a board, using the other end as a lever. You understand?" I nodded. "Well, even then it was all we could do to force the shutters back into place. But we did it. We *had* to do it.

"The rest of the night was passed in momentary expectation that the building would be blown over into Tuckerman's Ravine, and we with it. At four in the morning the wind registered one hundred and eighty-six miles. It had shifted then from east to north-east. From this time it steadily fell to ten miles at nine o'clock — as calm as a daisy. This was the heaviest blow ever experienced on the mountain."

"Suppose this house had gone, and the hotel stood fast, could you have effected an entrance into the hotel?" I asked.

"No, indeed. We could not have faced the wind."

"Not for a hundred feet, and in a matter of life and death?"

"In that gale? We should have been lifted clean off our feet and smashed upon the rocks like this bottle," flinging one out at the door.

"So then for all those hours you expected from one moment to another to be swept into eternity?"

"We did what we could. Each of us wrapped himself up in blankets and quilts, tying these tightly around him with ropes, to which were attached bars of iron, so that if the house went by the board we might stand a chance—a slim one—of anchoring, somehow, somewhere."

I tried to make him admit that he was afraid; but he would not.

THE TORNADO FORCING AN ENTRANCE.

Only he forgot, he said, in the excitement of that terrible night, that he was ill, until the danger was over.

"We are going to have a blow," observed Doyle, glancing at the barometer—"barometer falling, wind rising. Besides, that blue haze, creeping over the valley, is a pretty sure sign of a change of weather." His prognostic was completely verified in the course of a few hours.

"Now," said Doyle, rising, "I must go and feed my chick."

We retraced our steps to the point of rocks overhanging the southern slope, where he stopped and began to scatter crumbs, I watching him curiously meanwhile. Pretty soon he went down on his hands and knees and peered underneath the rocks. "Ah!" he exclaimed, with vivacity, "there you are!"

"What is it?" I asked; "what is there?"

"My mouse. He is rather shy, and knows I am not alone," he replied, chirruping to the animal with affectionate concern.

Brought to the mountain top in some barrel or box, the little stowaway had become domesticated, and would come at the call of his human playmate. The incident was trifling enough of itself, yet there was something touching in this companionship, something that sharply recalled the sense of loneliness I had myself experienced. In reality, the disparity between the man and the mouse seemed not greater than that between the mountain and the man.

While we were standing among the rocks the sun touched the western horizon. The heavens became obscured. All at once I saw an immense shadow striding across the valley below us. Slowly and majestically it ascended the Carter chain until it reached the highest summit. I could not repress an exclamation of surprise; but what was my astonishment to see this immense phantom, without pausing in its advance, lift itself into the upper air to an incredible height, and stand fixed and motionless high above all the surrounding mountains. It was the shadow of Mount Washington projected upon the dusky curtain of the sky. All the other peaks seemed to bow their heads by a sentiment of respect, while the actual and the spectre mountain exchanged majestic salutations. Then the vast gray pyramid retreated step by step into the thick shades. Night fell.

The expected storm which the observer had predicted did not fail to put in an appearance. By the time we reached the house the wind had risen to forty miles an hour, driving the clouds in an unbroken flight against the summit, from which they rebounded with rage equal to that displayed in their vindictive onset. The Great Gulf was like the crater of some mighty volcano on the eve of an eruption, vomiting forth volumes of thickening cloud and mist. It seemed the mustering-place of all the storm-legions of the Atlantic, steadily pouring forth from its black jaws, unfurling their ghostly standards as they advanced to storm the battlements of the mountain. Occasionally a break in the column disclosed the opposite peaks looming vast and black as midnight. Then the effect was indescribable. At one moment everything seemed resolving into its original elements; the next I was reminded of a gigantic mould, not from mortal hands, in which all these vast forms were slowly cooling. The moon shed a pale, wan light over this unearthly scene, in which creation and annihilation seemed confusedly struggling. The sublime drama of the Fourth Day, when light was striving with darkness for its allotted place in the universe, seemed enacting under my eyes.

The evening passed in comparative quiet, although the gale was now moving from east to west at the rate of sixty miles an hour. Rain rattled on the roof like shot. Now and then the building shuddered and creaked, like a good ship breasting the fury of the gale. Vivid flashes of lightning made the well-lighted room momentarily dark, and checked conversation as suddenly as if we had felt the electric shock. Under such novel conditions, with strange noises all about him, one does not feel quite at ease. Nevertheless the kettle sung on the stove, the telegraph instrument ticked on the table. We had Fabyan's, Littleton, and White River Junction within call. We had plenty of books, the station being well furnished from voluntary gifts of the considerate-benevolent. At nine Doyle went out, but immediately returned and said he had something to show me. I followed him out to the platform behind the house. A forest fire had been seen all day in the direction of Fabyan's, but at night it looked like a burning lake sunk in depths of infernal blackness. I had never seen anything so nearly realizing my idea of hell. No other object was visible—only this red glare as of a sun in partial eclipse shining at the bottom of an immense hole. We watched it a few minutes and then went in. I attempted to be cheerful, but how was one to rise above such surroundings? Alternately the storm roared and whined for admittance. Worn out with the tension, physical and moral, of this day, I crept into bed and tried to shut the storm out. The poor exile in the next room murmured to himself, " Ah, this horrible solitude !"

The next morning, while looking down from this eagle's nest upon the southern peaks to where the bridle-path could be distinctly traced across the plateau, and still winding on around the peaked crest of Monroe, I was seized with a longing to explore the route which on a former occasion proved so difficult, but to-day presenting apparently nothing more serious than a fatiguing scramble up and down the cone. Accordingly, taking leave of my companion, I began to feel my way down that cataract of granite, fallen, it would seem, from the skies.[1]

In proportion as I descended, the mountain ridge below regained, little by little, its actual character. Except where patches of snow mottled it with white, it displayed one uniform and universal tinge of faded orange where the soft sunshine fell full upon it, toned into rusty brown when overshadowed, gradually deepening to an intense blue-black in the ravines. But so insignificant did the summits look, when far below, that I hardly recognized them for the same I had seen from Fabyan's and had traversed from Crawford's. Monroe, the nearest, has, however, a most striking resemblance to an enormous petrified wave on the eve of dashing itself down into the valley. The lower you descend the stronger this impression becomes; but from the summit of Mount Washington this peak is so belittled that the mountains seemed saying to each other, "Good-morning, Mole-hill!" "Good-morning, Big Bully!"

When I reached the stone-corral, the ground, if ground it can be called, descended less abruptly, over successive stony terraces, to a comparative level, haired over with a coarse, wiry, and tangled grass, strewed with bowlders, and inundated along its upper margin by torrents of stones. Upon closer inspection these stones arranged themselves in irregular semicircular ridges. In the eyes of the botanist and entomologist this seemingly arid region is more attractive than the most beautiful gardens of the valley. Among these grasses and these stones lie hid the beautiful Alpine flowers of which no species exist in the lowlands. Only the arbutus, which puts forth its pink-and-white flowers earliest of all, and is warmed into life by the snows, at all resembles them in its habits. Over this grassy plain the wind swept continually and roughly; but on

---

[1] It was for a long time believed that the summit of Mount Washington bore no marks of the great Glacial Period, which the lamented Agassiz was the first to present in his great work on the glaciers of the Alps. Such was the opinion of Dr. C. T. Jackson, State Geologist of New Hampshire. It is now announced that Professor C. II. Hitchcock has detected the presence of transported bowlders not identical with the rocks in place.

putting the grass aside with the hand, the tiny blossoms greet you with a smile of bewitching sweetness.

These areas, extending between and sometimes surrounding the high peaks, or even approaching their summits, are the "lawns" of the botanist, and his most interesting field of research. Within its scope about fifty species of strictly Alpine plants vegetate. As we ascend the mountain, after the dwarf trees come the Lapland rhododendron, Labrador tea, dwarf birch, and Alpine willows, which, in turn, give place to the Greenland sandwort, diapensia, cassiope, and other plants, with arctic rushes, sedges, and lichens, which flourish on the very summit.

To the left, this plain, on which the grass mournfully rustled, sloped gently for, I should guess, half a mile, and then rolled heavily off, over a grass-grown rim, into Tuckerman's Ravine. In this direction the Carter Mountains appeared. Beyond, stretching away out of the plain, extended the long Boott's Spur, over which the Davis path formerly ascended from the valley of the Saco, but which is now, from long disuse, traced with difficulty. Between this headland and Monroe opened the valley of Mount Washington River, the old Dry River of the carbuncle hunters, which the eye followed to its junction with the Saco, beyond which the precipices of Frankenstein glistened in the sun, like a corselet of steel. Oakes's Gulf cuts deeply into the head of the gorge. The plain, the ravine, the spur, and the gulf transmit the names of those indefatigable botanists, Bigelow, Tuckerman, Boott, and Oakes.

On the other side of the ridge—for of course this plain has its ridge—the ground was more broken in its rapid descent toward the Ammonoosuc Valley, into which I looked over the right shoulder of Monroe.

But what a sight for the rock-wearied eye was the little Lake of the Clouds, cuddled close to the hairy breast of this mountain! On the instant the prevailing gloom was lighted as if by magic by this dainty nursling of the clouds, which seemed innocently smiling in the face of the hideous mountain. And the stooping monster seemed to regard the little waif, lying there in its rocky cradle, with astonishment, and to forego his first impulse to strangle it where it lay. Lion and lamb were lying down together.

Casting an eye upward, and finding the houses on the summit were hidden by the retreating curvature of the cone, I saw, with chagrin, light mists scudding over my head. It was a notice to hasten my movements idle to disregard here. Crossing as rapidly as possible Bigelow's Lawn

—the half-mile of grass ground referred to, where I sunk ankle-deep in moss, or stumbled twenty times in as many rods over concealed stones —I skirted the head of the chasm for some distance. But from above the ravine does not make a startling impression. I, however, discovered, lodged underneath its walls, a bank of snow. All around I heard water gurgling under my feet in rock-worn channels while making its way tranquilly to the brow of the ravine. These little underground runlets are the same that glide over the head-wall, and are the head tributaries of the Ellis.[1]

Retracing my way to the ridge and to the path, which I followed for some distance, startling the silence with an occasional halloo, I descended into the hollow, where the Lake of the Clouds seems to have checked itself, white and still, on the very edge of the tremendous gully, cut deep into the western slopes. The lake is the fountain-head of the Ammonoosuc. Its waters are too cold to nourish any species of fishes; they are too elevated for any of the feathered tribe to pay it a visit.

Strange spectacle! A fairy haunt, rock-rimmed and fringed about with Alpine shrubs, half-disclosing, half-concealing its bare bosom, coyly reposed on this wind-swept ridge, like "a good deed in a naughty world." From its crystal basin a tiny rill trickled through soft moss to the dizzy verge beyond, where, like some airy sprite, clothed with the rainbow and

---

[1] In going to and returning from the ravine, I must have walked over the very spot which has since derived a tragical interest from the discovery, in July, 1880, of a human skeleton among the rocks. Three students, who had climbed up through the ravine on the way to the summit, stumbled upon the remains. Some fragments of clothing remained, and in a pocket were articles identifying the lost man as Harry W. Hunter, of Pittsburg, Pennsylvania. This was the same person whom I had seen placarded as missing, in 1875, and who is referred to in the chapter on the ascent from Crawford's. A cairn and tablet, similar to those erected on the spot where Miss Bourne perished, had already been placed here when I last visited the locality, where the remains had so long lain undiscovered in their solitary tomb. An inscription upon the tablet gives the following details: "Henry W. Hunter, aged twenty-two years, perished in a storm, September 3d, 1874, while walking from the Willey House to the summit. Remains found July 14th, 1880, by a party of Amherst students." The place is conspicuous from the plain, and is between the Crawford Path and Tuckerman's. By going a few rods to the left, the Summit House, one mile distant, is in full view. This makes the third person known to have perished on or near the summit of Mount Washington. Young Hunter died without a witness to the agony of his last moments. No search was made until nearly a year had elapsed. It proved ineffectual, and was abandoned. Thus, strangely and by chance, was brought to light the fact that he sunk exhausted and lifeless at the foot of the cone itself. I can fully appreciate the nature of the situation in which this too adventurous but truly unfortunate climber was placed.

LAKE OF THE CLOUDS.

tossing its white tresses to the sport of the breeze, it tripped gayly over the grisly precipice and fell in a silvery shower from height to height. Where it passed, flowers, ferns, and rich herbage sprung forth upon the hard face of the granite.   Tapering fir-trees exhaled a dewy freshness; aspens quivered with the delight of its coming, and aged trees, tottering, decrepit, piteous to see, stretched their withered limbs toward heaven. On it went, and still on, leaving its white robe clinging to the mountain side. All the forest seemed crowding forward to catch it; but, now reverently kissing the feet of the old trees, now saucily flinging a handful of crystal in the faces of scowling cliffs, it eluded the embrace of the forest, which thrilled with its musical laughter from lowest deeps to the summit of high-rocking pines. When it was no longer visible a sonorous murmur heralded its triumphal progress. No wonder the bewildered eye roved from bleak summit to voluptuous vale; from the handful of drops above to the brimming river below. The miracle of Horeb was being repeated hour by hour, like an affair of every-day life.

This hand-mirror of Venus has two tiny companion pools close by. The weary explorer may sip a draught of sweetest savor while admiring their exceeding beauty—a beauty heightened by its unexpectedness, and teaching that not all is barren even here. A benison on those little lakes!

Stone houses of refuge are much needed on the mountains over which the Crawford trail reaches the summit. They should always be provided with fagots for a fire, clean straw or boughs for a bed, and printed directions for the inexperienced traveller to follow. A fireplace, furnished with a crane and a kettle for heating water, would be absolute luxuries. Being done, this glorious promenade—the equal of which does not exist in New England—would be taken with confidence by numbers, instead of, as now, by the few. It is the appropriate pendant of the ascent from the Glen by the carriage-road, or from Fabyan's by the railway. One can hardly pretend to have seen the mountains in their grandest aspects until he has threaded this wondrous picture-gallery, this marvellous hall of statues.[1]

While recrossing the plateau, from which Washington has the appearance of one mountain piled upon another, I suddenly came upon a dead sparrow in my path. Poor little fellow! he was too adventurous, and sunk on stiffening pinions beneath the frozen wind. Ten steps farther on a large brown butterfly flew up and fluttered cheerily along the path. Why, then, did the bird die and the butterfly live?

---

[1] A log-hut has been built near the summit of Mount Clinton since this was written. It is a good deed. But the long miles over the summits remain as yet neglected. Had one existed at the base of Monroe, it is probable that one life, at least, might have been saved. It is on the plain that danger and difficulties thicken.

This mountain butterfly, which endured cold that the bird could not, has excited the attention of naturalists, it is said. The mountain is 6293 feet high, and the butterflies never descend below an elevation of about 5600 feet. Here they "disport during the month of July of every year," thriving upon the scanty deposits of honey found in the flowers of the few species of hardy plants that grow in the crevices of the rocks at this great altitude, and upon other available liquid substances. The insect measures, from tip to tip of the expanded fore-wings, about one and eight-tenths inches. It is colored in shades of brown, with various bands and marblings diversifying the surface of the wings. The butterfly is known to naturalists as the *Œneis semidea*, and was first described, in 1828, by Thomas Say. An allied species occurs on Long's Peak and other elevated heights in Colorado; and another is found at Hopedale, Labrador; but they are confined to these widely separated localities. It is surmised that the butterfly, like the Alpine flora, beautifully illustrates the presence, or rather the advance and retreat, of the glacier.

I took up the little winged chorister of the vale who was not able to make spring come to the mountain for all his warbling. Truly, was not the little bird's fate typical of those ambitious climbers for fame who, chilled to death by neglect or indifference, die singing on the heights? So the sparrow's fall gave me food for reflection, during which I reached the little circular enclosure at the foot of the cone.

Once more I climbed the rambling and rocky stairs leading to the summit; but long before reaching it clouds were drifting above and below me. The day was to end like so many others. The crabbed old mountain had exhausted his store of benevolence. I hurried on down the Glen road. After descending a mile I heard a rumbling sound, deep and prolonged, like distant thunder. The thought of being overtaken on the mountain by a thunder-storm made me quicken my pace almost to a run. On turning the corner where the snow-bank had lain, like a lion in the path, devoutly wishing myself well and safely over, I felt something rise in my throat. The bank was no longer there. Every vestige of it had disappeared, and, in all probability, its sudden plunge down the mountain was what I had taken for thunder. Ten minutes sooner and I should have been upon its treacherous bridge.

I passed the Half-Way House, entered the dusk forest, where the tree-tops were swaying wildly to and fro, the birds flitting silently, and the tall pines discordantly humming, as if getting the pitch of the storm.

Suddenly it ·grew dark. A stream of fire blinded me with its glare. Then a deafening peal shook the solid earth. Another and another succeeded: Olympian salvos greeted the arrival of the storm king.

The rain was pattering among the leaves when I emerged into the open vale, guided by the lights of the Glen House shining through the darkness. My heavy feet almost refused to carry me farther, and I walked like the statue in " Don Juan."

THIRD JOURNEY.

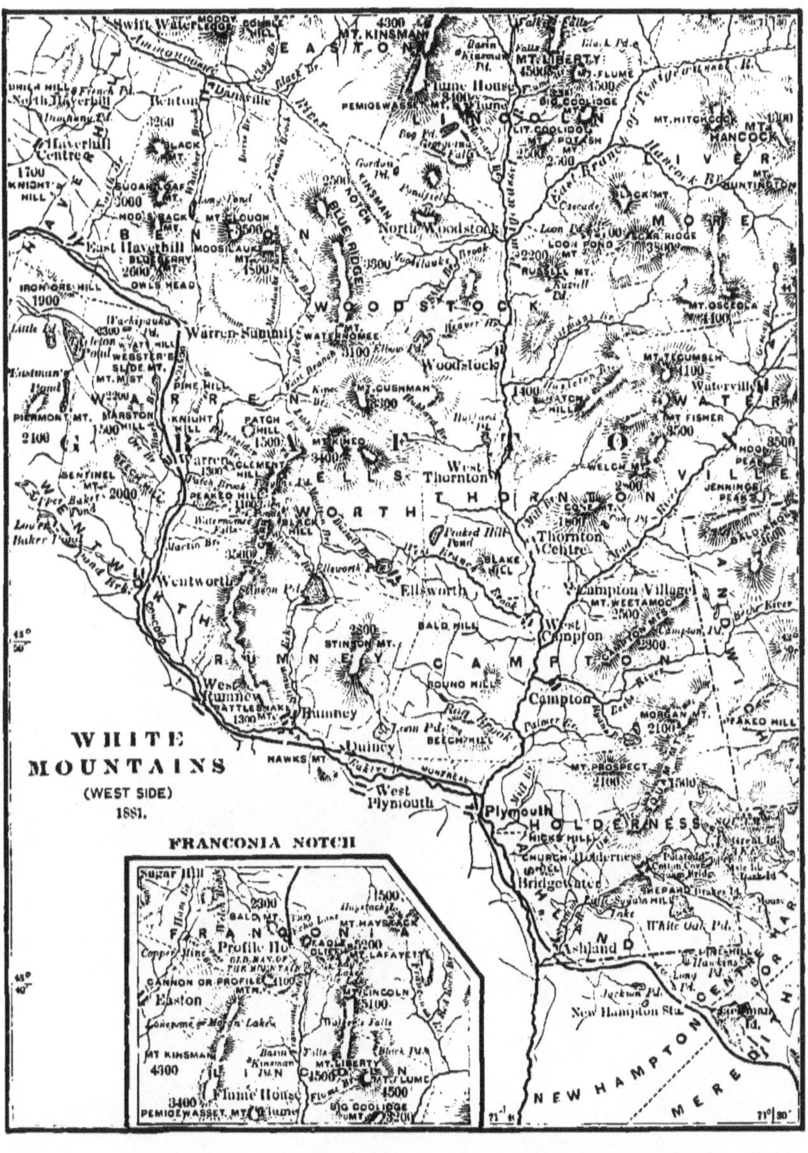

WHITE
MOUNTAINS
(WEST SIDE)
1881.

FRANCONIA NOTCH

THIRD JOURNEY.

I.

O child of that white-crested mountain whose springs
Gush forth in the shade of the cliff-eagle's wings,
Down whose slopes to the lowlands thy wild waters shine,
Leaping gray walls of rock, flashing through the dwarf-pine!

WHITTIER.

PLYMOUTH lies at the entrance to the Pemigewasset Valley, like an encampment pitched to dispute its passage. At present its design is to facilitate the ingress of tourists.

I am sitting at the window this morning looking down the Pemigewasset Valley. It is a gray, sad morning. Wet clouds hang and droop heavily over. In the distance the frayed and tattered edges are rolled up, half-disclosing the humid outlines of the hills on the other side of the valley. The trees are budded with rain-drops. Through a lattice of bordering foliage I look down upon the river, shrunken by drought to half its usual breadth, and exposing its parched bed of sand and pebbles. It gives an expiring gurgle in its stony throat. It is one of those mornings that, in spite of our philosophy, strangely affect the spirits, and are like a presentiment of evil. The clouds are funereal draperies; the river chants a dirge.

In this world of ours, where events push each other aside with such appalling rapidity, perhaps it is scarcely remembered that Hawthorne breathed his last in this house on the night of May 18th, 1864. He who was born in sight of these mountains had come among them to die.

In company with his old college mate and loving friend, General Pierce, he came from Centre Harbor to Plymouth the day previous to the sad event. Devoted friends—and few men have known more devoted—had for some time seen that his days were numbered. The fire

16

had all but gone out from his eye, which seemed interrogating the world of which he was already more than half an inhabitant. A presentiment of his approaching end seemed foreshadowed in the changed look and faltering step of Hawthorne himself: he walked like a man consciously going to his grave. Still, much was hoped—it could hardly be that much was expected—from this journey, and from the companionship of two men grown gray with care, each standing on the pinnacle of his ambition, each disappointed, but united, one to the other, by the ties of life-long friendship; turning their backs upon the gay world, and walking hand-in-hand among the sweet groves and pleasant streams like boys again. It was like a dream of their lost youth: the reality was no more.

On this journey General Pierce was the watchful, tender, and sympathetic nurse. Without doubt either of these men would have died for the other.

But these hopes, these cares, alas! proved delusive. The angel of death came unbidden into the sacred companionship; the shadow of his wings hovered over them unseen. In the night, without a sigh or a struggle, as he himself wished it might be, the hand of death was gently and kindly laid on the fevered brain and fluttering heart. In the morning his friend entered the chamber to find only the lifeless form of Nathaniel Hawthorne plunged in the slumber that knows no awakening. Great heart and mighty brain were stilled forever.

While the weather gives such inhospitable welcome let us employ the time by turning over a leaf from history. According to Farmer, the intervales here were formerly resorted to by the Indians for hunting and fishing. At the mouth of Baker's River, which here joins the Pemigewasset, they had a settlement. Graves, bones, gun-barrels, besides many implements of their rude husbandry, have been discovered. Here, it is said, the Indians were attacked by a party of English from Haverhill, Massachusetts, led by Captain Baker, who defeated them, killed many, and destroyed a large quantity of fur. From him Baker's River receives its name.

Before the French and Indian war broke out this region was debatable ground, into which only the most celebrated and intrepid white hunters ventured. Among these was a young man of twenty-three, named Stark, who lived near the Amoskeag Falls, in what is now Manchester. In April, 1752, Stark was hunting here with three companions, one of whom was his brother William. They had pitched their camp on Baker's

River, in the present limits of Rumney, and were prosecuting their hunt with good success, when they suddenly discovered the presence of Indians in their vicinity. Though it was a time of peace, they were not the less apprehensive on that account, and determined to change their position. But the Indians had also discovered the white hunters, and prepared to entrap them. When Stark went out very early the next morning to collect the traps he was intercepted and made prisoner. The Indians then took a position on the bank of the river to ambush his companions as they came down. Eastman, who was on the shore, next fell into their hands; but the two others were in a canoe floating quietly down the stream out of reach. Stark was ordered to hail and decoy them to the shore. He obeyed; but, instead of lending himself to the treachery, shouted to his friends that he was taken, and to save themselves. They instantly steered for the opposite shore, receiving a volley as they did so. Stinson, one of those in the boat, was shot dead; but William Stark escaped through the heroism of his brother, who knocked up the guns of the savages as they covered him with fatal aim.

Stark and his fellow-prisoner were taken to St. Francis by Actæon and his prowling band, with whom they had had the misfortune to fall in. At St. Francis the Indians set Stark hoeing their corn. At first he cut up the corn and spared the weeds; but this expedient not serving to relieve him of the drudgery, he threw his hoe into the river, telling his captors that hoeing corn was the business of squaws, not of warriors. This answer procured him recognition among them as a spirit worthy of themselves. He was adopted into the tribe, and called the "Young Chief." The promise of youth was fulfilled. The young hunter of the White Mountains and the conqueror of Bennington are the same.

The choice is open to leave the railway here and enter the mountains by the Pemigewasset Valley, or to continue by it the route which conducts to the summit of Mount Washington, by Bethlehem and Fabyan's. To journey on by rail to the Profile House is seventy-five miles, while by the common road, following the Pemigewasset, the distance is only thirty miles. A daily stage passes over this route, which I risk nothing in saying is always one of the delightful reminiscences of the whole journey. Deciding in favor of the last excursion, my first care was to procure a conveyance.

At three in the afternoon I set out for Campton, seven miles up the valley, which the carriage-road soon enters upon, and which by a few unregarded turnings is presently as fast shut up as if its mountain gates had in reality swung noiselessly together behind you. Hardly had I recovered from the effect of the deception produced by seeing the same mountain first in front, next on my right hand, and then shifted over to the other side of the valley, when I saw, spanned by a high bridge, the river in violent commotion far down below me.

The Pemigewasset, confined here between narrow banks, has cut for itself two deep channels through its craggy and cavernous bed; but one of these being dammed for the purpose of deepening the other, the general picturesqueness of the fall is greatly diminished. Still, it is a pretty and engaging sight, this cataract, especially if the river be full, although you think of a mettled Arabian harnessed in a tread-mill when you look at it. Livermore Fall, as it is called, is but two miles from Plymouth, the white houses of which look hot in the same brilliant sunlight that falls so gently upon the luxuriant green of the valley. The feature of this fall is the deep water-worn chasm through which it plunges.

By crossing the bridge here the left bank of the stream may be followed, the valley towns of Campton, Thornton, and Woodstock being divided by it into numerous villages or hamlets, frequently puzzling the uninitiated traveller, who has set out in all confidence, but who is seized by the most cruel perplexity, upon hearing that there are four villages in Campton, each several miles distant from the other. One would have pleased him far better.

Crossing this bridge, and descending to the level meadow below the falls, I made a brief inspection of the establishment for breeding and stocking with trout and salmon the depleted mountain streams of New Hampshire. The breeding-house and basins are situated just below the falls, on the banks of the river. This is a work undertaken by the State, with the expectation of repeopling its rivers, brooks, and ponds with their finny inhabitants. All those streams immediately accessible from the villages are so persistently fished by the inhabitants as to afford little sport to the angler from a distance, who is compelled to go farther and fare worse; but the State is certainly entitled to much credit for its endeavor to make two trout grow where only one grew before. It is feared, however, that the experiment of stocking the Pemigewasset with salmon will not prove successful. The farmers who live along the banks say that one of these fish is rarely seen, although the fishery is protected by the most rigid regulations. No one who has not visited the mountains be-

ON THE PROFILE ROAD.

tween May 1st—the earliest date when fishing is permitted—and the middle of June, can have an idea of the number of sportsmen every year resorting to the trout streams, or of the unheard-of drain upon those streams. Not the least of many ludicrous sights I have witnessed was that of a man, weighing two hundred pounds, excitedly swinging aloft a trout weighing less than two ounces, and this trophy he exhibited to me with unfeigned triumph—the butcher! This is mere slaughter, and ought not to be tolerated. A pretty sight is to see the breeding-trout follow you in your walk around the margin of their little basin to be fed from your hand. They are tame as pigeons and ravenous as sharks.

Mount Prospect, in Holderness, is the first landmark of note. It is seen, soon after leaving Plymouth, rising from the opposite side of the valley, its green crest commanding a superb view of the lake region below, and of the lofty Franconia Mountains above. It is worth ascending this mountain were it only to see again the beautiful islet-spotted Squam Lake and far-reaching Winnipiseogee quivering in noonday splendor.

The beautiful valley is now open throughout its whole extent. Of course I refer only to that portion lying above Plymouth. But it is an anomaly of mountain valleys. Its length is about twenty-five miles, and its greatest width, I should judge, not more than three or four. For twenty miles it is almost as straight as an arrow. There is nothing to hinder a perfectly free and open view up or down. Contrast this with the wilful and tortuous windings of the Ammonoosuc, or the Saco, which seem to grope and feel their way foot by foot along their cramped and crooked channels. The angle of ascent, too, is here so gradual as to be scarcely noticed until the foot of the mountain wall, at its head, is reached. True, this valley is not clothed with a feeling of overpowering grandeur, but it is beautiful. It is not terrible, but bewitching.

The vista of mountains on the east side of the valley becomes every moment more and more extended, and more and more interesting. A long array of summits trending away to the north, with detached mountains heaved above the lower clusters, like great whales sporting in a frozen sea, is gradually uncovered. Green as a carpet, level as a floor, the valley, adorned with clumps of elms, groves of maples, and strips of tilled land of a rich chocolate brown, makes altogether a picture which sets the eye fairly dancing. Even the daisies, the clover, and the buttercups which so plentifully spangle the meadows seem far brighter **and** sweeter in this atmosphere, nodding a playful welcome as you **pass** them by. We are in the country of flowers.

Since passing Blair's and the bridge over the river to Campton Hollow I was on the alert for that first and most engaging view of the Franconia Mountains which has been so highly extolled. Perhaps I should say that one poetic nature has revealed it to a thousand others. Without doubt this landscape is the more striking because it is the first, and consequently deepest, impression of grand mountain scenery obtained by those upon whom at a turn of the road, and without premonition, it flashes like the realization of some ecstatic vision.

Half a mile below the little hamlet of West Campton the road crosses the point of a hill pushed well out into the valley. It is here that the circlet of mountains is seen enclosing the valley on all sides like a gigantic palisade. In one place, far away in the north, this wall is shattered to its centre, like the famous Breach of Roland; and through this enormous loop-hole we see golden mists rising above the undiscovered country beyond. We are looking through the far-famed Franconia Notch. On one side the clustered peaks of Lafayette lift themselves serenely into the sky. On the left a silvery light is playing on the ledges of Mount Cannon, softening all the asperities of this stern-visaged mountain. The two great groups now stand fully and finely exposed; though the lower and nearer summits are blended with the higher by distance. Remark the difference of outline. A series of humps marks the crest-line of the group, which culminates in the oblique wall of Mount Cannon. On the contrary, that on the right, culminating in Lafayette, presents two beautiful and regular pyramids, older than Cheops, which sometimes in early morning exactly resemble two stately monuments, springing alert and vigorous as the day which gilds them. At a distance of twenty miles it demands good eyes and a clear atmosphere to detect the supporting lines of these pyramidal structures, which in reality are two separate mountains, Liberty and Flume. This exquisite landscape seldom fails of producing a rapturous outburst from those who are making the journey for the first time.

There are many points of resemblance between this view and that of the White Mountains from Conway Corner. Both unfold at once, and in a single glance, the principal systems about which all the subordinate chains seem manœuvring under the commanding gaze of Washington or Lafayette.

Soon after starting it was evident that my driver's loquaciousness was due to his having "crooked his elbow" too often while loitering about Plymouth. The frequent plunge of the wheels into the ditches by the roadside, accompanied with a shower of mud, was little conducive to the calm and free enjoyment of the beauties of the landscape. The driver alone was unconcerned, and as often as good fortune enabled him to steer clear of upsetting his passengers would articulate, thickly. "Don't be alarmed, Cap': no one was ever hurt on this road."

Silently committing myself to that Providence which is said to watch over the destinies of tipplers, I breathed freely only when we drew up at the hospitable door of the village inn, bespattered with mud, but with no broken bones.

Sanborn's, at West Campton, is the old road-side inn that long ago swung the stag-and-hounds as its distinctive emblem. A row of superb maples shades the road. Here we have fairly entered the renowned intervales, that gleam among the darker forests or groves like patches of blue in a storm-clouded sky. Looking southward, across the level meadows, the hills of Rumney flinging up smooth, firm curves, and the more distant, downward-plunging outline of Mount Prospect, in Holderness, close the valley. Upon the left, where the clearings extend quite to the summits of the near hills, the maple groves interspersed among them resemble soldiers advancing up the green slopes in columns of attack. Following this line a little, the valley of Mad River is distinguished by the deep trough through which it descends from the mountains of Waterville. And here, peering over the nearer elevations, the huge blue-black mass of Black Mountain flings two splendid peaks aloft.

For a more intimate acquaintance with these surroundings the hillside pasture above the school-house gives a perspective of greater breadth; while that from the Ellsworth road is in some respects finer still. About two miles up this road the valley of the East Branch, showing the massive Mount Hancock, cicatriced with one long, narrow scar, is lifted into view. The other features of the landscape remain the same, except that Mount Cannon is now cut off by the hill rising to the north of us. As often as one of these hidden valleys is thus revealed we are seized with a longing to explore it.

One need not push inquiry into the antecedents of Campton or the neighboring villages very far. The township was originally granted to General Jabez Spencer, of East Haddam, Connecticut, in 1761. In 1768 a few families had come into Campton, Plymouth, Hebron, Sandwich, Rumney, Holderness, and Bridgewater. No opening had been made for civilized men on this side of Canada except for three families, who

had gone fifty miles into the wilderness to begin a settlement where Lancaster now is. The name is derived simply from the circumstance that the first proprietors built a camp when they visited their grant. The

WELCH MOUNTAIN, FROM MAD RIVER.

different villages are much frequented by artists, who have spread the fame of Campton from one end of the Union to the other. But a serpent has entered even this Eden—the villagers are sighing for the advent of the railway.

Having dedicated one day to an exploration of the Mad River Valley, I can pronounce it well worth any tourist's while to tarry long enough in the vicinity for the purpose. It is certainly one of the finest exhibitions of mountain scenery far or near. Here is a valley twelve miles long, at the bottom of which a rapid river bruises itself on a bed of broken rock, while above it are heaped mountains to be picked out of a thousand for peculiarity of form or structure. The Pemigewasset is passed by a ford just deep enough at times to invest the journey with a little healthy excitement at the very beginning. The ford has, however, been carefully marked by large stones placed at the edge of the submerged road.

Fording the river and climbing the hill which lies across the entrance to this land-locked valley, I was at once ushered upon a scene of great and varied charm. Right before me, sunning his three peaks four thousand feet above, was the prodigious mass of Black Mountain. Far up the valley it stretched, forming an unbroken wall nearly ten miles long, and apparently scaling all access from the Sandwich side. A nipple, a pyramid, and a flattened mound protruding from the summit ridge constitute these eminences, easily recognized from the Franconia highway among a host of lesser peaks. At the southern end of this mountain the range is broken through, giving passage to a rough and straggling road—fourteen hundred feet above the sea-level—to Sandwich Centre, and to the lake towns south of it. This pass is known as Sandwich Notch.

Campton Village lies along the hill-slope opposite to Black Mountain. Completely does it fill the artistic sense. Its situation leaves nothing to be desired in an ideal mountain village. So completely is it secluded from the rest of the world by its environment of mountains, that you might pass and repass the Pemigewasset Valley a hundred times without once surprising the secret of its existence. All those houses, half hid beneath groves of maples, bespeak luxurious repose. Opposite to Black Mountain, whose dark forest drapery hides the mass of the mountain, is the immense whitish-yellow rock called Welch Mountain. Only a scanty vegetation is suffered to creep among the crevices. It is really nothing but a big excrescent rock, having a principal summit shaped somewhat like a Martello tower; and, indeed, resembling one in ruins. The bright ledges brilliantly reflect the sun, causing the eye to turn gratefully to the sombre gloom of the evergreens crowding the sides of the neighboring mountains. Welch Mountain reminded me, I hardly know why, of Chocorua; but the resemblance can scarcely extend farther than to the meagreness, mutually characteristic, and to the blistered, almost calcined ledges, which in each case catch the earliest and latest beams of day. In fact, I could think only of a leper sunning his scars, and in rags.

At the head of the vale, alternately coming into and retreating from view—for we are still progressing—is the mysterious triple-crowned mountain known on the maps as Tripyramid. When first seen it seems standing solitary and alone, and to have wrapped itself in a veil of thinnest gauze. As we advance it displays the white streak of an immense slide, which occurred in 1869. This mountain is visible from the shore of the lake at Laconia. It is one of the first to greet us from the elevated summits, though from no point is its singularly admirable and well-proportioned architecture so advantageously exhibited as when approaching by this valley. Its northern peak stands farthest from the others, yet not so far as to mar the general grace and harmony of form. Hail to thee, mountain of the high, heroic crest, for thy fortunate name and the gracious, kingly mien with which thou wearest thy triple crown! Prince thou art and potentate. None approach thy forest courts but do thee homage.

The end of the valley was reached in two hours of very leisurely driving. The road abruptly terminated among a handful of houses scattered about the bottom of a deep and narrow vale. This is, beyond question, the most remarkable mountain glen into which civilization has thus far penetrated. On looking up at the big mountains one experiences a half-stifled feeling; and, on looking around the scattered hamlet, its dozen houses seem undergoing perpetual banishment.

This diminutive settlement, in which signs of progress and decay stand side by side—progress evidenced by new and showy cottages; decay by abandoned and dilapidated ones—is at the edge of a region as shaggy and wild as any in the famed Adirondack wilderness. It fairly jostles the wilderness. It braves it. It is really insolent. Yet are its natural resources so slender that the struggle to keep the breath in it must have been long and obstinate. A wheezy saw-mill indicates

BLACK AND TRIPYRAMID MOUNTAINS.

at once its origin and its means of livelihood; but it is evident that it might have remained obscure and unknown until doomsday, had not a few anglers stumbled upon it while in pursuit of brooks and waters new.

The glen is surrounded by peaks that for boldness, savage freedom, and power challenge any that we can remember. They threaten while maintaining an attitude of lofty scorn for the saucy intruder. The curious Noon Peak—we have at length got to the end of the almost endless Black

Mountain—nods familiarly from the south. It long stood for a sun-dial for the settlement; hence its name. Tecumseh, a noble mountain, and Osceola, its worthy companion, rise to the north. A short walk in this direction brings Kancamagus[1] and the gap between this mountain and Osceola into view. All these mountains stand in the magnificent order in which they were first placed by Nature; but never does the idea of inertia, of helpless immobility, cross the mind of the beholder for a single moment.

The unvisited region between Greeley's, in Waterville, and the Saco is destined to be one of the favorite haunts of the sportsman, the angler, and the lover of the grand old woods. It is crossed and recrossed by swift streams, sown with lakes, glades, and glens, and thickly set with mountains, among which the timid deer browses, and the bear and wild-cat roam unmolested. Fish and game, untamed and untrodden moun-tains and woods, welcome the sportsman here. With Greeley's for a base, encampments may be pitched in the forest, and exploration carried into the most out-of-the-way corners. The full zest of such a life can only be understood by those to whom its freedom and unrestraint, its health-ful and vigorous existence, have already proved their charm. The time may come when the mountains shall be covered with a thousand tents, and the summer-dwellers will resemble the tribes of Israel encamped by the sweet waters of Sion.

Waterville maintains unfrequent communication with Livermore and the Saco by a path twelve miles long—constructed by the Appalachian Mountain Club—over which a few pedestrians pass every year. I have explored this path for several miles beyond Beckytown while visiting the great slide which sloughed off from the side of Tripyramid, and the cas-cades on the way to it. Osceola, Hancock, and Carrigain, three remark-ably fine mountains, offer inviting excursions to expert climbers. I was reluctantly compelled to renounce the intention of passing over the whole route, which should occupy, at least, two days or parts of days, one night being spent in camp.

The Mad River drive is a delightful episode. In the way of moun-tain valley there is nothing like it. Bold crag, furious torrent, lonely cabin, blue peak, deep hollow, choked up with the densest foliage, con-stitute its varied and ever-changing features. The overhanging woods

---

[1] Kancamagus, the Pennacook sachem, led the Indian assault on Dover, in 1689.

FRANCONIA NOTCH, FROM THORNTON.

looked as if it had been raining sunshine; the road like an endless grotto of illuminated leaves, musical with birds, and exhaling a thousand perfumes.

The remainder of the route up the Pemigewasset is more and more a revelation of the august summits that have so constantly met us since entering this lovely valley. Boldly emerging from the mass of mountains, they present themselves at every mile in new combinations. Through Thornton and Woodstock the spectacle continues almost without intermission. Gradually, the finely-pointed peaks of the Lafayette group deploy and advance toward us. Now they pitch sharply down into the valley of the East Branch. Now the great shafts of stone are crusted with silvery light, or sprayed with the cataract. Now the sun gilds the slides that furrow, but do not deface them. Stay a moment at this rapid brook that comes hastening from the west! It is an envoy from yonder great, billowy mountain that lords it so proudly over

> "many a nameless slide-scarred crest
> And pine-dark gorge between."

That is Moosehillock. Facing again the north, the road is soon swallowed up by the forest, and the forest by the mountains. A few poor cottages skirt the route. Still ascending, the miles grow longer and less interesting, until the white house, first seen from far below, suddenly stands uncovered at the left. We are at the Flume House, and before the gates of the Franconia Notch.

II.

THE FRANCONIA PASS.

Beyond them, like a sun-rimmed cloud,
The great Notch Mountains shone,
Watched over by the solemn-browed
And awful face of stone!—WHITTIER.

WHEN Boswell exclaimed in ecstasy, "An immense mountain!" Dr. Johnson sneered, "An immense protuberance!" but he, the sublime cynic, became respectful before leaving the Hebrides. Charles Lamb, too, at one time pretended something approaching contempt for mountains; but, after a visit to Coleridge, he made the *amende honorable* in these terms:

"I feel I shall remember your mountains to the last day of my life. They haunt me perpetually. I am like a man who has been falling in love unknown to himself; which he finds out when he leaves the lady."

Notwithstanding their prepossessions against nature, and their undisguised preference for the smoke and dirt of London, the mountains awoke something in these two men which was apparently a revelation of themselves unto themselves. I have felt a higher respect for both since I knew that they loved mountains, as I pity those who have only seen heaven through the smoke of the city. It is not easy to explain two ideas so essentially opposite as are presented in the earlier and later declarations of these widely famous authors, unless we agree, keeping "Elia's" odd simile in mind, that in the first case they should, like woman, be taken, not at what she says, but what she means.

The Flume House is the proper tarrying-place for an investigation of the mountain gorge from which it derives both its custom and its name. It is also placed opposite to the Pool, another of those natural wonders with which the pass is crowded, and which tempt us at every step to turn aside from the travelled road.

Fronting the hotel is a belt of woods, with two massive mountains rising behind. In the concealment of these woods the Pemigewasset, contracted to a modest stream, runs along the foot of the mountains. A rough, zigzag path leads through the woods to the river and to the Pool. Now raise the eyes to the summit-ridge of yonder mountain. The peak finely reproduces the features of a gigantic human face, while the undulations of the ridge fairly suggest a recumbent human figure wrapped in a shroud. The outlines of the forehead and nose are curiously like the profile of Washington; hence the colossal figure is called Washington Lying in State. This immortal sculpture gave rise to the idea that the tomb of Washington, like that of Desaix, on the St. Bernard, should be on the great summit that bears his name.

A GLIMPSE OF THE POOL.

From the Flume House I looked up through the deep cleft of the Notch— an impressive vista. To the left is Cannon, or Profile Mountain; to the right the beetling crags of Eagle Cliff; then the pointed, shapely peaks of Lafayette; and so the range continues breaking off and off, bending away into lesser mountains that finally melt into pale-blue shadows. Now a stray cloud atop a peak gives it a volcanic character. Now a puff scatters it like thistle-down. It is a sultry summer's morning, and banks of film hang like huge spider's-webs in the tree-tops. Soon they detach themselves, and, floating lazily upward, are seized by a truant breeze, spun mischievously round, and then settle quietly down on the highest peaks like young eaglets on their nest.

Let us first walk down to the Pool. This Pool is a caprice of the river. Imagine a cistern, deeply sunk in granite, receiving at one end a weary cascade, which seems to crave a moment's rest before hurrying on down the rocky pass. In the mystery and seclusion of ages, and with only the rude implements picked up by the way, the river has hollowed a basin a hundred feet wide and forty deep out of the stubborn rock. Without doubt Nature thus first taught us to cut the hardest marble with sand and water. Cliffs traversed by cracks rise a hundred feet higher. The water is a glossy and lustrous sea-green, and of such marvellous transparency that you see the brilliant pebbles sparkling at the bottom, shifting with the waves of light like bits of glass in a kaleidoscope. Overtopping trees lean timidly over and peer down into the Pool, which coldly repulses their shadows. Only the colorless hue of the rocks is reflected; and the stranger, seeing an old man with a gray beard standing erect in a boat, has no other idea than that he has arrived on the borders and is to be accosted by the ferryman of Hades.

The Flume is reached by going down the road a short distance, and then diverging to the left and crossing the river to the Flume Brook. A carriage-way conducts almost to the entrance of the gorge. Then begins an easy and interesting promenade up the bed of the brook.

This is a remarkable rock-gallery, driven several hundred feet into the heart of the mountain, through which an ice-cold brook rushes. The miracle of Moses seems repeated here sublimely. Some unknown power smote the rock, and the prisoned stream gushed forth free and lightsome as air. You approach it over broad ledges of freckled granite, polished by the constant flow of a thin, pellucid sheet of water to slippery smoothness. Proceeding a short distance up this natural esplanade, you enter a damp and gloomy fissure between perpendicular walls, rising seventy feet above the stream, and, on lifting your eyes suddenly, espy an enormous bowlder tightly wedged between the cliffs. Now try to imagine a force capable of grasping the solid rock and dividing it in halves as easily as you would an apple with your two hands.

At sight of the suspended bowlder, which seems, like Paul Pry, to have "just dropped in," I believe every visitor has his moment of hesitation, which he usually ends by passing underneath, paying as he goes with a tremor of the nerves, more or less, for his temerity. But there is no danger. It is seen that the deep crevice, into which the rock seems jammed with the especial purpose of holding it asunder, also hugs the intruder like a vise; so closely, indeed, that, according to every appearance, it must stay where it is until doomsday, unless released by some passing earthquake from its imprisonment. Sentimental tourists do not omit to find a moral in this curiosity, which really looks to be on the eve of dropping, with a loud splash, into the torrent beneath. On top of the cliffs I picked up a visiting-card, on which some one with a poetic turn had written, "Does not this bowlder remind you of

THE FLUME, FRANCONIA NOTCH.

the sword of Damocles?" To a civil question, civil reply: No; to me it looks like a nut in a cracker.

Over the gorge bends an arcade of interlaced foliage shot through and through with sunshine; and wherever cleft or cranny can be found young birches, sword-ferns, trailing vines, insinuating their long roots in the damp mould, garland the cold granite with tenderest green. The exquisite white anemone blooms in the mossy wall wet with tiny streams that do not run but glide unperceived down. What could be more cunning than the persistency with which these hardy waifs, clinging or drooping along the craggy way, draw their sustenance from the rock, which seems to nourish them in spite of itself? Underneath your feet the swollen torrent storms along the gorge, dashing itself recklessly against intruding bowlders, or else passing them with a curl of disdain. How gallantly it surmounts every obstacle in its way! How crystal-clear are its waters! On it speeds, scattering pearls and diamonds right and left, like the prodigal it is; unpolluted, as yet, by the filth of cities, or turned into a languid, broken-spirited drudge by dams or mill-wheels. 'Stop me?" it seems exclaiming. "Why, I am offspring of the clouds, their messenger to the parched earth, the mountain maid-of-all-work! Stay; step aside here in the sun and I will show you my rainbow-signet! When I rest, do you not behold the mother imaged in the features of the child? Stop me! Put your hand in my bosom and see how strong and full of life are my pulse-beats. To-morrow I shall be vapor. Thought is not freer. I do not belong to earth any more than the eagle sailing above yonder mountain-top."

Overhead a fallen tree-trunk makes a crazy bridge from cliff to cliff. The sight of the gorge, with the flood foaming far below, the glitter of falling waters through the trees, the splendid light in the midst of deepest gloom, the solemn pines—the odorous forest, the wildness and the coolness—impart an indescribable charm to the spot that makes us reluctant to leave it. Many ladies ascend to the head of the gorge and, crossing on the rude bridge, leave their visiting-cards on the other side; one had left her pocket-handkerchief, with the scent fresh upon it. I picked it up, and out hopped a toad.

After the Pool and the Flume, an ascent of the mountain behind the hotel will be found conducive to enjoyment of another kind. This mountain commands delicious views of the valley of the Pemigewasset. A short hour is usually sufficient for the climb. It was a very raw, windy morning on which I climbed it, but the uncommon purity of the air and the exceeding beauty of the landscape were most rarely combined with cloud effects seen only in conjunction with a brisk north-west wind. I had taken a station similar to that occupied by Mount Willard with respect to the Saco Valley, now opening a vista essentially different from that most memorable one in my mountain experience. The valley is not the same. You see the undulating course of the river for many leagues, and but for an intercepting hill, which hides them, might distinguish the houses of Plymouth. The vales of Woodstock, Thornton, and Campton, spotted with white houses, lie outspread in the sun, between enclosing mountains; and the windings of the Pemigewasset are now seen dark and glossy, now white with foam, appearing, disappearing, and finally lost to view in the blended distance. The sky was packed with clouds. Over the vivid green of the intervales their black shadows drifted swiftly and noiselessly, first turning the light on, then off again, with magical effect. To look up and see these clouds all in motion, and then, looking down, see those weird draperies darkly trailing over the land, was a reminiscence of

> "The dim and shadowy armies of our unquiet dreams—
> Their footsteps brush the dewy fern and paint the shaded streams."

The mountain ridges flowed southward with marvellous smoothness to the vanishing-point, on one side of the valley bright green, on the other indigo blue. This picture was not startling, like that from the Crawford Notch, but, in its own way, was incomparable. The sunsets are said to be beautiful beyond description.

One looks up the Notch upon the great central peaks composing the water-shed—Cannon, Lafayette, Lincoln, and the rest—to see crags, ridges, black forests, rising before him in all their gloomy magnificence.

On one side all is beauty, harmony, and grace; on the other, a packed mass of bristling, steep-sided mountains seem storming the sky with their gray turrets. Could we but look over the brawny shoulders of the mountains opposite to us, the eye would take in the vast, untrodden solitudes of the Pemigewasset forests cut by the East Branch and presided over by Mount Carrigain—a region as yet reserved for those restless and adventurous spirits whom the beaten paths of travel have ceased to charm or attract. But an excursion into this "forest primeval" is to be no holiday promenade. It is an arduous and difficult march

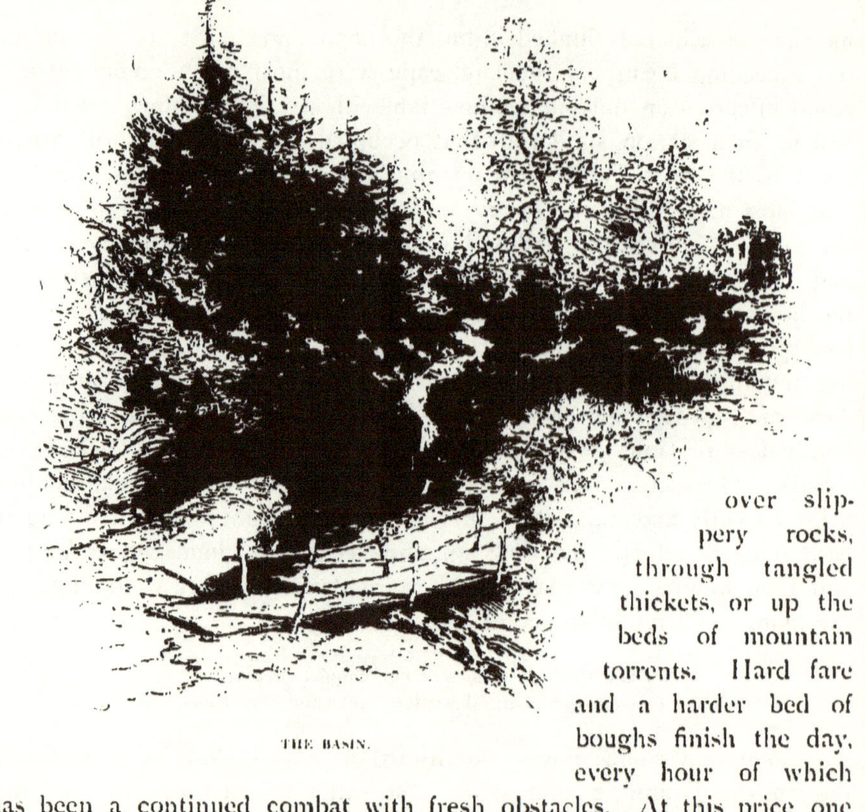

THE BASIN.

over slippery rocks, through tangled thickets, or up the beds of mountain torrents. Hard fare and a harder bed of boughs finish the day, every hour of which has been a continued combat with fresh obstacles. At this price one may venture to encounter the virgin wilderness or, as the cant phrase is, "try roughing it." It is a curious feeling to turn your back upon the last cart-path, then upon the last foot-path; to hear the distant baying of a hound grow fainter and fainter—in a word, to exchange at a single step the sights and sounds of civilized life, the movement, the bustle, for a silence broken only by the hum of bees and the murmur of invisible waters.

I left the Flume House in company with a young-old man, whom I met there, and in whom I hoped to find another and a surer pair of eyes, for, were he to have as many as Argus, the sight-seer would find employment for them all.

While gayly threading the green-wood, we came upon a miniature edition of the Pool, situated close to the highway, called the Basin. A basin in fact it is, and a bath fit for the gods. It is plain to see that the stream once poured over the smooth ledges here, instead of making its exit by the present channel. A cascade falls into it with hollow roar. This cistern has been worn by the rotary motion of large pebbles which the little cascade, pouring down into it from above, set and kept actively whirling and grinding at its own mad caprice. But this was not the work of a day. Long and constant attrition only could have scooped this cavity out of the granite, which is here so clean, smooth, and white, and filled to the brim with a grayish-emerald water, light, limpid, and incessantly replenished by the effervescent cascade. In the beginning this was doubtless an insignificant crevice, into which a few pebbles and a handful of sand were dropped by the stream, but which, having no way of escape, were kept in a perpetual tread-mill, until what was at first a mere hole became as we now see it. The really curious feature of the stone basin is a strip of granite projecting into it which closely resembles a human leg and foot, luxuriously cooling itself in the stream. Such queer freaks of nature are not merely curious, but they while away the hours so agreeably that time and distance are forgotten.

As we walked on, the hills were constantly hemming us in closer and closer. Suddenly we entered a sort of crater, with high mountains all around. One impulse caused us to halt and look about us. In full view at our left the inaccessible precipices of Mount Cannon rose above a mountain of shattered stones, which ages upon ages of battering have torn piecemeal from it. Its base was heaped high with these ruins. Seldom has it fallen to my lot to see anything so grandly typical of the indomitable as this sorely battered and disfigured mountain citadel, which nevertheless lifts and will still lift its unconquerable battlements so long as one stone remains upon another. Hewed and hacked, riven and torn, gashed and defaced in countless battles, one can hardly repress an emotion of pity as well as of admiration. I do not recollect, in all these mountains, another such striking example of the denuding forces with which they are perpetually at war. When we see mountains crumbling before our very eyes, may we not begin to doubt the stability of things that we are pleased to call eternal? Still, although it seems erected solely for the pastime of all the powers of destruction, this one, so glorious in its unconquerable resolve to die at its post—this one, exposing its naked breast to the fury of its deadliest foes—so stern and terrific of aspect, so high and haughty, so dauntlessly throwing down the gauntlet to Fate itself—assures us that the combat will be long and obstinate, and that the mountain will fall at last, if fall it must, with the grace and heroism of a gladiator in the Roman arena. The gale flies at it with a shriek of impotent rage. Winter strips off its broidered tunic and flings white dust in its aged face. Rust corrodes, rains drench, fires scorch it; lightning and frost are forever searching out the weak spots in its harness; but, still uplifting its adamantine crest, it receives unshaken the stroke or the blast, spurns the lightning, mocks the thunder, and stands fast. Underneath is a little lake, which at sunset resembles a pool of blood that has trickled drop by drop from the deep wounds in the side of the mountain.

We are still advancing in this region of wonders. In our front soars an insuperable mass of forest-shagged rock. Behind it rises the absolutely regal Lafayette. Our footsteps are stayed by the glimmer of water through trees by the road-side. We have reached the summit of the pass.

Six miles of continued ascent from the Flume House have brought us to Profile Lake, which the road skirts. Although a pretty enough piece of water, it is not for itself this lake is resorted to by its thousands, or for being the source of the Pemigewasset, or for its trout—which you take for the reflection of birds on its burnished surface—but for the mountain rising high above, whose wooded slopes it so faithfully mirrors. Now lift the eyes to the bare summit! It is difficult to believe the evidence of the senses! Upon the high cliffs of this mountain is the remarkable and celebrated natural rock sculpture of a human head, which, from a height twelve hundred feet above the lake, has for uncounted ages looked with the same stony stare down the pass upon the windings of the river through its incomparable valley. The profile itself measures about forty feet from the tip of the chin to the flattened crown which imparts to it such a peculiarly antique appearance. All is perfect, except that the forehead is concealed by something like the visor of a helmet. And all this illusion is produced by several projecting crags. It might be said to have been begotten by a thunder-bolt.

Taking a seat within a rustic arbor on the high shore of the lake, one is at liberty to peruse at leisure what, I dare say, is the most extraordinary sight of a lifetime. A change of position varies more or less the character of the expression, which is, after all, the marked peculiarity of this monstrous *alto relievo;* for let the spectator turn his gaze vacantly upon the more familiar objects at hand—as he inevitably will, to assure himself that he is not the victim of some strange hallucination—a fascination born neither of admiration nor horror, but strongly partaking of both emotions, draws him irresistibly back to the Dantesque head stuck, like a felon's, on the highest battlements of the pass. The more you may have seen, the more your feelings are disciplined, the greater the confusion of ideas. The moment is come to acknowledge yourself vanquished. This is not merely a face, it is a portrait. That is not the work of some cunning chisel, but a cast from a living head. You feel and will always maintain that those features have had a living and breathing counterpart. Nothing more, nothing less.

But where and what was the original prototype? Not man; since, ages before he was created, the chisel of the Almighty wrought this sculpture upon the rock above us. No, not man; the face is too majestic, too nobly grand, for anything of mortal mould. One of the antique gods may, perhaps, have sat for this archetype of the coming man. And yet not man, we think, for the head will surely hold the same strange converse with futurity when man shall have vanished from the face of the earth.

This gigantic silhouette, which has been dubbed the Old Man of the Mountain, is unquestionably the greatest curiosity of this or any other mountain region. It is unique. But it is not merely curious; nor is it more marvellous for the wonderful accuracy of outline than for the almost superhuman expression of frozen terror it eternally fixes on the vague and shadowy distance—a far-away look; an intense and speechless amazement, such as sometimes settles on the faces of the dying at the moment the soul leaves the body forever—untranslatable into words, but seeming to declare the presence of some unutterable vision, too bright and dazzling for mortal eyes to behold. The face puts the whole world behind it. It does everything but speak—nay, you are ready to swear that it is going to speak! And so this chance jumbling together of a few stones has produced a sculpture before which Art hangs her head.

I renounce in dismay the idea of reproducing the effect on the reader's mind which this prodigy produced on my own. Impressions more pronounced, yet at the same time more inexplicable, have never so effectually overcome that habitual self-command derived from many experiences of travel among strange and unaccustomed scenes. From the moment the startled eye catches it one is aware of a *Presence* which dominates the spirit, first with strange fear, then by that natural revulsion which at such moments makes the imagination supreme, conducts straight to the supernatural, there to leave it helplessly struggling in a maze of impotent conjecture. But, even upon this debatable ground, between two worlds, one is not able to surprise the secret of those lips of marble. The Sphinx overcomes us by his stony, his disdainful silence. Let the visitor be ever so unimpassioned, surely he

THE OLD MAN OF THE MOUNTAIN.

must be more than mortal to resist the impression of mingled awe, wonder, and admiration which a first sight of this weird object forces upon him. He is, indeed, less than human if the feeling does not continually grow and deepen while he looks. The face is so amazing, that I have often tried to imagine the sensations of him who first discovered it peering from the top of the mountain with such absorbed, openmouthed wonder. Again I see the tired Indian hunter, pausing to slake his thirst by the lake-side, start as his gaze suddenly encounters this terrific apparition. I fancy the half-uttered exclamation sticking in his throat. I behold him standing there with bated breath, not daring to stir hand or foot, his white lips parted, his scared eyes dilated, until his own swarthy features exactly reflect that unearthly, that intense amazement stamped large and vivid upon the livid rock. There he remains, rooted to the spot, unable to reason, trembling in every limb. For him there are no accidents of nature; for him everything has its design. His moment of terrible suspense is hardly difficult to understand, seeing how careless thousands that come and go are thrilled, and awed, and silenced, notwithstanding you tell them the face is nothing but rocks.

If the effect upon minds of the common order be so pronounced, a first sight of the Great Stone Face may easily be supposed to act powerfully upon the imaginative and impressible. The novelist, Hawthorne, makes it the interpreter of a noble life. For him the Titanic countenance is radiant with majestic benignity. He endows it with a soul, surrounds the colossal brow with the halo of a spiritual grandeur, and, marshalling his train of phantoms, proceeds to pass inexorable judgment upon them. Another legend—like its predecessor, too long for our pages—runs to the effect that a painter who had resolved to paint Christ sitting in judgment, and who was filled with the grandeur of his subject, wandered up and down the great art palaces, the cathedrals of the Old World, seeking in vain a model which should in all things be the embodiment of his ideal. In despair at the futility of his search he hears a strange report, brought by some pious missionaries from the New World, of a wonderful image of the human face which the Indians looked upon with sacred veneration. The painter immediately crossed the sea, and caused himself to be guided to the spot, where he beheld, in the profile of the great White Mountains, the object of his search and fulfilment of his dream. The legend is entitled *Christus Judex*.

Had Byron visited this place of awe and mystery, his "Manfred," the scene of which is laid among the mountains of the Bernese Alps, would doubtless have had a deeper and perhaps gloomier impulse; but even among the eternal realms of ice the poet never beheld an object that could so arouse the gloomy exaltation he has breathed into that tragedy. His line—

> "Bound to earth, he lifts his eye to heaven"—

becomes descriptive here.

Again and again we turn to the face. We go away to wonder if it is still there. We come back to wonder still more. An emotion of pity-mingles with the rest. Time seems to have passed it by. It seems undergoing some terrible sentence. It is a greater riddle than the gigantic stone face on the banks of the Nile.

All effects of light and shadow are so many changes of countenance or of expression. I have seen the face cut sharp and clear as an antique cameo upon the morning sky. I have seen it suffused, nay, almost transfigured, in the sunset glow. Often and often does a cloud rest upon its brow. I have seen it start fitfully out of the flying scud to be the next moment smothered in clouds. I have heard the thunder roll from its lips of stone. I recall the sunken cheeks, wet with the damps of its night-long vigil, glistening in the morning sunshine—smiling through tears. I remember its emaciated visage streaked and crossed with wrinkles that the snow had put there in a night; but never have I seen it insipid or commonplace. On the contrary, the overhanging brow, the antique nose, the protruding under-lip, the massive chin, might belong to another Prometheus chained to the rock, but whom no punishment could make lower his haughty head.

I lingered by the margin of the lake watching the play of the clouds upon the water, until a loud and resonant peal, followed by large, warm drops, admonished me to seek the nearest shelter. And what thunder! The hills rocked. What echoes! The mountains seemed knocking their stony heads together. What lightning! The very heavens cracked with the flashes.

> " Far along
> From peak to peak the rattling crags among
> Leaps the live thunder! not from one lone cloud,
> But every mountain now hath found a tongue,
> And Jura answers, through her misty shroud,
> Back to the joyous Alps, who call to her aloud!"

III.

THE KING OF FRANCONIA.

> Hills draw like heaven
> And stronger, sometimes, holding out their hands
> To pull you from the vile flats up to them.
>
> E. B. BROWNING.

AT noon we reached the spacious and inviting Profile House, which is hid away in a deep and narrow glen, nearly two thousand feet above the sea. No situation could be more sequestered or more charming. The place seems stolen from the unkempt wilderness that shuts it in. An oval, grassy plain, not extensive, but bright and smiling, spreads its green between a grisly precipice and a shaggy mountain. And there, if you will believe me, in front of the long, white-columned hotel, like a Turkish rug on a carpet, was a pretty flower-garden. Like those flowers on the lawn were beauties sauntering up and down in exquisite morning toilets, coquetting with their bright-colored parasols, and now and then glancing up at the grim old mountains with that air of elegant disdain which is so redoubtable a weapon—even in the mountains. Little children fluttered about the grass like beautiful butterflies, and as unmindful of the terrors that hovered over them so threateningly. Nurses in their stiff grenadier caps and white aprons, lackeys in livery, cadets in uniform, elegant equipages, blooded horses, dainty shapes on horseback, cavaliers, and last, but not least, the resolute pedestrian, or the gentlemen strollers up and down the shaded avenues, made up a scene as animated as attractive. There is tonic in the air: there is healing in the balm of these groves. Even the horses step out more briskly. Peals of laughter startle the solemn old woods. You hear them high up the mountain side. There go a pair of lovers, the gentleman with his book, whose most telling passages he has carefully conned, the lady with her embroidery, over which she bends lower as he reads on. Ah, happy days! What is this youth, which, having it, we are so eager to escape, and, when it is gone, we look back upon with such longing?

EAGLE CLIFF AND THE ECHO HOUSE.

The lofty crag opposite the hotel is Eagle Cliff, a name at once legitimate and satisfying, although it is now untenanted by the eagles which formerly made their home in the security of its precipitous rocks. The cliff is also seen to great advantage from Echo Lake, half a mile farther on, of which it constitutes a striking feature. In simple parlance it is an advanced spur of Mount Lafayette. The high and curving wall of this cliff encloses on one side the Profile Glen, while Mount Cannon forms the other. The precipices tower so far above the glen that large trees look like shrubs. Behind Eagle Cliff, almost isolating it from the mountain, of which it is the barbacan, a hideous ravine yawns upon the pass. Here and there, among the thick-set evergreen trees, beech and birch and maple, spread masses of rich green, and mottle it with softness. The purple rock bulges daringly out, forming a parapet of adamant.

The turf underneath the cliff was most beautifully and profusely spangled with the delicate pink anemone, the *fleur des fées*, that pale darling of our New England woods, to which the arbutus resigns the sceptre of spring. It is a moving sight to see these little drooping flowers, so shy and modest, yet so meek and trustful, growing at the foot of a bare and sterile rock. The face hardened looking up; grew soft looking down. "Don't tread on us!" "May not a flower look up at a mountain?" they seem to plead. Lightly fall the dews upon your upturned faces, dear little flowers! Soft be the sunshine and gentle the winds that kiss those sky-tinted cheeks! In thy sweet purity and innocence I see faces that are beneath the sod, flowers that have blossomed in Paradise.

We see also, from the hotel, the singular rock that occasioned the change of name from Profile to Cannon Mountain. It nearly resembles a piece of heavy ordnance protruding, threateningly, from the parapet of a fortress.

Taking one of the well-worn paths conducting to the water-side, a few minutes' walk brings us to the shore of Echo Lake, with Eagle Cliff now rising grandly on our right. Nowhere among the White Hills is there a fuller realization of a mountain lake than this. Light flaws frost it with silver. Sharp keels cut it as diamonds cut glass. The water is so transparent that you see fishes swimming or floating indolently about.

Echo Lake is somewhat larger than Profile Lake, and is only a step from the road. Its sources are in the hundred streams that descend the surrounding mountains, and its waters are discharged by the valley, lying between us and the heights of Bethlehem, into the Ammonoosuc. Therefore, in coming from one lake to the other we have

crossed the summit of the pass. On one side the waters flow to the Merrimac, on the other to the Connecticut. An idle fancy tempted me to bring a cup of water from Profile and cast it into Echo Lake, forgetting that, although divided in their lives, the twin lakes had yet a common destiny in the abyss of the ocean. I found the outlook from the boat-house on the whole the most satisfying, because one looks back directly through the deep chasm of the Notch.

In this beautiful little mountain-tarn the true artist finds his ideal. The snowy peak of Lafayette looked down into it with a freezing stare. Cannon Mountain now showed his retreating wall on the right. The huge, castellated rampart of Eagle Cliff lifted on its borders precipices dripping with moisture, and glistening in the sun like casements. Except for the lake, the whole aspect would be irredeemably savage and forbidding—a blind landscape; but when the sun sinks behind the long ridge of Mount Cannon, purpling all these grisly crags, and the cloaked shadows, groping their way foot by foot up the ravines, seem spectres risen from the depths of the lake, you see, underneath the cliffs, long and slender spears of golden light thrust deep into its black and glossy tide, crimsoning it as with its own life-blood. Then, too, is the proper moment for surprising these vain old mountains viewing themselves in their mountain mirror, in which the bald, the wrinkled, and the decrepit appear young, vigorous, and gloriously fair; to see them gloating over their swarthy features like the bandit in "Fra Diavolo." Their ragged mantles are changed to gaudy cashmeres, picturesquely twisted about their brawny shoulders, their snows to laces. Oh the pomp, the majesty of these sunsets, which so glorify the upturned faces of the haggard cliffs; which transmute, as in the miracle, water into wine; which instantly transform these rugged mountain walls into gates of jasper, and ruby, and onyx—glowing, effulgent, enrapturing! And then, after the sun drops wearily down the west, that gauze-like vapor, spun from the breath of evening, rising like incense from the surface of the lake, which the mountains put on for the masque of night; and, finally, the inquisitive stars piercing the lake with ice-cold gleams, or the full-moon breaking in one great burst of splendor on its level surface!

The echo adds its feats of ventriloquism. The marvel of the phonograph is but a mimicry of Nature, the universal teacher. Now the man blows a strong, clear blast upon a long Alpine horn, and, like a bugle-call flying from camp to camp, the martial signal is repeated, not once, but again and again, in waves of bewitching sweetness and with the exquisite modulations of the wood-thrush's note. From covert to covert, now here, now there, it chants its rapturous melody. Once again it glides upon the entranced ear, and still we lean in breathless eagerness to catch the last faint cadence sighing itself away upon the palpitating air. A cannon was then fired. The report and echo came with the flash. In a moment more a deep and hollow rumbling sound, as if the mountains were splitting their huge sides with suppressed laughter, startled us.

The ascent of Mount Lafayette fittingly crowns the series of excursions through which we have passed since leaving Plymouth. This mountain dominates the valleys north and south with undisputed sway. It is the King of Franconia.

At seven in the morning I crossed the little clearing, and, turning into the path leading to the summit, found myself at the beginning of a steep ascent. It was one of the last and fairest days of that bright season which made the poet exclaim,

"And what is so fair as a day in June?"

The thunder-storm of the previous afternoon, which continued its furious cannonade at intervals throughout the night, had purified the air and given promise of a day favorable for the ascension. No clouds were upon the mountains. Everything betokened a pacific disposition.

MOUNT CANNON, FROM THE BRIDLE-PATH, LAFAYETTE.

The path at once attacks the south side of Eagle Cliff. A short way up, openings afford fine views of Mount Cannon and its weird profile, of the valley below, and of the glen we have just left. The stupendous mass of Eagle Cliff, suspended a thousand feet over your head, accelerates the pace.

After an hour of steady, but not rapid, climbing, the path turned abruptly under the shattered, but still formidable, precipices of the cliff, which rose some distance higher, skirted it awhile, and then began to zigzag among huge rocks along the narrow ridge uniting the cliff with the mass of the mountain. Two deep ravines fall away on either side. For two or three hundred yards, from the time the shoulder of the cliff is turned until the mountain itself is reached, the walk is as romantic an episode of mountain climbing as any I can recall, except the narrow gully of Chocorua. But this passage presents no such difficulties as must be overcome there. Although heaped with rocks, the way is easy, and is quite level. In one place, where it glides between two prodigious masses of rock dislodged from the cliff, it is so narrow as to admit only a single person at a time. When I turned to looked back down the black ravine, cutting into the south side of the mountain, my eye met nothing but immense rocks stopped in their descent on the very edge of the gulf. It is among these that a way has been found for the path, which was to me a reminiscence of the high defiles of the Isthmus of Darien; to complete the illusion, nothing was now wanting except the tinkling bells of the mules and the song of the muleteer. I climbed upon one of the high rocks, and gazed to my full content upon the granite parapet of Mount Cannon.

In a few rods more the path encountered the great ravine opening into the valley of Gale River. Through its wide trough brilliant strips of this valley gleamed out far below. The village of Franconia and the heights of Lisbon and Bethlehem now appeared on this side.

I think that the perception of a distance climbed is greater to one who is looking down from a great height than to one looking up. Doubtless the imagination, which associates the plunging lines of a deep gorge with the horror of a fall, has much to do with this impression. Upon crossing a bridge of logs, the peak of Lafayette leaped up; yet so distant as to promise no easy conquest. Somewhere down the gorge I heard the roar of a brook ; then the report of the cannon at Echo Lake; but up here there was no echo.

The usual indications now assured me that I was nearing the top. In three-quarters of an hour from the time of leaving the natural bridge, joining Eagle Cliff with the mountain, I stood upon the first of the great billows which, rolling in to a common centre, appear to have forced the true summit a thousand feet higher.

The first, perhaps the most curious, thing that I noticed — for one hardly suspects the existence of considerable bodies of water in these high regions, and, therefore, never comes upon them except unawares — was two little lakelets, nestling in the hollow between me and the main peak. Reposing amid the sterility of the high peaks, these lakes surround themselves with such plants as have survived the ascent from below, or, nourished by the snows of the summit, those that never do descend into temperate climates. Thus an appearance of fertility—one of those deceptions that we welcome, knowing it to be such—greets us unexpectedly. But its appearance is weird and forbidding. Here the extremes of arctic and temperate vegetation meet and embrace; here the flowers of the valley annually visit their pale sisters, banished by Nature to these Siberian solitudes; and here the rough, strong Alpine grass, striking its roots deep among the atoms of sand, granite, or flint, lives almost in defiance of Nature herself; and when the snows come and the freezing north winds blow, and it can no longer stand erect, throws itself upon the tender plants, like a brave soldier expiring on the body of his helpless comrade, saved by his own devotion.

But these Alpine lakes always provoke a smile. When some distance beyond the Eagle Lakes, as they are called, and higher, I caught, underneath a wooded ridge of Cannon, the sparkle of one hidden among the summits on the opposite side of the Notch. The immense, solitary Kinsman Mountain overtops Cannon as easily as Cannon does Eagle Cliff. In its dark setting of the thickest and blackest forests this lake blazed like one of the enormous diamonds which our forefathers so firmly believed existed among these mountains. They call this water— only to be discovered by getting above it—Lonesome Lake, and in summer it is the chosen retreat of one well known to American literature, whom the mountains know, and who knows them.

I descended the slope to the plateau on which the lakes lie, soon gaining the rush-grown shore of the nearest. Its water was hardly drinkable, but your thirsty climber is not apt to be too fastidious. These lakes are prettier from a distance; the spongy and yielding moss,

CLOUD EFFECTS ON MOUNT LAFAYETTE.

the sickly yellow sedge surrounding them, and the rusty brown of the brackish water, do not invite us to tarry long.

The ascent of the pinnacle now began. It is too much a repetition, though by no means as toilsome, of the Mount Washington climb to merit particular description. This peak, too, seems disinherited by Nature. The last trees encountered are the stunted firs with distorted little trunks, which it may have required half a century to grow as thick as the wrist. I left the region of Alpine trees to enter that of gray rocks, constantly increasing in size toward the summit, where they were confusedly piled in ragged ridges, one upon another, looming large and threateningly in the distance. But as often as I stopped to breathe I scanned "the landscape o'er" with all the delight of a wholly new experience. The fascination of being on a mountain-top has yet to be explained. Perhaps, after all, it is not susceptible of analysis.

After gaining the highest visible point, to find the real summit still beyond, I stopped to drink at a delicious spring trickling from underneath a large rock, around which the track wound. I was now among the ruin and demolition of the summit, standing in the midst of a vast atmospheric ocean.

Had I staked all my hopes upon the distant view, no choice but disappointment was mine to accept. Steeped in the softest, dreamiest azure that ever dull earth borrowed from bright heaven, a hundred peaks lifted their airy turrets on high. These castles of the air—for I will maintain that they were nothing else—loomed with enchanting grace, the nearest like battlements of turquoise and amethyst, or, receding through infinite gradations to the merest shadows, seemed but the dusky reflection of those less remote. The air was full of illusions. There was bright sunshine, yet only a deluge of semi-opaque golden vapor. There were forms without substance. See those iron-ribbed, deep-chested mountains! I declare it seemed as if a swallow might fly through them with ease! Over the great Twin chain were traced, apparently on the air itself, some humid outlines of surpassing grace which I recognized for the great White Mountains. It was a dream of the great poetic past: of the golden age of Milton and of Dante. The mountains seemed dissolving and floating away before my eyes.

Stretched beneath the huge land-billows, the valleys—north, south, or west—reflected the fervid sunshine with softened brilliance, and all those white farms and hamlets spotting them looked like flakes of foam in the hollows of an immense ocean.

Heaven forbid that I should profane such a scene with the dry recital of this view or that! I did not even think of it. A study of one of Nature's most capricious moods interested me far more than a study of topography. How should I know that what I saw were mountains, when the earth itself was not clearly distinguishable? Alone, surrounded by all these delusions, I had, indeed, a support for my feet, but none whatever for the bewildered senses.

I found the mountain-top untenanted except by horse-flies, black gnats, and active little black spiders. These swarmed upon the rocks. I also found buttercups, the mountain-cranberry, and a heath, bearing a little white flower, blossoming near the summit. There were the four walls of a ruined building, a cairn, and a signal-staff to show that some one had been before me. This staff is 5259 feet above the ocean, or 3245 feet above the summit of the Franconia Pass.

The ascent required about three, and the descent about two hours. The distance is not much less than four miles; but, these miles being a nearly uninterrupted climb from the base to the summit of the mountain, haste is out of the question, if going up, and imprudent, if coming down. There are no breakneck or dangerous places on the route; nor any where the traveller is liable to lose his way, even in a fog, except on the first summit, where the new and old paths meet, and where a guide-board should be erected.

IV.

FRANCONIA, AND THE NEIGHBORHOOD.

Believe if thou wilt that mountains change their places, but believe not that men change their dispositions.—*Oriental Proverb.*

ALTHOUGH one may make the journey from the Profile House to Bethlehem with greater ease and rapidity by the railway recently constructed along the side of the Franconia range, preference will unquestionably be given to the old way by all who would not lose some of the most striking views the neighborhood affords. Beginning near the hotel, the railway skirts the shore of Echo Lake, and then plunges into a forest it was the first to invade. By a descent of one hundred feet to the mile, for nine and a half miles, it reaches the Ammonoosuc at Bethlehem station. I have nothing to say against the locomotive, but then I should not like to go through the gallery of the Louvre behind one.

FRANCONIA IRON WORKS AND NOTCH.

From Echo Lake the high-road to Franconia, Littleton, and Bethlehem winds down the steep mountain side into the valley of Gale River.

To the left, in the middle distance, appear the little church-tower and white buildings constituting the village of Franconia Iron Works. This village is charmingly placed for effectively commanding a survey of the amphitheatre of mountains which isolates it from the neighboring towns and settlements.

As we come down the three-mile descent, from the summit of the pass to the level of the deep valley, and to the northern base of the notch-mountains, an eminence rises to the left. Half-way up, occupying a well-chosen site, there is a hotel, and on the high ridge another commands not only this valley, but also those lying to the west of it. On the opposite side to us rise the green heights of Bethlehem, Mount Agassiz being conspicuous by the observatory on its summit. Those farm-houses dotting the hill-side show how the road crooks and turns to get to the top. Following these heights westward, a deep rift indicates the course of the stream dividing the valley, and of the highway to Littleton. Between these walls the long ellipse of fertile land beckons us to descend.

I am always most partial to those grassy lanes and by-ways going no one knows where, especially if they have well-sweeps and elm-trees in them; but here also is the old red farm-house, with its antiquated sweep, its colony of arching elms, its wild-rose clustering above the porch, its embodiment of those magical words, " Home, sweet home." It fits the rugged landscape as no other habitation can. It fits it to a T, as we say in New England. More than this, it unites us with another and different generation. What a story of toil, privation, endurance these old walls could tell! How genuine the surprise with which they look down upon the more modern houses of the village! Here, too, is the Virginia fence, on which the king of the barn-yard defiantly perches. There is the field behind it, and the men scattering seed in the fallow earth. Yonder, in the mowing-ground, a laborer is sharpening his scythe, the steel ringing musically under the quick strokes of his " rifle."

Over there, to the left, is the rustic bridge, and hard by a clump of peeled birches throw their grateful shade over the hot road. Many stop here, for the white-columned trunks are carved with initials, some freshly cut, some mere scars. But why mutilate the tree? What signify those letters, that every idler should gratify his little vanity by giving it a stab? Do you know that the birch does not renew its bark, and that the tree thus stripped of its natural protection is doomed? Cease, then,

I pray you, this senseless mutilation; nor call down the just malediction of the future traveller for destroying his shade. Unable to escape its fate, the poor tree, like a victim at the stake, stoically receives your barbarous strokes and gashes. Refrain, then, traveller, for pity's sake! Have a little mercy! Know that the ancients believed the tree possessed of a soul. Remember the touching story of Adonis, barbarously wounded, surviving in a pine, where he weeps eternally. Consider how often is the figure of "The Tree" used in the Scriptures as emblematic of the life eternal! Who would wish to inhabit a treeless heaven?

The stream—which does not allow us to forget that it is here—is a vociferous mountain brook. Hardly less forward is the roadside fountain gushing into a water-trough its refreshing abundance for the tired and dusty wayfarer. It makes no difference in the world whether he goes on two legs or on four. "Drink and be filled" is the invitation thus generously held out to all alike. With what a sigh of pleasure your steaming beast lifts his reluctant and dripping muzzle from the cool wave, and after satisfying again and again his thirst, luxuriously immersing his nose for the third and fourth time, still

THE ROADSIDE SPRING.

pretends to drink! How deliciously light and limpid and sparkling is the water, and how sweet! How it cools the hot blood! You quaff nectar. You sip it as you would champagne. It tastes far better, you think, pouring from this half-decayed, moss-crusted spout than from iron, or bronze, or marble. Come, fellow-traveller, a bumper! Fill high! God bless the man who first invented the roadside fountain! He was a true benefactor of his fellow-man.

Turn once more to the house. A little girl tosses corn, kernel by kernel, to her pet chickens. There go a flight of pigeons: they curvet and wheel, and settle on the ridge-pole, where they begin to flirt, and strut, and coo. The men in the field look up at the top of the mountain, to see if it is not yet noon. And now a woman, with plump bare arms, coming briskly to the open door, puts the dinner-horn to her lips with one hand while placing the other lightly upon her hip. She does not know that act and attitude are alike inviting. How should she?

Let us follow the pretty stream that is our guide. Franconia has the reputation of being the hottest in summer and in winter the coldest of the mountain villages. It *is* hot. The houses are strung along the road for a mile. People may or may not live in them: you see nobody. One modest church-tower catches the eye for a moment, and then, as we enter the heart of the village, a square barrack of a building, just across the stream, is pointed out as the old furnace, which in times past gave importance to this out-of-the-way corner. But the old furnace is now deserted except by cows from the neighboring pastures, who come and go through its open doors in search of shade. At present the river, which brings its music and its freshness to the very doors of the villagers, is the only busy thing in the place.

During the Rebellion the furnace was kept busy night and day, turning out iron to be cast into cannon. The very hills were melted down for the defence of the imperilled Union. In the adjoining town of Lisbon the discovery of gold-bearing quartz turned the heads of the usually steady-going population. The precious deposits were first found on the Bailey farm, in 1865, and similar specimens were soon detected on the farms adjoining. It is said the old people could scarcely be made to credit these reports until they had seen and handled the precious metal; for the country had been settled nearly a century, and the presence of any but the baser ores was wholly unsuspected and disbelieved.

There is one peculiarity, common to all these mountain villages, to which I must allude. A stranger is not known by any personal peculiarity, but by his horse. If you ask for such or such a person, the chances are ten to one you will immediately be asked in return if he drove a bay horse, or a black colt, or a brown mare with one white ear; so quick are these lazy-looking men, that loll on the door-steps or spread themselves out over the shop-counters, to observe what interests them most. The girls here know the points of a horse better than most men, and are far more reckless drivers than men. To a man who, like myself, has lived in a horse-stealing country, it does look queerly to see the barn-doors standing open at night. But then every country has its own customs.

One seeks in vain for any scraps of history or tradition that might shed even a momentary lustre upon this village out of the past. Yet its situation invites the belief that it is full of both. Disappointed in this, we at least have an inexhaustible theme in the dark and tranquil mountains bending over us.

Mount Lafayette presents toward Franconia two enormous green billows, rolled apart, the deep hollow between being the great ravine dividing the mountain from base to summit. Over this deep incision, which, from the irregularity of one of its ridges, looks widest at the top, presides, with matchless dignity, the bared and craggy peak whose dusky brown gradually mingles with the scant verdure checked hundreds of feet down. With what hauteur it seems to regard this effort of Nature to place a garland on its bronzed and knotted forehead! One can never get over his admiration for the savage grace with which the mountain, which at first sight seems literally thrown together, develops a beauty, a harmony, and an intelligence giving such absolute superiority to works of Nature over those of man.

The side of Mount Cannon turned toward the village now elevates two almost regular triangular masses, one rising behind the other, and both surmounted by the rounded summit, which, except in its mass, has little resemblance to a mountain. It is seen that on two-thirds of these elevations a new forest has replaced the original growth. Twenty-five years ago a destructive fire raged on this mountain, destroying all the vegetation, as well as the thin soil down to the hard rock. Even that was cracked and peeled like old parchment. This burning mountain was a scene of startling magnificence during several nights, when the village was as light as day, the sky overspread an angry glow, and the river ran blood-red. The hump-backed ridges, connecting Cannon with Kinsman, present nearly the same appearance from this as from the other side of the Notch—or as remarked when approaching from Campton.

The superb picture seen from the upper end of the valley, combining, as it does, the two great chains in a single glance of the eye, is extended and improved by going a mile out of the village to the school-house on the Sugar Hill road. It is a peerless landscape. I have gazed at it for hours with that ineffable delight which baffles all power of expression. It will have no partakers. One must go there alone and see the setting sun paint those vast shapes with colors the heavens alone are capable of producing.

Distinguished by the beautiful groves of maple that adorn its crest, Sugar Hill is destined to grow more and more in the popular esteem. No traveller should pass it by. It is so admirably placed as to command in one magnificent sweep of the eye all the highest mountains; it is also lifted into sun and air by an elevation sufficiently high to reach the cooler upper currents. The days are not so breathless or so stifling as they are down in the valley. You look deep into the Franconia Notch, and watch the evening shadows creep up the great east wall. Extending beyond these nearer mountains, the scarcely inferior Twin summits pose themselves like gigantic athletes. Passing to the other side of the valley, we see as far as the pale peaks of Vermont, and those rising above the valley of Israel's River. But better than all, grander than all, is that kingly coronet of great mountains set on the lustrous green cushion of the valley. Nowhere, I venture to affirm, will the felicity of the title, "Crown of New England,"[1] receive more unanimous acceptance than from this favored spot. Especially when a canopy of clouds overspreading permits the pointed peaks to reflect the illuminated fires of sunset does the crown seem blazing with jewels and precious stones. All the great summits are visible here, and all the ravines, except those in Madison, are as clearly distinguished as if not more than ten instead of twenty miles separated us.

The high crest of Sugar Hill unfolds an unrivalled panorama. This is but faint praise. Yet I find myself instinctively preferring the landscape from Goodenow's; for those great horizons, uncovered all at once, like a magnificent banquet, are too much for one pair of eyes, however good, or however unwearied with continued sight-seeing. As we cannot look at all the pictures of a gallery at once, we naturally single out the masterpieces. The effort to digest too much natural scenery is a species of intellectual gluttony the overtaxed brain will be quick to revenge, by an attack of indigestion or a loss of appetite.

I was very fond of walking, in the cool of the evening, either in this direction or to the upper end of the village, on the Bethlehem road.

---

[1] This name was given to his picture of the great range, in possession of the Prince of Wales, by Mr. George L. Brown, the eminent landscape-painter. The canvas represents the summits in the sumptuous garb of autumn.

There is one point on this road, before it begins in earnest its ascent of the heights, that became a favorite haunt of mine. Emerging from the concealment of thick woods upon a sandy plain, covered here with a thick carpet of verdure, and skirted by a regiment of pines seemingly awaiting only the word of command to advance into the valley, a landscape second to none that I have seen is before you. At the same time he would be an audacious mortal who attempted to transfer it to page or canvas. Nothing disturbs the exquisite harmony of the scene. To the left of you are all the White Mountains, from Adams to Pleasant; in front, the Franconia range, from Kinsman to the Great Haystack. Here is the deep rent of the Notch from which we have but lately descended. Here, too, overtopped and subjugated by the superb spire of Lafayette, the long and curiously-distorted outline of Eagle Cliff pitches headlong down into the half-open aperture of the pass. Nothing but an earthquake could have made such a breach. How that tremendous, earth-swooping ridge seems battered down by the blows of a huge mace! Unspeakably wild and stern, the fractured mountains are to the valley what a raging tempest is to the serenest of skies: one part of the heavens convulsed by the storm, another all peace and calm. Thus from behind his impregnable outworks Lafayette, stern and defiant, keeps eternal watch and ward over the valley cowering at his feet.

From this spot, too, sacred as yet from all intrusion, the profound ravine, descending nearly from the summit of Lafayette, is fully exposed. It is a thing of cracks, crevices, and rents; of upward curves in brilliant light; of black, mysterious hollows, which the eye investigates inch by inch, to where the gorge is swallowed up by the thick forests underneath. The whole side of the principal peak seems torn away. Up there, among the snows, is the source of a flashing stream which comes roaring down through the gorge. Storms swell it into an ungovernable and raging torrent. Thus under the folds of his mantle the lordly peak carries peace or war for the vale.

After the half-stifled feeling experienced among the great mountains, it is indeed a rare pleasure to once more come forth into full breathing-space, and to inspect at leisure from some friendly shade the grandeur magnified by distance, yet divested of excitements that set the brain whirling by the rapidity of their succession. If the wayfarer chances to see, as I did, the whole noble array of high summits presenting a long, snowy line of unsullied brilliance against a background of pale azure, he will account it one of the crowning enjoyments of his journey.

The Bridal Veil Falls, lying on the northern slope of Mount Kinsman, will, when a good path shall enable tourists to visit them, prove one of the most attractive features of Franconia. Truth compels me to say that I did not once hear them spoken of during the fortnight passed in the village, although fishermen were continually bringing in trout from the Copper-mine Brook, on which these falls are situated. The height of the fall is given at seventy-six feet, and its surroundings are said to be of the most romantic and picturesque character. Its marvellous transparency, which permits the ledges to be seen through the gauze-like sheet falling over them, has given to it its name.

From Franconia I took the daily stage to Littleton, which lies on both banks of the Ammonoosuc, and, turning my back upon the high mountains, ran down the rail to Wells River, having the intention of cultivating a more intimate acquaintance with that most noble and interesting entrance formed by the meeting of the Ammonoosuc with the Connecticut.

V.

THE CONNECTICUT OX-BOW.

Say, have the solid rocks
Into streams of silver been melted,
Flowing over the plains,
Spreading to lakes in the fields?
                    LONGFELLOW.

THE Connecticut is justly named "the beautiful river," and its valley "the garden of New England." Issuing from the heart of the northern wilderness, it spreads boundless fertility throughout its stately march to the sea. It is not a rapid river, but flows with an even and majestic tide through its long avenue of mountains. Radiant envoy of the skies, its mission is peace on earth and good-will toward men. As it advances the confluent streams flock to it from their mountain homes. On one side the Green Mountains of Vermont send their hundred tributaries to swell its flood; on the other side the White Hills of New Hampshire pour their impetuous torrents into its broad and placid bosom. Two States thus vie with each other in contributing the wealth it lavishes with absolutely impartial hand along the shores of each.

Unlike the storied Rhine, no crumbling ruins crown the lofty heights of this beautiful river. Its verdant hill-sides everywhere display the evidences of thrift and happiness; its only fortresses are the watchful and everlasting peaks that catch the earliest beams of the New England sun and flash the welcome signal from tower to tower. From time to time the mountains, which seem crowding its banks to see it pass, draw back, as if to give the noble river room. It rewards this benevolence with a garden-spot. Sometimes the mountains press too closely upon it, and the offended stream repays this temerity with a barrenness equal to the beneficence it has just bestowed. Where it is permitted to expand the amphitheatres thus created are the highest types of decorative nature. Graciously touching first one shore and then the other, making the loveliest windings imaginable, the river actually seems on the point of retracing its steps; but, yielding to destiny, it again resumes its slow march, loitering meanwhile in the cool shadows of the mountains, or indolently stretching itself at full length upon the green carpet of the level meadows. Every traveller who has passed here has seen the Happy Valley of Rasselas.[1]

Such is the renowned Ox-Bow of Lower Coös. Tell me, you who have seen it, if the sight has not caused a ripple of pleasurable excitement?

Here the Connecticut receives the waters of the Ammonoosuc, flowing from the very summit of the White Hills, and, in. its turn, made to guide the railway to its own birthplace among the snows of Mount Washington. Here the valley, graven in long lines by the ploughshare, heaped with fruitful orchards and groves, extends for many miles up and down its checkered and variegated floor. But it is most beautiful between the villages of Newbury and Haverhill, or at the Great and Little Ox-Bow, where the fat and fecund meadows, extending for two miles from side to side of the valley, resemble an Eden upon earth, and the villages, prettily arranged on terraces above them, half-hid in a thick fringe of foliage, the mantel-ornaments of their own best rooms. Only moderate elevations rise on the Vermont side; but the New Hampshire shore is upheaved into the finely accentuated Benton peaks, behind which, like a citadel within its outworks, is uplifted the gigantic bulk of Mooschillock—the greatest mountain of all this valley, and its natural landmark—keeping strict watch over it as far as the Canadian frontiers.

The traveller approaching by the Connecticut Valley holds this exquisite landscape in view from the Vermont side of the river. The tourist who approaches by the valley of the Merrimac enjoys it from the New Hampshire shore.

The large village of Newbury, usually known as the "Street," is built along a plateau, rising well above the intervale, and joined to the foot-hills of the Green Mountains. The Passumpsic Railway coasts the intervale, just touching the northern skirt of the village. The village of Haverhill is similarly situated with respect to the skirt of the White Mountains; but its surface is much more uneven, and it is elevated

---

[1] The true source of the Connecticut remained so long in doubt that it passed into a by-word. Cotton Mather, speaking of an ecclesiastical quarrel in Hartford, says that it was almost as obscure as the rise of the Connecticut River.

higher above the valley than its opposite neighbor. The Boston, Concord, and Montreal Railway, having crossed the divide between the waters of the Merrimac and the Connecticut, now follows the high level, after a swift descent from Warren Summit. These plateaus, or terraces, forming broken shelves, first upon one side of the valley, then upon the other, strongly resemble the remains of the ancient bed of a river of tenfold the magnitude of the stream as we see it to-day. They give rise at once to all those interesting conjectures, or theories, which are considered the special field of the geologist, but are also equally attractive to every intelligent observer of Nature and her wondrous works.

Of these two villages, which are really subdivided into half a dozen, and which so beautifully decorate the mountain walls of this valley, it is no treason to the Granite State to say that Newbury enjoys a preference few will be found to dispute. It has the grandest mountain landscape. Mooschillock is lifted high above the Benton range, which occupies the foreground. The whole background is filled with high summits—Lafayette feeling his way up among the clouds, Mooschillock roughly pushing his out of the throng. Meadows of emerald, river of burnished steel, hill-sides in green and buff, and etched with glittering hamlets, gray mountains, bending darkly over, cloud-detaining peaks, vanishing in the far east—surely fairer landscape never brought a glow of pleasure to the cheek, or kindled the eye of a traveller, already sated with a panorama reaching from these mountains to the Sound.

We are now, I imagine, sufficiently instructed in the general characteristics of the famed Ox-Bow to pass from its picturesque and topographical features into the domain of history, and to summon from the past the details of a tragedy in war, which, had it occurred in the days of Homer, would have been embalmed in an epic. Our history begins at a period before any white settlement existed in the region immediately about us. No wonder the red man relinquished it only at the point of the bayonet. It was a country worth fighting for to the bitter end.

VI.

"L'histoire à sa vérité; la legende a la sienne."

IN the month of September, 1759, the army of Sir Jeffrey Amherst was in cantonments at Crown Point. A picked corps of American rangers, commanded by Robert Rogers, was attached to this army. One day an aide-de-camp brought Rogers an order to repair forthwith to head-quarters, and in a few moments the ranger entered the general's marquee.

"At your orders, general," said the ranger, making his salute.

"About that accursed hornet's-nest of St. Francis?" said the general, frowning.

"When I was a lad, your excellency, we used to burn a hornet's-nest, if it became troublesome," observed Rogers, significantly.

"And how many do you imagine, major, this one has stung to death in the last six years?" inquired General Amherst, fumbling among his papers.

"I don't know; a great many, your excellency."

"Six hundred men, women, and children."

The two men looked at each other a moment without speaking.

"At this rate," continued the general, "his Majesty's New England provinces will soon be depopulated."

"For God's sake, general, put a stop to this butchery!" ejaculated the exasperated ranger.

"That's exactly what I have sent for you to do. Here are your orders. You are commanded, and I expect you to destroy that nest of vipers, root and branch. Remember the atrocities committed by these Indian scoundrels, and take your revenge; but remember, also, that I forbid the killing of women and children. Exterminate the fighting-

ROBERT ROGERS.

men, but spare the non-combatants.   That is war.   Now make an end
of St. Francis once and for all."

Nearly a hundred leagues separated the Abenaqui village from the
English; and we should add that once there, in the heart of the enemy's country, all idea of help from the army must be abandoned, and
the rangers, depending wholly upon themselves, be deprived of every
resource except to cut their way through all obstacles.   But this was
exactly the kind of service for which this distinctive body of American
soldiers was formed.

Sir Jeffrey Amherst had said to Rogers, "Go and wipe out St. Francis for me," precisely as he would have said to his orderly, "Go and saddle my horse."

But this illustrates the high degree of confidence which the army reposed in the chief of the rangers. The general knew that this expedition demanded, at every stage, the highest qualities in a leader. Rogers had already proved himself possessed of these qualities in a hundred perilous encounters.

That night, without noise or display, the two hundred men detailed for the expedition left their encampment, which was habitually in the van of the army. On the evening of the twenty-second day since leaving Crown Point a halt was ordered. The rangers were near their destination. From the top of a tree the doomed village was discovered three miles distant. Not the least sign that the presence of an enemy was suspected could be seen or heard. The village wore its ordinary aspect of profound security.• Rogers therefore commanded his men to rest, and prepare themselves for the work in hand.

At eight in the evening, having first disguised himself, Rogers took Lieutenant Turner and Ensign Avery, and with them reconnoitred the Indian town. He found it the scene of high festivity, and for an hour watched unseen the unsuspecting inhabitants celebrating with dancing and barbaric music the nuptials of one of the tribe. All this marvellously favored his plans. Not dreaming of an enemy, the savages abandoned themselves to unrestrained enjoyment and hilarity. The *fête* was protracted until a late hour under the very eyes of the spies, who, finding themselves unnoticed, crept boldly into the village, where they examined the ground and concerted the plan of attack.

At length all was hushed. The last notes of revelry faded on the still night air. One by one the drowsy merry-makers retired to their lodges, and soon the village was wrapped in profound slumber—the slumber of death. This was the moment so anxiously awaited by Rogers. Time was precious. He quickly made his way back to the spot where the rangers were lying on their arms. One by one the men were aroused and fell into their places. It was two in the morning when he left the village. At three the whole body moved stealthily up to within five hundred yards of the village, where the men halted, threw off their packs, and were formed for the assault in three divisions. The village continued silent as the grave.

St. Francis was a village of about forty or fifty wigwams, thrown together in a disorderly clump. In the midst was a chapel, to which the inhabitants were daily summoned by matin and vesper bell to hear the holy father, whose spiritual charge they were, celebrate the mass. The place was enriched with the spoil torn from the English and the ransom of many miserable captives. We have said that these Indians had slain and taken, in six years, six hundred English: that is equivalent to one hundred every year.

The knowledge of numberless atrocities nerved the arms and steeled the hearts of the avengers. When the sun began to brighten the east the three bands of rangers, waiting eagerly for the signal, rushed upon the village.

A deplorable and sickening scene of carnage ensued. The surprise was complete. The first and only warning the amazed savages had were the volleys that mowed them down by scores and fifties. Eyes heavy with the carousal of the previous night opened to encounter an appalling carnival of butchery and horror. Two of the stoutest of the rangers — Farrington and Bradley — led one of the attacking columns to the door where the wedding had taken place. Finding it barred, they threw themselves so violently against it that the fastenings gave way, precipitating Bradley headlong among the Indians who were asleep on their mats. All these were slain before they could make the least resistance.

On all sides the axe and the rifle were soon reaping their deadly harvest. Those panic-stricken, half-dazed wretches who rushed pell-mell into the streets either ran stupidly upon the uplifted weapons of the rangers or were shot down by squads advantageously posted to receive them. A few who ran this terrible gauntlet plunged into the river flowing before the village, and struck boldly out for the opposite shore; but the avengers had closed every avenue of escape, and the fugitives were picked off from the banks. The same fate overtook those who tumbled into their canoes and pushed out into the stream. The frail barks were riddled with shot, leaving their occupants an easy target for a score of rifles. The incessant flashes, the explosions of musketry, the shouts of the assailants, and the yells of their victims were all mingled in one horrible uproar. For two hours this massacre continued. Combat it cannot be called. Rendered furious by the sight of hundreds of scalps waving mournfully in the night-wind in front of the lodges, the pitiless assailants hunted the doomed savages down like blood-hounds. Every shot was followed by a death-whoop, every stroke by a howl of agony. For two horrible hours the village shook with explosions and echoed with frantic outcries. It was then given up to pillage, and then to the torch, and all those who from fear had hid themselves perished miserably in the flames. At seven o'clock in the morning all was over. Silence once more enveloped the hideous scene of conflagration and slaughter. The village of St. Francis was the funeral pyre of two hundred warriors. Rogers had indeed taken the fullest revenge enjoined by Sir Jeffrey Amherst's orders.

From this point our true history passes into the legendary.

While the sack of St. Francis was going on a number of the Abenaquis took refuge in the little chapel. Their retreat was discovered. A few of their assailants having collected in the neighborhood precipitated themselves toward it, with loud cries. Others ran up. Two or three blows with the butt of a musket forced open the door, when the building was instantly filled with armed men.

An unforeseen reception awaited them. Lighted candles burnt on the high altar, shedding a mild radiance throughout the interior, and casting a dull glow upon the holy vessels of gold and silver upon the altar. At the altar's foot, clad in the sacred vestments of his office, stood the missionary, a middle-aged, vigorous-looking man, his arms crossed upon his breast, his face lighted up with the exaltation of a martyr. Face and figure denoted the high resolve to meet fate half-way. Behind him crouched the knot of half-crazed savages, who had fled to the sanctuary for its protection, and who, on seeing their mortal enemies, instinctively took a posture of defence. The priest, at two or three paces in advance of them, seemed to offer his body as their rampart. The scene was worthy the pencil of a Rembrandt.

At this sight the intruders halted, the foremost even falling back a step, but the vessels of gold and silver inflamed their cupidity to the highest pitch; while the hostile attitude of the warriors was a menace men already steeped in bloodshed regarded a moment in still more threatening silence, and then by a common impulse recognized by covering the forlorn group with their rifles.

Believing the critical moment come, the priest threw up his hands in an attitude of supplication, arresting the fatal volley as much by the dignity of the gesture itself, as by the resonant voice which exclaimed, in French, "Madmen, for pity's sake, for the sake of Him on the Cross, stay your hands! This violence! What is your will? What seek ye in the house of God?"

A gunshot outside, followed by a mournful howl, was his sole response.

The priest shuddered, and his crisped lips murmured an *ave*. He comprehended that another soul had been sent, unshriven, to its final account.

"Hear him!" said a ranger, in a mocking undertone; "his gabble minds me of a flock of wild geese."

A burst of derisive laughter followed this coarse sally.

In fact, they had not too much respect for the Church of Rome, these wild woodsmen, but were filled with ineradicable hatred for its missionaries, domesticated among their enemies, in whom they believed they saw the real heads of the tribes, and the legitimate objects, therefore, of their vengeance.

"Yield, Papist! Come, you shall have good quarter; on the word of a ranger you shall," cried an authoritative voice, the speaker at the same time advancing a step, and dropping his rifle the length of his sinewy arms.

"Never!" answered the ecclesiastic, crossing himself.

A suppressed voice from behind hurriedly murmured in his ear, "*Écoutez: rendez-vous, mon père: je vous en supplie!*"

"*Jamais! mieux vaut la mort que la miséricorde de brigands et meurtriers!*" ejaculated the missionary, rejecting the counsel also, with a vehement shake of the head.

"*Grand Dieu! tout, donc, est fini*," sighed the voice, despairingly.

The rangers understood the gesture better than the words. An officer, the same who had just spoken, again impatiently demanded, this time in a higher and more threatening key,

"A last time! Do you yield or no? Answer, friar!"

The priest turned quickly, took the consecrated Host from the altar, elevated it above his head, and, in a voice that was long remembered by those who heard it, exclaimed,

"To your knees, monsters! to your knees!"

What the ranger understood of this pantomime and this command was that they conveyed a scornful and a final refusal. Muttering under his breath, "Your blood be upon your own head, then," he levelled his gun and pulled the trigger. A general discharge from both sides shook the building, filling it with thick and stifling smoke, and instantly extinguishing the lights. The few dim rays penetrating the windows, and which seemed recoiling from the frightful spectacle within, enabled the combatants vaguely to distinguish each other in the obscurity. Not a cry was heard; nothing but quick reports or blows signaled the progress of this lugubrious combat.

This butchery continued ten minutes, at the end of which the rangers, with the exception of one of their number killed outright, issued from the chapel, after having first stripped the altar, despoiled the shrine of its silver image of the Virgin, and flung the Host upon the ground. While this profanation was enacting a voice rose from the heap of dead at the altar's foot, which made the boldest heart among the rangers stop beating. It said,

"The Great Spirit of the Abenaquis will scatter darkness in the path of the accursed Pale-faces! Hunger walks before and Death strikes their trail! Their wives weep for the warriors that do not return! Manitou is angry when the dead speak. The dead have spoken!"

The torch was then applied to the chapel, and, like the rest of the village, it was fast being reduced to a heap of cinders. But now something singular transpired. As the rangers filed out from the shambles the bell of the little chapel began to toll. In wonder and dread they listened to its slow and measured strokes until, the flames having mounted to the belfry, it fell with a loud clang among the ruins. The rangers hastened onward. This unexpected sound already filled them with gloomy forebodings.

After the stern necessities of their situation rendered a separation the sole hope of successful retreat, the party which carried along with it the silver image was so hard pressed by the Indians, and by a still more relentless enemy, famine, that it reached the banks of the Connecticut reduced to four half-starved, emaciated men. More than once had they been on the point of flinging their burden into some one of the torrents every hour obstructing their way; but as one after another fell exhausted or lifeless, the unlucky image passed from hand to hand, and was thus preserved up to the moment so eagerly and so confidently looked for, during that long and dreadful march, to end all their privations.

But the chastisement of heaven, prefigured in the words of the expiring Abenaqui, had already overtaken them. Half-crazed by their sufferings, they mistook the place of rendezvous appointed by their chief, and, having no tidings of their comrades, believed themselves to be the sole survivors of all that gallant but ill-fated band. In this conviction, to which a mournful destiny conducted, they took the fatal determination to cross the mountains under the guidance of one of their number who had, or professed, a knowledge of the way through the Great Notch of the White Hills.

For four days they dragged themselves onward through thickets, through deep snows and swollen streams, without sustenance of any kind, when three of them, in consequence of their complicated miseries, aggravated by finding no way through the wall of mountains, lost their senses. What leather covered their cartouch-boxes they had already scorched to a cinder and greedily devoured. At length, on the last days of October, as they were crossing a small river dammed by logs, they discovered some human bodies, not only scalped, but horribly mangled, which were supposed to be some of their own band. But this was no time for distinctions. On them they accordingly fell like cannibals, their impatience being too great to await the kindling of a fire to dress their horrid food by. When they had thus abated somewhat the excruciating pangs they before endured, the fragments were carefully collected for a future store.

My pen refuses to record the dreadful extremities to which starvation reduced these miserable wretches. At length, after some days of fruitless wandering up and down, finding the mountains inexorably closing in upon them, even this last dreadful resource failed, and, crawling under some rocks, they perished miserably in the delirium produced by hunger and despair, blaspheming, and hurling horrible imprecations at the silver image, to which, in their insanity, they attributed all their sufferings. One of them, seizing the statue, tottered to the edge of a precipice, and, exerting all his remaining strength, dashed it down into the gulf at his feet.

Tradition affirms that the first settlers who ascended Israel's River found relics of the lost detachment near the foot of the mountains; but, notwithstanding the most diligent search, the silver image has thus far eluded every effort made for its recovery.

VII.

MOOSEHILLOCK.

And so, when restless and adrift, I keep
Great comfort in a quietness like this,
An awful strength that lies in fearless sleep,
On this great shoulder lay my head, nor miss
The things I longed for but an hour ago.

SARAH O. JEWETT.

MOOSEHILLOCK, or Moosilauke,[1] is one of four or five summits from which the best idea of the whole area of the White Mountains may be obtained. It is not so remarkable for its form as for its mass. It is an immense mountain.

Lifted in solitary grandeur upon the extreme borders of the army of peaks to which it belongs, and which it seems defending, haughtily overbearing those lesser summits of the Green Mountains confronting it from the opposite shores of the Connecticut, which here separates the two grand systems, like two hostile armies, the one from the other, Moosehillock resembles a crouching lion, magnificent in repose, but terrible in its awakening.

This immense strength, paralyzed and helpless though it seems, is nevertheless capable of arousing in us a sentiment of respectful fear—respect for the creative power, fear for the suspended life we believe is there. The mountain really seems lying extended under the sky listening for the awful command, " Arise and walk!"

---

[1] This orthography is of recent adoption. By recent I mean within thirty years. Before that time it was always Moosehillock. Nothing is easier than to unsettle a name. So far as known, I believe there is not a single summit of the White Mountain group having a name given to it by the Indians. On the contrary, the Indian names have all come from the white people. That these are sometimes far-fetched is seen in Osceola and Tecumseh; that they are often puerile, it is needless to point out. Moosehillock is probably no exception. It is not unlikely to be an English nickname. The result of these changes is that the people inhabiting the region contiguous to the mountain do not know how to spell the name on their guide-boards.

This mountain received a name before Mount Washington, and is in some respects, as I hope to point out, the most interesting of the whole group. In the first place, it commands a hundred miles of the Connecticut Valley, including, of course, all the great peaks of the Green Mountain and Adirondack chains. Again, its position confers decided advantages for studying the configuration of the Franconia group, to which, in a certain sense, it is allied, and of the ranges enclosing the Pemigewasset Valley, which it overlooks. Mooschillock stands in the broad angle formed by the meeting waters of the Connecticut and the Ammonoosuc. In a word, it is an advanced bastion of the whole cluster of castellated summits, constituting the White Mountains in a larger meaning.

Therefore no summit better repays a visit than Mooschillock; yet it is astonishing, considering the ease of access, how few make the ascent. The traveller can hardly do better than begin here his experiences of mountain adventure, should chance conduct him this way; or, if making his exit from the mountain region by the Connecticut Valley, he may, taking it in his way out, make this the appropriate pendant of his tours, romantic and picturesque.

Having been so long known to and frequented by the Indian as well as white hunters, the mountain is naturally the subject of considerable legend,[1] which the historian of Warren has scrupulously gathered together. One of these tales, founded on the disaster of Rogers, recounts the sufferings of two of his men, hopelessly snared in the great Jobildunk ravine. But that tale of horror needs no embellishment from romance. This enormous rent, equally hideous in fact as in name, cut into the vitals of the mountain so deeply that a dark stream gushes from the gaping wound, conceals within its mazes several fine cascades. Owing to long-continued drought, the streams were so puny and so languid when I visited the mountain that I explored only the upper portion of the gorge, which bristles with an untamed forest, levelling its myriad spears at the breast of the climber.

The greater part of the mountain lies in the town of Benton, or, perhaps, it would be nearer the truth to say that fully half the township is appropriated by its prodigious earthwork. But, to reach it without un-

---

[1] Speaking of legends, that of Rubenzal, of the Silesian mountains, is not unlike Irving's legend of Rip Van Winkle and the Catskills. Both were Dutch legends. The Indian legends of Mooschillock are very like to those of high mountains, everywhere.

dergoing the fatigues of a long march through the woods, it is necessary to proceed to the village of Warren, which is twenty miles north of Plymouth, and about fourteen south of Haverhill. Behind the village rises Mount Carr. Still farther to the north the summits of Mounts Kineo, Cushman, and Waternomee, continuing this range now separating us from the Pemigewasset Valley, form also the eastern wall of the valley of Baker's River, which has its principal source in the ravines of Moosehillock. There is a bridle-path opening communication with the mountain from the Benton side, on the north; and so with Lisbon and Franconia. A carriage-road is also contemplated on that side, which will render access still more feasible for a large summer population; while a bridle-path, lately opened between two peaks of the Carr range, facilitates ingress from the Pemigewasset side.

I set out from the village of Warren on one of the hottest afternoons of an intensely hot and dry summer. The five miles between the village and the base of the mountain need not detain the sight-seer. At the crossing of Baker's River I remarked again the granite-bed honeycombed with those curious pot-holes sunk by whirling stones, first set in motion and then spun around by the stream, which here, breaking up into several wild pitches, pours through a rocky gorge. But how gratefully cool and refreshing was even the sound of rushing water in that still, stifling atmosphere, coming, one would think, from a furnace! Then for two miles more the horse crept along the road, constantly ascending the side of the valley, until the last house was reached. Here we passed a turnpike-gate, rolled over the crisped turf of a stony pasture through a second gate, and were at the foot of Mooschillock.

In a trice we exchanged the sultriness, the dryness, the dust, parching or suffocating us, of a shadeless road, for the cool, moist air of the mountain-forest and the delectable sound of running water. A brook shot past; then another; then the horse, who stopped when he liked, and as often as he liked, like a man forced to undertake a task which he is determined shall cost his task-masters dearly, began a languid progress up the increasing declivity before us. His sighs and groans, as he plodded wearily along, were enough to melt a heart of stone. I therefore dismounted and walked on, leaving the driver to follow as he could. The question was, not how the horse should get us up the mountain, but how we should get the horse up.

They call it four and a half miles from the bottom to the top. The distances indicated by the sign-boards, nailed to trees, did not appear to me exact. They are not exact; and the reason why they are not is sufficiently original to merit a word of explanation. Having long observed the effect of imagination, especially in computing distances, the builder of the road, as he himself informed me, adopted a truly ingenious method of his own. He lengthened or shortened his miles according as the travelling was good or bad. For example: the first mile, being an easy one, was stretched to a mile and a quarter. The last mile is also very good travelling. That, too, he lengthened to a mile and a half. In this way he reduced the intervening two and a half miles of the worst road to one and three-fourth miles. This absolutely harmless piece of deception, he averred, considerably shortened the most difficult part of the journey. No one complained that the good miles were too long, while the bad ones were now passed over with far less grumbling than before they were abbreviated by this simple expedient, which very few, I am convinced, would have thought of. In fact, the sum of the whole distance being scrupulously adhered to, it is the most civil piece of engineering of which I have any knowledge.

The road up is rough, tedious, and, until the ridge at the foot of the south peak is reached, uninteresting. It crooks and turns with absolute lawlessness while climbing the flanks of the southern peak, skirting also the side of the profound ravine eating its way into the mountain from the south. Nearing this summit we obtained through an opening a glimpse of Mount Washington, veiled in the clouds. The trees now visibly dwindled. Just before reaching the ridge, where it joins this peak, a fine spring, deliciously cold, gushed from the mountain side. A few rods more of ascent brought us quite out upon the long, narrow, curving backbone of the mountain, uplifting its sharp edge between two profound gorges, connecting the peaks set at its two extremes, between which Nature has decreed a perpetual divorce. The sun was just setting as we emerged upon this natural way conducting from peak to peak along the airy crest of the mountain.

Although this, it will be remembered, is one of the longest miles, according to the scale of computation in vogue here, the unexpected speed which the horse now put forth, the sight of the squat, little Tip-Top House, clinging to the summit beyond, the upper and nether worlds floating or fading in splendor, while the night-breezes sweeping over cooled our foreheads, and rudely jostled the withered trees, drawn a little apart to the right and left to let us pass, quickly replaced that weariness of mind and body which the mountain exacts of all who pass over it on a sultry midsummer's day.

At the extremity of the ridge, which is only wide enough for the road, a gradual ascent led to the high summit and to a level plateau of a few acres at its top. This was treeless, but covered with something like soil, smooth, and, being singularly free from the large stones found everywhere else, affords good walking in any direction. The house is built of rough stone, and, though of primitive construction, is comfortable, and even inviting. Furthermore, its materials being collected on the spot, one accepts it as still constituting a part of the mountain, which, indeed, at a little distance it really seems to be. In the evening I went out, to find the mountain blindfolded with clouds. Soon rain began to drive against the window-panes in volleys. At a late hour we heard wheels grinding on the rocks outside, and then a party of tourists drove up to the door, dripping and crestfallen at having undertaken the ascent with a storm staring them in the face. But they had only this one day, they said, and were "bound" to go up the mountain. So up they toiled through pitch darkness, through rain and cloud, passed the night in a building said to be on the summit, and returned down the mountain in the morning, to catch their train, through as dense a fog as ever exasperated a hurried tourist. But they had been to the top! Are there anywhere else in the world people who travel two hundred miles for a single day's recreation?

It is very curious, this being domesticated on the top of a mountain. We go to bed wondering if the scene will not all vanish in our dreams. It was very odd, too, to see the tourists silently mount their buck-board in the morning, and disappear, within a stone's throw, in clouds. Detaching themselves to all intents from earth, they began a flight in air. Walking a short distance, perhaps a gunshot, from the house, I groped my way back with difficulty. The case seemed desperate.

But grandest scene of all was the breaking up of the storm. Shortly after noon the high sun began to exert a sensible influence upon the clouds. A perceptible warmth, replacing the chill and clammy mists, began to pervade the mountain-top. Presently a dim sun-ray shot through. Then, as if a noiseless explosion had suddenly rent them, the whole mass of clouds was torn in ten thousand tatters flying through space. All nature seemed seized with sudden frenzy. Here a summit and there a peak was seen, struggling fiercely in the grasp of the storm. Coming up with rushing noise, the west wind charged home the routed storm-clouds with fresh squadrons. What indescribable yet noiseless tumult raged in the heavens! Even the mountains seemed scarcely able to stem the tide of fugitives. A panic seized them. Fear gave them wings. They rushed pell-mell into the ravines and clung to the tree-tops; they dashed themselves blindly against the adamant of Lafayette, only to fall back broken into the deep fosse beneath. Bolts of dazzling sunshine continually tore through them. The gorges themselves seemed heaped with the wounded and the dying. But the rushing wind, trampling the fugitives down, dispersed and cut them mercilessly to pieces. One was irresistibly carried away by this rage of battle. In ten minutes I looked around upon a clear sky. One cloud, impaled on the gleaming spear of Lafayette, hung limp and lifeless; another floated like a scarf from the polished casque of Chocorua; a third, taken prisoner *en route*, humbly held the train of Washington. All the rest of the phantom host, using its power to render itself invisible, vanished from sight as if the mountains had swallowed it up.

The landscape being now fully uncovered, I enjoyed all its rare perfection. It is a superb and fascinating one, invested with a powerful individuality, surrounded by a charm of its own. You wish to see the two great chains? There they are, the greater rising over the lesser, in the order fixed by Nature. That sunny space in the softened coloring of old tapestry, more to the right, is the Pemigewasset Valley, and the spot from where not long ago we looked up at this mountain looming large in the distance. We raise our eyes to glance up the East Branch upon Mount Hancock and the peaks of Carrigain peeping over. We touch with magic wand the faint cone of Kearsarge, so dim that it seems as if it must rise and float away; then, continuing to call the roll of mountains, Moat, Tripyramid, Chocorua, and all our earlier acquaintances rise or nod among the Sandwich peaks. Some draw their cloud-draperies over their bare shoulders, some sun their naked and hairy breasts in savage luxury. We alight like a bird upon the glassy bosom of Winnepiseogee the incomparable, and, like the bird, again rise, refreshed, for flights still more remote. We sweep over the Uncanoonucs into Massachusetts, steadying the eye upon far Wachusett as we pass from the Merrimac Valley. Now come thronging in upon us the mountains of the Connecticut Valley. We rest awhile upon the transcendently beautiful expanse of the Ox-Bow, and its playthings of villages, strung along the glittering necklace of the river. Across this valley, lifting our eyes, we wander among the loftiest peaks of the Green Mountains—those colossal *verd-antiques*—exchanging frozen glances across the placid expanse of Champlain with the haughtiest summits of the Adirondacks. We grow tired of this. One last look, this time up the valley, reveals to us the wide and curious gap between two distant mountains, and far beyond Memphremagog, where these mountains rise, we scan all the route travelled by Rogers, the perils of which are fresh in our memory. We pass on unchallenged into the dominions of Victoria.

Is not this a landscape worth coming ten miles out of one's way to see? And yet the half is not told. I have merely indicated its dimensions. Now let the reader, drawing an imaginary line from peak to peak, go over at leisure all that lies between. I merely prick the chart for him. Moosehillock, not quite five thousand feet high, overlooks all New Hampshire, pushes investigation into Maine and Massachusetts, is familiar with Vermont, distant with New York, and has an eye upon Canada. It is said the ocean has been seen, but I did not see it.

Circumstances compelled me to drive the old horse, who has made more ascensions of the mountain than any living thing, back to Warren. No other was to be had for love or money. Had there been time I would have preferred walking, but there was not. This horse measured sixteen hands. His thin body and long legs resembled a horse upon stilts. He looked dejected, but resigned. I argued that he would be able to get down the mountain somehow; and, once out of the woods, I could count on his eagerness to get home, to some extent, perhaps. I was not deceived in either expectation.

The road, as I have said, is for most of the way a rough, steep, and stony one. In order to check the havoc made by sudden showers, and to hold the thin soil in place, hemlock-boughs were spread over it, artfully concealing those protruding stones which the scanty soil refused to cover. He who intrusted himself to it did not find it a bed of roses. The buck-board was the longest, clumsiest, and most ill-favored it has ever been my lot to see. This vehicle, being peculiar to the mountains, demands, at least, a word. It is a very primitive and ingenious affair, and cheaply constructed. Naturally, therefore, it originated where the farmers were poor and the roads bad. But what is the buck-board? Every one has seen the spring-board of a gymnasium or of a circus. A smooth plank, ten feet long, resting upon trestles placed at either end, assists the acrobat to vault high in the air. Each time he falls the rebound sends him up again. This is the principle of the buck-board. Remove the trestles, put a pair of wheels in the place of each, and you have the vehicle itself, *minus* shafts or pole, according as one or two horses are to draw it. Increased weight bends the board or the spring more and

THE BUCK-BOARD WAGON.

more until it is in danger of touching the ground. The passengers sit in the hollow of this spring, the natural tendency of which is to shoot them into the air.

I am justified in speaking thus of the road and the vehicle. But who shall describe the horse? That animal was possessed of a devil, and, like the swine of the miracle, ran violently all the way down the mountain, without stopping for water or breath. Fortunate indeed for me was it that the sea was not at the bottom. In three-quarters of an hour, half of which was spent in the air, I was at the foot of the mountain which had required two tedious hours to ascend. How the quadruped managed to avoid falling headlong fifty times over the concealed stones I have no idea. How I contrived to alight, when a wheel, coming violently against one of these stones, put the spring-board in play — how I contrived to alight, I remark, during this game of battledoor and shuttlecock, never twice in the same place, is to this day an enigma.

The houses of ancient Rome frequently bore the inscription for the benefit of strangers, "*Cave canem.*" This could be advantageously replaced here, upon the first turnpike-gate, at the mountain's foot, with the warning, " Beware of the horse!"

VIII.

BETHLEHEM.

Ros. O Jupiter! how weary are my spirits!
Touch. I care not for my spirits, if my legs were not weary.
As You Like It.

HAVING finished with the western approach to the White Mountains, I was now at liberty to retrace my route up the Ammonoosuc Valley, which so abounds in picturesque details—farms, hamlets, herds, groups of pines, maples, torrents, roads feeling their way up the heights—to that anomaly of mountain towns, Bethlehem. Thanks to the locomotive, the journey is short. The villages of Bath, Lisbon, Littleton, are successively entered; the same flurry gives a momentary activity to each station, the same faces crowd the platforms, and the same curiosity is exhibited by the passengers, whose excitement receives an increase with every halt of the laboring train.

Bethlehem is ranged high up, along the side of a mountain, like the best china in a cupboard. The crest of Mount Agassiz[1] rises behind it. Beneath the village the ground descends, rather abruptly, to the Ammonoosuc, which winds, through matted woods, its way out of the mountains. There are none of those eye-catching gleams of water which so agreeably diversify these interminable miles of forest and mountain land.

It is only by ascending the slopes of Mount Agassiz that we can secure a stand-point fairly showing the commanding position of Bethlehem, or where its immediate surroundings may be viewed all at once. It is so situated, with respect to the curvature of this mountain, that at one end of the village they do not know what is going on at the other. One

---

[1] In the valley of the Aar, at the head of the Aar glacier, in Switzerland, is a peak named for Agassiz, who thus has two enduring monuments, one in his native, the other in his adopted land. The eminent Swiss scientist spent much time among the White Mountains.

end revels in the wide panorama of the west, the other holds the unsurpassed view of the great peaks to the east.

Bethlehem has risen, almost by magic, at the point where the old highway up the Ammonoosuc is intersected by that coming from Plymouth, the Pemigewasset Valley, and the Profile House. In time a small roadside hamlet naturally clustered about this spot. Dr. Timothy Dwight, the pioneer traveller for health and pleasure among these mountains, passed through here in 1803. Speaking of the appearance of Bethlehem, he says: "There is nothing which merits notice, except the patience, enterprise, and hardihood of the settlers which have induced them to stay upon so forbidding a spot; a magnificent prospect of the White Mountains; and a splendid collection of other mountains in their neighborhood, particularly on the south-west." It was then reached by only one wretched road, which passed the Ammonoosuc by a dangerous ford. The few scattered habitations were mere log-cabins, rough and rude. The few planting-fields were still covered with dead trees, stark and forbidding, which the settlers, unable to fell with the axe, killed by girdling, as the Indians did.

From this historical picture of Bethlehem in the past, we turn to the Bethlehem of to-day. It is turning from the post-rider to the locomotive. Not a single feature is recognizable except the splendid prospect of the White Mountains, and the magnificent collection of other mountains, which call forth the same admiration to-day. Fortunate geographical position, salubrity, fine scenery — these, and these alone, are the legitimate cause of what may be termed the rise and progress of Bethlehem. All that the original settlers seem to have accomplished is to clear away the forests which intercepted, and to make the road conducting to the view.

It is the position of Bethlehem with respect to the recognized points or objects of interest that gives to it a certain strategic advantage. For example, it is admirably situated for excursions north, south, east, or west. It is ten miles to the Profile, twelve to the Fabyan, seventeen to the Crawford, fifteen to the Waumbek, and eighteen to the base of Mount Washington. One can breakfast at Bethlehem, dine on Mount Washington, and be back for tea; and he can repeat the experience with respect to the other points named as often as inclination may prompt. Moreover, the great elevation exempts Bethlehem from the malaria and heat of the valleys. The air is dry, pure, and invigorating, rendering it the paradise of those invalids who suffer from periodical attacks of hay-fever. Lastly, it is new, or comparatively new, and possesses the charm of novelty—not the least consideration to the thousands who are in pursuit of that and that only.

Bethlehem Street is the legitimate successor of the old road. This is a name *sui generis* which seems hardly appropriate here, although it is so commonly applied to the principal thoroughfares of our inland New England villages. It has a spick-and-span look, as if sprung up like a bed of mushrooms in a night. And so, in fact, it has; for Bethlehem as a summer resort dates only a few years back its sudden rise from comparative obscurity into the full blaze of popular fame and favor. The guide-book of fifteen years ago speaks of the *one* small but comfortable hotel, kept by the Hon. J. G. Sinclair. In fact, very little account was made of it by travellers, except to remark the magnificent view of the White Mountains on the east, or of the Franconia Mountains on the south, as they passed over the then prescribed tour from North Conway to Plymouth, or *vice versa*.

But this newness, which you at first resent, besides introducing here and there some few attempts at architectural adornment, contrasts very agreeably with the ill-built, rambling, and slip-shod appearance of the older village-centres. They are invariably most picturesque from a distance. But here there is an evident effort to render the place itself attractive by making it beautiful. Good taste generally prevails. I suspect, however, that the era of good taste, beginning with the incoming of a more refined and intelligent class of travellers, communicated its spirit to two or three enterprising and sagacious men,[1] who saw in what Nature had done an incentive for their own efforts. We walk here in a broad, well-built thoroughfare, skirted on both sides with hotels, boarding-houses, and modern cottages, in which three or four thousand sojourners annually take refuge. All this has grown from the "one small hotel" of a dozen years ago. Shade-trees and grass-plots beautify the way-side. An immense horizon is visible from these houses, and even the hottest summer days are rendered endurable by the light airs produced and set in motion by the oppressive heats of the valley. The sultriest season is, therefore, no bar to out-of-door exercise for persons of average health,

---

[1] Such, for example, as the Hon. J. G. Sinclair, Isaac Cruft, Esq., and ex-Governor Howard of Rhode Island.

rendering walks, rambles, or drives subject only to the will or caprice of the pleasure-seeker. But in the evening all these houses are emptied of their occupants. The whole village is out-of-doors, enjoying the coolness or the panorama with all the zest unconstrained gratification always brings. The multitudes of well-dressed promenaders surprise every new-comer, who immediately thinks of Saratoga or Newport, and their social characteristics. Bethlehem, he thinks, must be the ideal of those who would carry city or, at least, suburban life among the mountains; who do not care a fig for solitude, but prefer to find their pleasures still connected with their home life. They are seeing life and seeing nature at the same time.

Sauntering along the street from the Sinclair House, a strikingly large and beautiful prospect opens as we come to the Belleview. Here the road, making its exit from the village, descends to the Ammonoosuc. The valley broadens and deepens, exposing to view all the town of Littleton, picturesquely scattered about the distant hill-sides. Its white houses resemble a bank of daisies. The hills take an easy attitude of rest. Six hundred feet below us the bottom of the valley exhibits its rich savannas, interspersed with cottages and groves. Above its deep hollow the Green Mountains glimmer in the far west. "Ah!" you say, "we will stop here."

Let us now again, leaving the Sinclair House behind, ascend the road to the Profile. It is not so much travelled as it was before the locomotive, in his coat-of-mail, sounded his loud trumpet at the gates of Franconia. A mile takes us to the brow of the hill. We hardly know which way to look first. Two noble and comprehensive views present themselves. To the left Mount Agassiz rears his commanding peak. In front of us, across a valley, is the great, deeply-cloven Franconia Notch. Lafayette is superb here. Now the large, compact mass of Mooschillock looms on the extreme right, together with all those striking objects lately studied or observed from the village of Franconia, which so quietly reposes beneath us. But this landscape properly belongs to the environs of Bethlehem, and never is it so incomparably grand as when the summits are fitfully revealed, battling fiercely with storm-clouds. Every phase of the conflict is watched with eager attention. Seeing all this passion above, it calls up a smile to look down at the unbroken and unconscious tranquillity of the valley.

Facing now in the direction of Bethlehem, the eye roves over the

MOUNT LAFAYETTE, FROM BETHLEHEM.

broad basin of the Ammonoosuc for many
miles up and down. The hills of Littleton, Whitefield, Dalton, Carroll, and Jefferson bend away from the opposite
side; and over the last the toothed Percy Peaks[1] rise blue and clear

---

[1] The twin Percy Peaks, which we saw in the north, rise in the south-east corner of Strat-
ford. Their name was probably derived from the township now called Stark, and formerly
Percy. The township was named by Governor Wentworth in honor of Hugh, Earl of North-

at the point where the waters of the Connecticut and the Androscoggin, approaching each other, conduct the Grand Trunk Railway out of the mountains. The west is packed with the high summits of the Green Mountain chain. The great White Mountains are concealed, as yet, by the swell of the mountain down whose side the road conducts to the village. "This," you exclaim, "this is the spot where we will pitch our tents!" But there is no public-house here, and we are reluctantly forced to descend. In proportion as we go down, this seemingly limitless panorama suffers a partial eclipse. The landscape changes from the high-wrought epic to the grand pastoral, if such a distinction may be applied to differing forms of mountain scenery. This approach is, without doubt, the most striking introduction to Bethlehem. It is curiously instructive, too, as regards the relative merits of successive elevations, each higher than the other, as proper view-points.

A third ramble is altogether indispensable before we can say that we know Bethlehem of the Hills. The direction is now to the east, by the road to the Crawford House, or Fabyan's, or the Twin. We continue along the high plateau, in the shade of sugar-maples or Lombardy poplars, to the eastern skirt of the village, the houses getting more and more unfrequent, until we come upon the edge of the slope to the Ammonoosuc, where the road to Whitefield, Lancaster, and Jefferson, leaving the main thoroughfare, drops quietly down into Bethlehem Hollow. No envious hill now obstructs the truly "magnificent view." Through the open valley the lordly mountains again inthrall us with the might of an overpowering majesty.

This locality has taken the name of the great hotel erected here by Isaac Cruft, whose hand is visible everywhere in Bethlehem. The Maplewood, as it is called, easily maintains at its own end the prestige of Bethlehem for rapid growth. When I first visited the place, in 1875, I found a modest roadside hostelry accommodating sixty guests; five years later a mammoth structure, in which six hundred could be accommodated, had risen, like Aladdin's palace, on the same spot. Instead of our little musical entertainment, our mock-trial, our quiet rubber of whist, of an evening, there were readings, lectures, balls, masquerades, theatricals, *musicales*, for every day of the week.

---

umberland, who figured in the early days of the American Revolution. The adjoining township of Northumberland is also commemorative of the same princely house.

But Bethlehem is emphatically the place of sunsets. In this respect no other mountain resort can pretend to equal it. From no other village are so many mountains visible at once; at no other has the landscape such length and breadth for giving full effect to these truly wonderful displays. More because the sublimity of the scene deserves a permanent chronicle than from any confidence in my own ability to reproduce it, I attempt in black and white to describe one of unparalleled intensity of color, one that may never be repeated, certainly never excelled, while the sun, the heavens, and the mountains shall last.

A cold drizzle having set in on the day of my arrival, the mountains were invisible when I rose in the morning. I looked, but they were no longer there. I was much vexed at the prospect of being storm-bound, or of making under compulsion a sojourn I had beforehand resolved to make at my own good will and pleasure. So strongly is the spirit of resistance developed in us. After a critical investigation of the weather, it crossed my mind like an intuition that something extraordinary was preparing behind the enormous masses of clouds clinging like wet draperies to the skirts of the mountains, forming an impenetrable curtain, now and then slowly lifted by the fresh north wind, now suddenly distended or collapsing like huge sails, but noiselessly and mysteriously as the ghostly canvas of the *Flying Dutchman.*

Toward the middle of the afternoon, the wind having freshened, the lower clouds broke apart here and there — just enough to reveal to us that ever-new picture of the White Mountains, beautifully robed in fresh snow, above the darker line of forest; but so thoroughly were the high summits blended with the dull silver-gray of upper sky that the true line of separation defied the keenest scrutiny to detect it. This produced a curious optical illusion. Extended sumptuously along the crest-line, rivalling the snow itself, a bank of white clouds rendered the deception perfect, since just above them began that heavy and dull expanse which overspread and darkened the whole heavens, thus imperfectly delineating a second line of summits mounting to a prodigious height. They seemed miles upon miles high.

Up stretched this gigantic and shadowy phantasm of towers, domes, and peaks, illimitably, as if mountains and heavens were indeed come together in eternal alliance. At the same time the finger dipped in water could trace a more conclusive outline on glass than the eye could find here. The summits, a little luminous, emitted a cold, spectral glare. It gave you a chill to look at them. No sky, no earth, no deep gorges, no stark precipices—no anything except that dead wall, so sepulchral in its gray gloom that equally mind and imagination failed to find one familiar outline or contour. The true peaks seemed clouds, and the clouds peaks. But this phantasm was only the prologue.

At the hour of sunset all the lower clouds had disappeared. The upper heavens now wore that deep grape-purple impervious to light or warmth, and producing the effect of a vast dome hung with black. The storm replaced the azure tint of the sky with the most sombre color in its laboratory. The light visibly waned. The icy peaks still reflected a boreal glitter. But in the west these funereal draperies fell a little short of touching the edge of the horizon—a bare hand's-breadth—leaving a crevice filled with golden light, pure and limpid as water, clear and vivid as winnowed sunshine. The sun's eye would soon be applied to this peep-hole. A feverish impatience seized us. We could see the people at their doors and in the street standing silent and expectant, with their faces turned to the heavens. From a station near Cruft's Ledge we watched intently for the moment when this splendid light, concentrated in one level sheet, should fall upon the great mountains.

In a few seconds a yellow spot of piercing brilliancy appeared in this narrow band of light. One look at it was blinding; a second would have paralyzed the optic nerve. Mechanically we put up our hands to shut it out. Imagine a stream of molten iron—hissing-hot and throwing off fiery spray — gushing from the side of a furnace! Even that can give but a feeble idea of the unspeakable intensity of this last sun-ray. It blazed. It flooded us with a suffocating effulgence. Suppose now this cataract of liquid flame suddenly illuminating the pitchy darkness of a cavern in the bowels of the earth. The effect was electrifying. Confined between the upper and nether expanse — dull earth and brooding sky—rendered tenfold more dazzling by the blackness above, beneath, the sun poured upon the great mountains one magnificent torrent of radiance. In an instant the broad land was deluged with the supreme glories of that morning when the awful voice of God uttered the sublime command,

"Let there be light, and there was light."

An electric shock awoke the torpid earth, transfigured the mountains. On swept the mighty wave, shedding light, and warmth, and splendor where a moment before all was dark, cold, and spiritless. Like Ajax before Troy, the giant hills braced on their dazzling armor. Like Achilles's shield, they threw back the brightness of the sun. Every tree stood sharply out. Every cavern disclosed its inmost secrets. Twigs glittered diamonds, leaves emitted golden rays. All was ravishingly beautiful.

This superb exhibition continued while one might count a hundred. Then all the lower mountains took on that ineffable purple that baffles description. Starr King, Cherry Mountain, were resplendent. As if the livid and thick-clustered clouds above had been trodden by invisible feet, these peaks seemed drenched with the juice of the wine-press. The high summits, buried in snow and cloud, were yet coldly impassive, but presently, little by little, the light crept up and up. Now it seized the topmost pinnacles. Heavens, what a sight! Ineffable glory seemed quenched in the sublime terrors of that moment. On our right the Twin and Franconia mountains glowed, from base to summit, like coals of fire. The lower forests were wrapped in flame. Then all the snowy line of peaks, from Adams to Clinton, turned blood-red. No pale rose or carnation tints, as in those enrapturing summer sunsets so often witnessed here. The stupendous and flaming mountains of hell seemed risen before us, clothed with immortal terrors. We stood rooted to the spot, like men who saw the judgment-day dawning, the solid earth consuming, before their doubting eyes. Everlasting, unquenchable fires seemed encompassing us about. Nothing more weird, more unearthly, or more infernal was ever seen. Even the country-people, stolid and indifferent as they usually are, regarded it with mingled stupefaction and dismay.

The drama approached its climax. Before we were aware, the valley grew dark. But still, the granite peaks of Lafayette, and of that admirable pyramid, Mount Garfield, which even the greater mountain cannot reduce to impotence, glowed like iron drawn from the fire. Their incandescent points, thrust upward into the black gulf of the heavens, towered above the blacker gulfs below unspeakably. By degrees the scorching heat cooled. The great Franconia spires successively paled. But long after they seemed reduced to ashes, the red flame still lingered upon the snows of Mount Washington. At last that, too, faded out. Life was extinct. The great summit took on a wan and livid hue. Night kindly spread her mantle over the lifeless form of the mountain, which still disclosed its larger outlines rigid, majestic, even in death.

Twilight succeeded—twilight steeped in silence and coolness, in the thousand odors exhaled by the teeming earth. One by one the birds hushed their noisy twitter. Overcome by their own perfumes, flowers shut their dewy petals and drooped their tender little heads. The river seemed a drowsy voice rising from the depths of the forest, complaining that it alone should toil on while all else reposed. With night comes the feeling of immensity. With sleep the conviction that we are nothing, and that the order of nature disturbs itself in nothing for us. If we awake, well; if not, well again. What if we should never wake? One such splendid pageant as I have attempted to describe instinctively quenches human pride. It is true, a sunset is in itself nothing, but it compels you to admit that the world moves for itself, not for you. Believe it not a gorgeous display in which you, the critical spectator, assist, but the signal that the day ends and the night cometh. A spectacle that can arouse the emotions of joy, fear, hope, suspense—nothing? Perhaps. God knows.

There are very pleasant walks, affording fine views of all the highest mountains, around the eastern slope or to the summit of the mountain rising at the back of the hotel. The bare but grassy crest of this mountain, one of my favorite haunts, enabled me to reconnoitre my route in advance up the valley, and to look over into the yet unvisited region of Jefferson, or back again, at the environs of Franconia. The glory that pours down upon these hills, the vales they infold, the wild streams, the craggy mountain spurs, the soft, velvety clearings that turn their dimpled cheeks to be kissed by the sunshine, may all be seen and fully enjoyed from this spot.

The heights behind us are well-wooded on the summits, but below this belt of woodland extends a broad band of sunny clearings checkered with fields of waving grain. These fields are among the highest cultivated lands in New England. Long tillage was necessary to reduce this refractory soil to subjection. Farther down, toward the railway-station, the pastures are so encumbered with stones that a sheep would turn from them in dismay. To mow among these stones a man would have to go down on his knees.

There is a beautiful orchard of sugar-maples down the road to the Hollow; but it always makes me sad to see these trees standing with their naked sides pierced and bleeding from gaping wounds.

At the corner of this road my attention was arrested by a sign-board planted in front of an unpainted cottage, behind which rose a clump of magnificent birches. I walked over to see what it could mean. The sign-board bore the name "Sir Isaac Newton Gay," in large black letters. Here was a spur to curiosity! A knight, or at least a baronet, living in humble seclusion, yet parading his quality thus in the face of the world! Going to the gate, my perplexity increased upon seeing the grass-plot in front of the dwelling literally covered with broken glass, lamp-chimneys, bits of colored china, bottles of every imaginable shape and size stuck upright upon sticks, interspersed with lumps of white quartz. Some cabalistic meaning, doubtless, attached to the display. This brilliant rubbish sparkled in the sun, filling the enclosure with the cheap glitter of a pawnbroker's shop-window. The thing so far announced a little eccentricity, at least, so I made bold to push my investigation still farther, and was rewarded by finding, piled against the trunk of a tree, at the back of the house, a heap of skulls of animals as high as my head. The recluse's intent was now plain. Here was a lesson that he who ran might read. The rubbish in the front yard illustrated the pomp, glitter, and emptiness of life; the monument of skulls its true estate, divested of all false show or pretence. Without doubt this was a philosopher worthy of his name.

I was admitted by a singular-looking being, with dry, straight, lank hair, weak features, watery eyes, and a shuffling gait. Some accident having partially closed one eye, gave him a look of preternatural wisdom. He was ready to give an opinion on any subject under the sun, no matter how difficult or abstruse, as soon as broached, and stroked his scanty beard while doing so with evident self-complacency. I had a moment to see that the walls were papered with old handbills of county fairs, travelling shows, and the like, the floor covered with patches of carpet as various as Joseph's coat, when my man began a formula similar to what the Bearded Lady drawls out or the Tattooed Man recites through his nose to gaping rustics at a country muster, at ten cents a head. He told where he was born, how old he was, and how long he had lived in Bethlehem. At the proper moment I put my hand in my pocket and took out a dime, which he thankfully accepted, and dropped inside a broken coffee-pot.

"Sir," I observed, "seeing you are American-born, I infer your title must have been conferred by some foreign potentate?"

"No; that is my name."

" But," I pursued, "has it not an unrepublican sound in a country where titles are regarded with distrust, not to say aversion ?"

" I tell you it is my name," with some heat; "I was named for the great *Sir* Isaac Newton."

" Your pardon, Sir Isaac. May I ask if you inherit the genius of your distinguished namesake ?"

" Well, yes, to some extent I do; I philoserphize a good deal. I read a good many books folks leaves here, besides what newspapers I can pick up; but you see it costs a lifetime to get knowledge."

Jaques, the misanthrope, wandering in the Forest of Arden, was not more astonished at Touchstone's philosophy than I at this answer. " Very true," I assented. " What is your philosophy of life ?"

He tapped his forehead with his forefinger, but it was only too evident the apartment was untenanted. He remained a moment or two as if in deep thought, and then began,

" Well, I'm eighty-six years of age, come next July."

My flesh began to creep: he was beginning, for the third time, his eternal formula. The hermit, fumbling a red handkerchief, resumed,

" I can say I've never wanted for necessaries, and don't propose to give myself any trouble about it." And then he expatiated on the folly of fretfulness.

The Hermit of Bethlehem, as he is called, but who opens his door wide for the world to enter, is· a very ordinary sort of hermit indeed. Still, his very feebleness of intellect, his vanity even, should be a shield instead of a target for those who, like myself, are lured by the unmeaning trumpery at his door, which has no other significance in the world than a childish passion for objects that glitter in the sun.

The constituents of hotel life do not belong to any locality: they are universal. It is curious to see here people who have spent half their lives in India, or China, or Australia moving about among the untravelled with the well-bred ease and adaptation to circumstances that newly-fledged tourists can neither understand nor imitate. It is very droll, too, that people who have lived ten years in the same street, at home, without knowing each other, meet here for the first time.

I beg to introduce another acquaintance picked up by the roadside while walking from the Twin Mountain House to Bethlehem. Had I been driving, the incident would still have waited for a narrator.

Climbing the hill-side at a snail's pace was a peddler's cart, drawn by a scrubby little white horse, and bearing a new broom for an ensign, which seemed to symbolize that this petty trader meant to sweep the road clean of its loose cash. The sides of the cart were gayly decorated with pans, basins, dippers by the dozen, and bristled with knickknacks for barter or ready money, from a gridiron to a door-mat. The movement of the vehicle over the stony road kept up a lively clatter, which announced its coming from afar. There being, for the moment, no house in sight, the proprietor was engaged in picking raspberries by the road-side.

The peddler—well, he was little, and stubby too, like his horse, for whom he had dismounted to lighten the pull up-hill. The animal seemed to know his business, for he stopped short as often as he came to a water-bar, blew a cloud from his nostrils, champed his bit, and distended his sides so alarmingly with a long, deep respiration, that the patched-up harness seemed in danger of bursting. He then glanced over his shoulder toward his master, shook his head deprecatingly, and, with a deep sigh, moved on.

The little merchant of small wares and great had on a rusty felt hat, rakishly set on one side of his bullet head, and a faded olive-green coat, rather short in the skirts, to conceal two patches in his trousers. The latter were tucked into a pair of dusty boots very much turned up at the toes. His face was a good deal sunburnt, and his hair, eyebrows, and mustache were the color of the road—sandy. Except a pair of scissors, the points of which protruded from his left-hand vest-pocket, I perceived no weapon offensive or defensive about him. He was a very innocent-looking peddler indeed.

As I was passing him he held out a handful of ripe fruit. The hand was disfigured with an ugly cicatrice: it was rather dirty. He accompanied the offer with an invitation to "hop on" his cart and ride. This double civility emanated from a gentleman and a peddler.

The walk from Crawford's to Bethlehem *is* rather fatiguing; but I said, as in duty bound, "No" (I said it because the thought of riding through Bethlehem Street on the top of a peddler's cart appeared ridiculous in my eyes—with shame I confess it), "thank you; your horse already has all he can pull, and I have only a mile or two farther to go."

The peddler then fell into step with me, taking a long, even stride that brought back old recollections. I said, ·

" You have been a soldier."

" How know you dat?"

" By your gait—you do not walk, you march: by that sabre-cut on your right hand."

" Ha! you goot eyes haf; but it a payonet vas."

Believing I saw a veteran of our great civil war, I asked, with undisguised interest,

" Where did you serve?   Where were you wounded?"

" Von year und half in war mit Danemark, von year und half mit Oustria, und two mit Vrance."

I looked at him again. What!   That undersized, insignificant appearing little chap, whom I could easily have pitched into the ditch, he a soldier of Sadowa, of Metz, of Paris.   Bah!

" So, the wars over, you emigrated to America?"

" Right avay.   Ven I get home from Baris I tell Linda, my vife, 'Look here, Linda: I been soldier six year.   Now I plenty fighting got.   Dere's two hunder thaler in the knapsack.   Shut your mouth tight, open your eye close, and we get out of dis double-quig.'   She say 'Where I go?' und I tell her the *U*-nited States, by hell, befor anoder var come.   She begin to cry, I begin to schwear, und we settle it right avay."

I asked if he minded telling how he came by the wound in his hand.   This is what he told me in his broken English:

When Marshal Bazaine made his last desperate effort to shake off the deadly gripe the Prussians had fastened upon Metz, a battalion of *tirailleurs* suddenly surrounded an advanced post established by the Germans in the suburbs.   The morning was foggy, and the surprise complete.   The picket had hardly the time to run to their arms before they were driven back pell-mell on the reserve, amid a shower of balls.   The reserve took refuge in a stone building surrounded by a thick hedge, maintaining an irregular fire from the windows.   One of the last to cross the court-yard, with the French at his heels, was our German.   Before he could gain the friendly shelter of the house he stumbled and fell headlong, his gun flying through the air as he came to the ground, so that he was not only prostrate but disarmed.

Half-stunned, he scrambled to his knees just as his nearest pursuer made a savage lunge with his sabre-bayonet.   The Prussian instinctively grasped it.   While trying 'thus to parry the deadly thrust, the keen weapon pierced his hand, and he was a second time borne to the earth, or, rather, pinned to it by his adversary's bayonet.

"*Rendez-vous Allemand, cochon!*" screamed the Frenchman, bestriding the little Prussian with a look of mortal hatred.

"*Je ne fous combrends,*" replied the wounded man, drawing a revolver with his free hand and shooting his enemy dead. "I couldn't helb it, I vas so mad," finished the ex-soldier, running to serve two of his customers, who stood waiting for him at a gate by the roadside. I left him exhibiting ribbons, edgings, confectionery—heaven knows what! —with all the volubility of an experienced shopman.

IX.

JEFFERSON, AND THE VALLEY OF ISRAEL'S RIVER.

Through the valley runs a river, bright and rocky, cool and swift,
Where the wave with many a quiver plays around the pine-tree's drift.

Good Words.

IT remains to introduce the reader into the valley watered by Israel's River, and for this purpose we take the rail from Bethlehem to Whitefield, and from Whitefield to Jefferson.

Like Bethlehem, Jefferson lies reposing in mid-ascent of a mountain. Here the resemblance ends. The mountain above it is higher, the valley beneath more open, permitting an unimpeded view up and down. The hill-side upon which the clump of hotels is situated makes no steep plunge into the valley, but inclines gently down to the banks of the river. Instead of crowding upon and jostling each other, the mountains forming opposite sides of this valley remain tranquilly in the alignment they were commanded not to overstep. The confusion there is reduced to admirable order here; the smooth slopes, the clean lines, the ample views, the roominess, so to speak, of the landscape, indicate that everything has been done without haste, with precision, and without deviation from the original plan, which contemplated a paradise upon earth.

Issuing from the wasted sides of Mount Jefferson and Mount Adams, Israel's River runs a short north-westerly course of fifteen miles into the Connecticut at Lancaster. This beautiful stream received its name from Israel Glines, a hunter, who frequented these regions long before the settlement of the country. The road from Lancaster to Gorham follows the northern highlands of its valley to its head, then crossing the dividing ridge which separates its waters from those of Moose River, descends this stream to the Androscoggin at Gorham.

On the north side Starr King Mountain rises 2400 feet above the valley and 3800 feet above the sea. On the south side Cherry Mountain lifts itself 3670 feet higher than the tide-level. These two mountains form the broad basin through which Israel's River flows for more than half its course. The village of Jefferson Hill lies on the southern slope of Starr King, and, of course, on the north side of the valley. Cherry Mountain, the most prominent object in the foreground, is itself a fine mountain study. It looks down through the great Notch, greeting Chocorua. It is conspicuous from any elevated point north of the Franconia group — from Fabyan's, Bethlehem, Whitefield, Lancaster, etc.

THE NORTHERN PEAKS FROM JEFFERSON.

Owl's Head is a conspicuous protuberance of this mountain. Over the right shoulder of Cherry Mountain stand the great Franconia Peaks, and to the right of these, its buildings visible, is Bethlehem. Now look up the valley.

We see that we have taken one step nearer the northern wing of the great central edifice whose snowy dome dominates New England. We are advancing as if to turn this magnificent battle-line of Titans, on whose right Madison stands in an attitude to repel assault. Adams next erects his sharp lance, Jefferson his shining crescent, Washington his broad buckler, and Monroe his twin crags against the sky. Jefferson, as the nearest, stands boldly forward, showing its tremendous ravines, and long, supporting ridges, with great distinctness. Washington loses something of its grandeur here; at least it is not the most striking object; that must be sought for among the sable-sided giants standing at his right hand. The southern peaks, being foreshortened, show only an irregular and flattened outline which we do not look at a second time. From Madison to Lafayette, our two rallying points, the distance can hardly be less than forty miles as the eye travels: the entire circuit it is able to trace cannot fall short of seventy or eighty miles. As at Bethlehem, the view out of the valley is chiefly remarkable for its contrast with every other feature.

I took a peculiar satisfaction in these views, they were so ample, so extensive, so impressive. Here you really feel as if the whole noble company of mountains were marshalled solely for your delighted inspection. At no other point is there such unmeasured gratification in seeing, because the eye roves without hinderance over the grandest summits, placed like the Capitol at the head of its magnificent avenue. It alights first on one pinnacle, then flits to another. It interrogates these immortal structures with a calm scrutiny. It dives into the cool ravines; it seeks to penetrate, like the birds, the profound silence of the forests. It toils slowly up the broken crags, or loiters by the cascades, hanging like athletes from dizzy brinks. It shrinks, it admires, it questions; it is grave, gay, or thoughtful by turns. I do not believe the man lives who, looking up to those mountains as in the face of the Deity, can deliberately utter a falsehood: the lie would choke him.

Furthermore, you get the best idea of height here, because the long amphitheatre of mountains is seen steadily growing in stature toward the great central group; and comparison is, by all odds, the best of teachers for the eye.

If for no other reason than the respect due to age, Jefferson deserves a moment to itself. It was granted, October 3d, 1765, to John Goffe, under the name of Dartmouth. The road diverging here, and crossing Cherry Mountain to Fabyan's, is the oldest, as it long was the only highway through the White Mountains. In those early times the travelled way was by the Connecticut River and Lancaster through this valley to the White Mountain Notch. The divergent road is the old turnpike between Vermont and Portland. Gradually, as settlements were pushed farther and farther up the Ammonoosuc, a way was made by Bath, Lisbon, Littleton, and Dalton, to Lancaster; but to pass beyond it was still necessary to follow the old route; nor was it until after the settlement of Bethlehem cleared the way that an execrable horse-path was made over the present great highway up the Ammonoosuc. In 1803 President Dwight passed over this new road on his second excursion to the great Notch. Few travellers would now be willing to undergo what he did to see the mountains. There were then only three or four houses in the sixteen miles between Bethlehem and the Notch.

One of the first settlers of Jefferson was Colonel Joseph Whipple, mentioned in the narrative of Nancy, the ill-starred mountain-maid, who died while following her faithless lover in his flight from Jefferson out of the mountains. Colonel Whipple lived on the road to Cherry Mountain, near the mill. In 1797 his was the only house on the road. During the Revolution a party of Indians, led by a white man, surrounded the house, and made Whipple their prisoner. Inventing some pretext, the colonel obtained leave to go into another room, from which he made his escape by a window and fled to the woods, where he successfully eluded pursuit.

Finding myself already well advanced toward the summit of Starr King, I finished the ascent of this mountain during an afternoon's stroll. Nothing worthy of remark, except the exquisite view from the summit, presented itself. Here I met again a throng of old acquaintances, and encountered a crowd of new ones. Here I saw something like a shadow darken the side of Mount Washington, and watched it creep steadily up and up to the summit. The shadow was the smoke of the locomotive making its last ascent for the day, under the eyes of thousands of spectators, who look at it to turn away with a smile, a shrug, or a shake of the head.

The name of Starr King has become a household word with all travellers in the White Mountains. It was most fitting that he who interpreted Nature so well and so truly should receive his monument at her hands. To him the mountains were emblematic of her highest perfection. He loved them. His tone when speaking of them is always tender and caressing. They appealed to his rare and exquisite perception of the beautiful, to his fine and sensitive nature, capable of detecting intuitively what was hid from common eyes. He felt their presence to be ennobling and uplifting. He opened for us the charmed portal. We accompanied him through an earthly paradise then first revealed to us by the fervor and wealth of his description. He led us to the shadiest retreats, the coolest groves, the most secluded glens. He guided our footsteps up the steep mountain-side to the bleak summit. Thrice fitting was it that a mountain should perpetuate the name of Thomas Starr King. As was said at the grave of Gautier, he too dated "from the creation of the beautiful."

I have now rested four days at Ethan Crawford's, who lives on the side of Boy Mountain, five miles east of Jefferson Hill, on the road to Gorham. This Ethan is a son of the celebrated guide and host so well known to former travellers by the *sobriquet* of Keeper of the Mountains.

I go to the window, and facing toward the setting sun look down the broadening valley of Israel's River, over the glistening house-tops of Whitefield, into and beyond the Connecticut Valley. I have Mitten Mountain and Cherry Mountain, both heavily wooded, just over the way, although the view of these elevations is in part intercepted by a nearer mountain, also covered with a vigorous forest. At this moment I hear the rush of the stream far down in the Hollow; and, following the serpentine line its dark course makes among the press of hills, am confronted by the massive slopes of Madison and Adams, the sombre ravine and castled crags of Jefferson, and the hoary crest of Washington. I am really in the heart of the mountains.

Swiftly from these mountains descend, with exquisite grace, enormous billows of deep sea-green, which do not subside but lift themselves proudly at the foot of those great overhanging walls of olive and malachite. Here rolling together, their foliage, bright or dark, repeats the effect of flaws sweeping over a sunny sea. Their deep hollows, arching sides, and limpid crests perfect the resemblance to the moment when, having exerted its utmost energy, the panting ocean stands exhausted and motionless in the grasp of the north wind.

These lower mountains, interposing a barrier between the two valleys of the Ammonoosuc and of Israel's River, seem, you think, pushed up from the yielding earth simply by the enormous weight of the higher and neighboring mountains whose keen summit-lines cut New England in halves. At this hour these lines are edged with dull gold. All along the wavering heights I can detect with the naked eye isolated black crags, and can plainly see the deep dents in the broken cornices and capitals of the grand old mountains—those vestiges of their primordial architecture. Here the inclined ridge of the plateau, connecting the pinnacle of Washington with the peaks of Monroe, is traced along its whole extent. At this distance its craggy outline breaks in light ripples, announcing nothing of that wilderness of stones assailing the climber. All the asperities are softened into capricious harmonies. Below yawn the ravines.

The tracks of old slides and torrents in the side of Monroe remind you of the branches of a gigantic fossil tree, exposed by a fracture dividing the mountain in two. Such is, in fact, the impression received by looking at this mountain; but the object which most excites my attention is the broad and deep rent in the side of Jefferson, over which hang on one side the crumbling counterfeits of towers and battlements, while on the other cataracts, like necklaces, are suspended over its unfathomed abysses. Cloud-shadows drift noiselessly along the warm steeps. Cataracts glisten brightly in the sun. The grave peaks look down unmoved on the play of the one and the sport of the other.

The picture of life in East Jefferson would not be complete without the old hound dozing in the sun, the turkey-cocks strutting consequentially up and down, the barn-swallows darting swiftly in and out, the ring of young Ethan's anvil, and the bleating of sheep far up the mountain-side. I see them nibbling the fresh herbage, and watch the gambols of the lambs like a child — only the child laughs aloud, and I do not laugh. Voices come down the hill-side, and I see the slow movement of a hammock and the flutter of a dress in the maple-grove. Poetry and perfume mingle with the scent of wild-flowers and songs of golden-mouthed birds.

Evening does not drive us within doors, the nights are so enchanting. Day fades imperceptibly out. Even the stars seem disconcerted. One by one they peep, and then flit from view. We watch the slow mustering of the celestial host in silence. A meteor leaps from heaven to earth. The fire-flies resemble a shower of sparks, or, as darkness deepens, a phosphorescent sea. Dorbeetles hurtle the still air, and frogs sing barcarolles in the misty fens. Now the mountains put on their sable armor that is to render them invisible. Here the poet must assist us:

"It is the hush of night; and all between
Thy margin and the mountains, dusk, yet clear,
Mellowed and mingling, yet distinctly seen—
Save darkened Jura, whose capped heights appear
Precipitously steep."

Light seems reluctant to leave the summits. It does not wholly fade out of the west until a late hour. In a clear and starry night all the surrounding mountains can be distinguished long after the valley is steeped in darkness. At half-past nine I could easily tell the time by my watch; and even at this hour a pale, nebulous light still lingered where the sun had gone down. So at near two thousand feet above the full sea one peers over into that deeper horizon where twilight and dawn meet and embrace on the dusky threshold of midnight.

While in the neighborhood, I devoted a day to an exploration of the Ravine of the Cascades. This ravine is entered from a point on the Gorham road about three miles distant from the Mount Adams House. A cart-way crosses the meadow here to an abandoned mill which is on the stream coming from the ravine, and by which you must ascend. A more beautiful example of a mountain brook it has never been my lot to see. The ascent is, however, tedious and toilsome in the extreme over the smooth and slippery rocks in its bed. Four hours of this brought me to the region of low trees, and to the foot of the first fall, which, I judged, descended about thirty feet. This way to the summit is open only to the most vigorous climbers. Even then it is better to descend into the ravine from the gap between Adams and Jefferson in order to visit these cascades.

The two most profitable excursions to be made here are undoubtedly the ascent of Mount Adams and the drive to the top of Randolph Hill. I have found on the first summit irrefragable evidence that, next to Washington and Lafayette, Adams is the peak which summer tourists are most desirous of ascending. A good path, on which there is a camp, leads to the summit. Having other views in regard to this mountain, which I had so often admired from a distance, I made a third reconnoisance of its outworks and its remarkable ravine, while *en route* for Randolph Hill.

Unquestionably fine as the views are along this road, on which you are at one time rolling smoothly over meadow or upland, with the great northern peak rising to its full height, or again toiling up a stony hill-side to obtain a much better idea of its real character and prodigious dimensions, the climax is reserved until, turning from the high-way, you begin a slow advance up the long hill-side that makes an almost uninterrupted descent for five miles to the Androscoggin. Here I saw from a balcony what I had before seen from the ground-floor. The view is large and expansive. You look down the surging land into the Androscoggin. You look over among the mountains circling its head, huddled together like a frightened herd. You look down into the valley of the Moose, and through the gap in the great chain you again see the valley of the Peabody and the Carter Notch. Now you hold the great northern peaks admiringly at arm's-length, as you would an old friend. Putting an imaginary hand on each broad shoulder, you scan them from head to foot. They submit calmly and with condescension to your lengthened scrutiny. Presently the low sun floods them with royal purple and gilds the topmost crags with refined gold. You glance up the valley. The little river comes like a stream of fire which the huge mountains seem crowding forward to trample out. Now look down. The same mountains seem spurning the glittering serpent away from their feet.

King's Ravine is as well seen from this point, perhaps, as any. It is a huge natural niche excavated high up the mountain. You see everything — grizzled spruces, blackened shafts of stone, rifted walls, tawny crags—all in one glance. It is formidable and forbidding, though a way has been made through it by which to ascend Mount Adams. Now that there is a good path skirting the ravine and avoiding it, that look will usually suffice to deter sensible people from attempting to reach the summit by it. It is far better to descend into it and grope one's way down through and underneath the bowlders. The same, and even greater, obstacles are encountered as in Tuckerman's. In early spring the walls of the ravine are streaked with slowly-melting snows. These gulches, all converging toward the bottom, send a torrent roaring down with noise equal to surf on a hard sea-beach. This torrent is the principal source of the Moose.

Well do I remember my first venture here. I had walked from Gorham. Seeing a man chopping wood by the side of the road, I entered into conversation with him; but at the first suggestion I let fall of an intention to climb to the ravine he gaped open-mouthed. To ascend the brook to the ravine, the escarpment of the ravine to the high precipices, the precipices to the gate-way, was an exploit in those days.

But this was long ago. A good climber now puts King's Ravine down in his list of excursions with the same nonchalance that a belle of the ball-room enters an additional waltz on her card of engagements.[1]

One day I had fished along the Moose without success. Nothing could give a better idea of a mountain stream than this one, fed by snows and gushing from the breached side of Mount Adams. But either the water was too cold or the trout too wary. They persistently refused my fly. I tried red and brown hackle, then a white moth-miller; all to no purpose. Feeling downright hungry, I determined to seek a dinner elsewhere. Unjointing my rod, I returned, rather crestfallen, down the mountain into the road.

I knocked at the first house. Pretty soon the curtain of the first window at my left hand was partly drawn aside. I felt that I was under the fire of a pair of very black eyes. An instant after the door was half-opened by a woman past middle life, who examined me with a scared look while wiping her hands on a corner of her apron. Two or three white heads peeped out from the folds of her dress like young chickens from the old hen's wing, and as many pairs of widely-opened eyes surveyed me with innocent surprise.

Perceiving her confusion, I was on the point of asking some indifferent question, about the distance, the road—I knew not what—but my stomach gave me a twinge of disdain, and I stood my ground. Hunger has no conscience: honor was at stake. In two words I made known my wants, I confess with confidence oozing away at my fingers' ends.

Her confusion became still greater—so evident, indeed, that I took a backward step and stammered, quite humbly, "A hunch of bread-and-cheese or a cup of milk—" when the good-wife nailed me to the threshold.

Quoth she, "The men folks have all *et* their dinners, and there hain't no more meat; but if you could put up with a few trout?"

Put up with trout! Did I hear aright? The word made my mouth water. I softly repeated it to myself—"Trout!"—would I put up with trout? Not to lower myself in this woman's estimation, I replied that, seeing there was nothing else in the house, I would put

---

[1] The greater part of the ascent so nearly coincides, in its main features, with that into Tuckerman's, that a description would be, in effect, a repetition. To my mind Tuckerman's is the grander of the two; it is only when the upper section of King's is reached that it begins to be either grand or interesting by comparison.

up with trout. Let it suffice that I made a repast fit for a prince, and, like a prince, being served by a bashful maiden with cheeks like the arbutus, which everybody knows shows its most delicate pink only in the seclusion of its native woods.

My hours of leisure in Jefferson being numbered, having now made the circuit of the great range by all the avenues penetrating or environing it, the reader's further indulgence is craved while his faithful guide points his well-worn alpenstock to the last stage of our mountain journeys.

Behold us at last, after many capricious wanderings, after calculated avoidance, approaching the inevitable end. We are *en route* for Fabyan's by the road over Cherry Mountain. This road is twelve miles long. As we mount with it the side of Cherry Mountain the beautiful vistas continually detain us. We are now climbing the eastern wall of the valley, so long the prominent figure from the heights of Jefferson. We now look back upon the finely-traced slopes of Starr King, with the village luxuriously extended in the sun. For some time we are like two travellers going in opposite directions, but who turn again and again for a last adieu. Now the forest closes over us and we see each other no more.

Noonday found me descending that side of the mountain overlooking the Ammonoosuc Valley. Where the Cherry Mountain road joins the valley highway the White Mountain House, an old-time tavern, stands. The railway passes close to its door. A mile more over the level brings us to Fabyan's, so called from one of the old mountain landlords, whose immortality is thus assured. Now that mammoth caravansary, which seems all eyes, is reached just as the doors opening upon the great hall disclose a long array of tables, while permitting a delicious odor to assail our nostrils.

To speak to the purpose, the Fabyan House really commands a superb front view of Mount Washington, from which it is not six miles in a bee-line. All the southern peaks, among which Mount Pleasant is undoubtedly the most conspicuous for its form and its mass, and for being thrown so boldly out from the rest, are before the admiring spectator; but the northern peaks, with the exception of Clay and Jefferson, are cut off partly by the slopes of Mount Deception, which rises directly before the hotel, partly by the trend of the great range itself to the north-east. The view is superior from the neighborhood of the Mount

Pleasant House, half a mile beyond Fabyan's, where Mount Jefferson is fully and finely brought into the picture.

The railway is seen mounting a foot-hill, crossing a second and higher elevation, then dimly carved upon the massive flanks of Mount Washington itself, as far as the long ridge which ascends from the north in one unbroken slope. It is then lost. We see the houses upon the

MOUNT WASHINGTON, FROM FABYAN'S.

summit, and from the Mount Pleasant House the little cluster of roofs at the base. A long and well-defined gully, exactly dividing the mountain, is frequently taken to be the railway, which is really much farther to the left. The smoke of a train ascending or descending still further indicates the line of iron, which we admit to the category of established facts only under protest.

Sylvester Marsh, of Littleton, New Hampshire, was the man who dreamed of setting aside the laws of gravitation with a puff of steam. Like all really great inventions, his had to run the gauntlet of ridicule. When the charter for a railway to the summit of Mount Washington was before the Legislature a member moved that Mr. Marsh also have leave to build one to the moon. Had the motion prevailed, I am persuaded Mr. Marsh would have built it. Really, the project seemed only a little more audacious. But in three years from the time work was begun (April, 1866) the track was laid and the mountain in irons.[1] The summit which the superstitious Indian dared not approach, nor the most intrepid white hunter ascend, is now annually visited by thousands, without more fatigue than would follow any other excursion occupying the same time. The excitement of a first passage, the strain upon the nerves, is quite another thing.

In a little grass-grown enclosure, on the other side of the Ammonoosuc, is a headstone bearing the following inscription :

IN MEMORY OF

CAP ELIEZER ROSBROOK

WHO DIED SEP. 25

1817

In the 70 Year

Of His Age.

When I lie buried deep in dust,
My flesh shall be thy care
These withering limbs to thee I trust
To raise them strong and fair.

WIDOW

HANNAH ROSEBROOK

Died May 4, 1829

Aged 84

Blessed are the dead who die in the Lord For they rest from their labors
And their works do follow them.

So far as is known Rosebrook was the first white settler on this spot. One account[2] says he came here in 1788, another fixes his settlement in 1792.[3] His military title appears to have been derived from services ren-

---

[1] The road up the Rigi, in Switzerland, was modelled upon the plans of Mr. Marsh.
[2] Dr. Timothy Dwight.   [3] Rev. Benjamin G. Willey.

dered on the Canadian frontier during the Revolutionary War. Rosebrook was a true pioneer, restless, adventurous, and fearless. He was a man of large and athletic frame. From his home in Massachusetts he had first removed to what is now Colebrook, then to Guildhall, Vt., and lastly here, to Nash and Sawyer's Location, exchanging the comforts which years of toil had surrounded him with, abandoning the rich and fertile meadow-lands of the Connecticut, for a log-cabin far from any human habitation, and with no other neighbors than the bears and wolves that prowled unharmed the shaggy wilderness at his door. With his axe this sturdy yeoman attacked the forest closely investing his lonely cabin. Year by year, foot by foot, he wrested from it a little land for tillage. With his gun he kept the beast of prey from his little enclosure, or provided venison or bear's meat for the wife and little ones who anxiously awaited his return from the hunt. Hunger and they were no strangers. For years the strokes of Rosebrook's axe, or the crack of his rifle, were the only sounds that disturbed the silences of ages. Little by little the circle was enlarged. One after another the giants of the forest fell beneath his blows. But years of resolute conflict with nature and with privation found him at last in the enjoyment of a dearly-earned prosperity. Travellers began to pass his doors. The Great White Mountain Notch soon became a thoroughfare, which could never have been safely travelled but for Rosebrook's intrepidity and Rosebrook's hospitality. In this way began the feeble tide of travel through these wilds. In this way the splendidly equipped hotel, with its thousands of guests the locomotive every hour brings to its door, traces its descent from the rude and humble cabin of Eleazer Rosebrook.

X.

THE GREAT NORTHERN PEAKS.

> Cradled and rocked by wind and cloud,
> Safe pillowed on the summit proud,
> Steadied by that encircling arm
> Which holds the Universe from harm,
> I knew the Lord my soul would keep,
> Upon His mountain-tops asleep!
>
> LUCY LARCOM.

THUS I found myself again at the base of Mount Washington, but on the reverse, opposed to the Glen. Before the completion of the railway from Fabyan's to the foot of the mountain I had passed over the intervening six miles by stage—a delightful experience; but one now steps on board an open car, which in less than half the time formerly occupied leaves him at the point where the mountain car and engine wait for him. The route lies along the foaming Ammonoosuc, and its justly admired falls, cut deep through solid granite, into the uncouth and bristling wilderness which surrounds the base of the mountain. The peculiarity of these falls does not consist in long, abrupt descents of perturbed water, but in the neatly excavated caves, rock-niches, and smoothly rounded cliffs and basins through which for some distance the impatient stream rears and plunges like a courser feeling the curb. Imperfect glimpses hardly give an idea of the curious and interesting processes of rock-cutting to one who merely looks down from the high banks above while the train is in rapid motion. It is better, therefore, to visit these falls by way of the old turnpike.

The advance up the valley which has first given us an outlook through the great Notch, on our right, presents for some time the huge green hemisphere of Mount Pleasant as the conspicuous object. The track then swerves to the left, bringing Mount Washington into view, and in a few minutes more we are at the ill-favored clump of houses and sheds at its base.

The mechanism of the road-way is very simple. The track is formed of three iron rails, firmly clamped to stout timbers, laid lengthwise upon transverse pieces, or sleepers. These are securely embedded, where the surface will allow, or raised upon trestles, where its inequalities would compel a serious deflection from a smooth or regular inclination. One of these, about half-way up the mountain, is called Jacob's Ladder. Here the train achieves the most difficult part of the ascent. After

MOUNTAIN RAILWAY-STATION IN STAGING TIMES.

traversing the whole line on foot, and inspecting it minutely and thoroughly, I can candidly pronounce it not only a marvel of mechanical skill, but bear witness to the scrupulous care taken to keep every timber and every bolt in its place. In two words, the structure is nothing but a ladder of wood and iron laid upon the side of the mountain.[1]

---

[1] The greatest angle of inclination is twelve feet in one hundred.

The propelling force employed is equally simple. The engine and car merely rest upon and are kept in place by the two outer rails, while the power is applied to the middle one, which we have just called a rail, but is, more properly speaking, a little ladder of steel cogs, into which the corresponding teeth of the locomotive's driving-wheel play—a firm hold being thus secured. The question now merely is, how much power is necessary to overcome gravity and lift the weight of the machine into the air? This cogged-rail is the fulcrum, and steam the lever. Mr. Sylvester Marsh has not precisely lifted the mountain, but he has, nevertheless, with the aid of Mr. Walter Aiken, reduced it, to all intents, to a level.

The boiler of the locomotive, inclined forward so as to preserve a horizontal position when the engine is ascending, the smoke-stack also pitched forward, give the idea of a machine that has been in a collision. Everything seems knocked out of place. But this queer-looking thing, that with bull-dog tenacity literally hangs on to the mountain with its teeth, is capable of performing a feat such as Watt never dreamed of, or Stephenson imagined. It goes up the mountain as easily as a bear climbs a tree, and like a bear.

I had often watched the last ascension of the train, which usually reaches the summit at sunset, and I had as often pleased myself with considering whether it then most resembled a big, shining beetle crawling up the mountain side, or some fiery dragon of the fabulous times, dragging his prey after him to his den, after ravaging the valley. My own turn was now come to make the trial. It was a cold afternoon in September when I entered the little carriage, not much larger than a street-car, and felt the premonitory jerk with which the ascent begins. The first hill is so steep that you look up to see the track always mounting high above your head; but one soon gets used to the novelty, and to the clatter which accompanies the incessant dropping of a pawl into the indentures of the cogged-rail, and in which he recognizes an element of safety. The train did not move faster than one could walk, but it moved steadily, except when it now and then stopped at a water-tank, standing solitary and alone upon the waste of rocks.

By the time we emerged above the forest into the chill and wind-swept desolation above it—a first sight of which is so amazing—the sun had set behind the Green Mountain summits, showing a long, serrated line of crimson peaks, above which clouds of lake floated in a sea of amber. It grew very cold. Great-coats and shawls were quickly put on. Thick darkness enveloped the mountain as we approached the head of the profound gulf separating us from Mount Clay, which is the most remarkable object seen at any time either during the ascent or descent. Into this pitchy ravine, into its midnight blackness, a long and brilliant train of sparks trailed downward from the locomotive, so that we seemed being transported heavenward in a chariot of fire. This flaming torch, lighting us on, now disclosed snow and ice on all sides. We had successfully attained the last slope which conceals the railway from the valley. Up this the locomotive toiled and panted, while we watched the stars come out and emit cold gleams around, above, beneath. The light of the Summit House twinkled small, then grew large, as, surmounting the last and steepest pitch of the pinnacle, we were pushed before a long row of lighted windows crusted thick with hoar-frost. Stiffened with cold, the passengers rushed for the open door without ceremony. In an instant the car was empty; while the locomotive, dripping with its unheard-of efforts, seemed to regard this desertion with reproachful glances.

Reader, have you ever sat beside Mrs. Dodge's fire after such a passive ascension as that just described? After a two hours' combat with the instinct of self-preservation, did you dream of such comforts, luxuries even, awaiting you on the bleak mountain-top, where nothing grows, and where water even congeals and refuses to run? Could you, in the highest flights of fancy, imagine that you would one day sit in the courts of heaven, or feast sumptuously amid the stars? All this you either have done or may do. And now, while the smartly-dressed waiter-girl, who seems to have donned her white apron as a personal favor, brings you the best the larder affords, pinch yourself to see if you are awake.

In several ascensions by the railway I have always remarked the same symptoms of uneasiness among the passengers, betrayed by pale faces, compressed lips, hands tightening their grasp of the chairs, or subdued and startled exclamations, quickly repressed. To escape the influence of such weird surroundings one should be absolutely stolid—a stock or a stone. So for all it is an experience more or less acute, according to his sensibility, strength of nerve, and power of self-control. However well it may be disguised, the strong equally with the weak, and more deeply than the weak, feel the strain which ninety minutes' combat with gravitation, attraction, ponderosity, engenders. The mind does not for a single instant quit its hold of this defiance of Nature's laws. As long as iron and steel hold fast, there is no danger; but you think iron and steel are iron and steel, and no more. An anecdote will illustrate this feeling.

After pointing out to a lady-passenger the skilful devices for stopping the engine—the pawl, the steam, and the atmospheric brakes—and after patiently explaining their mechanism and uses, the listener asked the conductor, with much interest,

"Then, if the pawl breaks while we are going up?"

"The engine will be stopped by means of these powerful brakes, applied directly to the axles, which will, of course, render the train motionless. As the locomotive has two driving-wheels, the engineer can bring a double power to bear, as you see. Each is independent of the other, so that if one gives way the other is still more than sufficient to keep the engine stationary."

"Thank you; but the car?"

"Oh, the car is not attached to the engine at all; and should the engineer lose the control of his machine, which is not at all likely, the car can be brought to a stand-still by independent brakes of its own. You see the engine goes up behind, and in front, down; and the car is simply pushed forward, or follows it."

"So that you consider it—"

"Perfectly safe, madam, perfectly safe."

"Thank you. One question more. Suppose all these things break at once. What then? Where would we go?"

"That, madam, would depend on what sort of a life you had led."

I have still a consolation for the timid. Ten years' trial has confirmed the declaration of its projectors, that they would make the road as safe or safer than the ordinary railway. No life has been lost by an injury to a passenger during that time. Besides, what is the difference? After its day, the railway will pass like the stage-coach—that is, unless you believe, as you do not, that the world and all progress are to stop with ourselves.

The affable lady hostess told me that she paid an annual rental of ten thousand dollars for her palace of ice; nominally for a year, but really for a term of only seventy-six days, this being the limit of the season upon the summit. During the remaining two hundred and

ASCENT BY THE RAILWAY.

eighty-nine days the house is closed.
During four or five months it is buried,
or half-buried, in a snow-drift. Of this large sum,
three thousand dollars go to the Pingree heirs.   These
facts may tend to modify the views of those who think the
charges exorbitant, if such there are.

Raising my eyes to look out of the window, the light from within fell upon a bank of snow. A man was stooping over it as if in search of something. Going out, I found him feeling it with his hands, and examining it with childish wonder and curiosity. I approached this eccentric person very softly; but he, seeing my shadow on the snow beside him, looked up.

"Can I assist you in recovering what you have lost?" I inquired.

"Thank you; no. I have lost nothing. Ah! I see," he continued, laughing quietly, "you think I have lost my wits. But it is not so. I am a native of the East Indies, and I assure you this is the first time in my life I have ever seen snow near enough to handle it. Imagine what an experience the ascent of Mount Washington is for me!"

We took a turn down the hard-frozen Glen road together in order to see the moon come up. The telegraph-poles, fantastically crusted with ice to the thickness of a foot, stretched a line of white-hooded phantoms down the dark side of the mountain. From successive coatings of frozen mist the wires were as thick as cables. Couches of snow lay along the rocks, and fresh snow had apparently been rubbed into all the inequalties of the cliffs rising out of the Great Gulf. The scene was supremely weird, supremely desolate.

From here we crossed over to the railway, and, ascending by it, shortly came upon the heap of stones, surmounted by its tablet, erected on the spot where Miss Bourne perished while ascending the mountain, in September, 1855. The party, of which she was one, setting out in high spirits in the afternoon from the Glen House, was overtaken near the summit by clouds, which hid the house from view, and among which they became bewildered. It was here Miss Bourne declared she could go no farther. Overcome by her exertions, she sunk exhausted and fainting upon the rocks. Her friends were scarcely awakened to her true condition when, amid the surrounding darkness and gloom, this young and lovely maiden of only twenty expired in the arms of her uncle. The mourners wrapped the body in their own cloaks, and, ignorant that a few rods only separated them from the summit, kept a vigil throughout the long and weary night. We hasten over this night of dread. In the morning, discovering their destination a few rods above them, they bore the lifeless form of their companion to it with feelings not to be described. A rude bier was made, and she who had started up the mountain full of life now descended it a corpse.

The evening treated us to a magnificent spectacle. The moon, in full-orbed splendor, moved majestically up the heavens, attended by her glittering retinue of stars. Frozen peaks, reflecting the mild radiance, shone like beaten silver. But the immense hollows between, the deep valleys that had been open to view, were now inundated with a white and luminous vapor, from which the multitude of icy summits emerged like a vast archipelago—a sea of islands. This spectral ocean seemed on the point of ingulfing the mountains. This motionless sea, these austere peaks, uprising, were inconceivably weird and solemnizing. An awful hush pervaded the inanimate but threatening host of cloud-girt mountains. Upon them, upon the sea of frozen vapor, absorbing its light, the clear moon poured its radiance. The stars seemed nearer and brighter than ever before. The planets shone with piercing brilliancy; they emitted a sensible light. The Milky Way, erecting its glittering nebula to the zenith, to which it was pinned by a dazzling star, floated, a glorious, star-spangled veil, amid this vast sea of gems. One could vaguely catch the idea of an unpeopled desolation rising from the fathomless void of a primeval ocean. The peaks, incased in snow and ice, seemed stamped with the traces of its subsidence. Pale and haggard, they lifted their antique heads in silent adoration.

Going to my room and extinguishing the light, I stood for some time at the window, unable to reconcile the unwonted appearance of the stars shining far below, with the fixed idea that they ought not to be there. Yet there they were. To tell the truth, my head was filled with the surpassing pomp I had just witnessed, of which I had not before the faintest conception. I felt as if I was silently conversing with all those stars, looking at me and my petty aspirations with such inflexible, disdainful immobility. When one feels that he is nothing, self-assurance is no great thing. The conceit is taken out of him. On a mountain the man stands naked before his Maker. He is nothing. That is why I leave him there.

That night I did not sleep a wink. Twenty times I jumped out of bed and ran to the window to convince myself that it was not all a dream. No; moon and stars were still bright. Over the Great Gulf, all ghastly in the moonlight, stood Mount Jefferson in his winding-sheet. I dressed myself, and from the embrasure of my window kept a vigil.

Sunrise did not produce the startling effect I had anticipated. The morning was fine and cloudless. A gong summoned the inmates of the hotel to the spectacle. Without dressing themselves, they ran to their windows, where, wrapped in bed-blankets, they stood eagerly watching the east. To the pale emerald of early dawn a ruddy glow succeeded. Before we were aware, the rocky waste around us grew dusky red. The crimsoned air glided swiftly over the neighboring summits. Now the brightness was upon Adams and Jefferson and Clay, and now it rolled its purpled flood into the Great Gulf, to mingle with the intense blackness at the bottom. For some moments the mountain-tops held the color, then it was transfused into the clear sunshine of open day; while the vapors, heavy and compact, stretched along the valleys, still smothering the land, retained their leaden hue.

It was still early when I descended the carriage-road on my way to Mount Adams. The usual way is to keep the railway as far as the old Gulf Tank, near which is a house of refuge, provided with a cooking-stove, fuel, and beds. I continued, however, to coast the upper crags of the Great Gulf, until compelled to make directly for the southern peak of Mount Clay. The view from this *col* is imposing, embracing at once, and without turning the head, all the southern summits of the chain. Here I was joined by two travellers fresh from Mont Blanc and the Matterhorn.

Each choosing a route for himself, we pushed on to the high summit of Clay, from which we looked down into the deep gap dividing this mountain from Jefferson. Arrived there, we resolutely attacked the eastern slopes of this fine peak, whose notched summit rose more than seven hundred and fifty feet above our heads. Patches of Alpine grasses, of reindeer-moss, interspersed with irregular ridges of stones, extended quite up to the summit, which was a mere elongated stone-heap crowning the apex of its cone. Those undulating masses encircling its bulk, half hid among the grass, were like an immense python crushing the mountain in its deadly folds. We picked our way carefully among this chaotic débris, which the Swiss aptly call "cemeteries of the devil," tripping now and then in the long, wiry grass, or burying our feet among the hummocks of dry moss, which were so many impediments to rapid progress. This appearance and this experience were common to the whole route.

At each summit we threw ourselves upon the ground, to feast upon the landscape while regaining breath. Each halt developed more and more the grand and stupendous mass of Washington receding from the depths of the Great Gulf, along whose edge the carriage-road serpentined and finally disappeared. We saw, a little softened by distance, the horribly mutilated crags of the head wall stripped bare of all verdure, presenting on its knobbed agglomerates of tempest-gnawed granite a thousand eye-catching points and detaining as many shadows. Nothing— not even the glittering leagues of mountains and valleys shooting or slumbering above, beneath—so riveted the attention as this apparently bottomless pit of the five mountains. It was a continued wonder. It drew us by a strange magnetism to its dizzy brink, chained us there, and then abandoned us to a physical and moral vertigo, in which the power of critical investigation was lost. An invisible force seemed always dragging us toward it. Whence comes this horrible, this uncontrollable desire to throw ourselves in?

Out of the death-like torpor which eternally shrouds the ravine the smiling valley seems escaping. The crystal air of the heights grows thick in its depths. Beasts and birds of prey haunt its gloomy solitudes. An immense grave seems yawning to receive the mountains. The aged mountains seem standing with one foot in the grave.

This gulf makes an impression altogether different from the others. It is an immense ravine. Each of the five mountains pushes down into it massive buttresses of granite, forming lesser ravines between of considerable extent. Through these streams trickle down from invisible sources. But these buttresses, which fall lightly and gracefully as folds of velvet from summit to base of the highest mountains, these ravines, are hardly noticed. The insatiable maw of the gulf swallows them as easily as an anaconda a rabbit. In immensity, which you do not easily grasp, in grandeur, which you do not know how to measure, this has no partakers here. Even the great Carter Mountain, rising from the Peabody Valley, seems no more than a stone rolled away from the entrance of this enormous sepulchre.

Our first difficulties were encountered upon the reverse of Mount Jefferson, from whose side rocky spurs detached themselves, and, jutting out from the side of the mountain, formed an irregular line of cliffs of varying height, in the way we had selected for the descent. But these were no great affair. We now had the Ravine of the Castles upon our left, the stately pyramid of Adams in front, and, beneath, the deep hollow between this mountain and the one we were descending. We had the little hamlet of East Jefferson at the mouth of the ravine.

and that crowd of peaks, tightly wedged between the waters of the Connecticut and the Androscoggin, looming above it.

A deviation to the left enabled us to approach the Castellated Ridge, which is, beyond dispute, the most extraordinary rock-formation the whole extent of the range can show. As it is then fully before you, it is seen to much better advantage when approached from Mount Adams. I do not know who gave it this name, but none could be more felicitous or expressive. It is a sloping ridge of red-brown granite, broken at its summit into a long line of picturesque towers and battlements, rising threateningly over an escarpment of débris. Such an illusion is too rarely encountered to be easily forgotten. It is hardly possible to doubt you are really looking at an antique ruin. One would like to wander among these pre-Adamite fortifications, which curiously remind him of the old Spanish fortresses among the Pyrenees. From the opposite side of the ravine—for I had not the time requisite for a closer examination—the rock composing the most elevated portion of the ridge appears to have been split perpendicularly down, probably by frost, allowing these broken columns and shafts to stand erect upon the verge of the abyss. In the warm afternoon light, when the shadows fall, it is hardly possible to conceive a finer picture of a crumbling but still formidable mountain fortress. Bastions and turrets stand boldly out. Each broken shaft sends a long shadow streaming down into the ravine, whose high and deeply-furrowed sides are thus beautifully striped with dusk-purple, while the sunlit parts retain a greenish-gray.

At the foot of Jefferson we found, concealed among rushes, a spring, which refreshed us like wells of the desert the parched and fainting Arab. From here two routes offered themselves. One was by keeping the curved ridge, rising gradually to a subordinate peak (Samuel Adams),[1] and to the foot of the summit itself; a second was by crossing the ground sloping downward from this ridge into the Great Gulf. We chose the latter, notwithstanding the dwarf-spruce, advancing well up to the foot of the ridge, promised a warm reception.

At last, after sustaining a vigorous tussle with the scrub-firs, and stopping to unearth a brook whose waters purred underneath stones, I

---

[1] Samuel Adams at the feet of John Adams is not the exact order that we have been accustomed to seeing these men. Better leave Samuel Adams where he stands in history—alone.

THE CASTELLATED RIDGE.

stood at the foot of
the pointed shaft I had so often
seen wedged into the sky. Five hundred feet
or more of the apex of this pyramid is apparently
formed of broken rocks, dropped one by one into place.
Nothing like a ledge or a cliff is to be seen: only these
ponderous, sharp-edged masses of cold gray stone, lifted
one above another to the tapering point. Up this mutilated pyramid
we began a slow advance. It was necessary to carefully choose one
step before taking another, in order to avoid plunging into the deep cre-

vasses traversing the peak in every direction. At last I placed my foot upon the topmost crag.

No one can help regarding this peak with the open admiration which is its due. You conceive that every mountain ought to have a pinnacle. Well, here it is. We could easily have stood astride the culminating point. But how came these rocks here? and what was the primitive structure, if these fragments we see are its relics? One hardly believes that an ice-raft could have first transported and then deposited such misshapen masses in their present symmetrical form. Still less does he admit that the original shaft, crushed in a thousand pieces by the glacier itself, fell with such grace as to rise again, as he now sees it, from its own ruins. If, again, it proceeds from the eternal hammering of King Frost, what was the antique edifice that first rose so proudly above the frozen seas of the great primeval void? But to science the things which belong to science. We have a book describing heaven, but not one that resolves the problems of earth. The "*Veni, vidi, vici,*" of the Book of Genesis leaves us at the beginning. We are still staring, still questioning, still vacillating between this theory and that hypothesis.[1]

We had from the summit an inspiring though not an extensive view. A bank of dun-colored smoke smirched the fair western sky as high as the summits of the Green Mountains. At fifty miles mountains and valleys melted confusedly into each other. Water emitted only a dull glimmer. Here a peak and there a summit surveyed us from afar. All else was intangible; almost imaginary. At twenty-five miles the land, resuming its ordinary appearance, was bathed in the soft brilliance caused by the sun shining through an atmosphere only half transparent.

Upon this obscure mass we traced once more the well-known objects environing the great mountain. To the south Mount Washington divided the landscape in two. For some time we stood admiring its magnificent *torso*, its amplitude of rock-land, its easy preponderance over every other summit. Again we followed the road down the great northeast spur. Once more we caught the white specks which denote the line of the railway. We plunged our eyes down into the Great Gulf,

---

[1] It is only forty years since Agassiz advanced his now generally adopted theory of the Glacial Period. The Indians believed that the world was originally covered with water, and that their god created the dry land from a grain of sand.

and lifted them to the shattered protuberances of Clay, which seemed to mark the route where the glacier crushed and ground its way through the very centre of the chain. A second time we descended Jefferson to the deep dip, opening like a trough between two enormous sea-waves, where we first saw the little Storm Lake glistening. Following now the long, rocky ridge, rolling downward toward the hamlets of Jefferson and Randolph, the mountains yawned wide at our feet. We were looking over into King's Ravine—to its very bottom. We peered curiously into its remotest depths, traced the difficult and breathless ascent through the remarkable natural gateway at its head out upon a second ridge, on which a little pond (Star Lake) lies hid. We then crossed the gap communicating with Mount Madison, whose summit, last and lowest of the great northern peaks, dominates the Androscoggin Valley with undisputed sway. To-day it made on us scarcely an impression. Its peak, which from the valley holds a rough similitude with that of Adams, is dwarfed here. You look down upon it.

More applicable to Adams than to any other, for our eyes grow dazzled with the glitter and sparkle of countless mica-flakes incrusting the hard granite with clear brilliancy as from the facets of a diamond; more applicable, again, from the stern, unconquerable attitude of the great gray shaft itself, lifted in such conscious pride beyond the confines of the vast ethereal vault of blue—a tower of darkness invading the bright realms of light; a defiance flung by earth in the face of high heaven—is the magnificent description of the Matterhorn from the pen of Ruskin:

"If one of these little flakes of mica-sand, hurried in tremulous spangling along the bottom of the ancient river, too light to sink, too faint to float, almost too small for sight, could have had a mind given to it as it was at last borne down with its kindred dust into the abysses of the stream, and laid (would it not have thought?) for a hopeless eternity in the dark ooze, the most despised, forgotten, and feeble of all earth's atoms; incapable of any use or change; not fit, down there in the diluvial darkness, so much as to help an earth-wasp to build its nest, or feed the first fibre of a lichen — what would it have thought had it been told that one day, knitted into a strength as of imperishable iron, rustless by the air, infusible by the flame, out of the substance of it, with its fellows, the axe of God should hew that Alpine tower;—that against it—poor, helpless mica-flake!—the snowy hills should lie bowed like flocks of sheep, and the kingdoms of the earth fade away in unregarded blue; and around it — weak, wave-drifted mica-flake! — the great war of the firmament should burst in thunder, and yet stir it not; and the fiery arrows and angry meteors of the night fall blunted back from it into the air; and all the stars in the clear heaven should light, one by one, as they rose, new cressets upon the points of snow that fringed its abiding-place on the imperishable spire!"

Myself and my companions set out on our return to the Summit House early in the afternoon, choosing this time the ridge in preference to the scrubby slope. From this we turned away, at the end of half an hour, by an obscure path leading to a boggy pool, sunk in a mossy hollow underneath it, crossed the area of scattered bowlders, strewn all around like the relics of a petrified tempest, and, filling our cups at the spring, drank to Mount Adams, the paragon of mountain peaks.

As we again approached the brow of Mount Washington the sun resembled a red-hot globe of iron flying through the west and spreading a conflagration through the heavens. Again the colossal shadow of the mountain began its stately ascension in the east. One moment the burning eye of the great luminary interrogated this phantom, sprung from the loins of the hoary peak. Then it dropped heavily down behind the Green Mountains, as it has done for thousands of years, the landscape fading, fading into one vast, shadowy abyss, out of which arose the star-lit dome of the august summit.

TOURIST'S APPENDIX.

PREPARED FOR "THE HEART OF THE WHITE MOUNTAINS."

GEOGRAPHY.—The White Mountains are in the northern central part of the State of New Hampshire. They occupy the whole area of the State between Maine and Vermont, and between Lake Winnipiseogee and the head-streams of the Connecticut and Androscoggin rivers.

Two principal chains, having a general direction from south-west to north-east, constitute this great water-shed of New England. These are the Franconia and the White Mountains proper, sometimes called the "Presidential Range."

Grouped on all sides of the higher summits are a great number of inferior ridges, among which, as in the Sandwich Range, rise some very fine peaks, widely extending the mountainous area, and diversifying it with numerous valleys, lakes, and streams.

Two principal rivers, the Saco and Merrimack, flowing from these two chief clusters, form the two great valleys of the White Mountain system; and by these valleys the railways enter the mountains from the seaboard. Lake Winnipiseogee, which washes the southern foot of the mountains, is also a thoroughfare, as are the valleys of the Connecticut and Androscoggin rivers.

DISTANCES.—It is 430 miles from Philadelphia to Fabyan's; 340 from New York, *via* Springfield; 190 from Montreal, *via* Newport; 208 *via* Groveton; 169 from Boston, *via* North Conway (Eastern R.R.); 208 *via* Concord (B., C., & M. R.R.); 91 from Portland, *via* North Conway (P. & O. R.R.); 91 from Portland to Gorham (G. T. R.); 199 from Boston to Gorham, *via* Eastern and Grand Trunk roads; and 206 *via* Boston and Maine and Grand Trunk roads.

ROUTES.—Procure, before starting, the official time-tables of the railroads running to the mountains or making direct connection with them, by application to local agents, by writing to the ticket-agents of the roads, or by consulting a railway guide-book. The roads reaching the mountains are—

From Washington: The Pennsylvania, and New York & New England.

From Philadelphia: The Pennsylvania, and New York & New England.

From Montreal: The Grand Trunk, and The South-eastern.

From Quebec: The Grand Trunk Railway.

From Saratoga: The Delaware & Hudson Canal Co.

From New York: New York, New Haven, & Hartford (all rail *via* Springfield, White River Junction, and Wells River to Fabyan's; or all rail *via* Springfield, Worcester, Nashua, and Concord, N. H.; or all rail *via* "Shore Line," Boston & Albany, or New York & New

England roads to Boston); or by Fall River, Norwich, or Stonington "Sound Lines" to Boston; thence by either of the following railroads:

From Boston: Eastern R.R., *via* Beverly (18 miles, branch to Cape Ann); Hampton (46 miles, Boar's Head and Rye Beaches); Portsmouth (56 miles, Newcastle and Isles of

Shoals and York Beach); Kittery (57 miles); Wolfborough Junction (98 miles, branch to Lake Winnipiseogee); North Conway (138 miles; connects with Portland and Ogdensburg); Intervale (139 miles); Glen Station (144 miles, for Jackson and Glen House); Crawford's (165 miles); Fabyan's (169 miles; connects with B., C., & M. for Summit of Mount Washington, Bethlehem, Profile House, and Jefferson; or by same route to Portland, thence by P. & O. R.R. to North Conway, or Grand Trunk Railway to Gorham).

Boston, Lowell & Concord, and Boston, Concord & Montreal Railroads, *via* Lowell (26 miles); Nashua, Manchester, Concord (75 miles); Plymouth (123 miles); Woodsville (166 miles, Wells River); Littleton (185 miles, for Sugar Hill); Wing Road (192 miles, branch to Jefferson); Bethlehem (196 miles, branch road to Profile House, also to "Maplewood," and Bethlehem Street); Twin Mountain House, Fabyan's (208 miles, branch to

Summit of Mount Washington, 217 miles); connects at Fabyan's with P. & O. and Eastern roads for North Conway, Portland, and Boston.

Boston & Maine R.R. *via* Lawrence (26 miles); Haverhill, Exeter (50 miles); Dover (68 miles); Rochester (78 miles); Alton Bay (96 miles), connecting with steamer for Wolfborough and Centre Harbor, on Lake Winnipiseogee; or by the same road to Portland, thence by P. & O. to North Conway and Fabyan's, or Grand Trunk to Gorham and Glen House.

From Portland: Portland & Ogdensburg R.R. *via* Sebago Lake (17 miles); Fryeburg (49 miles); Conway Centre, North Conway (60 miles); Glen Station (66 miles, Jackson and Glen House); Bartlett (72 miles); Crawford's (87 miles); Fabyan's (91 miles; connects with B., C., & M. R.R. for Summit of Mount Washington, Bethlehem, Profile House, Sugar Hill, Jefferson, etc.).

Grand Trunk Railway: Danville Junction (27 miles); Bethel (70 miles); Shelburne (86 miles); Gorham (91 miles, for Glen House).

A good way to do the mountains by rail is to buy an excursion-ticket over the route entering on the west, and, passing through, leave them by the roads on the east side *via* Boston or Portland, or *vice versa*. At Fabyan's, where the two great routes meet, the traveller coming from either direction may pursue his journey without delay. From *Boston to Boston, Portland to Portland*, there is continuous rail without going twice over the same line.

Lake Winnipiseogee.—At Alton Bay, Wolfborough, and Weirs steamer is taken for Centre Harbor, at the head of the lake. Here the traveller may either take the daily stages for West Ossipee (E. R.R.) or steamer to Weirs (B., C., & M.), and thus be again on the direct rail routes.

HOW TO CHOOSE A LOCATION.—Do you wish a quiet retreat, off the travelled routes, where you may have rest and seclusion, or do you desire to fix yourself in a position favorable to exploring the whole mountain region?

In either case consult (1) some friend who has visited the mountains; (2), consult the maps in this volume; (3), consult the landlord in any place you may fancy for a limited or a lengthened residence; (4), apply to the agents of the Eastern, Portland, & Ogdensburg, Boston, Concord, & Montreal, Boston & Maine, or Grand Trunk Railways, for books or folders containing a list of the mountain hotels reached by their lines, and the charge for board by the day and week. (The Eastern, and B., C., & M. print revised lists every year, for gratuitous distribution.)

Wolfborough, Weirs, Centre Harbor, and Sandwich (all on or near Lake Winnipiseogee); Blair's, Sanborn's, Campton Village, Thornton, and Woodstock, in the Pemigewasset Valley; Tamworth, Conway Corner, Fryeburg, the Intervale (North Conway), Jackson, the Glen House, Bethel (Me.), Shelburne, Randolph, East Jefferson, Jefferson Hill, Lancaster, Littleton, Franconia, Sugar Hill, Haverhill, and Newbury (Vt.)—all come within the category first named; while the second want will be supplied at such points as North Conway, Crawford's, Fabyan's, Twin Mountain House, Bethlehem, and the Profile House. North Conway and Bethlehem are the keys to the whole mountain region. Fabyan's and the Glen House are the proper points from which to ascend Mount Washington.

To aid in locating these places on the map, refer constantly to the Index at the end of the volume.

Leaving Boston or Portland in the morning, any of the points named may be reached in from four to eight hours.

HINTS FOR TOURISTS.—Select your destination, if possible, in advance; and if you require apartments, telegraph to the hotel where you mean to stop, giving the number of persons in your party, thus avoiding the disappointment of arriving, at the end of a long journey, at an over-crowded hotel.

Should you fix upon a particular locality for a long or short stay, write to one (or more) of the landlords for terms, etc.; and if his house is off the line of railway, inform him of the day and train you mean to take, so that he may meet you with a carriage at the nearest station.   But if you do not go upon the day named, remember to notify the landlord.

U. S. METEOROLOGICAL STATION, MOUNT WASHINGTON, IN SUMMER.

Always take some warm woollen clothing (inside and outside) for mountain ascensions. It is unsafe to be without it in any season, as the nights are usually cool even in mid-summer.

From the middle of June to the middle of October is the season of mountain travel. The best views are obtained in June, September, and October.   From the middle of September to the middle of October the air is pure and invigorating, the mountain forests are then in a blaze of autumnal splendor, the cascades are finer, and out-of-door jaunts are less fatiguing than in July and August.

Should you wish merely to make a rapid tour of the mountain region, it will be best so to arrange your route before starting that the first day will bring you where there is something to be seen, to a comfortable hotel, and from which your journey may be continued with an economy of time and money.

The three journeys described in this volume will enable you to see all that is most desirable to be seen ; but the excellent facilities for traversing the mountains render it immaterial whether these routes are precisely followed, taken in their reverse order, or adopted as a general plan, with such modifications as the tourist's time or inclination may suggest.

Upon arriving at his destination the traveller naturally desires to use his time to the best advantage possible. But he is ignorant how to do this. "What shall I do?" "Where shall I go?" are the two questions that confront him. Let us suppose him arrived, first, at NORTH CONWAY.

As he stands gazing up the Saco Valley, Moat Mountain is on his left, Kearsarge at his right, and Mount Washington in front. (Refer to the Chapter and Index articles on North Conway.) The high cliffs on the side of Moat are called the Ledges. This glorious view may be improved by going a mile up the railroad, or highway, to the Intervale. The Ledges contain the local celebrities. Taking a carriage, or walking, one may visit them in an afternoon, seeing in turn Echo Lake, the Devil's Den, the Cathedral, and Diana's Baths. The picturesque bits of river, meadow, and mountain seen going and returning will make the way seem short, and are certain to detain the artistic traveller. Artists' Falls, on the opposite side of the valley, will repay a visit, if the stream is in good condition. Artists' Brook, on which these falls are, runs from the hills east of the village. A carriage-road leads to the Artists' Falls House, from which a short walk brings one to the falls. This excursion will require not more than two hours. Then there are the drives to Kearsarge village, under the mountain, and back by the Intervale ; to Jackson, over Thorn Hill, and back by Goodrich Falls (three to four hours each); to Bartlett Bowlder, by the west, and back by the east side of the valley ; to Fryeburg and Mount Chocorua—the last two requiring each half a day at least. The ascent of Kearsarge (from Kearsarge village) or of the Moats (from Diana's Baths) each demands a day to itself. But by starting early in the morning a good climber may ascend and descend Kearsarge, getting back to the village by two o'clock in the afternoon.

At the Intervale he can easily repeat all these experiences, as this is a suburb of North Conway. Let him take his first stroll over the meadows to the river, or among the grand old pines in the forest near the railway station, while preparing for more extended excursions.

At Glen Station.—While waiting for the luggage to be put on, if the day is perfectly clear, the traveller, by going up the track a few rods, to the bridge over the Ellis, may get a glimpse of the summit of Mount Washington, with the hotel upon the apex ; also of Carter Notch. On the way to Jackson he will pass over Goodrich Falls by a bridge. He should not fail to remark the fine cliffs of Iron Mountain, at his left hand, before entering the village. Should he be *en route* for the Glen House, let him be on the lookout for the Giant's

Stairs, on the left, after leaving Jackson, and then for the grand view of Pinkham Notch, with Mount Washington at the left, about four miles beyond Jackson. The summit of Spruce Hill—the scene of the highway robbery in 1881—is the top of the long rise beyond the bridge over Ellis River.

At Jackson we have moved eight miles nearer Mount Washington, in the direction of the Glen House (12 miles) and Gorham (20 miles), and also toward the Carter Notch, distant from the village 9 miles. The excursions back to North Conway are similar to those described from that place. The first thing to do here is to stroll up the Wildcat, and pass an hour or two among the falls on this stream, which begin at the village. A walk or drive up this valley to Fernald's Farm, and back by the opposite side, or over Thorn Hill, are two tempting half-day excursions. In an hour one may walk to Goodrich Falls (road to Glen Station) and back to the village. He may start after breakfast, and drive to Glen Ellis Falls (road to Glen House), eight miles, returning to the hotel for dinner; or, lunching at Glen Ellis, go on one mile farther to the Crystal Cascade; then, dining at the Glen House (3 miles), return at leisure. But it is a mistake to take two such pieces of water in one day. The pedestrian whose base is Jackson, and who makes this trip, should pass the night at the Glen House and return by the Carter Notch, the distance being about the same as by the highway. But he should never try this alone, for fear of a disabling accident. Or he may take the Glen House stage at Jackson early in the afternoon, and, letting it drop him at Glen Ellis, make his own way to the hotel (4 miles) on foot, after a visit to the falls. Apply to Mr. Osgood, the veteran guide, at the Glen House, for services, or directions how to enter the Carter Notch from the Glen House side; and to Jock Davis, who lives at the head of the Wildcat Valley, if going in from the Jackson side.

Ladies who are accustomed to walking can reach Carter Notch with a little help now and then from the gentlemen. But the fatigue of going and returning on the same day would be too great. A party could enter the Notch in the afternoon, pass the night in Davis's comfortable cabin, and return the next morning. The path in is much easier and plainer from the Jackson than from the Glen House side; but there is no difficulty about keeping either. Davis will take up everything necessary for camping out, except food, which may be procured at your hotel before starting. There is plenty of water in the Notch.

At the Glen House one may finish the afternoon by walking back a mile on the Jackson road to the Emerald Pool; or, if he is in the vein, go one mile farther on to Thompson's Falls, and, ascending to the top, look over the forest into Tuckerman's Ravine. The Crystal Cascade (3 miles) and Glen Ellis (4 miles) from the hotel, ought to occupy half a day, but three hours (driving) will suffice, if one is in a hurry. The drive to Jackson, or march into the Notch, are just noted under Jackson. To go into Tuckerman's Ravine by the Crystal Cascade, or by Thompson's Path (Mount Washington carriage-road), will take a whole day. Ladies have been into Tuckerman's; but the trial cannot be recommended except for the most vigorous and courageous. The Appalachian Club has a camp near Hermit Lake, where a party going into the ravine in the afternoon may pass a comfortable night, ascend to the Snow Arch in the morning, and return to the hotel for dinner.

A three-mile walk on the Gorham road, crossing the Peabody River to the Copp Farm-house, gives a view of the celebrated "Imp" profile, on the top of the opposite mountain. This walk is an affair of two hours and a half. (See art. "Imp" in Index.) The Garnet

Pool (one mile from the hotel) may be taken on the way. Or, for a short and interesting stroll, go down this road a half-mile to where the Great Gulf opens wide before you its immense wall of mountains. The carriage-road to the summit requires four hours for the ascent by stage; a good climber can do it on foot in about the same time. Should a storm overtake him above the woods, he can find shelter in the Half-way House, just at the edge of the forest.

INTERIOR OF THE METEOROLOGICAL STATION, MOUNT WASHINGTON.

At Crawford's one can saunter into the woods at the left of the hotel, and enjoy himself in the sylvan retreat, "Idlewild;" or, going down the road, ascend the Elephant's Head by a path turning in at the left (sign-board), obtaining the view down the Notch; or, continuing on a short distance, enter and examine the Gate of the Notch. All these objects are in full view from the hotel. Other rambles of an hour are to Gibbs' Falls, entering the woods at the left of the hotel (guide-board), or, crossing the bridge over the railroad track on the right, to Beecher's Cascades. The ascent of Mount Willard (3 miles) should on no account be omitted. Good carriage-road all the way, and vehicles from the hotel. The celebrated Crawford Trail to the Summit of Mount Washington, the scene of many exploits, begins in the grove at the left of this hotel. The distance is fully nine miles, and six or seven hours will be none too many for the jaunt. Four intervening mountains, Clinton, Pleasant, Franklin, and Monroe, are crossed. There is a shelter-hut in the woods near the summit of Clinton.

At Fabyan's.—Three or four hours may be profitably spent on Mount Deception, opposite the hotel. The first summit is as much as one would care to undertake in an afternoon, to get the extended and magnificent view of the great range at sunset. Opposite the hotel is a cosy little cottage, kept open by the railroads for the use of travellers, and to give them information respecting routes, hotels, distances, fares, etc. The Upper Ammonoosuc Falls (3½ miles) are well worth a visit. They are on the Old Turnpike to the base of Mount Washington. The traveller has now at command all the important points in the moun-

METEOROLOGICAL STATION, MOUNT WASHINGTON, IN WINTER.

tains. He is 9 miles from the Summit, 4 from Crawford's, 29 from North Conway, 13 from Bethlehem, 22 from the Profile, and 18 from Jefferson—all reached by rail in one or two hours.

At Bethlehem.—If the tourist locates himself at the "Maplewood," the walk up the mountain to the Observatory, or to Cruft's Ledge, at sunset, or to the village (1¼ miles), or down the Whitefield road to The Hollow, is a good introduction. At "The Street" he will find the busiest thoroughfare in the mountains, leading him on to a beautiful panorama of the Ammonoosuc Valley, with Littleton in its lap ; or, ascending the old Profile House road above the Sinclair House for a mile, will see the great Franconia mountains from the best view-point. Bethlehem is 9 miles from the Profile House, 13 from Fabyan's, 17 from Crawford's, 42 from North Conway, 15 from Jefferson, and 22 from the Summit.

At Profile House.—If you arrive by rail *via* Bethlehem, you have crossed the broad flank and great ravine of Mount Lafayette to the shores of Echo Lake, a mile from the hotel. But the opposite side of this lake is a more eligible site for views of the surrounding mountains ; and the summit of Bald Mountain, at its north end, is still better. From the long piazza of the Profile House the great Notch mountains close in toward the south. Cannon Mountain is on your right, with the peculiar rocks giving it this name thrust out from the highest ridge in full view. The woods at the foot of this mountain, filling the pass in front of you, conceal the beautiful Profile Lake, the twin-sister of Echo Lake. The enormous rock at your left is Eagle Cliff, a spur of Mount Lafayette, the mountain being ascended on the south side of this cliff. Improve the first hour of leisure by walking directly down the road to Profile Lake. In a few minutes you will reach the shore near a rustic arbor (guide-board), furnished with seats, and here you command the best view of the renowned "Old Man of the Mountain." Boats may be had here for a sail upon the lake. Return to the hotel by the path through the woods. Walk next up the pass one mile to Echo Lake (boats and fishing-gear at the boat-house) ; or, extending your jaunt as far as Bald Mountain, obtain, by following the old path through the woods at the right, the best observation of the pass from the north. The trip to the Flume House (including the Basin, Pool, and Flume) is next in order, and will occupy a half day, although the distance is only six miles, and the road excellent. If the forenoon is taken, a party can either return to the hotel for dinner or dine well at the Flume House. The Pool is reached by a path half a mile long, entering the woods opposite the Flume House. It will take an hour to drive to the Flume ; and an hour to go into the chasm itself and return is little enough ; allowing another hour for the Pool makes four hours for the excursion.

The ascent of Mount Lafayette (3¾ miles) demands three to four hours. Saddle-horses can be procured at the hotel. Those unwilling to undertake the whole climb may, by ascending Eagle Cliff (1 mile on same path), secure a grand view of the Notch and lakes, the Profile, the ravines, and the Pemigewasset Valley. A stage leaves the Profile House every morning for Plymouth, connecting with trains for Boston and New York, and permitting the tourist to enjoy the beauties of the Pemigewasset Valley. But it is better to ascend this valley.

At the Flume House (refer to the preceding article).—It is a comparatively easy climb of an hour and a half to the top of Mount Pemigewasset, behind the hotel. See, from the hotel, the outline of the mountain ridge opposite, called Washington Lying in State.

At Jefferson.—The branch railway from Whitefield (B., C., & M. R.R.) leaves its passengers about three miles from the cluster of hotels and boarding-houses called Jefferson Hill, or five from East Jefferson (E. A. Crawford's, Highland, or Mount Adams House) ; but carriages are usually in waiting for all these houses. The walks and drives up and down this valley are numerous and interesting, especially so in the direction of Mount Adams and Randolph Hill, Cherry Mountain and Lancaster. The trip over Cherry Mountain, reaching Fabyan's (13 miles) by sunset, or from Fabyan's, reaching Jefferson at this hour, is a memorable experience of mountain beauty. Excursions to Mount Washington, Profile House, Glen House, or Gorham, demand a day. The ascent of Starr King, Owl's Head, Ravine of the Cascades, King's Ravine, or Mount Adams are the *pièces de résistance* for this locality.

ITINERARY OF A WALKING TOUR.—Two weeks of fine weather will enable a good pedestrian to traverse the mountains from Plymouth to North Conway, or *vice versa*, following the great highways throughout the whole journey, and giving time to see what is on the route. Good hotel accommodation will be found at the end of each day. Should bad weather unsettle his plans, he will nearly always be able to avail himself of regular stage or railway conveyance for a less or greater distance. Thus: First day, Plymouth to Woodstock (dine at Sanborn's, West Campton), 16 miles; second day, Flume House (visiting Flume and Pool), 8 miles; third day, Profile House (visiting Basin and "Old Man"), 5½ miles; fourth day, Bethlehem (*via* Echo Lake and Franconia), 9 miles; fifth day, Whitefield, 8 miles; sixth day, East Jefferson, 13 miles; seventh day, Glen House, 14 miles; eighth day, for vicinity of Glen House; ninth day, Summit of Mount Washington by carriage-road, 8 miles; tenth day, descent by mountain railway to Crawford's, 13 miles; eleventh day, through the Notch to Bartlett, 13 miles; twelfth day, Jackson and vicinity, 9 miles; thirteenth day, North Conway, 8 miles. Total, 124 miles.

Advice for Climbers.—Don't hurry when on a level road—keep your strength for the ascent. Always take the long route up a mountain, if it be the easier one. Be careful where you plant the foot in gullied trails or on icy ledges—a sprain is a serious matter if you are alone. Carry in your pocket a flask, fitted with a tumbler or cup; matches that will ignite in the wind, half a dozen cakes of pitch-kindling, a good glass, and a luncheon; in your hand a stout walking-stick; and upon your feet shoes that can be trusted—none of your gimcracks—but broad-soled ones, shod with steel nails. On a long march a rubber overcoat, a haversack, and an umbrella will be needed. Cold tea slakes thirst more effectually than water; but when you are exposed to wet and cold something stronger will be found useful. Should you have a palpitation of the heart, or an inclination to vertigo, do not climb at all. Take quiet rambles instead. My word for it, they are better for you than scaling breathless ascents or looking down over dizzy precipices. If you feel nausea, stop at once until you recover from it. If caught on the Crawford trail between Mounts Clinton and Washington, *go back* to the hut on the first-named mountain.

Newspapers for Tourists, at Bethlehem (*The Echo*) and on the Summit (*Among the Clouds*) are published during the season of travel, giving hotel arrivals, information concerning rail and stage routes, excursions, and whatever may be of interest to the summer population in general.

Telegraphic and telephone communication may be had at all the principal hotels and railway-stations.

The Appalachian Mountain Club prints every year a periodical made up of scientific and literary contributions from its members. Address the club at Boston.

Trout, pickerel, and *black bass* are found in all the mountain waters. The State stocks the ponds and streams with trout, bass, and salmon from its breeding-houses at Plymouth. Fishing legally begins May 1. There is good trout-fishing on Swift River (Albany), with Conway for head-quarters. From Jackson, or Glen House, the Wildcat and Ellis are both good trout streams; so are Nineteen-Mile Brook and the West Branch of Peabody; but the Wild River region (from Shelburne, Glen House, or Jackson) affords better sport, because less visited. To go in from Jackson or Glen House a guide will be necessary, and Davis, of Jackson, is a good one. From Jefferson and Randolph the upper waters of the Moose, and Israel's River (especially in the Mount Jefferson ravine), are fished with good success. E. A. Crawford, of East Jefferson, knows the best spots. From Bartlett there should be good fishing on Sawyer's River, above the Livermore mills. Consult Frank George, the veteran landlord of the Bartlett House. From Crawford's the best fishing-ground is Ethan's Pond, behind Mount Willey. At Franconia the writer has seen some fine strings brought from the Coppermine Brook (back of Mount Kinsman). Fair fishing may also be had on Lafayette Brook—ask Charles Edson, of the Edson House. Profile Lake is stocked with trout for the benefit of guests of the hotel. The upper streams of the Pemigewasset are all good fishing-ground. Apply to Mr. D. P. Pollard, North Woodstock, or Merrill Greeley, Waterville. The houses of both are resorted to by experienced fishermen who track the East Branch or Mad River tributaries. Pickerel and bass are caught in Lakes Winnipiseogee, Squam, Chocorua, Ossipee, and Silver, besides scores of ponds lying chiefly in the lake region.

N.B.—Those going exclusively to fish should go early in the season for the best sport.

Guides.—The landlords will either accompany you or procure a suitable person.

Camping Out.—A wall tent is preferable, but two persons get along comfortably in one of the "A" pattern. Get one with the fly, which can be spread behind the tent, thus giving an additional room, in which the cooking and eating may be done under cover. Set up your tent where there is natural drainage—where the surface water will run off during wet weather. Dig a shallow trench around it, on the outside, for this purpose, and if you can obtain them, lay boards for a floor. A kerosene-oil stove, with its utensils, folding cot-bed, camp-chairs, and mess-chest, containing dishes (tin is best), constitute a complete outfit, to be reduced according to convenience or pleasure. To make a woodsman's camp, first set up two crotched posts five feet high, and six or eight apart (according to number). On these lay a pole. From this pole three or four others extend to the ground. Then cut brush or bark for the roof and sides, and build your fire in front. For a camp of this sort a hatchet and packet of matches only are necessary. But always pitch your encampment in the vicinity of wood and water.

Mount Washington Railway.—Length, from base to summit, 3 miles. Rise in the three miles, 3,625 feet. Steepest grade, 13¼ inches in three feet, or 1980 feet to the mile. Begun in 1866; completed in 1869.

Mount Washington Carriage-road.—Length, 8 miles. Average grade, one foot in eight. Steepest grade, one foot in six. Begun in 1855; finished in 1861.

Mount Washington Signal Station.—The Summit was first occupied for scientific purposes in the winter of 1870-'71. Since then it has been attached to the Weather Bureau at Washington, and occupied by men detailed from the United States Signal Corps, the men volunteering for the service.

ALTITUDES.—The following list of altitudes of the more important and well-known points has been compiled from the publications of the Geological Survey of New Hampshire and of the Appalachian Mountain Club. The figures in **heavy-face** type are the results either of actual levelling or of trigonometrical survey, while the remainder depend upon barometrical measurement. Where the mean of two not widely-differing authorities is given, the fact is denoted by the letter "*m*" preceding the figures:

MOUNTAIN SUMMITS.

Adams	*m*	5785
Ascutney (Vermont)		3186
Black (Sandwich Dome)		**3999**
Boott's Spur		5524
Cannon		3850
Carrigain	*m*	4651
Carter Dome	*m*	4827
Chocorua		3540
Clay		5553
Clinton	*m*	4315
Crawford		3134
Giant's Stairs		3500
Gunstock		**2394**
Iron	*about*	2000
Jefferson		5714
Kearsarge, S. (Merrimack County)		**2943**
Kearsarge, N. (Carroll County)		**3251**
Lafayette		**5259**
Madison	*m*	5350
Moat (North peak)		3200
Monadnock	*m*	**3177**
Monroe	*m*	5375
Moosilauk		**4811**
Moriah		4653
Osceola	*m*	4408
Passaconnaway		4200
Percy (North peak)		3336
Pleasant (Great range)	*m*	4768
Pleasant (Maine)		**2021**
Starr King	*m*	3872
Twin	*about*	5000
Washington		**6293**
Webster		4000
Whiteface		**4007**
Willey		4300

VILLAGES AND HOTELS.

Bartlett (Upper)		**660**
Bethlehem (Sinclair House)	*m*	1454
Franconia		921
Crawford House		**1899**
Fabyan "		**1571**
Flume "		1431
Glen "		**1632**
Gorham		**812**
Jackson		759
Jefferson Hill		1440
Jefferson Highlands (Mt. Adams House)		1648
Lancaster		**870**
North Conway		**521**
Plymouth		**473**
Profile House		1974
Sugar Hill (Post Office)		1351
Waterville (Greeley's Hotel)	*m*	1544
Willey House		**1323**

NOTCHES.

Carter Notch		3240
Cherry Mt. Road (summit)	*m*	2180
Crawford or White Mt. Notch		**1914**
Dixville Notch		1831
Franconia Notch	*m*	2015
Pinkham Notch (south of Glen House)		2018
Carrigain Notch		2465

MISCELLANEOUS.

Ammonoosuc Sta. (base of Mt. Washington)		**2668**
Camp of Appalachian Mountain Club, on the Mt. Adams path		3307
Echo Lake (Franconia)	*m*	1928
Lake of the Clouds		5053
Lake Winnipiseogee		**500**

Distant Points Visible from Mount Washington (taken from "Appalachia").—Mount Megantic (Canada), 86 miles, seen between Jefferson and Adams; Mount Carmel, 65 miles, just over Mount Adams; Saddleback, 60 miles, head of Rangely Lakes; Mount Abraham, 68 miles, N., 47° E.; Ebene Mountain, 135 miles, vicinity of Moosehead Lake (rarely seen, even with a telescope); Mount Blue, 57 miles, near Farmington, Me.; Sebago Lake, 43 miles, over Mount Doublehead; Portland, 67 miles, over Lake Sebago; Mount Agamenticus, 79 miles, between Kearsarge and Moat Mountains; Isles of Shoals, 96 miles, to the right of Agamenticus (rarely seen); Mount Monadnock, 104 miles, between Carrigain and Sandwich Dome; Mount Ascutney (Vt.), 81 miles, S., 45° W.; Killington Peaks (near Rutland, Vt.), 88 miles, on the horizon between Moosilauk and Lincoln; Camel's Hump (Vt.), 78 miles, over Bethlehem Street; Mount Whiteface (Adirondack chain, N. Y.), 130 miles, over the right slope of Camel's Hump; Mount Mansfield (highest of Green Mountains). 77

miles, between Twin Mountain House and Mount Deception; Mount Wachusett (Mass.), 126 miles, is also visible under favorable conditions, just to the right of Whiteface (N. H.).

MOUNTAIN PATHS. [Those with an asterisk (*) were built by the Appalachian Mountain Club.] *Chocorua.*—There are three or four paths. The best leads from the Hammond Farm, 2½ miles from the Chocorua Lake House, and 14 miles from North Conway. The ascent, as far as the foot of the final peak, is feasible for ladies. From this point the easiest way is to flank the peak to the left until an old watercourse is reached, which may be followed nearly to the summit.

**Moat.*—An old path leads from the Swift River road to the summit of the South Peak. Another, from the clearings on an old road which extends along the base of the South Peak, leads to the top of the middle ridge; but the best path for tourists is the one from Diana's Baths, on Cedar Brook, following the stream to the foot of the ridge, thence over the ridge to the summit of the North Peak. Path well made, and plainly marked with signs and cairns; about 3½ miles in length.

**Middle Mountain, North Conway.*—Beginning at the ice-ponds near Artists' Falls House, the path extends around the base of Peaked Mountain, thence to the bare ledges which reach to the summit. Distance, 1¾ miles. Path well marked, and the view very beautiful.

Kearsarge, North Conway.—A bridle-path starts from a farm-house near Kearsarge Village, and extends to the summit. Distance, nearly 3 miles. Route plain, and not difficult.

**Mount Bartlett.*—The path starts near the Pequawket House, Lower Bartlett, follows old logging roads for some distance, runs thence directly to the summit. From the summit the path extends along the ridge until it joins the bridle-path to Kearsarge.

**Carrigain.*—The route leads from the mills at Livermore, which are reached by a road leaving the P. & O. R.R. at Livermore Station. From the mills, logging roads are followed —crossing Duck Pond and Carrigain Brooks—to the base; thence by a plain path through a fine forest to "Burnt Hat Ridge," from which it is only a short distance to the summit.

From mills to summit is about 5 miles. Station to mills, 2 miles.

**Livermore-Waterville Path.*—This is intended for a bridle-path. Starting from the mills at Livermore, a logging-road is followed nearly two miles on the southerly side of Sawyer's River. Here the path begins and runs along the north-west base of Green's Cliff, crosses Swift River at a beautiful fall, thence through the Notch south of Mount Kancamagus to Greeley's, in Waterville. The path is well marked by painted signs. Distance from Livermore to Swift River, 5 miles; to Greeley's, 12 miles.

**Mount Willey.*—Path leaves the P. & O. R.R. a little south of Willey Station. The rise is rapid until the Brook Kedron is reached; this brook is then followed to its source, thence the path leads direct to the summit. Distance, 1¼ miles. The climb is steep; but the view unsurpassed.

Crawford Bridle-path leads from the Crawford House to the summit of Washington. Path is plain, and the travelling along the ridge is easy; but it is not in condition for horses. *See* pp. 325, 326.

**Carter Notch.*—Path begins near the end of the Wildcat Valley road, about 5¼ miles from Jackson; thence it follows the valley of the brook to the ponds in the Notch. From the ponds it follows Nineteen Mile Brook to the clearing back of the Glen House. The travelling is easy; the view in the Notch grand.

Distance from the road to the ponds, about 4 miles; from the ponds to the Glen House, about the same.

Carter Dome.—The path starts from the larger pond in the Notch, and is well marked to the summit. It is very steep, and about 1½ miles in length.

Great Gulf.—A path beginning near the Glen House goes through this gorge. From the end of the path the carriage-road or railroad on Mount Washington may be reached by a severe climb up the side of the ravine.

Tuckerman's Ravine.—The Glen House path leaves the Mount Washington carriage-road about 2 miles up, then crosses through the forest to Hermit Lake.

Via Crystal Cascade.—The Mountain Club path begins about 3 miles from the Glen House, on the Jackson road, ascending the stream until it joins the Glen House path near Hermit Lake. Here the Club has a good camp for the use of travellers. Beyond, a single path extends to the Snow-field; and a feasible route has been marked with white paint on the rocks—up the head wall of the ravine, and thence to the summit.

Mount Adams.—This path starts opposite the residence of Charles E. Lowe, on the road from Jefferson Hill to Gorham, about 8½ miles from either town, and climbs the steep spur forming one wall of King's Ravine, following over the ledges to the westerly peak, thence to the summit. Distance, about 4 miles. Nearly half way up the spur a good camp has been built for the use of climbers. The way over the ledges is marked by cairns. Mount Jefferson may be reached by turning to the right before reaching the summit of the westerly peak; Madison by turning to the left.

King's Ravine.—The path branches from the Mount Adams path about 1½ miles from Lowe's. The bowlders in the Ravine are reached without great difficulty. From the bowlders up the head-wall, and through the gate-way, the climb is arduous; and the way is not very distinctly marked. From the gate-way, Madison and the several peaks of Adams may be reached.

Mount Madison.—There are several routes up Madison, but the best is probably that leading up the ridge from "Dolly" Copp's, on the Old Pinkham Road. The climb is tedious, and the path somewhat overgrown. The Mountain Club will probably clear and keep this path in good condition.

Bridal Veil Falls.—Path starts from Horace Brooks's, on the road from Franconia to Easton — 2 to 3 miles from Sugar Hill and Franconia Village. It follows an old road across the clearings to Copper-mine Brook, thence by the brook to the foot of the Falls. Distance, 2½ miles from Brooks's. Walking easy.

The path to the Flume on Mount Kinsman leads from the same highway about a mile beyond Brooks's.

Mount Lafayette.—The bridle-path begins near the Profile House, turning Eagle Cliff, and crossing over to the main ridge. It leads nearly to the summit of the ridge, thence across the *col* by the lakes, and up the main peak. Distance, 3½ to 3¾ miles.

Mount Cannon.—The path enters the forest near the cottages in front of the Profile House. The summit is reached by a steep climb of 1½ miles. The Cannon Rock is a short distance down the mountain-side, to the left of the path as it emerges from the forest; the forehead rock of the Profile can be reached by bearing down the mountain diagonally to the right from Cannon Rock until the edge of the cliff is reached. It is a hard scramble to the latter.

Black Mountain, Waterville.—The new path leaves the highway 2 miles below Greeley's, near Drake's Brook. It runs near the edge of the ravine of Drake's Brook, crosses the ridge between Noon and Jennings' Peaks—to each of which a branch path leads—thence up the northerly slope of the main summit. Distance from the road to the summit is $3\frac{1}{4}$ miles. The views are very fine, and the climb easy for ordinary walkers.

Osceola.—Path leaves the Greeley-pond path beyond the saw-mill above Greeley's, bearing to the left. Ascent easy. Distance, about 4 miles.

Tecumseh.—Path branches from the Osceola path at the crossing of the west branch of Mad River, $\frac{1}{4}$ of a mile from Greeley's. The grade is easy, except for a short distance near the summit. Distance from Greeley's, 3 miles.

Tri-Pyramid.—The great slide on Tri-Pyramid may be reached from Greeley's by a path across the pasture to the right from the rear of the house, thence about $1\frac{1}{2}$ miles through fine old woods to a deserted clearing known as Beckytown. From here the stream may be followed by clambering over the *débris* of the slide nearly 2 miles to the base of the South Peak. The summit is reached by climbing to the apex of the slide, thence bearing up to the right a short distance through low woods.

* *Thornton-Warren Path.*—This path was built to enable visitors in the Upper Pemigewasset Valley or in Warren to cross from one locality to the other, avoiding the long détour *via* Plymouth. It starts from the Profile House stage-road at the junction of the Tannery road, in West Thornton, crosses Hubbard Brook at this point, and passes over a long stretch of pasture until the woods are reached. At this point, and at all doubtful points, signs have been placed. For much of the distance the path follows Hubbard Brook, and passes out through the Notch between Mounts Kinco and Cushman to an old road-way leading to clearings on Baker's River, near the mountain-houses at the foot of Mount Moosilauke.

Distance from the stage-road to the road-way in Warren, 8 miles. A permanent camp has been built half-way on Hubbard Brook.

A trail has been spotted from a point in the path about 1 mile north of the camp to the summit of Kinco.

INDEX.

THE END.

NEW YORK & NEW ENGLAND RAILROAD.

THIS IS THE MOST CONVENIENT LINE BETWEEN

Boston, Philadelphia, Baltimore, and Washington,

AS IT IS THE **ONLY LINE** RUNNING

THROUGH PULLMAN CARS WITHOUT CHANGE.

The train leaving Washington, Baltimore, and Philadelphia in the afternoon, arrives in Boston the following morning in season to connect with trains on the Eastern, Boston & Maine, and Boston & Lowell Railroads, for points in the White Mountains and shore resorts. The morning trains from the White Mountains and shore resorts arrive in Boston in sufficient time to cross the city and take the 7 P.M. train for the South.

Berths in Pullman Sleepers can be secured in advance on application to the Company's Office.

322 Washington St., Boston, and Depot, foot of Summer St.; and at Pennsylvania Railroad Ticket Offices in Philadelphia, Baltimore, and Washington.

☞ Ask for Tickets via New England and Str. Maryland Lines.

S. M. FELTON, Jr., General Manager.   A. C. KENDALL, General Passenger Agent.

WILLIAM S. BUTLER & CO.

90 & 92 Tremont Street,

(Opposite Tremont House),   BOSTON. MASS.

DEALERS IN

Ribbons, Laces, Flowers, Montures, Velvets, Nets,

FEATHERS, SPRAYS, &c.

HATS, for Ladies and Misses; CORSETS—the Best Fitting and Most Sensible:
KID GLOVES A SPECIALTY—Latest Styles, Lowest Prices; BUTTONS, TRIMMINGS, &c.,
in endless variety; HOSIERY and UNDERWEAR, for Ladies and
Misses—an admirable assortment at low rates.

FANCY GOODS, PERFUMERY, TOILET ARTICLES, &c.

AND MANY OTHER NOVELTIES.

Ladies visiting Boston, or gentlemen wishing to make purchases for absent wives, sisters, or lady friends, will do well to inspect the admirably selected stock of Gloves, Laces, Velvets, Ribbons, Flowers, Millinery Goods, Hats, Hosiery, Small Wares, and Fancy Goods generally, offered by WILLIAM S. BUTLER & Co. at 90 and 92 Tremont Street (opposite the Tremont House). This firm has won an enviable reputation for the excellence of its goods, its courteous attendance, and the moderation of its prices; while its location renders it most convenient of access by horse cars, either from the hotels or from any of the railroad depots.

☞ **Orders by mail or express will receive prompt attention.**

WILLIAM S. BUTLER & CO.,   -   -   90 and 92 Tremont Street, Boston.

DRAKE'S NEW ENGLAND COAST.

NOOKS AND CORNERS OF THE NEW ENGLAND COAST. By Samuel Adams Drake. With numerous Illustrations. Square 8vo, Cloth, $3 50; Half Calf, $5 75.

My dear Sir,—I laid out your new and beautiful book to take with me to-day to my summer home, but before I go I wish to thank you for preparing a volume which is every way so delightful. All summer I shall have it at hand, and many a pleasant hour I anticipate in the enjoyment of it. I have *read* far enough in it already to feel how admirably you have done your part of it, and I have *seen*, in turning over the delectable pages, what a panorama of lovely nooks and rocky coast your artist has prepared for the pleasure of your readers. May they be a good many thousand this year, and continue to increase time onward. If I am not greatly out in my judgment, edition after edition will be called for. Truly yours,
JAMES T. FIELDS.

Thy "Nooks and Corners of the New England Coast" is a delightful book, and one of most frequent reference in my library. Thy friend,
JOHN G. WHITTIER.

I take this opportunity of acknowledging the pleasure I have received from your interesting book on our New England coast. It was my companion last summer on the coast of Maine. Yours truly,
F. PARKMAN.

Mr. Samuel Adams Drake does for the New England coast such service as Mr. Nordhoff has done for the Pacific. His "Nooks and Corners of the New England Coast"—a volume of 459 pages—is an admirable guide both to the lover of the picturesque and the searcher for historic lore, as well as to stay-at-home travellers. The "Preface" tells the story of the book; it is a sketch-map of the coast, with the motto, "On this line, if it takes all summer." "Summer" began with Mr. Drake one Christmas-day at Mount Desert, whence he went South, touching at Castine, Pemaquid, and Monhegan; Wells and "Agamenticus, the ancient city" of York; Kittery Point; "The Shoals;" Newcastle; Salem and Marblehead; Plymouth and Duxbury; Nantucket; Newport; Mount Hope; New London, Norwich, and Saybrook. What nature has to show and history to tell at each of these places, who were the heroes and worthies—all this Mr. Drake gives in pleasant talk—*N. Y. Tribune.*

My dear Mr. Drake.—I have given your beautiful book, "Nooks and Corners of the New England Coast," a pretty general perusal. It is one "after my own heart," and I thank you very much for it. Your Preface is an admirable "hit" in more ways than one. Like Grant, whom you have quoted, it took you, I imagine, *all winter* as well as *all summer* to accomplish your victory, for you speak of experiences with snow and sleet.

You have gathered into your volume, in the most attractive form, a vast amount of historical and descriptive matter that is exceedingly useful. I hope your pen will not be stayed. Your friend and brother of the pen,
BENSON J. LOSSING.

To-morrow I leave home for a week or two in Maine, and shall take your beautiful volume, "Nooks and Corners of the New England Coast," with me to read and enjoy at leisure. I am sure it cannot fail to be very interesting.
Yours faithfully,
HENRY W. LONGFELLOW.

I need not tell you with how much interest both my husband and myself—lovers of the valley—look forward to your work, nor how much pleasure your "Nooks and Corners" has already afforded us.
With most cordial regards,
HARRIET P. SPOFFORD.

His style is at once simple and graphic, and his work as conscientious and faithful to fact as if he were the dullest of annalists instead of one of the liveliest of essayists and historians. The legitimate charm of variety—characteristic of a work of this kind—makes the book more entertaining than any volume of similar size devoted exclusively to chronology, biography, essays, or anecdotes.—JOHN G. SAXE, in the *Brooklyn Argus.*

Mr. Drake's "Nooks and Corners of the New England Coast" ought to be in the hands of every one who visits our sea-side resorts. The artistic features serve to embellish a very interesting description of our New England watering-places, enlivened with anecdotes, bits of history connected with the various places, and pleasant gossip about people and things in general.—*Saturday Evening Gazette,* Boston.

Published by HARPER & BROTHERS, New York.

WHAT LEADING ENGLISH PAPERS

SAY OF

"PASTORAL DAYS;

OR,

MEMORIES OF A NEW ENGLAND YEAR."

By W. HAMILTON GIBSON.

4to, Illuminated Cloth, Gilt Edges, $7 50.

FROM "THE TIMES," LONDON.

The title of this very beautifully illustrated book conveys but a very faint idea of its merits, which lie, not in the descriptions of the varied beauties of the fields and fens of New England, but in the admirable wood-engravings, which on every page picture far more than could be given in words. The author has the rare gift of feeling for the exquisitely graceful forms of plant life and the fine touch of an expert draughtsman, which enables him both to select and to draw with a refinement which few artists in this direction have ever shown. Besides these essential qualities in a painter from nature, Mr. Gibson has a fine sense of the poetic and picturesque in landscape, of which there are many charming pieces in this volume, interesting in themselves as pictures, and singularly so in their resemblance to the scenery of Old England. Most of the little vignette-like views might be mistaken for Birket Foster's thoroughly English pictures, and some are like Old Crome's vigorous idyls. One of the most striking—a wild forest scene with a storm passing, called "The Line Storm"—is quite remarkable in the excellent drawing of the trees swept by the gale and in the general composition of the picture, which is full of the true poetic conception of grandeur in landscape beauty. But all Mr. Gibson's good drawing would have been nothing unless he had been so ably aided by the artist engravers, who have throughout worked with such sympathy with his taste, and so much regard for the native grace of wild flowers, grasses, ferns, insects, and all the infinite beauties of the fields, down to the mysterious spider and his silky net spread over the brambles. These cuts are exceptional examples of beautiful work. Nothing in the whole round of wood-engraving can surpass, if it has even equalled, these in delicacy as well as breadth of effect. Much as our English cutters pride themselves on belonging to the school which Bewick and Jackson founded, they must certainly come to these American artists to learn the something more which is to be found in their works. In point of printing, too, there is much to be learned in the extremely fine ink and paper, which, although subjected to "hot-pressing," are evidently adapted in some special condition for wood-printing. The printing is obviously by hand-press,* and in the arrangement of the type with the cuts on each page the greatest ingenuity and invention are displayed. This, too, has been designed with a sort of a Japanesque fancy; here is a tangled mass of grasses and weeds, with a party of ants stealing out of the shade, and there the dragon-flies flit across among the blossoms of the reeds, or the feathery seeds of the dandelion float on the page. Each section of the seasons has its suggestive picture : Springtime, with a flight of birds under a may-flower branch that hangs across the brook ; Summer, a host of butterflies sporting round the wild rose ; Autumn, with the swallows flying south and falling leaves that strew the page ; while for Winter the chrysalis hangs in the leafless bough, and the snow-clad graves in the village church-yard tell the same story of sleep and awakening. As many as thirty different artists, besides the author and designer, have assisted in producing this very tastefully illustrated volume, which commends itself by its genuine artistic merits to all lovers of the picturesque and the natural.

* The English reviewer is in error here. The letterpress and illustrations were printed together on an Adams press

FROM "THE SATURDAY REVIEW," LONDON.

This pleasant American book has brought to our remembrance, though without any sense of imitation, two old-fashioned favorites. In the first place, its descriptions of rural humanity, its rustic sweetness and humor, have a certain analogy with the delicately pencilled studies of life in Miss Mitford's "Our Village;" but the relation it bears to the second book is much closer. It is more than forty years since Mr. P. H. Gosse published the first of those delightful sketches of animal life at home which have led so many of us with a wholesome purpose into the woods and lanes. It was in the *Canadian Naturalist* that he broke this new ground; and though we do not think this has ever been one of his best-known books, we cannot but believe that there are still many readers who will be reminded of it as they glance down Mr. Gibson's pages.

People must be strangely constituted who do not enjoy such pages as Mr. Gibson has presented to us here. It is not merely that he writes well, but the subject itself is irresistibly fascinating. We plunge with him into the silence of a New England village in a clearing of the woods. The spring is awakening in a flush of tender green, in a fever of warm days and shivering nights, and we hasten with our companion through all the bustle and stir of the few busy hours of light so swiftly that the darkness is on us before we are aware. Then falls on the ear a pathetic, an intolerable silence ; a deep mist covers the ground, a few lights twinkle in scattered farms and cottages, and all seems brooding, melting, in the deep and throbbing hush of the darkness. * * * The wailing of the great owl upon the maple-tree takes our author back in memory to the scenes of his youth, where the owl was looked upon as a creature of most sinister omen, and his own partiality to it, as a proof that there was something uncanny or even "fey" about him. All this is described with great sympathy and delicacy; but perhaps Mr. Gibson is most felicitous in his little touches of floral painting. He has a few words about the earthy, spicy fragrance of the arbutus that might have been said in verse by the late Mr. Bryant; his description of the effect of biting the bulbs of the Indian turnip, or "Jack-in-the-pulpit," is inimitable in its quiet way; while the phrase about the fading dandelions — "the golden stars upon the lawn are nearly all burned out ; we see their downy ashes in the grass"—is perhaps the best thing ever said about a humble flower, whose vulgarity, in the literal sense, blinds us to the beauty of its evolution and decay.

In his studies of life and country manners Mr. Gibson is a very agreeable and amusing, if not quite so novel, a companion. Not seldom he reminds us not merely of Miss Mitford, but sometimes of Thoreau and of Hawthorne. The story of Aunt Huldy, the village crone who sustained herself upon simples to the age of a hundred and three, is one of those little vignettes, half humorous, half pathetic, and altogether picturesque, in which the Americans excel. Aunt Huldy was an old witch in a scarlet hood, whose long white hair flowing behind her was wont to frighten the village children who came upon her in the woods ; but she was absolutely harmless, a crazy old valetudinarian, who was always searching for the elixir of life in strange herbs and decoctions. At last she thought she had found it in sweet-fern, and she spent her last years in grubbing up every specimen she could find, smoking it, chewing it, drinking it, and sleeping with a little bag of it tied round her neck.

But although Mr. Gibson writes so well, he modestly disclaims all pretension as a writer, and lets us know that he is an artist by profession. His book is illustrated by more than seventy designs from his pencil, engraved in that beautiful American manner to which we have often called attention. The scenes designed are closely analogous to those described in the text. We have an apple-orchard in full blossom, with a group of idlers lounging underneath the boughs; scenes in the fields so full of mystery and stillness that we are reminded of Millet, or of our own Mason ; clusters of flowers drawn with all the knowledge of a botanist and the sympathy of a poet. It is hard to define the peculiar pleasure that such illustrations give to the eye. It is something that includes and yet transcends the mere enjoyment of whatever artistic excellence the designs may possess. We are directly reminded by them of such similar scenes as have been either the rule or the still more fascinating exception of every childish life, and at their suggestion the past comes back : in the familiar Wordsworthian phrase, "a river flows on through the vale of Cheapside."

We know so little over here of the best American art that it may chance that Mr. Gibson is very well known in New York. We confess, however, that we never heard of him before; but his drawings are so full of delicate fancy and feeling, and his writing so skilful and graceful, that, in calling attention to his book, we cannot but express the hope that we soon may hear of him again, in either function, or in both.

☞ "PASTORAL DAYS" is published by HARPER & BROTHERS, New York, who will send the work, postage prepaid, to any part of the United States, on receipt of $7 50.

HARPER'S GUIDE TO EUROPE.

HARPER'S HAND-BOOK FOR TRAVELLERS IN EUROPE AND THE EAST: being a Guide through Great Britain and Ireland, France, Belgium, Holland, Germany, Italy, Egypt, Syria, Turkey, Greece, Switzerland, Tyrol, Spain, Russia, Denmark, Norway, Sweden, United States, and Canada. By W. PEMBROKE FETRIDGE. With Maps and Plans of Cities. In Three Volumes. 12mo, Leather, Pocket-Book Form, $3 00 per vol. *The volumes sold separately.*

VOL. I. GREAT BRITAIN, IRELAND, FRANCE, BELGIUM, HOLLAND.

VOL. II. GERMANY, AUSTRIA, ITALY, SICILY AND MALTA, EGYPT, THE DESERT, SYRIA AND PALESTINE, TURKEY, GREECE.

VOL. III. SWITZERLAND, TYROL, DENMARK, NORWAY, SWEDEN, RUSSIA, SPAIN, UNITED STATES AND CANADA.

It has stood the test of trying experience, and has proved the traveller's friend in all emergencies. Each year has added to its attractions and value, until it is about as near perfect as it is possible to make it.—*Boston Post.*

Personal use of this Guide during several visits to various portions of Europe enables us to attest its merits. No American is fully equipped for travel in Europe without this Hand-Book.—*Philadelphia North American.*

Take "Harper's Hand-Book," and read it carefully through; then return to the parts relating to the places you have resolved to visit; follow the route on the maps, and particularly study the plans of cities. So you will start with sound pre-knowledge, which will smoothen the entire course of travel.—*Philadelphia Press.*

The book is not only unrivalled as a guide-book, for which it is primarily intended, but it is a complete cyclopedia of all that relates to the countries, towns, and cities which are described in it—their curiosities, most notable scenes, their most celebrated historical, commercial, literary, and artistic centres. Besides general descriptions of great value, there are minute and detailed accounts of everything that is worth seeing or knowing relative to the countries of the Old World. The great value of the book consists in the fact that it covers all the ground that any traveller may pass through—being exhaustive not only of one country or two, but comprising in its ample pages exact and full information respecting every country in Europe and the East.—*Christian Intelligencer, N. Y.*

It is a marvellous compendium of information, and the author has labored hard to make his book keep pace with the progress of events. * * * It forms a really valuable work of reference on all the topics which it treats, and in that way is as useful to the reader who stays at home as to the traveller who carries it with him abroad.—*N. Y. Times.*

I have received and examined with lively interest the new and extended edition of your extremely valuable "Hand-Book for Travellers in Europe and the East." You have evidently spared no time or pains in consolidating the results of your wide travel, your great experience. You succeed in presenting to the traveller the most valuable guide and friend with which I have the good fortune to be acquainted. With the warmest thanks, I beg you to receive the most cordial congratulations of yours, very faithfully, JOHN MEREDITH READ, Jr., *United States Minister at Greece.*

From having travelled somewhat extensively in former years in Europe and the East, I can say with entire truth that you have succeeded in combining more that is instructive and valuable for the traveller than is contained in any one or series of handbooks that I have ever met with.—T. BIGELOW LAWRENCE.

To make a tour abroad without a guide-book is impossible. The object should be to secure that which is most complete and comprehensive in the least compass. The scope, plan, and execution of Harper's makes it, on the whole, the most satisfactory that can be found.—*Albany Journal.*

PUBLISHED BY HARPER & BROTHERS, NEW YORK.

ENGLISH MEN OF LETTERS.

EDITED BY JOHN MORLEY.

The following volumes are now ready:

JOHNSON	LESLIE STEPHEN.
GIBBON	J. C. MORISON.
SCOTT	R. H. HUTTON.
SHELLEY	J. A. SYMONDS.
HUME	Professor HUXLEY.
GOLDSMITH	WILLIAM BLACK.
DEFOE	WILLIAM MINTO.
BURNS	Principal SHAIRP.
SPENSER	The DEAN OF ST. PAUL'S.
THACKERAY	ANTHONY TROLLOPE.
BURKE	JOHN MORLEY.
MILTON	MARK PATTISON.
SOUTHEY	Professor DOWDEN.
CHAUCER	Professor A. W. WARD.
BUNYAN	J. A. FROUDE.
COWPER	GOLDWIN SMITH.
POPE	LESLIE STEPHEN.
BYRON	JOHN NICHOL.
LOCKE	THOMAS FOWLER.
WORDSWORTH	F. W. H. MYERS.
DRYDEN	G. SAINTSBURY.
LANDOR	Professor SIDNEY COLVIN.
DE QUINCEY	Professor D. MASSON.
LAMB	The Rev. ALFRED AINGER.
BENTLEY	Professor JEBB.

12mo, Cloth, 75 cents per volume.

HAWTHORNE. By HENRY JAMES, Jr. .... 12mo, Cloth, $1 00.

VOLUMES IN PREPARATION:

SWIFT	JOHN MORLEY.
GRAY	E. W. GOSSE.
ADAM SMITH	LEONARD H. COURTNEY.
DICKENS	Professor A. W. WARD.

Others will be announced.

Published by HARPER & BROTHERS, New York.